This Love

MICHAELA JEAN TAYLOR

Copyright © 2023 by Michaela Jean Taylor (Spruce Media, LLC)

All rights reserved.

No part of this book may be reproduced, distributed, or transmitted in any form or by any electronic or mechanical means, including information storage and retrieval systems, without written permission from the author, except for the use of brief quotations in a book review and certain other noncommercial use permitted by copyright law.

Resemblance to actual persons and things living or dead, locales, or events is entirely coincidental.

THIS LOVE

Editor: Britt Tayler

Cover Designer: Michaela Jean Taylor

Formatting: Michaela Jean Taylor

If it all comes down to love and fear,
I hope you choose to live from a place of love.

Author's Note

This book contains on-page scenes with mature subject matter including grief, cancer, and drug use/abuse and is intended for mature audiences.

Chapter One

NORA

"Nora, are you listening?"

Parker's low voice pierced through my deep consciousness. I snapped my eyes to his, finding his blue hues swirling in question. "Oh—I'm sorry, what?"

The sigh that expelled from his lungs ignited a flair of annoyance within me. His gaze was sharp, judging, as if I were somehow disappointing him. As if he hadn't just caught me mid-chapter in a romance novel with an *excellent* slow burn. He knew how I got when I was reading—there was no reason for him to have an attitude about it. "The gala tonight," he pressed, "will you be ready in time for the car?"

I glanced at the clock on the wall and saw that it was five thirty. "It'll be here at seven, right?"

Parker nodded. "Yes. Seven, sharp."

It wasn't lost on me that he'd added the *sharp* to get his point across. I made a little show of focusing back on my book, finding the line I'd just been ripped away from. "I'll be ready."

There was a low level of tension building in the air as Parker continued to stare at me. I had no doubt that a heated debate was sounding off inside his head about whether he should ask me what I was planning to wear and if I was *sure* I'd have enough time.

This had been somewhat of a sore spot between us—my wardrobe, my style. Like pressing into an old bruise. It would take me forty-five minutes to get ready for the gala. An hour, tops—and that was only if I decided to curl my hair, which wasn't likely. And while I understood that most women who attended these kinds of events spent all day getting ready for them, a full glam team on standby, that just wasn't me. If Parker wanted a girl on his arm who was primped and plucked to the heavens and wearing some trendy designer number, he was *definitely* dating the wrong one. Which shouldn't have been a revelation, since we'd been together for three whole years. I heard another—albeit, softer—sigh from him before he walked out of the room, no doubt going to make himself a drink.

He loved his whiskey.

I allowed myself to read for another fifteen minutes before I tucked my worn bookmark between the pages and shelved the book, striding out of the den and down the long hallway to our massive primary suite. I looked around for Parker as I entered the room, but I didn't see him. He was likely enjoying his scotch in the private confines of his home office, with the door shut for an assured emphasis on his frustration with me.

I stepped into the large walk-in closet off the ensuite bathroom and perused the dresses that hung on my side. I didn't have many, and most of them I'd worn before, but that didn't bother me in the slightest. Who was I to care about repeating an outfit? The investment alone of each piece was enough to warrant *many* uses. While Parker came from so much wealth there was money basically oozing out of his ears, I came from much more humble beginnings where practicality was infused in my blood.

If only my mother could see me now.

I picked out a little black dress that was perfect for an event near the coast and hung it up in the bathroom where the steam from my shower could easily work out any wrinkles. I'd washed my hair this morning, so I pulled it up into a bun and tied it with a silk scrunchie before I turned on the faucet.

Allowing some time for the water to heat, I undressed and placed my clothes in the hamper, pausing in front of the full-length mirror. In the last three years, my body had slimmed down considerably. It stemmed less from a need to lose weight and more from an unintended change after my move out here.

Life was completely different in Los Angeles than it was in Denver. For instance, Parker had an in-home chef who cooked all of our meals. I thought it was a little excessive—I would have been happy to cook for us—but Parker insisted. "Besides," he'd said, "Clarke will make sure we get maximum nutritional benefits without so many calories." I knew it was a necessary evil that came with his job's territory, but it was exhausting.

Ever since I'd known him, Parker spent *hours* each day exercising with the ultimate goal of an almost non-existent body fat percentage. He'd even had a wing of the house converted into a home gym, complete with state-of-the-art equipment and a hydrotherapy setup. I'd be the first to admit his body was incredible, but I'd always felt like his desire to "look good" hinged on obsession. I learned fairly quickly to keep my opinions to myself, though, if I wanted to avoid *yet another* rundown on the ins and outs of the male modeling industry in L.A.

When we'd met, I was definitely on the softer side. I had a lot of fun in college, and I loved the curves that came as a result of it all—the many late-night Taco Bell runs with friends, drinking and dancing for hours in a club, living untamed and *free*. Those curves had made me feel sexy in my newfound womanhood. But now, even though I didn't exercise nearly as much as Parker did, my body had still changed dramatically. I was much leaner, those beloved curves mostly gone. I frowned at my reflection and felt, not for the first time, the struggle to recognize myself.

As the air in the bathroom hung heavy with steam from the running shower, I turned away from the mirror and stepped inside the giant glass cage, letting the scalding water cascade down my skin.

I MADE my way down the grand staircase in the foyer to find Parker already standing by the door. My heels made the descent a bit tricky—I still wasn't super comfortable walking in them since I'd only worn them a handful of times. Having always been the "tall girl" growing up, I hardly ever wore heels unless attending black-tie events like the one tonight.

Parker turned and looked up at me, and I saw a soft smile spread across his face. It was warm and bright, like a sudden burst of summer air through a rolled down window. I felt relief roll over me, the sensation both familiar and foreign. "You look beautiful, Nora."

My cheeks pulled in response. Maybe tonight things would feel lighter. Maybe we could just let go of the resentment that had built up between us and *enjoy* each other like we once did. "You don't look half bad, yourself," I responded. Parker looked like a dream right off a *GQ* cover in his black tuxedo. His hair was expertly styled to the side, his face freshly shaven. His bright blue eyes sparkled like the Pacific as they watched me approach.

"Perfect timing." He held out his arm for me when I reached the last step. "The car just arrived for us." I tucked my arm into his, and he led us down the front walkway toward a black Cadillac Escalade that sat idle on the curb.

I leaned most of my weight into Parker to avoid catching my heels in the cobblestone walkway, glancing over my shoulder as the door clicked behind us. The house was a mini-castle of concrete and glass that his parents had built for him when he was still just a teenager. Boasting six bedrooms and six bathrooms, it had always felt much too big for just Parker and me—and the few live-in staff members—but it was intended to be a starter home to bring up the next generation of Harts.

It was so exciting, back when I'd first moved in, to find myself in a place like this with a man as dashing as Parker. But over time, I had to get better at tamping down the feeling that this wasn't where I belonged, knowing it was easier to play house than to contemplate how I'd let so much of myself get lost.

Our driver, Jeremy, jumped out from his seat and jogged around the front of the SUV to open the back passenger door for us. "Good evening, sir." He nodded to Parker before his eyes shifted to me. "Miss," he said, and dipped his head. I felt a mild flush of embarrassment—it was still completely foreign to me when our staff acknowledged me as if I were someone like Parker: rich and poised with power. I always had the urge to tell them that it was okay, they didn't need to pay me any mind. That I was actually more like them than I'd ever be like him.

Parker got into the SUV first, ducking over to the far side of the back seat and gesturing me to slide in behind him. We got settled, and as Jeremy pulled us away from the curb, I looked out my window and watched as the other multi-million-dollar homes of Brentwood whirled by. It was a neighborhood dripping in luxury, nestled snugly within a city of dreamers.

Parker spent the majority of the hour-long drive to the Sunset Room on his phone, which would have bothered me in the beginning of our relationship, but was a routine I was used to by now. I should have known to bring my book to keep me company on the drive. When we finally pulled up to the venue, there was a crowd of people standing outside the building's front entrance, and immediately my stomach dipped, a tingling sensation settling in my fingers.

It wasn't that I didn't enjoy events like this—I did. Especially when the occasion was to promote the charitable efforts of local non-profits. Parker's mother had long ago founded Women in Color, an organization dedicated to the advocation of equal pay for women of *all* cultural backgrounds in Hollywood. Tonight's gala was celebrating some recently successful advocacy efforts. Knowing all that, I still fought the instinct to ask Jeremy to do another lap around the block.

Marjorie Barlow Hart, the daughter of the late Hollywood movie star, Miriam Barlow, was a successful actress in her own right, practically owning daytime television for decades with her role as Sophie Lastra in the wildly popular soap opera,

Sophie's World. The decades-long show had aired its final season five years ago, and since then, Marjorie continued to stay relevant in the industry through aggressive charitable efforts like this one.

Jeremy shifted the car into park and hustled to open the door for Parker and me. Through the commotion, I took stock of the red-carpet entrance lined with paparazzi on either side of the velvet ropes and braced myself. *Chin up, eyes bright, big smile. But not too big.* I heard the clicks of a few cameras as I stepped out of the car, a hasty attempt to get the first shot of whoever was arriving. There was a collective pause, though, as everyone pulled their eyes out of their camera lens to look at me directly, trying to place my face with a name.

Parker stepped out of the car behind me, his hand warm against my low back, and I quickly sidestepped to give him room. Immediately, the cameras began flashing in a frenzy.

"Parker, right here, please!"

"Parker, any words for us tonight?"

"Parker, are the rumors about your upcoming movie role true?"

Parker had always loved the attention, the opportunity to play the role of the effortlessly charming son of an incredibly famous actress, the grandchild of a Hollywood legend. Even now, as he skirted his bright blue eyes past mine as though we were in on a secret, he looked toward the cameras and teased them with a shy smile.

Parker was smart. He knew that by playing coy with the onlookers, they'd be hungrier to get to know him. To seek him out. You never would have guessed how much he thrived on the attention, from the calculated way he avoided the spotlight.

I took his outstretched hand and felt him turn toward me as we walked the carpet, his lips brushing against my ear. "You really do look great in that dress," he whispered, the words sending an involuntary chill down my spine. It had been a long time since I'd felt anything resembling intimacy with Parker, and I relished it—the aching reminder of how much chemistry used to exist between us. The thrill. Long looks across crowded rooms. The anticipation of another touch.

My grip on his arm tightened, drawing his body closer to mine. Halfway to the entrance of the venue, a step-and-repeat backdrop stood against tall hedges with the Women in Color logo splashed across it. We moved to stand in front of it, and Parker twirled us in the direction of the cameras.

I'd only been on a handful of red carpets with Parker, but I knew the drill. I kept my expression pleasantly neutral—not too excited and not too bored. My hand remained tucked into his arm, the practiced gesture bolstering his *attentive* and *doting* persona, as I stood half a step back from where he did to ensure he had the spotlight.

Not that I wanted it.

Parker led us away from the press after what might've been ten minutes or ten hours, and I took the opportunity to blink the moisture back into my eyes. Inside, vines of Jasmine and festoon lights hung from the ceiling, creating an ethereal atmosphere that could have put us in another place in time, rather than in downtown L.A. Round tables draped in white linen were set with beautiful clusters of hydrangeas and gleaming silver plates. There was a stage at the front of the hall where a beautiful floral arch stood, made from an assortment of wildflowers.

Guests were already milling around and talking in small

groups. These events were a socialite's dream, a gateway to new connections that might yield just the right kind of leverage to reach another rung on the social ladder. I had no doubt that everyone invited was either an actor, writer, producer, director, or held some other relevant role within the television or movie-making world. For someone up-and-coming, a seat at a table here tonight would be the opportunity of a lifetime.

"Oh, Parker, you made it just in time," I heard his mother croon from where she stood to the right, surrounded by her media and PR team—all of whom looking like they were in varying stages of panic. Marjorie, for her part, was her usual picture of grace and calm.

"Of course we did, Mom." I didn't miss the hint of annoyance in his tone. He hated when his parents treated him like their child in public settings, instead of as a colleague. An equal. Which, honestly, was ridiculous. His accomplishments were far from equal to *the* Marjorie Barlow Hart.

Marjorie stepped forward to kiss both sides of Parker's cheeks. "Traffic wasn't too wretched, I hope?"

"Not too bad, no."

"Good." Her eyes turned to me. "Hello, Nora, darling. You look"—she eyed my dress and shoes before quickly flicking her eyes back up to mine—"well."

I fought a flare of annoyance at that. Nevertheless, I smiled brightly. "Thank you, Marjorie. This venue is absolutely stunning."

Marjorie's eyes swept the room. "Yes, I suppose it came together quite nicely in the end, didn't it?" I watched her assistant's face fall.

"It's truly lovely."

A server in a white tuxedo holding a silver tray of champagne flutes approached us, and Marjorie beamed. "Oh, wonderful timing, dear boy!" She took a glass and tipped it back, draining half its contents in a single gulp. Parker grabbed two glasses and handed one of them to me with a charming smile.

"Let's head to the bar," he said, nodding his head over my shoulder. "I see a casting director that I want to say hi to. I heard he's working with Chris Evans on a new action movie, so it would be a good time to show face."

I followed Parker as he strode away with purpose, working hard to make sure my champagne didn't slosh out of my flute as I tried to keep up. My feet were already aching in these stupid heels.

For the rest of the night, Parker hardly spoke to me. I played my role with ease, standing at his side as he schmoozed with anyone he deemed important enough to hold a conversation with. He expelled an extra air of haughtiness tonight, knowing this was his mother's party. As if he was, by simple calculation, one of the more esteemed guests in attendance—despite the fact that he only had a few official credits to his name in his very young career.

The honest reality of his current public status was that he was only as famous as he was because of his mother, and although he would be hard pressed to admit it, he still needed her to succeed. But that didn't stop him from taking every opportunity to establish himself in the presence of others within the industry. I imagined there was a time when watching him work the room like this didn't give me second-hand embarrassment, but my memory simply didn't stretch that far back.

I wondered—as I had many times before—if this was why

Parker dated a girl like me. I wasn't someone he had to compete with. With his good looks and famous pedigree, he could probably have any young actress or model on his arm and in his bed, but three years into our relationship he still chose to have *me* by his side. Perhaps the idea of being with someone else, someone who had the potential to be more successful than him, was too much of a risk for his ego.

Over the years, plenty of other women had tried to come between us, had tried to convince Parker that they were better suited for a life with him. I'd seen the way they flocked to him at wrap parties and other industry events, always vying for his attention when I wasn't in the immediate vicinity. As long as Parker was still unmarried, I supposed they figured they had a chance to change his mind.

Truthfully, they probably *were* better suited for him. I knew what Parker and I looked like from the outside—hell, it wasn't lost on me that many of these people probably thought I was some kind of gold digger. I didn't blame them, even if opinions like that hurt. Our relationship didn't exactly make sense. In the beginning, things were different. We'd shared an easy chemistry that was undeniable. Over time, though, that chemistry morphed into something unexpected and unintended that resembled a moth more than a butterfly.

I didn't know what this was between us anymore.

Two years ago, Parker had been the undeniable love of my life—but now I wasn't so confident in that belief. The deep chasm that existed between us grew a little wider every day, and I wasn't sure I could go on ignoring how the important pieces of myself had been slipping off the edge and into the deep abyss this whole time.

Chapter Two

NORA

Parker and I were once again in the back seat of the Escalade, Jeremy having picked us up at eight, *sharp*. Despite a dull headache from last night's champagne, I'd managed to get ready with enough spare time to enjoy a banana and some toast from the kitchen. I was craving something greasier and more delicious, but Clarke the Chef didn't have those kinds of goods in his healthy arsenal.

I watched the palm trees whip past from my blessedly tinted window, mentally preparing for a full morning of Parker's family. I'd almost forgotten about the yacht excursion, but Marjorie was quick to remind us about it on our way out last night. I'd been surprised when Parker had assured her that he remembered—this was out of character for him, especially since his assistant usually handled everything for him and Parker almost never knew his own schedule—but I'd schooled my features as they discussed the day's expected forecast.

Outside of the Christmas holiday season, it wasn't exactly

normal for Parker's whole family to spend time together like this. They were all nice enough, but their dynamic was a lot different than what I was used to growing up. From past experience I knew to prepare myself for a certain level of *drama* that always somehow manifested when they got together.

Marjorie, the headstrong matriarch, was always terribly busy with her social calendar and self-indulgence. Making time for her children—unless there was publicity involved—was usually the last thing on her priority list.

Her painfully quiet husband, Thad, hardly ever came out of his office—but when he did, it was as if he hadn't been around anyone in ages and could barely be trusted to hold a conversation. Parker's father had been some sort of film investor in the early eighties, which was how he met Marjorie. In more recent years, he wasn't really doing a whole lot with his life . . . at least that I could tell.

Out of Parker's two siblings, his older sister, Priscilla, was Marjorie's single worst nightmare. She might've been a (younger, more beautiful) carbon copy of her mother, but she was hell-bent on doing everything she possibly could to publicly distance herself from the Hart family. Paparazzi were always scoring pictures of her stumbling out of clubs in the early morning hours, wrapped around her grungy new beau of the week.

Peyton was the star player of his high school's varsity football team, his large and bulky frame earning him plenty of recognition on the field. He was also a shameless flirt and had equal success with the ladies. Of everyone in the Hart family, Peyton was my favorite.

It didn't take long before Jeremy was pulling up to the small beachside parking lot that accessed Marina del Rey.

Dozens of large white vessels were docked, shining brightly against glittering sea. I spotted the eyesore we'd be spending the morning aboard almost immediately and smoothed on my smile in preparation. Parker and I exited the SUV and trudged over to where Marjorie and Thad were waiting.

"Good morning, Mom," Parker leaned in to kiss his mother on the cheek. "Dad," he said as he held out his hand to his father.

"Good morning, dear," Marjorie replied. She looked like she'd just crawled out of bed, although the copious amounts of Botox in her face made it harder to tell. I was surprised that an outing like this was scheduled for the morning after her big gala event. There was a time when Parker and I would've shared a knowing look about her appearance, but instead he placed himself in front of me, effectively cutting me out of the conversation.

"Is the yacht ready for us?" Parker asked.

"Yes, Peyton's already inside. The captain told us everything is set up and ready. We were just waiting for you and your sister . . ." She trailed off when her eyes caught somewhere behind me. "Oh, it looks like she's pulling in now."

I turned around in time to see a pastel pink Bentley pull into the parking lot. The sheer anxiety that I felt from simply looking at something worth so much money would have taken the joy right out of owning it for me. But to someone like Pricilla, the car was *owed* to her. A debt in the form of a graduation gift for the "difficult" childhood she'd had to endure.

Parker had given me his Range Rover when he upgraded to a Rolls-Royce at the beginning of the year, and I felt like a total imposter driving it around the city. I'd wanted to keep my trusty old Honda—there was nothing wrong with it—but

Parker insisted, saying that the Honda stuck out like a sore thumb in our driveway.

We all watched in silence as Priscilla pulled into a parking spot. She stepped out wearing a bright purple halter dress and a bag slung over her shoulder, but the true showstoppers were the black fishnet stockings that covered her thin, pale legs. I felt my lips curl into a smile at her bravery as she stepped toward us, despite being a little terrified of her.

"Morning, bitches." Priscilla raised her oversized sunglasses onto her head as she looked at each of us with a devilish smirk.

Marjorie scoffed. "Priscilla. *Please*. Mind your manners."

Priscilla's eyes rolled. "Mom, I literally just got here. Okay? Don't start this shit already."

"Who's ready to see the yacht?" Thad interjected.

The sleek, twenty-meter-long beauty—aptly named *Fantasea*—sparkled promisingly underneath the morning sun, and I let myself envision the day flying by, problem-free. An older man who I assumed to be the captain of the vessel stood proudly near where it was moored, a wide grin on his face as we approached. "Good morning!" he chirped.

Marjorie, who stepped right in front of her husband to assert herself as The Leader, returned a smile that twisted her tired features. "Thank you for having us this morning," she responded dryly.

"Pleasure's all mine, ma'am. Come on aboard, we have breakfast ready for you in the main cabin." He waved his arm and took off down a passageway lined with textured wallpaper and *literal* gold chandeliers.

One by one, we shuffled inside. Parker held his hand out to me after he'd crossed the threshold, giving me a chaste kiss on the cheek before we reached the grand cabin.

Inside, Peyton was inhaling what looked like an omelet. "Hey, guys," he greeted us, his mouth full of egg and spinach.

I exhaled a tight breath at the sight of him and walked over to give him a hug. "Hey, squirt."

Peyton rolled his eyes. "Nor, I'm bigger than my brother. And far more of a man, I can promise you that." He winked. "You ever want to find out what you're missing, you let me know."

My burst of laughter drowned out the sound of Parker clearing his throat behind me, and I gave the little brat a playful nudge.

I picked a blueberry lemon scone from a tray and placed it on a plate, grabbing a latte as well before looking for somewhere to sit outside with Parker. The yacht had begun sailing out of the marina and I found myself a little unsteady on my feet.

We found lounge chairs set up on the deck and stretched our legs on their white linen cushions. I was grateful for the sunlight on my face—the morning air was still chilly enough to raise goose bumps on my arms. "I take back all my grumbling from this morning . . . this is nice," I said as Parker crossed one leg over the other and leaned back to enjoy the view. The movement had my eyes zeroing in on his exposed ankle.

He was wearing his dreadful tapered pants that had a hemline a good three inches above his feet, a style that I absolutely hated. I always had to swallow the urge to laugh out loud when he put them on. It didn't help that he also wasn't wearing socks inside of his loafers. There was just so much . . . skin.

I forced my gaze back up to the horizon ahead, taking a

small bite out of my scone, and let the breeze whip my hair wildly around my face.

"It's beautiful, isn't it?" Parker asked.

I nodded in response as I chewed. "Mm-hm."

"Not as beautiful as you, of course."

I paused mid-chew, and when I looked over at him, I found his blue eyes on me. "Thank you."

His cheek twitched as the corner of his mouth pulled up, and he refocused on the water around us. While my hair was thrashing around and getting dragged through my latte's froth, Parker's was completely unaffected. The amount of product he must have used to achieve such a feat was borderline concerning. I hoped his scalp could breathe.

There was a sudden roaring in the sky above us that was getting louder by the second. I spun around in my seat to look up and found a helicopter hovering right above our yacht. Concern that someone had gone overboard flared through me, that this was a rescue crew—but my eyes caught on the door to the cabin where the rest of the Hart family was filing out of. Everyone was accounted for.

"Paparazzi," Parker said softly next to me, noting my concern. "Just ignore them."

What? Why would the paparazzi be here? I mean, sure, Marjorie was a famed television star, but she wasn't Angelina Jolie. The family wasn't usually followed *this* extensively by cameras. "Why would they have come out here today? We only just left the harbor." I had all my weight pressed into his chair and shouting the words right by his ear, the whirring from the chopper deafening.

Parker shook his head. On the surface he looked annoyed, as if the helicopter were a pesky fly inside his house that he couldn't escape. But I could see the thrill in his eyes, the revelry in this attention. "Who knows?" he responded casually.

Confusion etched itself into my mind. From the few times I'd been around the Harts in a public setting, there had only ever been paparazzi during publicity events with a red carpet. A photo of Marjorie at a lunch with her girlfriends would sporadically make it into a magazine, but we'd all gone out to dinner together on numerous occasions and had never run into anyone with a camera, aside from a few camera phones here and there. It felt invasive to have a helicopter simply floating above us like this. Was it even legal?

Even more confusing was that everyone was acting *really* nonchalant about it. I glanced back at the rest of the family again and found Marjorie and Thad peering over the railing into the water, distracted by something below. Peyton's gaze was stuck on the horizon. But Priscilla . . . her eyes were directly on me. There was an odd, knowing look in her expression. *Was she up to something?*

A smaller speedboat pulled up next to us, and I squinted my eyes to see more cameras. Frowning, I looked back at Parker. "Seriously, how would they have known we'd be out on the water today? And why are so many surrounding us?"

Parker shrugged. "You know paps, they can be ruthless." There was still that troublesome glint in his eye, as if he knew something that I didn't. And I didn't like it one bit. "Hey, Nora," he said, standing up out of his chair. His voice had dropped considerably. "Don't stress. It's a beautiful morning. Let's just . . . let's enjoy the view, okay?" He padded over to my chair and held out his hand to me. Who was going to tell him that the view was ruined and I couldn't enjoy anything with the wind kicking up my hair like I was being electrocuted?

I hesitated, staring at his expectant fingers. But eventually, I reached my own hand out to meet him—feeling the soft pads of his fingers wrapping around mine—and let him help me out of my chair. He guided me toward the railing and pulled me into his body, tucking me in so that my back was pressed against his chest. I felt his arms wrap around me in a warm embrace.

This was . . . nice. I could focus on this feeling, surely.

Standing with him here, now, in the rays of the morning sunlight . . . it was comfortable. And I found myself wondering again how we'd strayed so far in our relationship that a simple interaction like this felt special. It was the kind of affection that we should be giving each other all the time. Of course, said affection wouldn't typically include outrageously conspicuous paparazzi with their tongues lolling out attempting a high-speed chase.

Focus, Nora.

I frowned as I watched the ocean ripple in front of us and —Was that a second speedboat? What the *hell* was going on? I felt the wind whipping along my exposed back and knew that Parker had pulled away. When I turned to find him, he was kneeling in an unusual position—one knee on the sun-soaked deck, and one knee bent out in front of him.

Even more peculiar was the little velvet box that he held out in front of him. And the ginormous diamond ring resting inside of it. My eyes snapped to Parker's.

"Nora James, love of my life"—he was practically yelling the words over the sound of the helicopter and the speedboat and the wind thrashing between us—"will you marry me? Will you do me the great honor of being my wife?"

Suddenly, the loud pop of a champagne bottle rang out

from where Priscilla was standing, and I realized that the rest of the family had gathered just behind him. When had they snuck up so close? My eyes found Parker's again as a wave of nausea that had nothing to do with my lack of sea legs rolled through me.

The shuttering of what sounded like a hundred cameras echoed all around us, and suddenly it dawned on me. "Did you tell the paparazzi to be here for this?"

Parker grinned. "I thought it would be a special occasion for them to capture."

I squeezed my eyes shut and laid a hand on the railing to steady myself. "You *invited* the press to document your proposal to me? Do you hear how ridiculous that sounds? Something like this is supposed to be intimate—"

"Ridiculous? I . . . no, it's not like that." I opened my eyes when he cleared his throat, and that was when I saw the confusion flash across his face. "Honey, I want you to be my wife. Say yes?"

"You *want*?" A burst of white-hot anger rippled down my body, its intensity further throwing me off.

"Of course. Don't you?" His smile was faltering.

I heard Marjorie sniff loudly from somewhere in the distance, a subtle reminder of all of the eyes on us. This only fueled my irritation.

A flurry of thoughts stormed through my mind. I always expected that I'd spend the rest of my life with Parker, but now that the opportunity was staring me in the face, I couldn't help but think of the uncertainty that existed between us. Were we really even right for each other? Were we happy? There were happy *moments*, sure—but was that enough?

I knew Parker was waiting down there with bated breath. I

knew I needed to say something. I raised my chin and braced myself as a deep understanding locked into place. I wasn't a woman that Parker was crazy about. Maybe once upon a time, but not anymore. But I *was* a convenient pairing for him. I'd changed my whole life to be what he wanted me to be, gave up everything back home after—

What would Mom think?

The thought rose to the surface above all others, and I knew what needed to be done.

"No," I said, and I felt my shoulders release from where they'd been hitched to my ears.

Parker's eyes widened in a way I'd never seen before. "No?" His words were a sharp whisper.

I shook my head. "Parker, I'm so sorry. But I can't do this."

"But . . ." he said, fumbling. He rose to his feet and snapped the ring box shut. "Nora, I made reservations at the Beverly Hills Hotel for lunch to celebrate. My whole fucking family is here. What do you mean *no*?" His voice was laced with an unfamiliar venom.

I scoffed. There it was, plain as day. He wasn't even concerned about me. "I mean that I don't want to marry you. That I can't do this anymore." As I walked away, aiming for the cabin where I could lock myself in the bathroom and cry, I heard a new wave of fluttering cameras all around us.

The ride back to shore—and the subsequent car ride back to the house—was heavy with silence. Parker was furious with me, and I was just as furious with him for turning his attempted proposal into a fucking front-page story. To use our relationship as an *opportunity* for him to make it into the news . . . It made me feel cheap.

I was also furious with myself. I was furious at the life that I had here, at the woman staring at me from the mirror every day. How the hell had I let this happen? In all the years we'd dated, I was *always* the one who gave in. I always sacrificed, always made things easier for everyone around me. I'd allowed so much of who I was to fall to the wayside so that I could be a better fit for Parker and his life here.

He knew that I had no interest in being in the public eye. I'd made it clear to him since day one that his family's fame didn't bother me, him being in the spotlight didn't bother me, but that I wanted to keep my own life and our relationship as private as possible. To propose to me surrounded by the press . . . ? He was a fool.

Just last night at the gala, he'd barely spoken to me so that he could focus on brushing shoulders with L.A.'s elite. He wasn't motivated to share his undying love with me in front of anyone then. So to *use* me, to use our relationship now . . . I shook my head as Jeremy pulled the SUV up our driveway in Brentwood.

I looked up at our house—no, *Parker's* house, and realized that so much of our relationship had nothing to actually do with me. Every decision Parker made was for himself. Asking me to move here, to quit my teaching job in Denver and make a new life in L.A., to support him as he threw himself into a career under the spotlight . . . it was always for him.

I thought this life was my happily ever after, but I wasn't happy in the slightest. The sound of Parker slamming his door and storming away registered, and as I sat alone on the cool leather seat, I finally allowed myself to break through the dense fog that had been clouding my vision. It was time to get my life back, and I knew exactly where I needed to start.

Chapter Three

ANDRE

I leaned against the metal shelving and wiped the back of my hand across my forehead. It was only mid-morning, but I was mentally exhausted. Cameron and I were working the first bay and so far, we'd already replaced a faulty alternator, done four oil changes, and we'd just fastened the last twenty-two-inch rim on a tricked-out Tahoe.

I checked the clock that hung on the far wall and saw that it was time to start shifting the guys through lunch breaks. Logan was off today, so it was on me to make sure everyone ate, even though pulling the guys away would set us behind. "Yo, Cam," I yelled out to where he was taking the socket off an impact wrench. It was loud as hell with the air compressor running in the bay next to us, where Ernesto was replacing a blown-out tire on a Kia. The fucking rubber had shredded on the highway and took out the entire driver-side wheel well. The driver was lucky it didn't cause an accident.

Cameron's eyes snapped up. "Yeah?"

I nodded toward the small break room in the back. "Eat."

He dipped his chin and took off.

I called four of the other guys from their bays, and then headed for the front lobby to let Jess know that half the team was off the floor. I found her sitting at the desk, nose deep in a thick textbook with a pile of highlighters splashed across her lap. I walked closer, trying to make my steps heavy, as she absentmindedly pushed her glasses up on her nose. "Hey, Jessica?"

"Oh my gosh!" Her face flushed a cherry red and she clutched her book to her chest. "You scared me."

Shit. "Sorry, Jess. I wasn't trying to sneak up on you. Just wanted to let you know we're starting lunch rotation."

She nodded and moved to set her desk right, stacking piles of invoices and collecting the markers that'd fallen to the ground. "Got it, thank you."

"Sure," I said, and turned on my heel, but I didn't get far before my curiosity dragged me back. "What are you studying?"

She clicked the lid of her pen a few times and gave me a look I couldn't work out. "Oh . . . accounting. I'm in an accounting class right now, and it's honestly kicking my ass."

"Is that what you want to do? Be an accountant?"

Her eyebrows narrowed and she opened her mouth to say something but then closed it. It hit me that she probably thought I was trying to fuck with her. Some of the guys could be real assholes with their teasing, but I always made sure I wasn't one of them. I figured she had enough on her plate, being the only lady on the floor.

After a moment of hesitation, she answered. "No, not an

accountant. But I need to pass the course for my business degree. I want to own my own business someday."

Her face flushed again, like she was embarrassed for saying that out loud. She had no reason to be though. Fuck, I was never any good at school, but the type of shit she was learning —I could really use skills like that.

I had my own finish line picked out too, and as much as I loved working here, this wasn't the end of the game for me. "That's really cool, Jess. Good for you. Don't give up on that, okay?"

A small smile crept from her lips. "Okay." She nodded. "Thanks, Andre."

I heard the front door swing open behind me, the bells on the door handle signaling a customer. The one who stepped through looked around the lobby as if she'd never been inside an auto shop before. I took a step toward her, my black Converse squeaking on the linoleum floor. "Can I help you?" Jessica normally handled all customer interactions, but something about this girl had me moving. Maybe it was the panic in her eyes, or the way her blonde hair was sticking out in ten different directions.

"Yes," she breathed. Her eyes bounced back and forth between Jessica and me, and the jerky motion felt like the sharp edge of a knife, the slightest tremor of a tightrope. "My car . . . it's the steering wheel. It was rattling so hard I had to use both hands to steady it. I pulled off the highway after about ten miles. I probably should've stopped right away, but I was so close." She was rambling, and I couldn't help but think that I wouldn't mind if she never stopped. There was a prickle of familiarity in the back of my mind as she spoke, like a word stuck on the tip of my tongue, and I didn't know why. Maybe I'd seen her around here?

Doubtful—someone like her didn't run on the same streets as someone like me.

I took another step toward her, trying my hardest to look like the kind of guy she'd feel comfortable around: hands out to the side, big smile, slow steps. "Okay, no problem. We can help you figure it out. Where were you coming from?" Ten miles was a bit of a stretch to be driving when something felt wrong with your ride.

She bit her bottom lip between her teeth before letting it fall back out. "Los Angeles," she answered, a hint of something sour in her tone. I did a subtle once-over at that, noticing her clothes looked expensive. Her hair may have been messy, but her white shirt was definitely pressed and her navy shorts looked like they'd be in one of those nautical ads with a bunch of rich, white people smiling on a boat. So what was she doing *here*?

"You drove to Denver from L.A.? Shit, that must be over a thousand miles."

She nodded her head once. "Yeah, I left yesterday morning and stopped overnight in Utah." Another flicker of hesitation crossed her face.

I hummed, then doubled back to the counter where we kept the repair order forms, shaking my head when I met Jess's curious eyes. She didn't look so invested in her accounting textbook now, did she? I knew why she was surprised—head mechanics didn't usually concern themselves with paperwork and customer information—I just hoped she wouldn't call me out on it. For whatever reason, I didn't like that this woman felt uncomfortable. It made me want to sit her down, find out what was wrong, and *do* something about it.

The woman shifted on her feet and pushed a strand of hair over her shoulder. I caught sight of the soft arch of her neck and briefly wondered what her skin might feel like. She looked like she needed a hug. Or a shot of tequila—that always did me good. Maybe Logan kept some in his office. "What kind of car is it?"

Her mouth turned down in the corners. "A Range Rover." Again, that sour tone.

A Range Rover was a bougie-ass ride. She was definitely a rich girl. "Did you get it serviced before your trip?"

Her brown eyes locked in on mine. "What?"

I repeated my question, slower this time.

"What do you mean by 'serviced' though?" Her voice came out high-pitched and she started gnawing at the skin inside her cheek. She looked genuinely confused.

I couldn't decide if it was endearing or irritating. Normally a response like that would annoy the hell out of me . . . but no part of me rubbed wrong at her ignorance. Instead, I found myself cataloging all the ways I would take care of things like this for her if I was her man.

Jesus Christ, Andre, seriously?

"Did you take your car in for an oil change," I explained, "or have someone check the rest of your fluids before you left?"

I instantly regretted the question when her face collapsed. As an auto technician, it was a perfectly normal question for me to ask. But still. "Oh . . . um. No, I didn't. I just started driving, I wasn't really thinking." She put her hands on her hips and turned to face the notice board, like she might find the answer to her problems in the help-wanted ads.

"Hey." Her eyes flicked back to mine, so wide and brown and beautiful. I dropped my voice and gave her a look like *Totally fair, happens all the time. I'm sure you didn't fuck up your hundred-thousand-dollar car too badly.* I smiled. "Don't trip, all right? It's okay. We'll take a look at it." The tightness around her eyes relaxed a little. "Do you have anyone you can call to pick you up? It might take a while, depending on what we find under the hood."

She reached for her phone in her back pocket and took a big breath in. "Yeah, sorry. My friend . . . she's the one who told me to come here. I'll ask if she can come get me." She paused. "I called her right away, you know. Honestly like, the second my car started acting weird. I was going to pull over and call a tow truck but she gave me the name of this place." She was back to rambling now, and I knew this time it was because she thought I was judging her.

"Good, that's really good." She grinned, and I wanted her to do it again. "Do you have anything in your car you need to grab?"

I watched as a perfectly manicured finger tucked a piece of blonde hair behind her ear. Her nails were bright red, shining under the lights like candy paint on a newly restored Impala. "There's quite a bit of stuff in there. I'm . . . I'm moving back here . . . uh, to Denver. So all my things are packed in the back. But I don't really have a place where I can drop anything off yet. Is it okay if it all stays in there?"

My mind was caught on her words. She *was* from here. And she was staying. "No problem at all. As long as you don't need anything, I can take the keys from you and we'll get your car pulled in. Here, fill this in"—I dropped the clipboard on the shelf next to the notice board—"and Jessica will process your information. We'll call you as soon as we know what's going on, okay?"

She nodded, seeming more confident at the sound of my plan. I could give her plans all day if it made her feel better.

She pulled a key fob out of her front pocket and stepped forward to hand it to me. I stepped toward her as well, an urge to help close the distance between us. As I reached out to grab the fob, my fingers lightly grazed the back of her hand and I felt the zap of an electric current spark against her skin.

Her eyes widened slightly. A small chuckle escaped from my mouth as I pulled my hand back with the fob in tow. "Sorry, one of the hazards of the job. I'm always shocking people."

"Oh," her mouth curved upward, "don't worry about it." I watched her swallow before she spoke again. "Thank you."

I smiled at her, reassuring. "It's no problem at all . . ." I trailed off, hoping she'd fill the pause with her name.

"Nora. My name's Nora."

"Nora," I repeated. Again, it felt . . . familiar. "We'll be in touch, okay?"

"Sure." She nodded and gestured to her phone. "I'm just going to call my friend, and then I'll be back in to give you guys my information." When she turned for the door, I mumbled something that might've been another "okay," while my eyes stayed glued to her the whole way out.

Fuck. What the hell was that? Hundreds of women had come in to Logan's Auto, and none of them had ever gotten my head so fucking twisted like that.

I turned back around and faced a very bemused Jessica, but I did my best to casually play it off. The last thing I needed were rumors to spread around the shop—Logan damn sure wouldn't be happy. "I'm going to pull her car in as soon as one of the bays opens up. Tell her it might be a while?"

She looked back at her computer screen, and I caught the hint of a smile. "You got it, boss."

We didn't pull Nora's Range Rover into a bay until an hour before closing time, but I was hopeful that we'd be able to at least diagnose the issue before we closed up shop. "What's the deal with this one?" Cameron asked from under the hood.

"Customer drove it here from California and didn't get it serviced before she left. She heard rattling and her wheel seized up about ten miles out, so she drove it straight here." Cameron's eyes rolled, and it irritated me. "Hey," I said, and his eyes moved to me. "We don't judge."

His face twisted in confusion. "No problem, sorry." It might've been standard for the guys to talk shit in the bays, to rip into customers for their stupidity behind their backs, but Nora didn't deserve that. Whatever had her showing up like she did, whatever she was going through—because I was pretty positive she was going through something—she didn't deserve any extra bullshit. Cameron pulled the dipstick from the oil tank. "Yeah, the tank's dry."

"What does that tell us?" I asked. Cameron had been with the shop for over a year now, and he'd come a long-ass way from knowing practically nothing when he started, but I made sure to keep pushing him.

"Low oil level, pump not generating enough pressure.

Probably needs a new filter now too. Her check engine light should've warned, so I'll do a computer diagnostic to find out why it didn't."

"Good. Check it over and get back to me with a full rundown. I'll go give the customer a call and let her know we'll need it overnight. Get started on following the oil system through the pump—if you need to pull Manny in to help, go ahead." Manny had a decade's worth of experience, and he was one of our most patient guys. He'd been a big help getting Cam trained up. "Get as far as you can today and we can pick it back up in the morning, yeah?"

Cameron nodded. "Sounds good, boss."

I'd normally have Jessica reach out to a customer for an update like this, but I'd already come this far, I didn't see myself stopping now. Plus, she'd sounded so stressed before, I wanted to be the one to ease her worries if she had questions.

I was at the door to the shop's office a minute later, my eyes narrowing at the light pouring out through a crack. It was Logan's day off, and I was the only one with keys, so there was no reason for it to be open. I didn't even think before I lunged, pushing the rusty doorknob and swinging it open all the way.

Inside, Logan dropped the file he'd been holding and stumbled back a step. "Jesus, Andre, you scared the shit out of me."

I grimaced. *Second time today.* "Sorry, boss. I didn't know you were coming in today."

He'd taken the last few days off and was supposed to be in the mountains with his fiancée; I wasn't expecting him back until tomorrow. "We got back early and I wanted to get a head start on this paperwork." He hunched over his desk and tapped away on his keyboard before walking over to his printer. "How have things been going?" he asked over his shoulder.

I held my hands together in front of me as I spoke. "Good, really good. We've been busy, but the guys are handling it well. I submitted payroll for you to approve, and we got a parts shipment in last night. I had Manny and Damien enter the inventory into the system and then put it all away."

Logan nodded and turned back my way. "Sounds like you're on top of things. Good work."

It felt good to be acknowledged for the hard work I put in here. "Thanks."

"Oh." He cocked his head. "Did Nora come in?"

I stuffed down the urge to tug on my collar, suddenly hot. "Yeah, she came in this afternoon. I was actually about to give her a call. We need a little more time with her vehicle, but it should be good by tomorrow." *Don't ask, don't ask.* "You know her?"

The side of Logan's mouth curled up, and he looked up from the files in his hands. "Yeah, so do you. She's a friend of Amelia's . . . I thought you might've remembered. She was at my birthday party last summer."

Of course she was. Now I felt like a prick for not recognizing her, but we must not have spoken much because she was *definitely* a girl you didn't forget.

"And she drove here from L.A.? Amelia mentioned something about a breakup. She didn't even know she was coming back until she got the call earlier."

I let out a breath, my brain working through all the pieces of information. "She was pretty skittish. I don't even know how she made it all the way without the SUV overheating. I'm hoping she didn't fuck up her engine too bad—we still don't know why the oil light didn't trigger. Cameron's looking at it now."

"Well, let's consider her a friend of the shop and do what it takes. I trust you to handle it."

I dipped my chin and ran a hand over the back of my head. "You got it, boss. Consider it done."

Logan reached his arm out to grip my shoulder. "Thank you, Andre. For running this place while I was out. I'm lucky to have you."

I put my hand in my pocket and brushed the scrap of paper I'd written her number on between my fingers. "Happy to do it, boss."

Chapter Four

NORA

"You left? Just like that?" We were sitting on a plush white sofa in Mackenzie's living room, an assortment of eclectic throw pillows scattered around us. My elbow was currently propped on a round orange one with small mirrored beads forming a pattern in the center. I wouldn't have expected anything less.

"I couldn't stay for another minute, Mackenzie," I told her. "I literally . . . I couldn't do it anymore. Not after I said no, not after realizing how messed up my life had gotten, and definitely not when I stepped back and imagined what my mom would think." Her wide eyes softened a bit, and she closed the space between us to squeeze my leg. "I felt like I was climbing out of my skin being in that house, so I packed my things and bolted." I looked down at my lap where my fingers were tracing the scalloped hemline of my shorts, bracing myself for whatever was about to come out of her mouth. She'd been the one to rave about my relationship with Parker since the beginning, telling me that I'd finally found my Prince Charming.

Maybe I *had* found Prince Charming. He certainly had the castle, the money, the steady and secure future. But what good was finding the prince if the princess lost herself in the process? Maybe being swept away wasn't all it was cracked up to be— not if you were swept so far you didn't recognize yourself anymore.

Parker and I had only been dating a few months when my mother died. I'd met him at a bar on one of the few nights I'd actually let my friends take me out. I was my mom's main caregiver at that point, and I spent most of my time at home with her. But that night, Gwen—my other best friend from college—and Mackenzie wanted to see a live band downtown and practically forced me to go with them. Parker happened to be in Denver shooting for some commercial, and I remembered thinking he was the dreamiest man I'd ever laid eyes on.

Needless to say, he'd served as a wonderful distraction, and I threw myself into our new relationship as a way to escape the insurmountable sadness I was feeling. The truth was, as angry as I felt toward Parker for using me to serve his own image, I wasn't exactly innocent. Not back then, anyway.

Mackenzie sniffed, and my eyes moved up to meet hers. A dip of concern scrunched between her brows. "I'm sorry, Nora. I'm really glad you came here though. You can stay at our house for as long as you need to."

I smiled, even though her kindness sent a wave of anxiety through me. "I really appreciate it. I don't plan on being here too long, I promise."

"I'm serious, Nor. Take all the time you need. Eric and I

don't mind. And it means you can help me with some last-minute wedding planning!" She clapped her hands together as a wide grin bloomed on her face. "Having a live-in bridesmaid weeks before the wedding is kismet, don't you think?"

I brought a green velvet pillow up to my face and mock-groaned into it. "Okay, now I'm honestly scared. Go easy on me, Mack. You know I'm not an expert on all that girly shit."

"Okay, yeah right." She waved her arm across my body. "Look at you in these chic designer clothes. It's like you've transformed before my very eyes."

Rolling my eyes, I expelled a long breath. "Trust me, for every expensive article of clothing I own, a mile-long string of regret follows."

She leaned forward, placing her hand on the pillow. "Don't do that. Don't let yourself regret any of it. The time you spent with Parker wasn't wasted. First of all, you can say you've slept with a model. Regardless of how you feel about him now, that man is *hot*." I swiftly smacked her on the leg and a fit of giggles burst from her mouth before she continued. "Second, even if it didn't all pan out the way you envisioned, you still learned new things about yourself. Now you know what you want. Not to sound like the world's biggest cliché, but everything happens for a reason." She leaned into the couch, letting her head rest on the canary yellow quilt.

"Thanks." It was all I could manage with the swell of emotions thrumming under the surface of my skin. I wanted to tell her how scared I was, how anxious starting over made me feel. I wanted to cry. Without direction, the confidence I'd spent so much time building before I'd met Parker wilted. But at the same time, I knew I was strong enough to handle this, and I didn't want to ask for more help than absolutely necessary.

Eric got home from work late that night, which gave Mackenzie and I plenty of time to drink a bottle of wine together. It felt really, *really* good to have a comfortable night with one of my best friends—a reminder of how things used to be before I moved away.

Their cozy cottage was nothing like the cold surfaces and sharp edges of luxury you'd find in Brentwood. Instead, Mackenzie's personality was everywhere. The small dining room nook was painted a dusty rose, and the furniture was naturally distressed from following her and Eric through all their moves. Plants I didn't even know the names of made the room feel alive, their long vines hanging from the walls where colorful pots sat on floating shelves.

It was like pieces of a puzzle slotting into place, giving me an undeniable feeling of rightness. *This* was what I'd been craving from the sterile confines of Parker's "manor."

Later that night, as I lay beneath a vintage floral duvet in Mackenzie and Eric's guest bedroom, I stared wistfully at the ceiling and told myself over and over again that I could do this. I *could* rebuild my entire life, as long as I focused on one piece at a time. I'd need to find a more permanent place to stay— Mackenzie and Eric deserved their near-newlywed bliss without someone else shacking up inside their little slice of heaven.

There was a few hundred dollars in my checking account that I would have to make do with for now. I had a decent chunk of money stashed in a savings account from my mother's estate, but I never let myself touch it. I believed I would know what to use it for when the moment was right. This *wasn't* that moment, and I needed to do whatever I could to get some cash to keep from dipping into it.

Before I moved to California, I'd gotten my degree in education and worked at an elementary school teaching second grade. The gap in my employment over the last few years wouldn't look great, but there was always a shortage of teachers.

My thoughts flitted to the expensive Range Rover that I'd carelessly driven into the ground. I was such an idiot for thinking I could just drive it over a thousand miles without checking the basics. I hoped like hell I hadn't caused too much damage.

You got this, Nora. I repeated the mantra until I started to believe it, and willed my body to relax. It had been a whirlwind, but I'd successfully made it back to Colorado—the last place that I'd felt completely myself. I may have ruined my car in the process, but Mackenzie's words from earlier floated to the surface of my mind. *Everything happens for a reason.* She was right about it being cliché. And I loved it all the more for that reason.

My mind unwilling to cooperate, I let it roam to the phone call I'd gotten earlier. I hadn't expected to hear Andre's voice on the other end of the line, but he said he'd wanted to *personally* call and give me an update. Those words had elicited a full-body flush, naturally, and it was a reaction I still wasn't prepared to unpack. He said they'd need at least a full morning with it tomorrow, which was convenient because I knew I'd be spending the morning scouring the internet for apartment listings.

I pulled the blanket up around my neck and closed my

eyes, forcing every muscle in my body to relax one by one—a trick my mother had taught me when I was a little girl. I'd barely reached the muscles in my calves when thoughts of Andre's tattoos that covered both of his hands invaded my mind. The way he'd looked so intently at me with those cool, gray eyes. I felt a twinge of excitement at the prospect of seeing him again tomorrow.

Don't trip, all right?

Words from the mouth of a complete stranger. A stranger who, if I was being honest, had made me nervous when I'd first laid eyes on him. He was attractive, that part was clear. But he had that wayward look of someone who knew what trouble *really* looked like. And yet, when he'd sensed my discomfort, he found a way to cut through the noise in my head and reach me with his words.

It's okay.

And just like that, I slipped a hand under my pillow and fell into a deep sleep.

I GOT a call from Jessica at Logan's auto shop around noon. Her voice was cheerful as she told me that my Range Rover was ready to pick up. I was home alone, so I ordered an Uber and shot a text to Mack with an update.

When I got to the shop, Andre was in the lobby again. He turned to look at me with a lopsided grin and I kicked myself once more for how wrong I'd been about him yesterday. His thumbs were tucked into his pockets, hands hung lazily against either side of his black pants. The backs of his hands were covered in tattoos, and I let my eyes skate over the letters inked into his fingers—*LOVE* and *FEAR*. "Hey, Nora." His voice was like velvet as it purred against my senses and I looked back up to his face quickly.

"Hi," I stammered. "I'm here to pick up my car . . . the Range Rover? I brought it in yesterday—"

"I remember." His eyes sparkled. "Let me go grab it for you. I'll bring it around to the front."

"Sure. I'll just settle my bill first."

He shook his head. "Nah, you don't owe us a thing. Wasn't a big deal. We just flushed the lines and put some oil in your tank. It's on the house."

Dread pooled in my stomach. "I can't let you do that for me. I'm happy to pay whatever it costs."

His grin grew from one corner of his mouth as he pinned me with his sharp gaze. "Nothing to charge you for. Really. I'll meet you out front, yeah?" Before I had a chance at another rebuttal, Andre turned around and disappeared down the hallway.

Alone in the lobby with Jessica, I felt the silence turn awkward. What must she think of me, stumbling in here yesterday without a clue and then accepting handouts like this? I sidled up to her desk and ran my fingers along the edge. "Please, I'd really like to pay my bill." It was time I took care of myself. "I really insist."

Jessica blinked, and if I wasn't so frazzled, I might've commented on how gorgeous her wavy red hair was. "I wish I could help you, but when Andre makes a decision, that's usually the end of it. He hasn't processed any of your work in the system, so I wouldn't even know what to charge you for anyway." She gave me a gentle smile, and I knew it was a lost cause.

A long, resigned sigh poured out of my lungs as I thanked her. As soon as I stepped back through the door, Andre was pulling my Range Rover up. It looked like it'd been washed. I caught his eyes through the passenger-side window, and some of my earlier tension uncoiled when he winked at me.

"You're really not going to let me pay for anything?" I called out over the roof as he got out and shut the door.

He chuckled and walked around the front of the car, his swagger evident in the measured steps he took. "You're a stubborn one, aren't you?" His lips curved up in that lazy grin again, and my eyes caught on his throat, at the tattoo peeking out from his collar. It looked like a winged-creature of some sort.

"Listen, I realize that I made myself look like an oblivious airhead by not . . . *servicing* my car before driving all the way out here, but I was under a lot of stress and not really thinking straight. However," I pressed, meeting his eyes and swallowing a lump in my throat, "I assure you that I'm not a bumbling idiot. I can take care of myself. So really, please, I would like to pay for whatever work was done."

Andre's face fell, taking on more of an edge. "Nora," he said gently. Too gently. "I never doubted your ability to take care of yourself, and I definitely don't think you're a 'bumbling idiot.'" He bound his eyes tightly to mine, and they seemed to slip from a steel gray to a softer, more overcast silver. "I know you were anxious yesterday; I felt it. I don't know what it was about, and it's not my business. But I happen to have it in my power to ease your burden. I don't know you, Nora. At this point, I know your car better. But I do know that, at least in this, you're in good hands. Okay?"

My eyes burned with the sting of tears, and I had to look away. When was the last time I'd received such genuine kindness from another human being? Andre couldn't have been more different from the types of people I'd been surrounded by in Los Angeles—both in looks *and* sincerity. I'd always been a generous person myself, and felt happiest when I was helping others. Somewhere along the way, though, I'd forgotten how to accept kind gestures. Yet another way I'd let my life get away from me. *No more.* I huffed out a small breath and tipped my head back to look at him. "Okay."

He smiled again; his expression still gentle. "Good."

I reached my hand forward to take the keys from him, hesitating for a moment before my fingers made contact. "Are you going to zap me again?"

It was a joke, but I didn't miss the way Andre's gaze heated up a notch. "I guess we'll see, won't we?"

Clutching the fob, I tugged my hand back and watched as his focus moved down to his own fingers. "Um . . . can I ask you a quick question?"

Andre's posture straightened. "Of course."

I looked back at my car. "How much do you think I could sell this for?"

"Your Range Rover?"

"Yeah. I'm thinking of trading it in, but I need to figure out how much it's worth before I go to the dealership."

His eyes widened. "How soon are you trying to sell?"

"Today, if possible." I lifted both shoulders, my smile turning sheepish.

A muscle in Andre's cheek twitched. "Right. Tell you

what. Let me look up the resale value of its year and trim. I can be off in an hour and, if it helps, I'd be more than happy to go with you."

The urge to object flooded through me, and yet . . . my earlier thoughts knocked. The truth was that going into a dealership on my own scared the shit out of me, and after the stress of the past few days, I was exhausted. Besides, would he offer at all if it put him out?

"Are you sure?" Oh my god. What was I *doing*? I didn't know a thing about this guy.

But then his smile flashed brighter, like he was pleased to know that he had me, and for whatever reason it assured me that I could trust this tall, dark, tattooed mechanic. "Yes, Nora. I'm sure."

I sighed. "Okay."

He dipped his head and turned on his heel, but stopped halfway to the door. "Hey . . . did you know that we've met before?" Mischief glimmered in his eye.

"What?"

"Yeah . . . Logan's birthday party last year."

Oh. "You were there?" Logan was Amelia's fiancé, and Amelia was Mackenzie's best friend from childhood. He owned this auto shop, which was how I ended up here yesterday in the first place. I'd gotten to know Amelia pretty well during college and I'd met Logan on our graduation trip to Mexico.

"Sure was." He grinned. "Looks like we might run in some of the same circles, Nora James."

I heard him whistle to himself as he walked back inside.

I WAS STILL SITTING in my car an hour later when Andre exited the shop. I'd decided to just stay here and wait for him because I really didn't have anywhere else to go, and used the time to look up apartment listings in the area.

He stepped off the curb and into a patch of sunlight, his deep brown skin glowing in its bending rays, and it sprang to mind how handsome he was. He was also *really* tall. His uniform was loose-fitting and flecked with grease, and he wore a backward black hat over his shaved head.

I started my car and unlocked the doors, and when he pulled his open, his brows were scrunched together. "Have you been waiting here this whole time?"

I nodded. "Yeah, but I've kept myself busy."

"You could've waited inside in the lobby or something. You didn't need to stay out here."

"It's okay, I was looking up places for rent on my phone. Honestly, the hour flew by."

Andre didn't seem convinced, but he dropped the subject and got into the car, settling his black backpack in the footwell. "You know where you're going?"

"Yep." I got into gear and hit *Go* on my dashboard's GPS. "Thanks for coming. You really didn't have to."

"It's all good. Dealerships can be a lot, so I'd rather you have someone there with you."

His words hovered in the air between us. I felt caught off guard all over again. It was . . . really nice.

When I didn't say anything, he continued. "So this SUV

has a damn good resale value, and *I* happen to know it's in great condition." He offered me a smile. "What are you looking to trade it in for?"

I shrugged. "I don't have anything specific in mind, I just want something more affordable."

Andre rubbed his hands together as we pulled into the dealership a moment later. "All right, Nora, let's make this happen for you."

Chapter Five

ANDRE

Nora parked the Range Rover in the customer lot of the dealership and switched off the ignition. I watched her exhale and look out her window, a rogue piece of hair blowing across her face from the air conditioning vent. "I hate these places," she muttered.

I chuckled. "That's what I'm here for." She turned to face me, her teeth bearing down on her bottom lip. "I won't let anyone fuck with you. It's going to be okay, yeah?"

She nodded. "Okay."

"Are you sure you want to do this?" I looked around at the glossy interior, its dark oak veneer finish and tan leather seats. Even the steering wheel that she was still gripping had a heating feature—one that likely didn't mean much in California but would be a treat here in winter. "This is a nice-ass ride. You really want to give it up?"

Almost like my words snapped her into action, her eyes set

in determination, and she grabbed her purse from the back seat. "I'm sure. I hate this thing . . . Hate everything it represents."

Interesting. The urge to know more clawed at me. "Okay, let's go find something that makes you happy, then."

We got out and met halfway at the front of the car as I slung my backpack over my shoulder. The heat from the sun burned through the thick fabric of my work clothes, but this was worth it.

"Here's the deal," I said, leaning in and keeping my voice low. She smelled like fresh laundry and sugar, and the combination almost derailed me. "These places are always full of sales guys that can't wait for you to spend your money. They're like sharks, and they want you to help them pay their bills. The key is to act uninterested. Keep a poker face, and don't let them know what you're thinking. They talk fast and ask a lot of questions to try to confuse you into making a decision. You need to tune it all out."

Nora's eyes flashed again, and she nodded her pretty little head. "Okay."

"I'll be by your side. I'm right here if you have any questions, but I'm following your lead, okay?"

She didn't even have a chance to respond before a man approached. His hair was greased back and he was wearing a bright blue polo that was way too small—a strip of skin was exposed between the bottom of his shirt and the top of his pants. I watched as he honed in on Nora, a big fake smile plastered on his face. "Well, hello there!"

She took a step toward me and answered with a tight "Hello."

"Welcome to Denver's Car Masters! My name's Carl. What brings you in today?"

He kept his focus on Nora, completely ignoring me. "We're just looking around, *Carl*," I said. "But we'll be sure to let you know if we need anything." I placed my hand on the small of her back as I led her toward the far section of the lot.

"He was just trying to be nice," Nora whispered.

"I'm sure he was."

We zigzagged through the rows of used cars, and I took note of the first few that caught Nora's attention. She stopped to peek inside the window of an older model Ford Fusion. "Hm." All the ones she'd been interested in had been worlds away from her Range Rover, but this was the first she'd hummed at.

"You like it?"

"It's a little small." She gathered her hair and tucked it under the neck of her dress, then peered into the back seat. "I don't want anything too big, but I'd like to have *some* space."

"Let's keep going." I kept my eye out for something that might catch her attention but stayed quiet. She stopped again at a Honda Accord. It was a two-door coupe with a sunroof and leather seats. "Okay, you like this one," I guessed, noticing the smile on her lips.

Her eyes moved to me. "It's the same car I had before the Range Rover . . . my first car. I loved that thing." A chuckle fell from her lips, a quiet sound, but still—I felt it somewhere in my chest. "If cars could talk."

I wondered what kind of trouble she stirred up when she was younger. This Nora was reserved, careful to lay out only pieces of herself. But the evidence of something wilder lingered in her eyes. Logan's words about her recent breakup came to mind, and I couldn't imagine what kind of idiot would let her not only leave, but not even bother to make sure she was safe for her journey.

She gave the Honda another look and then turned around, her bright white sneakers crunching on the pavement. My eyes roved up the curve of her lean, tanned calf to the hem of her blue summer dress before I realized what I was doing and forced my eyes away.

I spotted a white Subaru Crosstrek in the distance. It looked like a newer model, and like something she'd want to see. When I spotted her to point it out, she was gazing at a bright red Hummer. "Nora."

She looked up, and for a split second it felt like the wind had been knocked out of me. From the reflection off all the cars, her brown eyes beamed, and she was the most beautiful thing I'd ever seen. I cleared my throat. "Check out that Subaru up ahead." I nodded in the direction of the crossover. My voice was strained, but there wasn't much I could do about that.

"Oh, good find, Andre!" She practically skipped across the concrete, her skirt dancing around her legs. My chest tightened again at the evidence of her joy.

She was walking half circles around it when I got closer, so I followed suit. I knew where to look for signs of accident restoration and aftermarket paintwork, but in general, signs of damage were easy to spot, and this one seemed clear of any. The body was in great shape and all four tires were damn near new. I found Nora looking at me, as if waiting for my opinion. "It looks good so far," I said, watching a smile ease onto her face. "Do you want to look inside?"

She nodded, and her smile widened. "Definitely."

I glanced at the dealership's main office that sat three parking rows away, and spotted Carl watching us from his perch on the sidewalk. As soon as I made eye contact with him, he hit the ground running. To Nora, I said, "Remember, you're in control of this, not anyone else. Okay?"

She responded with a nod.

"Find something that tickles your fancy?" Carl called out, a shit-eating grin spread across his face. Again, eyes for Nora only.

"Yes, I'd like to see the inside of this one, please." Her voice was confident, and I almost smiled. Almost. But not in front of Carl.

"Sure thing, let me go grab the keys," he said, and then jogged back toward the office.

Once he was halfway to the building, I said, "I'm going to check out a few things while we wait." I slid my backpack off my shoulder and rifled through it for my flashlight and rag. Lying down onto the asphalt, I scooted under the Subaru.

"What are you looking for?" I heard her ask.

"Making sure there's no damage to the undercarriage. And checking for fluid leaks. Rust damage. That's it, really."

I didn't have much to inspect, overall. For a used car, the previous owner had obviously taken great care of it. I began scooting my way back out from under the car just as Carl reappeared. He eyed me suspiciously. "Er, everything okay?" he asked. He clearly didn't like that I was helping myself.

"Everything's great, Carl," I muttered as I picked my backpack up and zipped it closed.

He frowned, and then as if realizing what he was doing, he suddenly smiled wide again and turned toward Nora. "I've got the keys, would you like a test drive?" He clicked the fob to unlock the car for emphasis.

"Yeah, that sounds great!" There was definitely a hint of sarcasm in her voice, and I chuckled softly under my breath. If Carl noticed, he didn't let on.

I moved to open the driver-side door for Nora and she raised her eyebrows, smiling in a way that had my chest puffing out of my Dickies button-up. Carl made a move to get into the passenger seat, but I stepped up to him with a menacing look that had him scrambling into the back seat.

Inside, the crossover was . . . *nice*. There was a decently sized entertainment screen within the media console, room to fit my six-six frame with enough to spare, and the interior was clean. It looked like it had been recently detailed. I was impressed.

"Okay," Slimy Carl said from the back, "let's exit the lot and turn right onto the main road. Another right gets us onto the freeway, and from there you can take the first exit and I'll guide you back. Sound good?"

"Sure," Nora responded, and slid her belt over her chest. She started the ignition, grinning at me as she adjusted the rear-view mirror before she pulled the car out of the parking space.

The first few minutes of the ride were quiet. I wanted to give Nora the space to get comfortable with the drive without putting any extra pressure on her. Luckily, Carl stayed quiet too. We made it on the on-ramp for the highway, and I could feel her overall confidence with the car growing.

She merged onto the highway and I subtly muttered to her under my breath, "Floor it."

Nora cocked her head to the side, keeping her eyes on the road. "What?"

"Floor it."

Looking at me then, her brown eyes sparked and a grin took over her mouth. She was so damn gorgeous.

And then she focused back on the road, gripped the steering wheel a little harder, and fucking gunned it.

NORA MISSED the first exit because she was so focused on letting the damn Subaru fly. Carl repeatedly directed her to exit the highway, but Nora's responding giggle was such an incredible sound that I was all for her ignoring him.

It was the first time I'd really seen a wide-open smile from her, and it twisted something inside of me—something foreign and unfamiliar. So I turned around in my seat to glare at Carl and said, "I thought this was a test drive? Let the girl get a feel for the car."

He muttered something under his breath and wrapped his hand around the grab handle.

She did eventually exit, expertly navigating the side streets to backtrack toward the dealership. Along the way, I told her to test the blinkers and horn—all of which worked as expected. By the time we made it back into the parking lot of the dealership, Nora was vibrating with an excited energy.

We all got out of the car and she handed the keys back to Carl, thanking him. He threw her one of his big fake smiles. "How did you feel driving it?"

She looked at me when she answered, "Free."

After a bit of negotiating—a conversation I was happy to

help lead at Nora's request—she successfully traded in her Range Rover for the Subaru. The dealership ended up cutting her a check for the difference, since the souped-up SUV was worth much more than what she was trading it in for.

Nora walked out of the dealership's front doors with a new set of keys and a crisp check in hand, smiling from ear to ear. And *damn* if it wasn't the best thing I'd ever seen.

Chapter Six

NORA

"Are you hungry?" I asked Andre. His gray eyes flicked to mine as he reached for his seatbelt.

"Uh . . . I could be. Why?"

"I owe you dinner."

His dark brows pulled together. "What do you mean?"

I ran my palm along the center console and darted my eyes around my spanking new Subaru. "This. For helping me today. I'm sure there are many things you would've rather done than back me up at a used car lot."

The smile that unfolded across his face was sweet and sticky inside of my stomach. "Trust me, Nora. There's nothing else I would've rather been doing than watch you make Carl sweat."

"No . . . *you* made Carl sweat," I corrected, giggling. "I'm pretty sure Carl almost shit his pants on a few occasions."

His smile grew wider as he stared at me for a moment. "You should do that more often."

"What?"

"Laugh," he said simply, his voice soft. "It suits you."

I felt my cheeks flush in response. He'd said the words so casually, and yet it felt anything but. "So . . ." I tried again, "can I take you to dinner? Seriously, between yesterday and today, you've done a lot for me and I'd like to return the favor."

He considered me for a moment before he dipped his head. "Okay, Nora, let's go get some dinner."

God, he was looking at me like I could be his meal, and it sent a surge of nervous energy throughout my body. But it didn't feel aggressive—nothing about him was. If anything, he felt . . . comforting. "You like burgers?" I asked.

He cocked an eyebrow. "Everybody likes burgers."

I scoffed. "If only that were true, Andre." And then I shifted the car into gear and took off.

I PARKED in front of my favorite diner in the whole world, feeling my heart skip a beat. It had been open since my mother was a little girl and was our spot as I grew up too. Some of my best memories with her happened here. I'd been surprised when the thought to come occurred, that I would be so willing to bring a near-stranger to a place that was etched into my soul.

I'd been feeling my mother's pull since returning to Denver, seeing her everywhere in the mountains that stood tall in the horizon and in the lush, shady trees surrounding the city. Coming here alone might've felt a little too hard, but facing the swell of emotions with Andre next to me was manageable— although I would never admit any of that to him.

Not only was Sunshine Shack nostalgic, but they had juicy, plate-sized cheeseburgers and the creamiest milkshakes in the whole damn city. "You ever been here before?" I asked, glancing at Andre. He took in the restaurant's facade, its tattered yellow sign flashing an arrow to the entrance near where a few people sat on picnic tables.

"Nope."

"Well, prepare to eat your heart out."

I didn't miss the lift of his cheeks as he pushed open his door.

It was still early in the evening, but the diner was already busy. Almost every table was full and the sound of clinking utensils and soft conversation filled the entire space. I eyed an open booth in the far corner and made a beeline for it.

As we sat down, I was struck by how much of the *same* everything was. The powder-blue vinyl table was peeling, and the dingy red booths were scratched and torn from decades of use. It looked exactly as it did the last time I was here with my mom.

Andre, with his dark clothes and tattoos, stood out in stark contrast to the family-friendly themes all around us. I noticed many patrons eyeing him warily from their tables, and felt a flare of annoyance in my chest. But then a twinge of guilt surfaced, because I'd had the same initial reaction to him in the shop yesterday. It felt so ridiculous now to have ever felt nervous around him.

I looked away from the booth next to us and found him watching me. "Why do you look anxious?"

"What?" I asked, feigning confusion.

Luckily, a waitress came by just in the nick of time. "Welcome to the Sunshine Shack, can I get you started with something to drink?"

Andre indicated for me to order first while he picked up a menu. I smiled up at the waitress. "May I please have the Strawberry Delight milkshake?"

"Sure thing." She wrote it down on her pad of paper. "And for you, sir?"

Andre flashed a grin before looking up at her. "I'll have what she's having, please."

"You got it," the waitress said, then sauntered away.

"Copycat," I teased.

"Hey, you're the one who's been here before." He picked up the menu again to look at the food options. "What's good to eat?"

"Honestly, I've eaten at this place hundreds of times and I always get the same thing—the Cheesy Belly. I'm sure there are other great options, but I wouldn't know."

His face scrunched up, and I realized he was trying to hold in a laugh.

"What?"

He looked me straight in the eye. "Did you just say *cheesy belly*, Nora?"

Oh. Well, when he put it like that. "I've never realized how bad that sounds." Images of dirty belly buttons swarmed my mind before I quickly shut them down. "I *swear* it's good—it's a cheeseburger with pork belly melted into it!"

He chuckled under his breath, and the glint in his eye told me he was enjoying this. "Whatever you say, sicko."

"I'm not a sicko!" I swatted his arm, and the feel of his smooth skin had me yanking my hand back and pressing it into my lap. Something about sitting under these fluorescent lights in front of this gorgeous man had me feeling jittery.

The wicked delight that sparkled in his eye burnt out. "I'm just teasing you." He was still smiling as the waitress approached the table with our strawberry milkshakes, setting them down in front of each of us.

"Are you ready to order?"

I kept my eyes on Andre as I ordered. "I'd *love* your Cheesy Belly, please. Medium rare, and an extra side of french fries."

His lips stretched all the way to his ears before he said again, "I'll have what she's having." He glanced up at the waitress. "Please."

It didn't take long for the food to come out, and everything was just as I remembered it. The burgers were huge, barely held together by long wooden toothpicks with the customary bright blue "Sunshine Shack" paper flags. Warm, gooey cheese melted onto the trays. I didn't hesitate before digging into mine, utterly ravenous.

After inhaling six bites, I remembered I wasn't alone and looked up at Andre, who was sitting back and observing my assault on the burger in my hands. "Wow, I don't think I've ever seen anyone get after a burger like that. I'm impressed."

I put the burger down on the tray and swallowed the food in my mouth. "Shit, sorry," I mumbled.

He cocked his head. "Sorry? For what?"

"My complete lack of manners," I replied. "I'm just starving and this is so good—"

"Nora," he interjected. "Don't apologize for enjoying a meal." He nodded down at the burger in front of me. "Go on."

I smiled at him and picked it up for another huge bite.

"You know," I said. "It's been years since I've eaten a cheeseburger."

"What? Why?"

Oh, where to start. I played with the paper straw in my glass, making patterns on the creamy pink drink. "I was dating this guy for a long time. It's why I was in California. He was like, super concerned about a healthy diet and hired an in-home chef to cook all our meals. I've had more salmon and chicken than anyone would ever care for. If I ever have any again in my entire life it'll be too soon." Andre ate his food as he listened. I picked up a french fry and stuffed it into my mouth. "I almost forgot what this was like."

"You're not with him anymore?"

"No." I don't know why I was sharing so much, but it felt nice to talk about. "He proposed on Sunday."

Andre paused with his milkshake in the air and stared at me for a minute. "And you said no?"

I nodded. "Yep. I said no."

"Can I ask why?" The question was laced with caution.

"Sure." I shrugged. "I wasn't happy."

"Because you couldn't eat Cheesy Bellies?"

I was amazed at how easily the giggle came out of me. "Yes, *that*, and there were plenty of other things that I realized I'd given up along the way in the relationship. I became this, like, muted version of myself. I had to shed so much of who I was to make it work, and for a long time I just let it happen. And then he proposed, and I knew I was looking at the rest of my life right in the eye, right in that ring. I didn't like what I saw. So I said no."

Andre was quiet for a while as he continued eating. Eventually, he asked another question. "What were you like before?"

I took a deep breath, finding the words. "I was . . . brave. Fearless."

He studied my face. "And now?"

"Now, I don't recognize who I see in the mirror. And I don't know what I want. It's like all the things that used to light me up aren't a part of my life anymore, and I wouldn't even know where to start on getting them back. I'm not in college . . . I can't just hit up some house party and find a thrill in a keg stand. I'm an adult now and I should have a plan and goals and maybe even a mortgage. I definitely shouldn't be back at the starting line." I paused, shaking my head. "Sorry. That was a lot."

Andre smirked and wiped his hands together on a napkin. "Don't apologize. It just sounds like you have some work to do."

"Yeah." But then I added, "Wait, what do you mean?"

He shrugged. "Spend the time to figure out what makes you happy."

"Oh," I said, thinking about his words and what they meant.

I must have looked confused because Andre spoke again. "You need to be completely open to the possibilities. One day at a time. And every choice you make should be rooted in the question, 'Does this make me happy?' or 'Is this getting me closer to what lights me up?' Trust yourself to figure it out and enjoy the process."

Wow. "You make it sound so easy."

"Oh, I don't think it's easy. But that's only because you'll get in your own way. You'll start pressuring yourself to figure it out quicker, or to make things work for other people and their opinions. When it starts to feel muddy, that's when you should take a step back and see that you're not being true to yourself. The spark in anything is either there or it isn't, and it's your job to be honest with yourself."

I stared at his dark brown eyes, letting his words cascade around me.

"Huh." I was honestly a little speechless. He made happiness feel so . . . attainable. The waitress came by with the check, and I saw Andre's hand reach out to grab it but I quickly beat him to it. "Hey, this is my treat, remember?"

He folded his hands on the table. "I would like to take care of this for you."

"Thank you. But no." I fished out a credit card from my purse, making sure that it was one with my name on it. I'd need to take scissors to the ones that had Parker's name. "You've taken care of enough for me."

"Hm." He rubbed a hand along his chin. "Well, can I buy you a drink, then?"

I set my card and the check at the end of the table and then looked at him. "They don't serve alcohol here."

"I don't mean here."

Oh. "Right now?"

The smirk that played on his lips was almost sinful. "I don't know, Nora. Would that make you happy?"

A buzzing sensation flared to life inside my chest, like the vibrating kick-start of a drum. I'd already spent almost half the day with Andre, and I had to admit . . . I wasn't ready for it to end. So I smiled and whispered, "Yes."

THE AMOUNT of pedestrians milling about downtown Denver on a Wednesday evening was shocking. It had always been a popular destination, but it was clear that even *more* tourists had been drawn into the city in the years since I'd lived here.

The setting sun cast a moody array of hazy purples and dusty oranges in the sky and cooled the hot summer air for the first time all day. And yet, the buzzing I still felt in my body from being here with Andre made me feel . . . warm.

I followed him down a busy street to a bar called Jackson's, a place he said he'd been a few times with his co-workers. It was dark and dimly lit, a variety of neon signs lining our path through the tight hallway. A spinning ball hanging from the ceiling propelled colorful specs of light around the entire place, but all I could register was the fact that Andre hadn't removed his hand from the small of my back since holding the door open and guiding me inside. I moved toward the large, wooden bar that took up the full back wall and found a couple of open stools.

"What would you like to drink?" he asked me as he sat down.

I glanced at the bottles sitting on glass shelves behind the bar, hoping something might seize my interest. Normally I drank wine, but this didn't feel like a place you ordered wine in. "Um," I said, considering. "I think I'll have a Jack and Coke, please."

He grinned. "Whiskey girl. Okay." Dipping his head in a single nod, he flagged a passing bartender and ordered my drink as well as a double shot of tequila for himself.

While we waited for our drinks, I turned to watch a group of guys near the back who were in the middle of a heated game of darts. The bar was packed, most people either waiting for drinks or sitting at the high-tops scattered around. The center of the floor was likely intended to be a space for dancing. And if there was a dance floor . . .

I spotted a digital jukebox tucked near the hallway leading to the bathrooms, and pounced.

It had been a long, long time since I browsed the music catalog of a jukebox in a dive bar, but the opportunity was too enticing to ignore. I pressed the touch screen and sifted through a bunch of top hits, selecting a handful of songs to play. I fed the machine a five-dollar bill and listened as Ed Sheeran began crooning from the speakers.

Back at the bar, my Jack and Coke was waiting for me, and I took a long pull from the straw before turning to Andre. "Thank you for the drink."

He dipped his head. "You deserve it, after the few days you've had." He raised his own drink, a lowball glass full of golden tequila, and clinked it against mine. "Congratulations on the new ride."

My eyes caught on his arm as he brought his glass to his lips. He'd taken off his black button-up after the diner, and was left only in the white T-shirt he'd had on underneath. His arms were covered in tattoos, and the bar lights pulsed against his skin as I traced the ink wrapping around his forearm. *Was that a dragon?*

"Is whiskey your go-to drink?" he asked, and I lifted my eyes from his arm.

"Why, are you impressed?"

He chuckled. "I like that you like whiskey, but I'm curious what your favorite drink is."

I lifted my shoulders and tilted my head. "I usually order wine, but this doesn't feel like a wine kind of night."

He nodded. "Makes sense."

Pulling my eyes away from him, I took another long sip from my drink, loving the way it warmed me from the inside out. The buzz hit me quickly, and I soon found myself asking the bartender for another round, despite Andre's still mostly full glass.

A loud cheer erupted from the guys playing darts, and I gathered the game had ended. A roar of laughter sounded from another side of the bar, and between that, the music, and the company, I was filled with a sense of . . . hope. Of belonging. Of being back in a place that felt so much more like *me* and so much less like Parker or his pretentious family or the thousands of fame-hungry people in L.A. that were honestly just so goddamn stiff and *boring*.

Already, I could feel my shoulders loosening. I could breathe a little easier. Maybe it was the whiskey's assault on my inhibitions, or maybe it was that I sensed Andre watching me, but I felt like I was right on the cusp of an entirely new adventure—if I could just hold on to this feeling, if I could hold tight to this new beginning, I might just make it out the other side unscathed.

I finished the thought as Harry Styles's "Kiwi" trilled through the sound system—one of my picks from the jukebox —and the high energy music made me want to *dance*. To let out everything I'd been holding in for so many fucking years.

Andre's words from the diner echoed in my head, and I shuffled off of my stool without another thought. My loose limbs carried me to the dance floor, and I felt my head floating in the clouds as the whiskey continued to coat me in its magic.

The fierce, heady beat of the song filled me up, and I pressed my eyelids shut and just *moved*.

Instantly, I was swept away.

I focused only on the lyrics in the song, on the bass that kept me in rhythm. Everything around me disappeared—I didn't care who was here or who might be watching. I didn't even care that I probably looked like a crazy person dancing alone in the middle of this bar.

It felt so good to give it all up as I swayed and twirled, consumed by the music. Eventually, I opened my eyes again to find Andre locked in on my movements. His eyes raked down my body in a way that made me feel . . . sexy. Emboldened by the darkness and the space between us, I watched him too. Watched his tall form stand up from the stool. Watched his eyes, blazing with intensity, stay planted on me as he came my way.

"You like this song?" I called out with a smile.

He hummed as he got closer to me, his smoky eyes falling to my hips. It felt like a dare, and it sent a rush through me—a familiar thrill that I'd been aching to uncover. A piece of me that had been stifled for so damn long.

He stepped into me, our noses so close they could graze each other. His warm breath, which was somehow fresh despite the burger and tequila, skated along my neck. Still, our bodies didn't touch, and yet . . . I hadn't felt this nervous around a man in years. The anticipation of being touched was almost as good as the real thing.

Almost.

Because then I felt him brush my hip, his calloused fingers hooking the fabric of my dress as he pulled me flush against him. His body swayed in tandem with mine, his movements light and sweeping as he followed my lead.

I wrapped my arms around his neck, looking up at him and fastening tightly to his warm gaze. I watched his eyes move down to my mouth and it filled me with such a force of pleasure that I almost kissed him right then. But then my thoughts finally caught up to what was happening and hesitation rushed through me.

What were we doing? Did he want to kiss me too? Or was he just trying to help me let loose, like he'd been supporting me with everything else?

I looked down at his mouth, at his full lips.

Does this make me happy?

Fuck it—I kissed him.

Chapter Seven

ANDRE

Her lips were like chaotic magic against mine, and it took everything in my power not to shove her against the wall of this bar and rip her pretty little dress right off in front of all these people. I knew they were watching us. Every guy in here had been watching her dance before I got off of my stool to join her—I'd been just as mesmerized as they were.

An eager sound escaped her throat, and my blood roared in response to the feel of it against my body. The feel of this. Of her in my arms. Her skin was soft beneath my fingers and she smelled like warm cotton candy. The sweetest treat.

My hand traveled to the back of her head where I sunk my fingers into her silky hair, deepening the kiss. Her tongue boldly darted out to lick my lips, and I let her in, savoring the taste of her.

Nora was a tall girl. She was still at least half a foot shorter than me, but would've been close to six feet in height. It felt so damn good to kiss a girl without having to hunch over. I enjoyed how perfectly we fit together. The way her teeth lightly nibbled against my bottom lip and her tongue swept into my mouth, just as avid in its exploration as my hands were on her body.

She removed her arms from my neck and I felt her hands trail down my back. She wrapped them around my ass and squeezed. I was so surprised by it that I couldn't help the chuckle that escaped between our kiss. Her confidence was sexy as hell, and so different from the apprehensive girl who walked into the shop yesterday.

She pulled away. There was a delicious flush on her face that cranked my smile wider. "Do you want to . . . meet me in the bathroom?" The words came out low and raspy and I caught myself thinking about all the things she could do with those rosy lips.

I watched as her eyes lingered on my own mouth. *Fuck.* There was nothing I wanted more than to follow her into that bathroom where I could give her much more than what was possible out here. She was so damn sexy. I would take my time teasing her, covering up her sweet moans with my mouth, savoring every moment.

Hesitation clogged my throat—no matter how confusing —and blocked the answer that I wanted to give her. I didn't know how much the whiskey was influencing her actions, and I wouldn't be able to live with myself if she regretted anything tomorrow.

"Nora, trust me when I say that I would *love* to do this." My voice was tight, the restraint I was trying like hell to hold on to thick between us. "I would love to take you into that dingy-ass bathroom and make you come so fucking hard that I'd need to carry you home after." Her sharp intake of breath sent blood rushing straight to my dick. "But I don't think it's a good idea, pretty girl. Not tonight."

Disappointment marred her features, and it nearly killed me. Her eyes dropped to my chest as her hands fell away to her sides. She took one solid step back, establishing distance between us. "Okay . . . yeah. No problem." She whirled around and rushed back to our spot at the bar.

"Nora," I said, following closely behind her. She ignored me. "*Nora*," I hissed.

Just as she reached her stool, she spun around to face me. "It's fine, Andre. Really. I'm sorry. I practically jumped you and that wasn't fair at all. It's just . . . it's been a while. And I thought maybe—"

"You thought right," I said, pleading, "*trust* me." Her eyes narrowed, but she didn't say anything, so I spoke again. "Look, there's nothing more I'd rather do than show you how right you were. But the last thing I want to do is take advantage of the situation, okay?"

It took a second, but eventually the shame and embarrassment unwound, and her face softened. "I get it," she said, her voice low. "Very kind of you." Her mouth formed a tight smile, but it didn't reach her eyes. I felt the urge to change the subject, to crack a joke and make her laugh so that I could see the light shine from them again. She took a deep breath and then stated casually, "I'm having at least two more drinks." She sat back down in her stool. "You want another one?"

I eyed my still-full glass of tequila from the last round she'd ordered. "Nah, I'm good. Go ahead and have mine, if you want." I sat down and nodded toward the drink. "I'll stop now so I can drive you home."

She gave me a look that I didn't quite understand before she reached to slide my tequila toward herself.

For a while, unspoken words hung heavy between us. I'd asked the bartender for a glass of water and was absentmindedly stabbing at the ice with my straw. I knew that stopping us from hooking up in the bathroom was the right thing to do, but the last thing I'd wanted was for Nora to feel rejected.

She seemed so fragile, so curled in on herself, and as soon as she'd begun to wield some semblance of confidence, I'd shut her down. I hated that. Especially after waxing on about happiness and joy and whatever else earlier.

Maybe she really did want to hook up with me. Maybe that *would* make her happy, to chase a one-night stand. With her recent breakup, I figured she wasn't looking for anything serious. She'd probably wanted to burn off some steam the way that only two bodies and zero thinking could.

I could be that for her. In fact, if she still wanted that after tonight, I'd make sure she knew that I was open to it. That I would love nothing more than to help her take the edge off. But . . . I wanted to be respectful, and I couldn't be sure that her actions tonight were influenced by the drinks or not. At least for right now, shutting this down was the right thing to do.

"So," I said, attempting to ignite some conversation. "Now that you got the new ride, what's your next move?"

She finished off the tequila and set the glass back down on the bar. "Well," she pondered, "the trade-in gave me plenty of cash to use as a down payment on an apartment, so finding a place to live in is next on the list." She didn't look at me when she spoke, but her tone was still friendly.

"Have you lived by yourself before?" I asked.

She shook her head. "No, I always had roommates in college. And then after my mom—" She stopped herself, looking down at her hands resting on the bar's surface. "After college I moved out to L.A. with Parker. I've never lived completely on my own."

I wanted to ask about her mom, but I left it alone for now. "I've never lived alone either," I said. Her eyes finally rose to mine and I could see the question laced in the tight set of her brow. "I live with my sister," I clarified. "I've always lived with my sister."

"Oh." She nodded. "How old is she?"

"Twenty-three. Going on forty."

Nora huffed out a small laugh, and it loosened some of the tightness in my chest. "What do you mean?"

I shook my head. "She's too damn responsible. Always mothering me and taking care of things. I want her to enjoy herself, to do what normal twenty-three-year-olds do. But . . ." I hesitated. "We haven't had the easiest life, and she had to grow up quickly. It was always hard for her to just be a kid, and now I worry that she's missed out on too much."

Nora nodded, though I could see more questions swirling in her mind. But she didn't ask them. Instead, she ordered another drink, and focused her attention on the neon lights that hung from the walls.

Uncertainty prickled. After spending only half a day with this girl, I already knew that it wasn't going to be enough. I knew I'd want to see her again . . . but after denying her on the dance floor, I wasn't sure if she would let me. I didn't lie to her

—I *was* interested in what she was offering earlier, but that wasn't what this was about. More than anything, I wanted to be her friend.

I wanted her to feel like she had someone to turn to if she ever needed it. Something about her panic yesterday had drilled through me, and I didn't think I'd be all right with never seeing her again after this. I wanted to know that she would be okay.

After Nora finished her fourth drink, she was undoubtedly good and drunk. She also seemed to have forgotten what happened between us and was singing loudly along with the music, giggling and holding on to my arm. The tension in her body had faded away and left her looking relaxed and happy. Her smiles were plentiful and came easy. If it weren't for her eyes, she would have looked at peace.

But those eyes gave her away. I could still see the weight of something dragging her down. Whether it was worry or fear or stress—I didn't know. But I wanted to help her through it.

Eventually, exhaustion set in her features, and she told me she was ready to go. I paid our tab and put my arm around her shoulders to tuck her body in close. She climbed into the passenger seat when we got to the Subaru and, after making sure she was safely buckled, I grabbed the keys from her.

The drive was quiet. She'd plugged her friend Mackenzie's address into my phone, and while I navigated the deserted city streets, I didn't press or force a conversation. By the time we pulled up to the small house she was staying at, Nora was asleep.

I heard the front door open behind me as I lifted Nora into my arms. Her head rested against my shoulder, and I carried her into the house where her friend had gotten some pillows and a blanket ready on the couch.

I laid Nora down, pulling the quilted blanket over her and gently moving a piece of hair out of her face. Leaning down, I pressed a soft kiss to her forehead before I focused back on Mackenzie, giving her the keys to the Subaru and asking her to keep an eye on Nora. She'd only had four drinks, but they'd hit her pretty hard and I didn't want her to be sick in the middle of the night.

Mackenzie assured me that she'd take over, and thanked me for getting Nora home safe. As I walked back out of the house, the feelings I'd had earlier came roaring back. I could only hope that I'd get to see her again, that this wasn't the last time.

I HAD an early morning at the shop the next day, and needed to get in by seven to unlock the doors and open the bays. It had only gotten busier as the summer wore on, and I knew we had a lot of work to get done to keep up with the demand. Anything I could do to help set the team up would go a long way. Still, I only made it to the shop with minutes to spare. I was moving slower this morning than I normally did, even after two cups of coffee.

After last night with Nora, I was *tired*. I'd barely pulled a few hours of sleep after Ubering back to my place. I didn't mind getting in late—not when it meant Nora had gotten home safe. But even after I'd showered and gotten into bed, I was restless all night.

I couldn't stop thinking about that kiss, how Nora's lips had felt so full and soft and bold against mine. It was . . .

different from any kiss I'd had before—and I'd had my fair share. Nora's made it seem like the kiss might have really meant something to her. Maybe not in a romantic sense . . . but like it was something she'd needed.

She'd taken hold of my attention, burrowing deep into my mind in a matter of days. My attraction to her was undeniable, but my draw to her was more than that. She was clearly going through some life-altering shit, and I knew what that felt like. I knew what it was like to wake up and not recognize yourself anymore.

Kissing me at Jackson's last night was part of her working to get back to herself. I *wanted* to be that for her. Better me than some other guy who might take advantage of her or hurt her in the process. That thought alone tightened an uncomfortable knot in my chest.

I unlocked the shop's doors and headed for the break room to brew a pot of coffee for the team. Jess, Cameron, and Ernesto were all scheduled to arrive at seven thirty to help open the shop at eight. We had a handful of scheduled oil changes and tire appointments this morning, as well as two bigger project vehicles that were still in the bays from yesterday.

I did a quick walkthrough of all six bays while the coffee brewed. I always liked to check that the previous day's closing team had kept things clean and organized. We'd hired a handful of new guys in the last six months, and it seemed like the shop's veterans were doing a fine job of ensuring they were properly trained.

"*Buenos días.*"

I turned to find Ernesto behind me, buttoning himself into his coveralls. "Morning, sir," I said, smiling. No one knew exactly how old Ernesto was, but he looked to be at least in his sixties, so we all treated him with respect accordingly. He also looked like could split a man in two back in his day, so there was that. "Coffee's on in the break room."

He grunted and nodded his head. I took in a deep breath, filling my lungs as I shifted my mind firmly back to the shop. I would worry over what to do about Nora later.

Chapter Eight

NORA

A DULL HEADACHE POUNDED IN MY TEMPLES AND anxiety filled my chest. I couldn't remember the last time I'd woken up and not remembered where I was or how I'd gotten there.

Squinting one eye open, I was thoroughly relieved to see that I was in Mackenzie and Eric's living room. A beaded blue pillow was pinned between my forehead and the back of the couch. I wasn't sure how I ended up here and not in the guest bedroom where I was supposed to be sleeping, but there was comfort in knowing I was at least in their house and not laid up somewhere strange and unfamiliar.

Flashes from the previous day slowly came back to me. The dealership with Andre . . . Cheesy Bellies at the Sunshine Shack . . . Drinks at Jackson's—

Shit.

Kissing Andre on the dance floor.

A groan escaped from my dry throat. I'd kissed plenty of

random guys at parties back in my college days, but that was just it. I wasn't in college anymore. And maybe if it *had* been a random stranger, I wouldn't feel so worried about it. But after everything he'd done to help me, I'd hurled myself at him like he was nothing but a piece of meat.

I was a terrible person.

I scrunched my brows together as I tried to remember how I'd gotten home, and slowly but surely the pieces came to me. Andre never had his second drink, and after the dance floor rejection, I was happy to take it from him. I remembered how I couldn't look him in the eye as I gulped down the double shot of tequila in just a few swigs. The tequila—mixed with the two whiskeys—had helped stave off *some* of the embarrassment I felt over throwing myself at Andre. At least in the moment. *Did I have another drink after that?* I couldn't remember.

But I did remember the smell of motor oil and spice on his work shirt after he put his arm around me to lead me back to my car. He must have driven me home, though the details of the drop-off were definitely hazy.

I wanted to text him and make sure he made it home okay, but I didn't even have his number. He'd been nothing but kind, and not only did I proposition him like a lunatic, I couldn't even reach out to apologize or check in.

Guilt swept through me as I forced myself to sit up on the couch, noticing the throw blanket I was tucked under. "Good morning, sunshine."

I turned my head to face Mackenzie, who was standing in between the living room and the kitchen. Her face was beet-red and she was sweating. "Have you been working out?"

Mackenzie smiled. "Yep. The Peloton is yours if you want to use it."

I grumbled. "No, thanks."

She giggled. "Rough night?"

"I don't think my body is used to whiskey anymore. Or dive bars. Definitely not tequila."

She sucked in a breath and her eyes danced as she went in for the kill. "Is that why your friend Andre had to carry you inside?"

Oh *fuck*. "What?!"

She smirked. "He carried your drunk, lifeless ass inside because you fell asleep in your new car. Which, by the way, congratulations."

I slapped my palm over my face, only to regret the movement as my head pulsed in pain. "Oh man, I'm such an idiot."

Her eyes softened. "Hey. None of that. The Nora I know would laugh something like that off."

I sighed. "Yeah, well, the Nora you *knew* turned into a Nora that no one knows anymore."

Her eyes flickered with concern, and she came to sit on the other end of the couch. "Are you okay?" she asked.

I nodded, moving my feet out of her way. "Yeah. It's just weird, being back here. Not knowing what I'm doing with my life. I know it's what I wanted, and that hasn't changed. I don't want to marry Parker. But . . . I just feel like I've lost so much. And now that I'm on my own again, it's hard to feel so stripped away from the *me* who used to exist."

Mackenzie nodded. "I get it, Nor. You assimilated. You gave up a lot of what makes you *you* to make things work in L.A. But you didn't lose yourself—not completely. You just have to chip away at the things you don't like anymore to find what makes you happy again." Her words were so similar to what Andre had said to me yesterday. "Try to have fun in the process, okay? Honestly . . . having a hot, tattooed bad boy carrying you in at the end of a night out isn't so terrible. Who is he anyway?"

I rolled my eyes. "He's just a . . . new friend. He works at Logan's shop."

Her face brightened. "I thought I recognized him! He's been at some shindigs over the last couple of years. Seriously, Nora—he's *hot*."

I smacked her shoulder. "Mack! The last thing I need right now is a man. I literally just detached myself from one. I need to focus on myself."

She shrugged, smiling. "Hey, you can focus on yourself and still get laid. In fact, you *should* get laid. It doesn't mean you have to settle down with anyone."

I snorted. "You're terrible. It's a good thing Eric locked you down so long ago. I have a feeling you'd be eating men alive if you were single."

Her laugh was loud and full. "Yeah, well, now I can live vicariously through you."

Shaking my head, I threw the blanket off my legs and stepped onto the floor. "I need coffee and something greasy."

Mackenzie sighed. "I'm trying to be healthy before the wedding, but a breakfast burrito sounds like heaven right now." She stared at me for a long moment before she got up and grabbed her keys off the counter. "I'll drive."

MACKENZIE and I ended up spending the entire day together. It was unexpected and unbelievably refreshing to have some solid girl time with one of my best friends. I hadn't been back to Denver to see any of my friends in over a year, and I didn't have any real friends out in L.A. Dating Parker had turned me into such an introverted homebody.

Eric was a hotshot architect and usually worked long days in a high-rise downtown. He was really only around on the weekends, but Mackenzie was a middle-school teacher, so the months-long summer break meant plenty of free time for her.

After grabbing some mouth-watering breakfast burritos from a place called Sam's only a few miles from her house, I told her that I needed to be productive and spend the day apartment hunting. Apparently, Mackenzie loved the idea so much she asked if she could tag along. I hadn't expected her to be interested, but I knew her type-A personality would come in handy, and I wasn't in any position to be turning down help today.

I had a decent chunk of money from the Range Rover that was now burning a hole in my checking account. It was more than enough for a deposit on an apartment *and* the first few months of rent as long as I found an affordable place. Unfortunately, there weren't many affordable apartments in Denver. Mackenzie and I had toured two studios and three one-bedroom units in four different buildings by the time the clock struck noon, and all of them had been way out of my budget range.

I would need to figure something out, and soon.

I'd loved my job as a second-grade teacher after college. My mother had taught in an elementary school for decades before she got sick, and seeing the impact she had on the children in her classes made her a hero in my eyes. I'd known pretty early on that I wanted to be a teacher too, and for the few years I was one, my passion had only heightened.

But she was gone now, and I knew that going back to a teaching role would bring up emotions I wasn't ready to face. And honestly, I might never be. It was still an open wound, and with all the other changes happening in my life, it was too daunting to think of going back.

This was a bit of a problem for me, though, because what else could I do to earn a decent income? Teaching was all I'd ever trained for. It was all I ever saw myself doing. And now . . . I didn't know.

"Okay," I grumbled as we got back into the car after the last tour. The apartment had looked amazing in pictures online, but it wasn't actually in the best shape even though the land-lord was still asking for an obscene amount in monthly rent. "Time to make some shifts in the plan. I can't afford anything in this area. There's a few places I want to check out in North Heights that are way cheaper than these money-sucking units."

I could feel Mackenzie's heavy glance from the passenger seat. "That's not exactly the safest area."

"Maybe," I said, "but the rental rates are better. Plus, it's not like I'll be hanging out on street corners at night looking for shady new friends. I just need a place that I can call home and make *mine*. And more than anything, I need to be able to afford it." I looked over and saw disapproval across her face. "Mack, I need to be on my own and I need to be smart about money. I can't afford the rates over here, at least not yet. And I refuse to be a third wheel in your house for longer than absolutely necessary."

She looked back out the windshield and blew out a breath. "It is nice having you around the house, you know." She snuck a quick peek back my way to see if the bait had worked. It hadn't. "Okay, fine. Let's go."

I rolled my eyes. "Don't be a diva."

Mackenzie let out a gasp in mock-horror, and then broke into a fit of giggles. "I am *not* a diva, you brat."

Smirking, I started the car and set off for North Heights. It was about a twenty-minute drive from the side of the city that we were currently on. We were halfway to the apartment building when my phone dinged from the center console. It was the sound of a new text message. "Would you mind checking who that's from?" I asked Mackenzie.

She picked up my phone and looked at the notification on my screen. "It's from a number you don't have saved. Want me to open it?"

Dread panged through me. I'd blocked Parker's number after he'd texted and called me incessantly during my drive to Denver. He might have gotten a new number just to try reaching out to me again—I wouldn't put it past him. "Is it a California area code?"

"Nope, Colorado."

Oh. *Maybe it's about an apartment?* I'd filled out a few contact forms online over the last couple of days. "Can you read it, please? My passcode is three-six-nine-zero-nine-six."

"Sure," she said, thumbing in the code. "Oh my gosh," Mackenzie squealed, "it's from your new man friend! He says: 'Hey Nora, hope it's okay I got your number from our records at the shop. Probably against a lot of rules, but I didn't get a chance to ask you for it like I meant to yesterday and I wanted to make sure you were okay this morning. Hope you're having a good day. Be happy.'"

My head was instantly floating. "He said all that?" I asked, eyes still on the road.

I saw Mackenzie's face turn toward me in my periphery. "Yeah. Nor"—she angled the screen of my phone toward me— "he told you to be *happy*. Pretty sweet of him, if you ask me."

I sighed. "Yeah, I know. He's actually really sweet. I told him a little bit about my situation yesterday, about Parker proposing and me saying no. And how I came out here to . . . I don't know, find myself? And he basically said that we over-complicate happiness. He told me if I make decisions that make me happy, it'll all work out. It was . . . kind. More than."

Mackenzie was silent for a moment, but I could still feel her eyes on me. Finally, she said, "Want me to respond with anything back?"

"No!" I blurted. "I'll text him back later."

She giggled, tucking my phone back into the console. "You like him." It wasn't a question.

"I do *not* like him, Mack. I literally just ended things with Parker, and I *just* got back here. I was serious this morning, I need to focus on prioritizing myself right now. He's a nice guy for sure. But I'm done with romance for a while."

I glanced over at my friend, knowing she was assessing me. "I hear you. And I support it."

I blew out a sigh. "But?"

Another giggle. "*But* the way he carried you in last night, and the way he covered you with that blanket . . . and now, seeing that text message . . . I just have a good feeling about him." She shrugged, like it was nothing.

I wanted to argue, but a small kernel of hope nestled in my

chest and gave me pause. Mackenzie was right. Andre was . . . different. I wasn't ready for any kind of romance—not even a casual fling. But maybe Andre and I could be friends. And maybe, someday—

"All right," Mackenzie said with a clap. "We've made it to the run down side of the city. Let's see some apartments!"

I laughed. "You're so annoying," I said. "It's actually this building, I think." I pulled the car over to the side of the street and checked the address that was stored in my phone. "Yep, this is it. Let's go!"

We spent the next twenty-five minutes touring a one-bedroom unit that, although was tucked inside a building that looked like it was falling apart at the seams, was clean and filled with natural light on the inside. The last tenant had clearly been considerate enough to keep things in good shape.

Even Mackenzie was surprised. It wasn't anything fancy, but it was perfect for what I needed right now. I asked the building manager for pricing details and was ecstatic at the rates she listed back to me. The building offered some pretty steep month-to-month rental rates, but with a year-long lease it was affordable. I had enough funds from trading in the Range Rover to last me almost six months.

It was a no-brainer. I spent the next fifteen minutes filling out a rental application, which the building manager assured me was just protocol. As long as I had proof of funds for the deposit and first month's rent, she'd approve me.

I walked out of the building on cloud nine. I'd only been back in Denver for two days and I'd already done so much to set myself up for my new start. I still needed to furnish the place, but I could get by without much for now. I'd also need to find a job soon, but I was ready to make that my next big goal. I'd take any opportunity, even if it was just to pay the bills while I figured out what I actually wanted to do for the rest of my life.

Mackenzie and I decided to stop at the grocery store on the way home to pick up a few things for dinner, and as I trailed behind her pushing a cart, I couldn't help but feel mind-numbing relief flow through me. It was as if my organs had been twisted around inside my body, making it impossible to breathe.

But now, as I watched Mackenzie read the label on a bag of pasta, the tension in my body was snapping loose. I was no longer bound to the mountain of expectations that had been stacking up for the last three years.

Be happy.

I was beginning to remember what happy felt like.

Chapter Nine

ANDRE

The wide smile that transformed Gabriel's *face as he pressed down on the accelerator was contagious. We'd been given a rare opportunity to take the orange Pontiac Sunbird drop-top out by ourselves—El Viejo was feeling good today—and I felt like a million bucks as we wound our way through the old neighborhoods, taking the long way to get to the market. The list of items we were told to buy was clutched in my hands so that it didn't blow away.*

Gabriel didn't have his license, but he knew how to drive and he was technically old enough. It didn't matter though. I wouldn't have missed this for anything. Sitting next to him felt more right *than sitting anywhere else in the world, even if it meant getting caught doing the wrong thing. Where he went, I'd always go, too.*

"Escucha, cerebro," he said loudly over the wind, glancing at me before focusing his eyes back on the road, "you're growing up.

You're fourteen now, and you'll be a man soon. It's time I talk to you about a few things—things I had to learn the hard way."

He pulled out a cigarette from the pack of Marlboro reds he kept in his front shirt pocket, placing it expertly between his lips. He didn't light it—it would have been near impossible without stopping the car—but he had a habit of just holding them there until he was ready.

His normally slicked back hair, thick with the hair glue he used to keep it in place, was blowing wildly around his face as he began speaking again. "I know being in high school can make you feel like you've made it, but you ain't made shit yet. It's just another step toward the future. You've got smarts, kid, so it's not time to start fucking around. There are plenty of people who will try to lead you down the wrong road, who will want to bring you down to their level, but only you *can keep yourself straight. Do you understand?" He glanced toward me again.*

"Sí," I answered.

"Same goes for girls. You ain't shit, and you'll never be if you get caught up in some bullshit desperation for pussy. Guys walk around here and act like girls owe them something, but that's not how the world works. Girls don't owe you fucking anything. *You treat them with respect, and you keep them at a fucking distance. Do you understand?"*

I felt compelled to remind him that I'd caught him in the basement with Serena just last week, but stopped myself before the words slipped out. Instead, I looked him in the eye and nodded.

"Good. When the time is right and you think you're in love, come to me before anything happens. No matter what, come to me first. Okay?"

"Okay."

"And, Andre, this one is important, so listen close." He

straightened his back as he shifted in his seat. "Family is all you'll ever really have. Everyone else, everything else—none of it matters. Not money, not fast cars—nothing, hermano. *The world can be a cruel and ugly place; you know that firsthand. People will turn on you in a heartbeat to save themselves.*

"There will come a time in the future when you make something of yourself and accomplish some real shit. You're so damn smart, Andre, and I know you're going to break out of here someday. But don't you dare forget about your family. Remember who you are, remember where you come from, and stay true to that.

"At the end of the day, it's you and me and Marisela. That's it, hermano. *Someday, when we're older, our little family might grow—but for now, it's just us. It's our responsibility as men to always make sure that Sela is taken care of. Whatever it takes, no matter what. You protect her. And you figure out how to give her everything that she needs. Do you understand?"*

The look he gave me this time was heavier, thick with emotion. I noticed the crease between his brows, a tightening of his muscles as he gripped the steering wheel. This was important. "Te lo prometo, Gabriel," I said firmly. "I promise."

He reached out his hand and cupped the back of my head with a strong grip as he nodded his own, focusing back on the road.

"Good."

We were quiet for the rest of the drive. I knew in my gut something monumental had just happened. A sacred pact between brothers. A notable step in the loss of my boyhood.

Gabriel was right, I was becoming a man now. And it was time to step up.

I woke with a start. Turning to the small clock that sat on my nightstand, I saw that it was almost six in the morning. I'd beaten my alarm by five minutes.

Reaching to shut it off so that it didn't wake Marisela, a groan rumbled out of my throat. My mind was fuzzy—blurry with images from the memories-turned-dreams that often consumed my nights. I'd gotten plenty of sleep, but I didn't feel rested at all.

Forcing myself to sit up, I put my feet on the ground and rubbed my eyes. The muscles in my back were sore from work yesterday, and I wanted nothing more than to ignore my responsibilities, to ignore everything that needed to get done today, and just fall back into bed. Maybe then I could see him again.

Missing my brother was like a full-time job. It took up so much of my energy—grief was fucking exhausting. But I was also thankful for the way I missed him. I was thankful for the memories that plagued me. It kept him alive, at least in my heart.

Guilt lanced up my spine, and I dropped my head in my hands. Not being able to save him . . . it had almost done me in. Almost put me in the ground right fucking next to him. But I made him a promise, and I intended to keep it. I had to get my shit together and do what was right for our little sister.

I stood up and ambled out of my bedroom, moving down the narrow hallway toward the kitchen. All of the lights were off in the house, but the sun had risen and was shining through the windows. The promise of a good day, if I could just escape this feeling.

Pulling the ground coffee out of the pantry, I measured out enough to give Marisela and me a couple of mugfuls each. I set the machine to brew and leaned against the counter, staring blankly into the sink and listening to the *drip, drip, drip* of the coffee. I flexed and unflexed my hands, focusing my thoughts on the cold surface.

"*¿Estás bien, Andre?*"

I startled at the sound of my sister's soft voice. "*Fuck*, Sela." I sucked in a breath. "I didn't hear you come in."

"You were lost somewhere in the sink." She shrugged, dropping her eyes to my now-clenched fists.

I followed her line of sight, and then stuffed my hands in my pockets. "Yeah. It was a long night."

She nodded. "I heard you talking in your sleep. You were dreaming of him again."

It wasn't a question—she knew. She'd known about them since they'd started, when I'd slipped quietly into the darkness and let it take me so far down that I wasn't sure I'd ever see the light again. They were so much worse back then—I used to wake up screaming, images of him lifeless in that fucking car rushing over me, again and again.

The dreams I woke from these days weren't as violent or horrific. They just hurt like fucking hell.

"I'm sorry I woke you." It was all I could say.

Her eyes softened. "Don't worry about me. I just want to make sure *you're* okay."

I nodded. "I'm good. I'm all right."

"You've been working a lot. Are you getting enough rest?"

Sometimes I wished she wasn't so perceptive. "Yeah, the

shop's been busy and Logan took time off with his girl. But I'll get a break soon, don't worry."

"I'm not worried," she insisted.

"Liar."

Her mouth ticked up into a smile. "Okay, I am. But it's only because I love you."

I smiled back at her, grateful for her big heart. Even as the youngest, Marisela had always looked out for Gabriel and me in this way—providing the emotional support for our little threesome that didn't come naturally to us. She was a strong nurturer. I hoped to see her as a strong mother someday, if that was what she wanted. "I know you do, Sela. I just . . . I have to keep my focus on that finish line."

The finish line—the day I could free us of financial insecurity. Our entire lives, we'd lived either at the mercy of the state or, as we got older and phased out of the system, the mercy of luck and opportunity. No one had been around to hand anything down to us, so we had to carve out every success for ourselves.

Gabriel had done his best to provide for us in meaningful ways, but the curse of being the oldest of three orphan siblings was that no one was looking out for him as he tried to make a name for himself in the world. He took dangerous risks in the hopes of yielding strong payoffs, finding shortsighted opportunities for income on the streets through petty theft and dealing drugs. And it did provide for us all, for a little while. But it also ended up taking Gabriel away forever.

Now, I was hell-bent on learning from his mistakes and doing things right—working hard and saving money so that Marisela could start a business one day. Since we were little kids, she'd always wanted her own restaurant. We didn't get to eat out very much as children, and she loved the idea of strangers coming together to enjoy a good meal under one roof. I never lost sight of that dream of hers, and I hoped like hell I could help her realize it.

She looked at me for a long moment, no doubt gauging whether there was anything else for her to worry about. I must have passed the test because she moved to the fridge and pulled out a carton of eggs. "I'll make us breakfast, okay?"

My smile widened. "Sounds great."

With Logan opening the shop, I wouldn't need to be there until early afternoon, and I'd stay to close everything up tonight. So, seeing as I had a few hours to kill, I decided to burn off the residual emotional baggage from Gabriel's appearance in my dream at the gym.

I tried to get myself there at least three times a week, but with how busy things had been lately, I was barely managing it once a week. I was starting to feel the effects of that lack of physical exertion—the dark shadows creeping around the corners of my soul threatening to lure me down again.

I walked through the doors a few hours after eating breakfast with Marisela. Head down like usual, I set out for the familiar octagon in the back of the facility, letting the musty smell of old equipment fill my nostrils.

Sela had tried to shake me from my mood all morning, and I loved her for it. "Do you own *anything* that isn't black?" she'd said on my way out, leaning against the front entrance and waving a hand at my simple tee, fighting shorts, and—also black—gym bag slung over my shoulder.

I'd pulled her into me and ruffled her hair, grinning as she squirmed out of my hold. I knew it was her way of telling me she was happy that I'd taken her advice and was doing something for myself.

The walkway through the center of the gym cut through the cardio machines on the right and the free weights on the left where a bunch of wise guys on juice threw dumbbells around like they were nothing.

I didn't make eye contact with anyone—the gym wasn't the place to start fucking around with any sort of alpha bullshit. I'd seen enough pointless fights start over the bar of a bench press after some idiot stared down another idiot in the mirror while they were in the middle of a set.

Nah, that wasn't my style. I preferred to make my presence known a bit more subtly, but with *much* more persuasion: in the fighting ring with skillful grappling, greater physical endurance, and—my personal favorite—fists.

I recognized Santiago and Javier circling each other on the mat, their footwork agile and honed, like panthers ready to strike. They were brothers from East Colfax who'd been fighting for years. Rumor had it that Santiago, the youngest brother, was being courted by the UFC—he was that good.

"Yo, is that Andre finally coming around?" Juan's voice reached me from the ropes where he stood on the other side of the octagon. Juan was the middle brother between Santiago and Javier, and had stepped into the role of their manager when they'd gained notoriety in the circuit. He threw down every now and then, but he mostly left the fighting to his brothers. "Been a while."

I nodded my head. "Yeah." I dropped my bag on the floor against the wall and pulled out black tape to wrap my hands with while I watched Santiago strike a quick jab at Javier, who blocked and used the opportunity to shoot his foot out for a hard kick to the shins.

"Good, Javier," Juan called out, approval blazing in his eyes as he looked my way again. "Your mechanic life keeps you too busy to come scrap with us?" I knew he was teasing, but there was a tone of bitterness beneath the jest. I used to spend almost every waking hour in this gym, throwing myself into any fight I could just to feel something in the aftershocks of losing Gabriel.

One night after a particularly brutal round against Javier, Juan tried to convince me to let him manage me too. He said he could help take care of me, that I had what it took to go pro. While I appreciated his vision, I lacked any sort of motivation to get myself behind it. I'd wanted to fight simply to feel my fists connect with flesh and bone, to pour my rage into something tangible—nothing more and nothing less.

After I started working at Logan's, Juan had taken it personally. He couldn't understand why anyone would want to work a nine-to-five when they could do something like this for a living. He had connections in the industry and a knack for marketing fighters, but the amount of guys who actually went pro and made good money was slim. And I hadn't felt like explaining to him that for me, financial freedom would *always* be the goal.

I ignored the bait, instead asking, "Chino here?" Chino was as close to family as Marisela and I had. He'd been Gabriel's best friend growing up, and it was through him that I'd ended up at this gym years ago.

"Nah, not yet. He's usually in around nine." I checked the clock. *Fifteen minutes.* I finished wrapping my hands and put on my gloves, using my teeth to seal the Velcro along my wrists before jogging over to the heavy bags near the octagon. I made quick work of warming up with shadowboxing, feeling the warmth in my limbs loosen the muscles still tight with tension.

Chino showed up right at nine, just as Juan said, when I was working through drills on the heavy bag. He was a big burly man with a thick mustache and hard eyes, but I saw his face light up when he noticed me. "What's up, *carnal*? Haven't seen you in a hot minute."

He reached his hand out to tap against my glove in greeting. "Hey, Chino. I know, I've been busy."

"Nothing wrong with that, bro. You gotta take care of yours."

I nodded and, noticing that Santiago and Javier were done with their sparring, jerked my head to the ring. "You want to throw some hands?"

Lighthearted cockiness sparked in Chino's eyes. "Boy, I'll lay your ass out. Let's go."

I knew he'd be good for a real spar and not some pussy-footing show that some of the other guys here liked to put on. He was one of the nicest motherfuckers you'd ever meet, but when given the chance, he could be downright brutal with his fists. I'd seen him sweep dudes up in the streets like they were nothing growing up, always finding myself in awe of the sharp duality of his kindness and his menace. That menace especially flared when someone messed with his family, and through his close friendship with Gabriel, my sister and I had become just that.

We sized each other up in the ring, dancing around to

maintain distance. It didn't take long for him to connect his glove square into my jaw, finding me open after a block. It was a hard enough hit that I felt my fucking spine rattle. Rookie mistake—I had to bite back the swift flare of irritation and anger that came with the pain. But I got a few good licks in during the half hour we spent in the ring, and each time my gloves made contact with his hard grooves of bone, I could breathe a little easier.

My mind was still spinning with memories of Gabriel, with the flashes of rejection on a retreating Nora's face two nights ago, with the hints of concern that always laced Marisela's face when she looked at me. But at least here, the brunt of it all was a bit more . . . bearable.

I couldn't bring Gabriel back—a surety that sickened me every time I thought about it—but the other two things were fixable. I'd continue to prove to my sister that I was doing okay, that she didn't need to worry about me so much. That in fact, *I* should be worrying while *she* lived boldly.

And Nora . . . I'd make that right too. I'd texted her yesterday, but she hadn't responded. It worried me that she could be out of my life for good. And after the other night, I would understand. But I wasn't going to have it. Not after the time we'd spent together, after getting to know her. The more I learned, the more I needed . . . more.

Nah, she wasn't getting off that easy. I'd give her a second to breathe—god knew she had a lot going on. But I'd prove myself to be a steady force for her to anchor herself to if she ever needed it.

Chapter Ten

NORA

Mackenzie, Eric, and I walked into Larkspur on Friday night, past the shiny leather Chesterfield sofa at the entrance and the black-and-white portraits of 1920s speakeasies adorning the walls. It was a newer bar in the city that had been open less than a year, and though I'd never been inside until now, I instantly *loved* it. It was full of dark, moody corners, loud music, and *so* many people—exactly the kind of place I liked to let loose in.

The anticipation of the night ahead felt like untapped electricity buzzing through my body. I was itching to drink, itching to dance . . . Maybe I would even meet a nice, good-looking guy to go home with in a no-strings-attached kind of situation. I still hadn't moved into my new apartment yet—I would get the keys on Sunday morning—but that didn't mean I couldn't convince a guy to bring me to *his* place.

Mackenzie and I trailed behind Eric, who'd taken the lead in looking for the rest of our friends. Amelia had arranged tonight's get-together, so I knew that her fiancé Logan and her brother Adam were both probably here, too. I was always a little nervous running into Adam in the years since our graduation trip to Mexico, where I'd *definitely* hooked up with him.

It was a piece of history I had no regrets about—we'd been on the same page that it was just a casual fling to enjoy during our celebratory trip. Once we were back in Colorado, we'd gone on with our lives like it never even happened. But still, *awkward.*

Eric spotted the group sitting at the end of the long wooden bar and led us in that direction. Logan and Adam were standing tall in collared shirts with beers in hand, and Amelia and another pretty brunette were seated in bar stools in front of them. There were two open stools next to Amelia, and after she saw us, she grabbed purses off both of them and handed one to the girl next to her. "Hey, guys!" Her thousand-watt smile was like a star beckoning us in the night as Mackenzie and I took turns giving her a hug. "You guys remember Adam's girlfriend, Rachel?" She pointed her thumb behind her to the smiling brunette. *That's right.* She'd been at Logan's birthday party last year.

"Of course!" Mackenzie said, leaning in to hug her. "How are you guys?"

I also gave Rachel a hug. I didn't know if she knew anything about my history with Adam—I wasn't even sure if Mackenzie or Amelia did either—but it didn't matter. That ship had long-ago sailed. "Hi, Rachel, good to see you again." Her hug back was warm and friendly.

Mackenzie and I took the empty seats as Adam leaned in to give us each a chaste kiss on the cheek. "Lovely to see you as always, ladies." Logan remained where he was and smiled his hello to us both—he was always more of a quiet one.

A shorter woman with platinum-blonde hair approached us from behind the bar. "I see some new people over here," she said with a smile, her dainty silver septum ring glinting in the low light. Her hair was up in a messy bun, and I spotted bright purple streaks poking through. She was beautiful. "Can I get you guys something to drink?"

After my night at Jackson's earlier this week, I had *no* interest in hard liquor. "Can I have a beer, please?" I asked. "An IPA?" She nodded and then looked at Mackenzie, who ordered a vodka cranberry and a beer for Eric.

Amelia turned in her stool to face my direction when it was just us again. "So, Nora, you're back in Denver! I'm so glad that you're going to be close to us again." There was a hint of question in her voice, but I knew it was just a good-natured invitation to explain if I wanted to—or not, if I didn't.

I decided to keep it short and sweet. "Yeah, it feels good to be home."

"You're staying with Mackenzie, right?" Her eyes moved back and forth between us.

"Yes, but not for long." I smiled, excitement bursting from me. "I actually found a place of my own and put down a deposit this week. I'll be moving in on Sunday."

Amelia's eyes lit up. "Oh my gosh. Congratulations! Am I sensing a girls' night in the near future to break the new place in?" She wagged her eyebrows at me.

I laughed. "I'm sure that could be arranged," I replied. Honestly, a girls' night sounded like the cure to everything I'd been missing in my life. "I just need to find a job. *Then* I'll feel like I can exhale."

Amelia cocked her head. "Will you go back to teaching?"

I shrugged. "I don't know . . . I think I want to find something that'll help me pay the bills until I figure it out. Like maybe something in retail? Or a restaurant?"

The bartender returned with our drinks, and as she set them in front of us, Amelia turned to face her. "Mara, are you guys hiring here?"

The bartender—Mara—smiled. "I didn't figure you for a downtown club kind of girl, Amelia."

Amelia giggled. "No, actually, Nora, here is looking for a job, and I thought maybe if you were hiring, she could apply."

Mara looked at me and I took a deep breath. I did *not* expect to get put on the spot like this. But if Larkspur *was* hiring—and Amelia seemed to know the bartender well enough for this introduction—maybe it could turn into something. "Have you bartended or served before?"

I nodded. "I was a cocktail server at a few places during college—nothing this big or busy, but I held my own. I've never bartended, but I'd be happy to learn."

Mara smiled. "You free tomorrow morning? Around nine? I'll be here getting some admin stuff done, maybe we can talk about it more then?"

"Oh my gosh, *really*? That would be amazing! Thank you so much." I looked around the bar with new appreciation, a huge grin on my face. It was the kind of place I loved being in, and the idea of *working* here, too . . .

"No problem at all. We're actually pretty desperate for help, this place gets busier every weekend." As if on cue, a group of rowdy guys from the other end of the bar whistled for her attention. I watched as Mara rolled her eyes. "I swear, I'm going to gut punch those fucking guys before the night is over." She flashed us a menacing grin before she disappeared.

I swung back toward Amelia. "Thank you! How do you know Mara?"

She gave me a sideways smile. "Actually, Logan used to date her in high school, and then they dated again for a hot second before we finally figured our own shit out and got together. She's the nicest. Went through some bad shit with her ex, but she came back swinging. This bar is so busy because of *her*. She's a killer bartender, and she started a social media account to promote her nights here. In her first six months, she gained like forty *thousand* followers. I don't even know how many she has now, but it's at least six figures."

"Daaaamn!" Mackenzie let out a long breath from between Amelia and I.

"Yeah, that's crazy," I muttered, looking back to the fast-moving bartender and watching as she made multiple drinks at once with seemingly effortless ease. I imagined myself in her shoes, taking orders of shots and drinks from hundreds of people a night. "I bet she makes great tips," I mused.

"Well, if your interview tomorrow doesn't pan out for any reason," Mackenzie said over the music, "you can always just sell foot pictures."

Amelia burst out laughing. "Wow, Mack. *Great* advice."

TWENTY MINUTES LATER, Eric had whisked Mackenzie off to the dance floor, and I'd taken over her stool next to Amelia, safeguarding the now empty one with my purse. Rachel was turned around in her stool on the other side of Amelia so that she could talk to Adam and Logan—but I couldn't hear their conversation over the music.

Amelia had just provided me with the Cliffs Notes version of the last year of her life, absolutely swooning whenever she mentioned Logan or their engagement. There was nothing surprising to me about their relationship being so damn perfect. The last time I'd been home was a few months into it and the love-magic radiating between the two of them was glaringly obvious. I was beyond happy that she and Mackenzie had found their happily ever afters.

"Do you have a date set for the wedding?" I asked. Mackenzie's wedding was only a few weeks away, and I knew the focus would turn toward her and Logan afterward.

"Not yet, we've honestly been a bit lazy about it. We want to do something small at my parents' house in Breckenridge, so with access to our dream venue anytime we want, it kind of takes the pressure off planning in advance.

"Makes sense." I nodded and blew out a breath. "It's crazy to think about you girls getting married. Your brother even looks like he might be wifed up soon. We're getting older. Everyone is . . . *adulting*. Well, except for me. I'm literally starting over."

Amelia's eyes creased and she leaned closer. "You wanna talk about it?"

I took a long sip of my beer, shaking my head. "Not really," I said simply. "Not tonight. Let's just enjoy ourselves."

Amelia smiled. "You got it, and—" She broke off as her eyes flared and she shifted to peer over my shoulder. Curious, I turned to see what had caught her attention.

There, standing by the front door, was Andre, sucking up every ounce of air from the bar. My chest tightened, and I let my eyes dance along his body—the dark tattoos that covered nearly every inch of his skin, his black T-shirt stretching over his broad shoulders, the way his jeans hung a bit baggy from his waist, and the delicious knowledge of what was hidden underneath that I'd felt with my own two hands—

I pushed down the thought, storing it in the same place I'd put all the others from that night. His gray eyes swept the room, and when they landed on mine, I felt a spark ignite. His full lips stretched from under a layer of stubble, stoking that little spark into roaring flames burning low in my belly. Flashes of his tongue skating along the inside of my mouth flooded my mind, and I had to pry my eyes off him to get a hold of myself.

I turned back to find Amelia smiling at me with a glint in her eyes. "You know Andre?" she asked. Her smile said she already knew the answer.

I cleared my throat. "Uh . . . yeah. I met him at Logan's shop when I brought my car in on Monday." I decided not to tell her about the dealership or the Cheesy Bellies. *Or* what happened at Jackson's that night.

"Mm-hm."

"Don't look at me like that."

"Like what?" she asked, feigning innocence.

"You *know* what!"

Amelia tipped her head back and barked a laugh. "It's just that you're looking at Andre like . . . like he's a fine piece of cheesecake. And I don't know if you've tasted that particular flavor of cheesecake, nor is it my business what flavors of cheesecake you choose to try, but I do know *that* particular piece of cheesecake deserves to be appreciated and . . . well . . .

you're looking at him like you might really appreciate it. And it makes me happy to see. For both of you. Maybe. You know?" She lifted her glass to her lips and took a sip of her cocktail.

I felt the tips of my ears grow hot as I scoffed a little over-dramatically, thankful that the dim lighting would hide my blush. "I most certainly do *not* know, Amelia, what his flavor of cheesecake tastes like." My voice came out like a screaming whisper, and I realized through the corner of my eye that Andre was making his way toward us. His towering height was almost too much, its effect doing interesting things to my still-tight chest. Amelia and I looked up at him as he approached.

"Hey, Amelia." He smiled at her politely.

"Hi, Andre! Haven't seen you in a few weeks. How have you been?"

"Oh, you know. Busy at the shop but can't complain. Life is good." His attention turned to me. "Hey, Nora."

I could feel my blush grow stronger. "Hi, Andre."

He nodded his head toward an empty corner of the bar. "Can I talk to you for a second?"

I felt the weight of Amelia's gaze but stayed focused on Andre. "Sure," I said, keeping my voice casual even though I felt anything *but*. I hadn't returned Andre's text message, which I knew was a shitty move, but I hadn't known what to say.

I followed him over to a pool table that wasn't in use, and he sat back on the table's edge. "Hey, so . . . I just wanted to check in and make sure you were okay." He folded his arms over his chest and I found myself lost in the ink that spread across them.

Even leaning down, he was still taller than me. Flashes of his body on mine swirled in my head. Seeing him again in the flesh made it really hard to forget about the night at Jackson's —which I had every intention of doing. I took a deep breath before responding. "Yeah, I'm good."

He nodded. "Okay. It's just . . . I texted you. And when you didn't text back, I thought maybe something was wrong." His brow furrowed, and I had the sudden urge to press my finger up to smooth out the wrinkles.

I sighed. "I know, I'm sorry. I didn't know what to say. I felt embarrassed about Jackson's and—"

"Embarrassed?" Andre cut in. "Nora, I told you not to be. There's no reason for you to feel embarrassed about anything, not with me." God, why did he have to be so *nice* while also sounding so . . . commanding. "And as far as what to say to my text, you could start by saying 'hey' back. You know . . . like a normal conversation."

A smile tugged at my lips. "A normal conversation, huh?"

He grinned. "Yeah, girl. I was just trying to check up on you. It's what friends do."

"Friends?" I asked, pulse quickening.

"I could be your friend." His eyes were so sure and clear as they stayed locked on mine. It was obvious that he was serious. "I could be a good one if you let me."

My breath caught. "I'm sorry, Andre. You're right. I should have responded to you—you didn't deserve to be ghosted."

Confusion flashed across his face. "I don't know what that means."

I giggled, and watched as his confusion turned into something else . . . something lighter. A grin pulled from the side of his mouth. "Never mind," I said. "I'm sorry."

"It's cool. Don't be sorry. I just wanted to make sure you were good. How's the new ride treating you?"

"Good! I love it, I feel so much more comfortable in it than the Range Rover. And the extra cash helped me put a deposit down on a new apartment."

His eyes lit up. "Yeah? That's awesome. Have you moved in already?"

"Soon," I said. "I get the keys on Sunday. I was thinking about having some people over once I get settled in. I'll text you when I do."

He flashed that grin again. "You better."

OUR WHOLE GROUP was crowded together at the far end of the bar, which had gotten significantly more packed as the night went on. It seemed that Mara did have quite the fanbase —so many people were lying in wait for a spot at the bar with her. I noticed some even ask to get pictures taken with her, to which she politely responded that she was way too busy and maybe to try again later when things wound down.

The more I watched her in action, the more I found myself almost memorizing her movements as she took care of the hundreds of people in here. She wasn't alone—there was another bartender working with her, but it was obvious that the patrons weren't here to see him. If anything, he was simply floating around her, assisting with whatever she yelled at him for over the music and the din of the crowd. If things went well in my interview with her tomorrow, I would need to make sure I could handle this kind of fast-paced pressure. It was so much different than teaching a class of second-graders.

I felt my phone vibrating from my purse. *That's weird,* I thought—it was kind of late for a phone call. I looked around at all my friends and realized with mild embarrassment that pretty much everyone I knew and cared about was standing right in front of me. So who would be calling?

Fishing the phone out from the bottomless depths of my purse, I looked at the screen to find an unknown number calling, though the location I knew. *Los Angeles, California.* Trepidation sprouted in my stomach—it looked like Parker *had* gotten a new number, after all.

The call eventually went to voicemail and I breathed out a sigh. Only my relief was tremendously short-lived as my phone started ringing again, vibrating fiercely in my hand. This one was from a different number that was *also* labeled with an L.A. area code. *What the hell?* Was Parker using other people's phones, hoping I would answer?

It was Friday night—maybe he was drunk at a party, or drunk with his family? I didn't have any of his friends or family's contact information saved. I'd never needed to reach out to them for anything—communication and transportation and the like had always been handled for us.

I let that call go unanswered as well, but yet again, my phone started rattling with a new incoming call within seconds.

This time, it was from New York.

Frowning at the screen, I looked up at my friends to find all of them engaged in conversation. Andre was the only one paying attention to me, and his eyes were alert. I gave him a small smile and shrugged my purse over my shoulder, moving toward the door to the bar's outdoor patio, hoping the warmer-than-usual summer evening meant most people were taking advantage of the building's air conditioning.

I pushed open the door and found a few people laughing loudly across a small table to my left, but the right side was empty. Perching against the secluded alcove, I slid my thumb across the screen. I had a harrowing feeling that it wasn't Parker trying to get a hold of me, but I needed to be sure.

"Hello?" I answered.

"Yes, hello, is this Nora James?" a sultry female's voice questioned from the other end of the line.

"Who is this?" I asked, feeling panic rise up my throat.

"This is Michelle Rasmusson from *Page Six*. I'd love to ask you a few questions about your relationship with Parker Hart. Do you have a moment for me now? I promise to be quick." I squeezed my eyes shut as I sat down a small brick planter wall, bracing for the impact of whatever was about to hit me.

I'd purposefully stayed off any media sites this week. I avoided looking at gossip blogs, avoided even reading the news app on my phone. The only time I'd spent on the internet was to look for apartments to rent in the city. It was never lost on me that, because of Parker's *ridiculous* planning, there had been numerous eyes on the boat. Hundreds of pictures taken that depicted the moment Parker was down on one knee proposing to me as I tried to piece together what the hell he'd done.

It was unlikely that anything we'd said to each other that morning would have been heard over the deafening sound of the helicopter above us—but I knew what the scene had looked like. I'd stormed off, hiding inside the cabin of the yacht while Parker had festered and yelled the whole way back to shore. When I left L.A. the next morning, I'd spent the entire drive to Colorado praying that Parker—no, that *Marjorie* had the influence to make those photos disappear. I knew that if those pictures got out, there was a potential that I'd be thrown into a media frenzy I had absolutely zero desire to be a part of.

"Nora? Is now a good time?" the woman asked again.

"I'm sorry, you have the wrong number," I croaked, swiftly ending the call.

I stared at the screen as another call came in again. And again. And again. And again.

Taking a few grounding breaths, I ignored the incoming calls and opened my internet browser to search Parker's name, fumbling with shaking fingers as I typed into the search engine. As soon as I clicked enter, I watched as countless articles popped up with varying images of us from that morning. The photo quality was crisp and clear on all of them—there was no question what the images showed: Parker Hart had proposed to his long-term girlfriend. And she said no.

What caught my eye beyond the initial onslaught of photos were the headlines.

Mystery Girlfriend Says NO to Parker Hart's Proposal
Parker's Hart's Broken Heart - But Who is the Girl
Capable of Breaking It?
What Do We Really Know About Parker Hart's Elusive
Lady?

The articles had appeared the morning I'd skipped town—there had clearly been no stopping them. Whatever effort Parker and Marjorie had made to put a kibosh on the story had failed. But it was clear that the media didn't know who I was, which would explain why I hadn't heard anything about it over the last few days.

So why was *Page Six* calling now? How had that Michelle woman known my name?

On instinct, I swiped down on my screen to refresh the page, watching as a new story appeared—posted just four minutes ago. This one didn't show pictures from the morning on the yacht. No, this one showed pictures of *me*. Of me before Parker.

I opened the article and found a video embedded within—the thumbnail depicting Parker in what looked to be an interview. Panic slid like ice through my veins as I clicked play.

Chapter Eleven

ANDRE

She's fine, I rumbled to myself. Nora had been outside on the patio for over fifteen minutes now, and her sudden absence from the group unsettled me. No one else seemed concerned, though, so I tried to push the worry down. These were her best friends—I barely knew her in comparison. If they weren't worried, why should I be?

"Who wants a shot?" Adam looked around at the group, the desire to make bad decisions written all over his face. Amelia, Mackenzie, and Eric raised their hands, and he turned to flag down the bartender.

Logan cocked his head at Amelia. "What?" she asked, innocently.

"You know you shouldn't encourage him. He's a thirty-one-year-old neurosurgeon, not a twenty-one-year-old party animal," he teased. Rachel giggled.

Amelia shrugged. "You can take the boy out of the college parties, but you can't take the college party out of the boy."

Logan rolled his eyes as she stood up to tuck her arms around his waist. He looked down at her and kissed the top of her head.

Their affection toward each other always made me feel a mixture of uncomfortable and happy. I wasn't used to seeing two people so in love—I'd never seen anything remotely close to it. Logan looked at Amelia like she was his sun, and she looked at him like he was her sky. Witnessing something so powerful made my chest ache a little.

Love stories like that didn't exist where I came from.

I'd seen the change in Logan when they'd first gotten together—when he'd started showing up to work a little brighter. His face was flushed with more color, and he smiled a lot more. When he brought Amelia around for the first time, telling us that she was helping him with the shop's marketing, it all made sense. He'd been had—and she got him good.

Adam turned back around, four shots between his hands. He passed three of them off to the others before he held the fourth one out in the middle of the group. "To living forever!"

They held their drinks out to clink to his. I tipped my beer bottle into Logan's while the shot-takers downed their glasses and the rest of us took a sip of whatever we were drinking. My eyes kept sliding to the black patio door on the other side of the bar, waiting for Nora to walk back inside.

"You know that we can't actually live forever, right?" Mackenzie yelled over the music. "I mean, you *are* a doctor."

"I am?" Adam's eyes went wide, sending Rachel into another fit of giggles. Logan shook his head again, his arm still wrapped around Amelia.

"I'll be right back," I finally said, giving in to the temptation. I stepped away from the group without waiting for a response, anxious to get my eyes on her.

Just to make sure. That was okay, right?

I knew she was probably fine. It looked like someone had been calling her when she stepped away, so maybe she was just on the phone. Or maybe she got to talking with some people outside and was making new friends. Maybe she'd even met a guy and was in some dark corner getting to know him better.

Flashes of her mouth on mine at Jackson's pulsed through my vision and I pushed the patio door open harder than intended, swinging it open with such force that it almost hit the brick wall on the other side.

My eyes quickly swept over the patio before they settled on Nora, who was sitting on a big planter box, alone. With a sudden glaring focus, I realized she was crying.

A primal urge to protect her came over me as I made the four strides needed to reach her. "Hey," I said, keeping my voice light as I sat down beside her, close enough that our legs brushed together. She rubbed at her eyes, wiping away the tears that were still cascading. It only made the skin around them more red. "What's wrong?" I put a hand on her shoulder, turning her toward me.

She scoffed. It took a long moment before she finally whispered, "Nothing." Her eyes were glued to her feet—she wouldn't look at me.

"Oh yeah? You just like to find dark places to hide from your friends so you can cry?"

Her mouth tilted up a few millimeters. "One of my favorite pastimes."

"Hm," I grunted. "Cute."

Finally, her eyes flashed to me. "This is *not* cute."

"Your attempt to make a joke when you're clearly sad could be considered cute." I shrugged.

She sighed. "If you say so."

"Maybe I do." I knocked my knee into hers. "For real, Nora, what's wrong?"

She looked at me curiously for a moment before she finally let it out. "Parker—my ex—he . . . he tipped the paparazzi off that he was going to propose to me. They were all around us when it happened."

"When you said no."

She nodded. "Yeah. When I said no. His family is sort of famous, but he knew that I didn't want any of that to be a part of our relationship. I never wanted to be publicly known like they were. I had nothing of my own to even *be* known for, and I wasn't okay with my name being associated solely with the label of 'Parker's girlfriend.' That's so . . . lame.

"Anyway, I'd assumed his family wouldn't want the proposal to leak and damage his image. But now I know they couldn't stop it. I didn't realize it was all over the news. I've been avoiding it, purposefully *not* looking. But this reporter just called, trying to get a statement, which means they know who I am, and I finally looked and the story is everywhere." She took a deep breath before she continued, her words coming out faster. "And Parker—he cares about public perception a *lot* and . . . and I opened one of the articles. It's an interview with him." A fresh wave of tears began falling down her face, and I had to stop myself from catching them.

"He said I'd just been using him. He knew damn well I *never* wanted any part of that life, and yet he's publicly telling people that I'm some fame-hungry clout-chaser. He's protecting himself by *shaming* me with lies. And I'm so fucking angry at him, because after all those years of supporting him, I can't be supported in return? For being honest about my feelings?"

"Damn," I said softly, taking it all in. I had no fucking clue what to say to help her feel better—this was all a little out of my league. My initial reaction was a desire to drive out to Los Angeles and kick this Parker guy's ass, but I didn't think that's what she wanted to hear. "How can I help?"

Her shoulders lifted in a sad little shrug. "I don't know. I honestly just wish I could call my mom."

A memory from the other night drifted just out of reach. "You can't?"

Her gaze moved somewhere on the wall of the building. "She's gone."

I didn't have to ask to know what *gone* meant. "I'm so sorry, Nora."

She smiled softly. "It's been a few years. Needing her has never gone away though."

"I know what you mean. I feel the urge to call my brother all the time—he passed away almost four years ago." She looked at me then, her big, brown eyes swimming with vulnerability.

After a moment of silence, I spoke again. "Look, I know I'm not your mom, and I could never do anything to fill that void. I know it's not easy to deal with the layers of grief on top of everything else you have going on in your life, how overwhelming it can all become. But I was serious earlier when I said I could be a friend to you, Nora. And I know how grief works . . . how sometimes it helps to just have someone understand. I could be that for you, if you want. If you ever need to talk, I mean.

"As for this Parker loser . . . *fuck* him." A small laugh escaped her at that, and it made me smile. "I admit, I'm just a no-name mechanic from Denver, and I won't pretend to understand anything about fame or clout. But I'm sorry this guy thinks it's okay to talk shit about you . . . sorry that someone who wanted to make you his wife could turn around and disrespect you like that just because he didn't get what he wanted." Anger coursed through my veins just thinking about it. "One of the hardest lessons I've had to learn in life is not to give energy to the enemy. I used to obsess about people who wronged my family, the people who broke my brother—and I wanted to hurt them so bad, Nora. I wanted to cut them out of this world, knowing it would be a better place without them in it. But I realized focusing on hate and anger made it *really* hard to experience joy.

"I'm not trying to tell you what to do, and I'm not saying to just let any of this go. There's nothing wrong with defending yourself. But being genuinely happy is the best revenge. And you deserve to be really fucking happy. Okay?"

Her eyes softened, and I watched her mouth curl into a smile. She turned away from me, taking a deep breath as she looked up at the ivy snaking along the trellis above us. "You know, I really misjudged you." She looked back at me with an edge in her expression.

My curiosity ballooned at her words. "What do you mean?"

She shook her head. "When I came into the shop with the Range Rover, and you were in the lobby. I thought you were some hard-ass tattooed mechanic. I never imagined the depth that you'd have . . . that you would turn out to be such a kind, caring person. I'm sorry for making assumptions."

I felt my defenses rise a little as I let out a forced laugh. "Yeah, well, you wouldn't be the first, Nora. I've been judged my whole life. My parents weren't around growing up . . . I was a product of the system, an orphan boy with absolutely nothing except my siblings. And then as we got older, I became just another hoodlum from the streets in the eyes of everyone around us. Even before I got all these tattoos, people feared us. Like we were bad to our core—especially Gabriel and I. Just because we had a hard life." I took a swig of my beer and shrugged. "I don't blame you for your assumptions. Everyone makes them."

She put her hand on my arm, and I felt warmth radiate from the contact. "Andre, I'm sorry. You don't deserve to be judged like that. And . . . I would love to take you up on your offer. I'd really like a friendship with you."

I stared at her for a minute, feeling my defenses already retreating. "As long as it makes you happy, Nora." And I meant it.

She beamed. "Yes," she said, resting her head on my shoulder. "It already does."

I WAS DISTRACTED the next morning as I opened up the shop. My head clearly wasn't attached to the rest of my body because things kept going wrong. I'd set the coffee to brew without putting the pot in its place, and when I'd walked back into the break room, I almost slipped on the hot liquid covering the floor. It took me fifteen minutes to mop up the mess I'd made.

Then, as I went to wash my hands in the sink after cleaning the floor, I turned the knob to the faucet and broke it clean off. I'd had to grab an extra pair of pliers to replace it, and was hoping I could get it repaired before Logan noticed, which meant I'd need to run to the hardware store at some point today.

But none of that held a candle to what happened shortly after. I'd been working to approve the team's time cards through our payroll system when I accidentally deleted the fucking company records. All of them. I couldn't imagine a bigger fuck up, and I didn't even know how it happened. One minute, I was reviewing Cameron's hours from last weekend, and the next, the screen went completely blank.

I logged out and back in a hundred times, each time finding that Logan's Auto Shop's company profile was completely empty in the system. I sent a quick prayer up to the heavens as I called the payroll company's support line, hoping to god someone could undo whatever I'd just done.

I was now on minute forty-six of waiting to be connected with a support team member. As I was about to upend the desk, I heard a light knock on the office door. Turning in the chair, I saw Manny standing in the door frame, waving hello.

"Sup, Andre. What's good?"

I huffed out a breath and shook my head.

He looked me up and down. "That bad, huh?"

"It's been a fucking morning," I grumbled with the phone between my ear and shoulder.

"Anything I can help with?"

"No, thanks—just make sure the team is doing what they

need to do out there. I'll be stuck in here for a bit dealing with some issues."

Manny nodded and threw me a thumbs-up. "You got it, boss." And then he disappeared back into the bays, where the rest of the team was hopefully ready to open.

I blew out another breath as I turned back around, annoyed at the lame-ass elevator music coming through the phone. Closing my eyes, I rested my forearm on my fist as I got a hold of myself.

What is my fucking problem this morning?

I'd actually gotten great sleep last night, although my dreams were riddled with a certain blonde-haired bombshell who seemed to be diving deeper and deeper into my mind. Nora's breakdown last night had been . . . tough. It was hard to see her so upset, especially over some loser who never deserved having her in the first place. If I was her man . . .

Shit. No. I couldn't let myself have any ideas like that, because I was *not* Nora's man. She'd only just agreed to a friendship, and that was the lane I needed to keep things in— even if I thought about our kiss at least a hundred times a day.

I don't recognize who I see in the mirror. And I don't know what I want.

It's like all the things that used to light me up aren't a part of my life anymore.

Nora was going through shit right now; she'd said as much at the Sunshine Shack. I needed to be a supportive friend because I meant what I'd said. That girl deserved to be happy.

A support agent finally came on the other end of the line, and within a few minutes was able to reset everything in the payroll system. *Thank fuck.* I stayed on to complete a customer satisfaction survey—because that kid deserved a raise—then rested the phone back on its cradle and went back to reviewing time cards so that I could submit all hours for the upcoming week's payroll.

Mercifully done, I went out to the bays to check on the rest of the team, and was pleased to find everyone busy in their respective areas, staying productive and focused on the work. The rest of the morning went off without a hitch, and by the time lunch rolled around, I was back to feeling in control of myself. Making my way out back behind the building for a little fresh air and sunlight, I pulled out my phone and dialed Nora before I could talk myself out of it.

She answered on the third ring. "Hello?" That sweet voice brushed along my senses.

"Hey, Nora, it's Andre. How are you?"

"I'm good. I actually just got back from a job interview and it went really well." She sighed. "I'm still pretty frustrated about the media thing, but I appreciate you being there for me last night. Thank you for that."

"Wasn't a problem at all. Happy to help you, always. That's actually why I was calling . . . sometimes when I get pissed, I need to burn off some of that negative energy, so I wondered if you might want to give it a try? I'm going to the gym later today, and I'd like to bring you, if you want." I dragged my Chucks along the concrete, waiting for her answer. Did she think I was crazy, inviting her to the *gym*? "No pressure at all, of course," I added quickly, "just a friendly offer."

She giggled, and the sound instantly cracked open my chest. "The gym? I'd actually love that! Thank you."

I nodded, as if she could see me. "Great, I can pick you up. Does four o'clock work?"

"Yeah, that's perfect. I'll be at Mackenzie's." She laughed

softly. "You know where it is." I could hear the embarrassment in her tone as she was no doubt thinking of me bringing her home after Jackson's.

"Yeah, I know where it is. I'll see you then. And hey, Nora?"

"Yeah?"

"Congratulations on the job interview. I want to hear all about it."

A pause on the other end of the line had me feeling slightly nervous again, but then Nora responded. "Thank you, Andre. That means a lot." I could hear the smile in her voice.

I hung up and found myself staring at the mountains in the distance, reveling in the fact that such a shitty day could turn around so quickly. Four o'clock couldn't come fast enough.

The back door burst open, and I turned to find Manny and Cameron coming outside. This was typically where the guys took smoke breaks between vehicles. "Hey, boss," Cameron said from beneath a beanie that hung low over his eyes.

I shook my head. "Cameron, how many times do I have to tell you to lose the fucking hat during work hours?" I yanked the beanie off his head and tousled his hair.

He groaned. "You're such a mom, dude."

I laughed. "No, *dude*, I'm looking out for the shop. You know Logan doesn't like when you guys look like wild animals." I chucked the beanie at him, and he caught it before it hit his chest.

Manny whistled. "Cameron's always pulling shit, huh, boss?"

I scoffed. "You should be looking out for him, Manny."

Manny smiled wide as he lit a cigarette. "Nah, you know I don't look out for anyone but my damn self, boss."

A laugh burst out of me. *Touché.* "All right, don't make me come back out here to remind your asses to get back to work."

"Ten-four, boss!" Cameron saluted. *Wise ass.*

As I made my way back inside, I could hear Manny yell from behind me. "Cameron, what the *fuck*, bro. You know how dangerous white lighters are. Don't bring that shit around me!" I shook my head again as the door shut behind me.

Chapter Twelve

NORA

Running to the guest bedroom, I grabbed my sneakers from the closet and hurried back toward the front of the house. I threw my shoes on and tied them, then grabbed my purse off the hook by the door. I took a brief moment to look at myself in the mirror in the entryway, making sure the ponytail I'd thrown up a few minutes ago looked decent enough before I swung open the front door and stepped outside to meet Andre.

It had been an absolutely gorgeous day with a gentle breeze that rustled the trees in the neighborhood. Big, fluffy clouds dotted the bright blue sky as birds sang their cheery summer songs. And there, parked on the curb in front of the house, was a gorgeous vintage black Mustang with the windows rolled down and music playing loudly from within. More than that, there was a gorgeous man leaning against the front fender, watching my journey down the front pathway with an intensity that nearly brought me to my knees. Andre looked positively dangerous in black ray bans and a backward hat—a small smile crept up his face and I felt my heart stutter in response. He looked downright edible.

"Hey!" I greeted him, throwing my arms out for a hug when I reached him.

He wrapped his strong arms around me and gave me a quick squeeze. "Hey, Nora," he said into my ear, and I felt a buzz shoot down my spine at the feel of his warm breath on my neck. He was dressed for the gym in a black T-shirt and black athletic shorts, but I could still smell the shop on him. The motor oil and gasoline mixed with his own scent of spice and sweat had a heady effect. I chanced a swift look down at his bare legs, realizing it was my first time seeing him in shorts. It was oddly pleasing to know that even his legs were covered in tattoos. My mind reeled as I wondered what parts of his body might still be bare of any ink.

The shirt he wore exposed most of his throat, and in the bright daylight I could finally make out the tattoo there. It was a large skull with roses for eyes. On either side, large hawk wings spread out wide, expanding across his neck and reaching to just beneath his earlobes. It was . . . beautiful. He moved to open the passenger door for me, tracing a thumb along his smirk. "What?" I asked.

He shook his head once, setting his face back to neutral, though his eyes still danced in amusement. "Nothing. Ready?"

I sat down in the seat. "Ready as I'll ever be. I should warn you though—it's been a while since I've stepped foot in any gym. We had a home gym at the house in L.A. and I can count on one hand the number of times I used it in three years."

His smirk reappeared, and the sight of it was like the first taste of ice cream melting on my tongue on a hot summer evening. "Don't worry, you're in good hands."

Shutting my door, he circled the car and climbed in, shifting the Mustang into gear and pulling away from the curb. The warm, summer breeze caressed my face and flowed through my ponytail as I felt the rumble of the engine beneath the leather seats. "This is a nice car. How long have you had it?"

"A few years. I bought it a couple months after I started working at the shop. Logan knows a lot of people with nice cars, and when he realized I was taking the bus to get to work every day he put some feelers out and helped me find this. One of his old customers was selling it, and Logan asked him to bring it by so I could see it."

"Wow, that was nice of him."

Andre nodded. "Logan invests a lot in everyone who works for him. He's a good man."

I didn't know Logan nearly as well as I knew Amelia, but I remembered him going above and beyond to help our friend Gwen when she was stung by a jellyfish during our trip to Mexico. We were out on a snorkeling excursion and she panicked; she wasn't the strongest swimmer. Logan, who was closest to her when it happened, helped her get safely back to the boat and then proceeded to check on her for the rest of the day. "It must be nice to work for someone like that."

"Speaking of work." He flashed a smile my way. "I want to hear about your job interview."

A giddiness erupted inside of me. "Okay, so last night at Larkspur, Amelia introduced me to the bartender, Mara. I guess Amelia and Logan grew up with her, and Amelia asked if they were hiring because I had just told her I put a down payment on an apartment and needed to find a job." I was talking fast, excitement making my words tumble together, but I couldn't help myself. "Mara said they could use my help and invited me to go in this morning to talk to her about it . . . and it went really well!" Andre nodded along, not at all fazed by my high-pitched rambling. "I'm going to start cocktail serving three nights a week and I'll train with her behind the bar two nights a week until I'm ready to be on my own."

"Damn, girl!" The excitement in his voice matched mine. "That's amazing. Have you worked in a bar like that before?"

I shrugged. "I had a few cocktail waitressing jobs in college. I've never bartended, but I'm down to try. I think I'll like it, at least for now."

He nodded. "As long as it makes you happy."

"Yeah." I nodded. "And if it doesn't—it's no pressure. I can just find something different and keep working on figuring out what I really want to do."

"Sounds like things are falling into place for you." Andre pulled the car into the lot of a white, single-story building with ROCKY MOUNTAIN MMA written in bold black lettering.

"MMA?" I asked. "As in martial arts?"

A playful grin cocked from the side of his mouth. "Like I said earlier . . . it's a great way to burn off negative energy."

I hummed nervously. Was he going to make me actually hit something? "I thought we'd be, like, running on a treadmill."

He chuckled. "They have those here, too—but I want you to try something else first. Do you trust me?"

I was still looking at the building, but I felt his eyes on me from his side of the car. I turned to look at him and found his expression soft, his playful amusement no longer teasing through his features. Now it was with earnest intensity. "Yes," I answered. I didn't even hesitate. My reason was right in front of me, looking at me like I was something to be admired.

Andre had continuously showed up for me in ways that meant so much more than he probably understood. I was out at a bar with plenty of my friends last night—*good* friends who loved and supported me—and yet it was Andre who'd come to look for me. Andre who found me crying on that patio, who sat beside me and grounded me with his words. Who managed to pull me out of my head and somehow even make me laugh.

This friendship of ours might have been new, but it was already driving its roots down deep inside of me. His kindness and generosity were rare qualities, and I knew it.

Did I trust him? *Yes*. I really did.

He stared at me for a long, quiet moment. And then he pushed open his door and came around the car to open mine. As I stepped out and stood in front of him, I met his eyes and smiled. And though I could see him fight it, his own smile back was wide and unfiltered.

We trekked side by side into the building, my arm sweeping along the smooth wall that looked to have been freshly painted a bold black and red. There was an underlying scent of sweat in the air as men lifted an obscene amount of weight, watching themselves bulge out in the floor-to-ceiling mirror. It felt like I'd walked right into a corner of the world that was strictly meant for men, for their motivations to become vicious predators in the martial arts realm. There wasn't another woman in sight, at least that I could see.

Andre didn't greet anyone as he led me to the back of the gym where a fighting ring took up most of the space. A large Hispanic man wearing a collared polo with the gym's logo was heaving padded equipment and setting it down on a bench to the side of the ring. He looked up as we approached, and beamed when he saw Andre.

"*Hola hermano, qué pasa?*" The man—who looked older, but not by much—pulled Andre into a firm embrace. I could tell right away that they knew each other well, but I didn't think they were related. Outside of sharing similar golden-brown skin, they didn't look anything alike.

"*Lo mismo. Qué pasa contigo?*" Andre replied, and *oh*—though I didn't understand the words, hearing him speak Spanish sent a spark of intrigue through my body.

"Not much, not much," the man responded before he looked at me, still smiling. "And who's *this*?"

Andre placed a warm hand on my back as he spoke. "Chino, this is my friend, Nora. Nora, this is Chino. He owns the gym, and more than that, he's like family."

Chino's eyes were warm when he addressed me. "Lovely to meet you, Nora."

I reached out to shake his hand. "It's nice to meet you too, Chino."

He looked back to Andre and nodded his head toward the ring. "Octagon is yours for an hour, *hermano*. I brought out the Thai pads and some spare gloves. Do you need anything else?"

"No, that's perfect. Thank you. Appreciate you for letting me have it at the last minute."

He waved a hand as he began to walk away. "Don't mention it. I'll be in the back if you need me."

Andre looked at me and I raised my eyebrows at him. "You *rented* this for us?"

He smirked. "I didn't rent it. I just asked Chino if we could have it to ourselves for an hour. No big deal." He tugged lightly on my ponytail as I looked back toward the pads on the bench.

"What exactly are we doing?" I asked.

"Punching some shit," he said simply, "and getting some frustration out." He went to pick up a roll of athletic tape from the bench. "I'm going to wrap your hands, and then we'll try out those gloves, yeah?"

I stared at him, deadpan. "You're serious?"

Warm delight danced in his gray eyes. "Nora, remember when I asked if you trusted me?" I rolled my eyes, earning myself a chuckle. "Come on, girl," he said, his voice low. "Aren't you a little curious?"

Those eyes of his seemed to pierce right through me. I looked down at the tape in his hands, then at the ring behind him, and I had to admit—I *was* curious. I'd never hit anything in my life, but I'd never shied away from trying something new, either. And what better way to go for it than with Andre, who had what it took to make me feel comfortable?

He was asking me to try. He was bringing me further into his world. *Does this make me happy?* Yes.

"Okay, let's do it," I said, holding my hands out in the air between us with my palms facing down.

His gaze brightened, and he dipped his head. "Atta girl," he said. "Spread out your fingers."

I did as he said, then Andre began to wrap my right hand with the tape. He started in the center, wrapping it around a couple of times before he moved to wind the tape in between my fingers with each rotation.

"How come you go between the fingers?" I asked.

"Well, even though we're using gloves and pads, a solid punch is still a hard hit. We don't want your fingers to smash together on impact. By wrapping the tape through each gap, we're stabilizing your fingers and creating more structure for your fist to take on that impact without as much risk of injury."

"So . . . hitting hurts?"

He grinned. "Depends on how hard you hit . . . but yes, it can sometimes hurt. I don't think you'll have anything to worry about, though." His eyes flicked up to me. "Not because I don't think you can hit hard, but because I'm pretty good with these wraps."

I watched as he wrapped the tape over my thumb before moving down to my wrist. After he brought the material around a couple more times, he lifted the tape—and subsequently, my hand—to his mouth to tear the tape from the roll with his teeth. I felt a warm brush of his breath expel across my arm as he did so, and it was like the world slowed down to half speed as my eyes zeroed in on the sight of those teeth baring themselves to my wrist. I was almost dizzy by the feel of that exhale on my skin. The whole encounter was . . . absurdly intimate.

But if Andre noticed any change in my ability to stand or breathe or see straight, he didn't let on. He simply picked up my other hand and began the same process.

"So when we get in there," he said as he wrapped the tape through my fingers again, "I want you to try to get back to that place you were in last night. Try to bring those emotions back up to the surface so we can work through them in the ring. Think about the way you felt when you got that call from the reporter, and the anger and frustration when you heard what your ex said in that interview.

"This is a safe space, okay? It's just you and me in there. So let those feelings come back over you. And use them to fuel the fire throughout your body as we work through the exercises. It's important that you let it all out so it doesn't fester and eat at you. Shit like that can rot inside, you know?" He looked back up at me, his face more serious. "No matter what, I'll be right there, and I can take whatever you throw at me."

He'd finished wrapping my left hand, and lifted it to his teeth as he did with my right. But this time, the movement didn't spark the same sexual tension. This time, as his words bounced around in my head, it felt like a different kind of intimacy. Like we were preparing for a battle against those who had wronged me, and he was right there on the front lines, standing next to me with his weapons ready, following me into the bloodshed to blow apart my enemies.

I let out a slow breath as he turned around to pick up a pair of black boxing gloves. He tucked one between his knees to hold before he peeled back the Velcro at the wrist of the other, and then held it out for me to tuck my hand into. I pushed my wrapped hand into the mouth of the glove, feeling like I was putting on a battle suit. He then held the other glove up, and when both of them were on and fastened, I swung my arms around me to get a feel for the extra weight.

"Ready?" Andre asked, and I looked up to find him watching me.

I nodded, still a little unsure. But any trepidation that I might've had—I pushed it down. He was going through all of this to help me work through my feelings. The least I could do was be a willing and active participant. I closed my eyes for a moment, letting all of those feelings from last night resurface. It didn't take long before my heart pounded faster and the anger settled in as I heard Parker's words from that interview.

I was honestly a bit blindsided.

I'm a romantic at heart, and I thought she was truly the one for me—I wanted to spend the rest of my life with her.

You know, it all makes sense now. I just hadn't wanted to see it.

She was only with me for the clout. She knew that I could propel her forward with her career.

You want to know why she said no to my proposal? Because asking her on a private yacht in front of my family wasn't big enough for her.

I felt my blood roar in my ears as I opened my eyes and looked back up at Andre. "Yeah," I said back to him, "I'm ready."

Chapter Thirteen

ANDRE

Nora opened her eyes, and it was like looking at a completely different girl than the one who'd stood before me mere seconds ago. Her soft, warm eyes were now cold and narrowed. A line carved its way through the middle of her brow, and her lips were pressed tight and turned down in the corners.

This Nora was pissed off. She looked eager for an outlet. Eager for revenge, to rip somebody's head off with the rage brewing beneath the surface.

Good. I knew all too well what that felt like.

"Yeah," she said tightly, "I'm ready."

I nodded once, appreciating that she was taking this seriously. That she wasn't looking at this like some silly game. That she'd heard me when I said *not* working through the hard shit could lead to a mental clusterfuck later. I knew all about that, too. "Then follow me." I picked up the set of pads that lay on the bench and then helped her climb through the ropes of the ring. I led her to the center as I pushed my arms through the straps, the pad-side facing outward.

"Okay, first I want you to warm your body up and get your blood pumping. Take a light jog around the ring a few times until you feel your heart rate has increased and your breathing starts to feel labored. The weight of the gloves will work your arms and get you ready for sparring." She nodded and took off, jogging along the ropes of the ring.

And I just *watched*.

Her long legs as they carried her swiftly around the circumference of the ropes, her torso twisting gracefully, her arms swinging out in front of her with each step she took. She wore a matching gym set, the gray spandex material hugging her every curve. There was a few inches of skin showing between her tank top and shorts, and I had to will my eyes not to get stuck there. Her long blonde ponytail bounced back and forth behind her, swooshing over her shoulders as she ran.

She looked good. No doubt about it.

After five rotations, she met me in the middle of the ring, her face flushed and her chest rising and falling more rapidly than before. A light shimmer of sweat gleamed from her forehead as she asked, "How's that?"

"Good," I said, a hint of gravel in my voice. I cleared my throat and forced it away. "Okay, we're going to start with some easy throws. I want you to focus on form—it's not about how hard you can hit right now but how accurate your movements are. We don't want you to get hurt with a wild swing. Watch my arms." I showed her a quick jab, slowing it down to demonstrate the movement a couple times. And then I did the same to show her a proper cross. "Got it?"

"Yeah, I think so," she said.

"Okay, let me see your fighting stance." Nora stepped her left foot forward and bent both of her knees as she held the gloves out in front of her. "Pretty damn close. Keep your left foot forward like you have it, but make sure both feet are shoulder width apart—your right foot is a bit too far back. It'll throw you off balance when you swing."

She corrected herself. "Like this?"

"Yes, good. Now keep your back straight, shoulders back, and keep your left glove in front of the right one. Look up at your opponent, never down at the ground."

She made a few adjustments, and then looked at me for approval. Something about the eagerness in her eyes spread warmth throughout my chest.

"You got it, Nora. Fucking perfect. Okay, from here, I want you to hit the pads on my arms with a jab-jab-cross combo. Okay?"

She nodded, and I held the pads up in front of me with my own stance ready. She took a deep breath, and then moved through the hits with surprising ease. She looked at me again after she was done, in that similar search for approval. "Like that?"

I couldn't help it, I smiled. "Exactly. Now try with a little more oomph."

Nora moved through the hits again with more power, and this time I watched as she gritted her teeth through it. I could see the satisfaction on her face when she was done.

"How do your hands feel?" I asked.

She looked at the gloves, considering for a moment, and then her eyes flashed to mine. "They feel great, no issues."

I nodded. "That's what I like to hear."

I led her through the foundations of a solid hook and

uppercut, and we continued to work through her form on both. Within about fifteen minutes, she was throwing solid hits nearly every time, her confidence growing through each one.

After working through a jab-hook-uppercut combo, she stood up straight for a moment and wiped her brow with the back of her glove, her face even more flushed from the exertion.

"Okay, Nora," I said, watching as her eyes found mine with fervor for whatever came next. "You have the basics down, and your form is looking real good. Now I want you to let those feelings flood through you as you hit the pads. You can choose whatever combos you'd like, whatever feels right. But I want you to look at these pads, visualize your target, and pour yourself into your hits."

The slightest trace of uncertainty dipped in her brows. "Any hit?"

I nodded. "Whatever feels comfortable. I might vocalize a few adjustments here and there if your form starts to slack, but I want you to spend the next ten minutes sparring with me in constant movement. You can be vocal too if you need to get some shit out—whatever you need. I can take it, okay?"

She got back into her fighting stance, and I had to take a second to marvel at the sight of her. "Okay, ready," she said, dipping her chin.

For the next ten minutes, Nora's hits came harder and faster, her breaths uneven with exertion. I knew her muscles had to have been burning, but it was as if she used that pain and discomfort to strengthen the fire that was pouring out of her.

A few minutes in, she began a glorious bout of shit-talking

that rivaled that of the men who trained in this very ring every day.

"I really don't care what anyone in that godforsaken city thinks of me," she grumbled, eyes narrowed on the pads.

Jab-Cross-Jab-Hook

"They have no idea who the *fuck* I am," she spat.

Jab-Jab-Uppercut

"The *audacity* of that man-child to call *me* a fucking clout-chaser . . ."

Cross-Jab-Hook

". . . little do they know he's the fucking *worst* of them all!"

Jab-Hook-Uppercut

"I should have fucking known not to trust a pretty boy," she growled. Her cheeks were bright red as she inhaled a deep breath and then pushed it out through her nose.

I watched as a tear spilled from her eye and ran down her cheek before she wiped it away with her shoulder. The sight of it unleashed something inside of me that I'd been holding down tight—the urge to grab her by the shoulders and tug her toward me, to wrap my arms around her, it became almost unbearable.

She'd been so focused that when she finally looked back up at me, I saw the wave of embarrassment wash across her face.

I shook my head and dropped the pads a touch. "Don't you dare, Nora. You should be proud of what you just allowed yourself to express." I stood up straight and let my arms fall to my sides. "You did so good."

She let out a breath. "I did?"

"Are you kidding? For someone who's never done this before, you looked real comfortable with those gloves on. You're a natural, Nora."

Despite my encouragement, she still looked unsure. Her eyes moved to somewhere on the ground as she shifted her weight from one foot to the other. "It's just . . . it's hard to work through these feelings, you know? I spent *three years* in L.A., and for most of that time, I really thought I was building a life with Parker—something that I would be a part of forever. And it's so obvious to me now that I wasn't actually building anything. I was merely molding myself to him. I wasted so much time . . ." Another tear fell down her cheek, and I wanted so badly to wipe it away with my thumb. "I wasted so much time that I should have been spending working through what *I* needed to work through.

"My mom was sick for like, five years before she . . . before she passed. She had cancer. At first, they kept saying they caught it early, that she just needed chemo and radiation and she'd be fine—and she was, for a while. But it kept coming back, and each time it took more and more of her with it. She was all the family I had, and without her . . . I just *couldn't* deal." She huffed out a long breath.

"I met Parker at a bar one night. He was in town for some shoot, and I let myself believe he was the answer to all the pain I was feeling. Like I could just run away with him to California and leave the sadness and anger behind. I thought I could just . . . flip a switch. Start over. But it was all a distraction. I made it so easy for him to change every aspect of my life because the alternative was facing the devastation of losing the person I loved most in the world. So as angry as I am at the shit he's pulling . . . I feel like I can only really be angry at myself. This is all a result of my decision to run in the first place."

Her eyes were swimming in tears now, and something about seeing her so upset rocked me to my core. My pulse tripped violently as it pounded in my ears. Everything around us disappeared except for her sadness and my rage in the face of it. The blaring, primal need to fix it so that she could smile again.

No one had ever looked at me like that—so hopeful and terrified all at once. Every thought exposed. She was showing me this part of her that she'd kept safely guarded. It had me itching to sweep her off her feet and reward her for the gift of her trust, to prove myself worthy of it.

"Nora," I said, voice low. I waited for her to look at me. "First of all, you couldn't have expected to deal with the loss of your mom immediately after it happened. It doesn't . . . it doesn't work like that. When Gabriel died"—there was a quiver in my voice as I said his name, but I slid my own rising emotion to the side—"I completely lost myself, too. It took me years to see any light through it all. Grief is fucking *hard*, Nora. And there's no blueprint on how to move through it.

"*So what* if you ran? You did what you needed to do to survive the heartbreak. Don't blame yourself for choosing wrong, because there is no right or wrong with trauma. There's simply survival."

Tears streamed freely down her face now, and while I wanted to navigate us away from this painful topic, I needed her to hear something else, first.

"As for that fool in L.A., you deserved a hell of a lot more from him, Nora. The way he's treating you is *not* your fault. He clearly has no idea . . . no idea what he's taking advantage of. He was crazy not to do everything in his power to worship the ground you walk on. Don't you dare go thinking you deserve any of this. You're a damn treasure. You hear me? *Fuck* that loser."

Her eyes widened at the anger seeping out of me, her mouth frozen as it curled in surprise. Then she buried her face into the gloves still attached to her hands, letting out a sob that tore clean through my chest.

Panic seized me. "Oh shit . . . Nora . . . I'm sorry. I'm not trying to upset you . . ."

And then in a move so completely unexpected, she flung herself forward, threw her arms around my neck, and buried her face into my chest. Her shoulders shuddered as sobs continued to escape into my shirt. I wrapped my arms tightly around her body, pulling her in closer and dropping the pads on the ground. "Nora, I'm sorry. Was that too aggressive? I'm so sorry. I didn't mean to make you cry. I know sometimes I come off a little strong . . ."

She pulled her face from my chest and looked up at me, a bright ring of gold within the chestnut brown of her eyes lighting up through her emotion. A fresh tear collected in the corner of one before it rolled down her cheek, and I couldn't help it this time as I reached to wipe it away with my thumb. "That's the nicest thing a man has ever, *ever* said to me," she whispered, and leaned into my touch.

My heart pounded harder in my chest as she nuzzled back into it. I slid one hand around her back in soothing circles, running the other through her ponytail as she clutched tightly to my neck. She'd been working so hard for so long to feel okay, and it was all clearly coming to a head. It stirred something within me, something fierce and protective—a desperate need to show her how a real man should treat her. How a real man should do everything in his power to support her happiness. I knew that the feelings were dangerous to the boundaries of our friendship, but right here and now, I couldn't stop them from tearing through me.

I was mad attracted to her, there was no doubt about it. Even still . . . she didn't need a man making moves on her. She needed a friend. She needed a rock-solid pillar of support, and I would be exactly that. Her safe place. Her biggest fan. I would do it to whatever end, even if I had to hold myself back in the process. Even if I could never have her the way I really wanted. I wouldn't let her see it . . . I wouldn't let her see me struggle.

It was a better alternative to her hurting.

"Listen, Nora," I finally said as I pulled myself back to look her in the eye. "I know things feel a little upside down for you right now, but this is an opportunity for you to *really* build a life that makes you happy. Just like I said before—be open to the possibilities. Take everything as it comes, step by step. The grief you feel . . . it will always be a part of you. But you can learn how to live with it, I promise. And this shit with your ex, it'll pass. Just stay focused. Make decisions that make *you* happy, and don't put pressure on yourself to figure it all out at once."

Nora sniffed and took a deep breath. Her tears were beginning to subside. As if realizing we were still in each other's arms, she released my neck and took a step back. She shook her head. "How are you so good at this?"

"At what?" I asked.

"Breaking things down so they make sense. Knowing exactly what to say to stop me from falling apart." She huffed out a throaty laugh. It sounded more forced than anything, but it was a good start.

I shrugged, grinning at her. "I believe that everything in life is an exchange of energy, and that all energy is rooted in either love or fear. If you can just figure out how to live more from a place of love—loving yourself, most importantly—the fear starts to subside over time. Trust me, though, it took a fucking long time for me to get to this place. I see your pain and I feel like I know it. I just want to help, you know?"

This time, there was nothing forced about the way she smiled up at me. "Yeah, I believe you. I'm starting to wonder how the hell I managed to manifest you. It's like you're exactly what I needed to come back home to."

Her words hit me like a punch. It took me a second to respond, but when I did, the honesty and vulnerability spilled from my mouth despite how foreign it tasted. "Maybe it was me who manifested you, Nora."

The air weighed heavy as we stared at each other, locked in the moment as our words settled around us. I didn't regret what I'd said—it was the truth—but I also couldn't tell what she was thinking. Her face stayed frozen as she looked at me with those shining chestnut eyes.

"How are you guys doing over here?" Chino's voice sounded from the side of the ring. "Haven't seen you move in a while. You okay? You need anything?"

Nora smiled as she looked away, wiping her face on the back of a glove to hide any trace of her tears. I finally tore my gaze off her and looked over at Chino. "We're good, *hermano*," I said. "Just wrapping up."

He nodded. "Okay, no rush. Just leave the pads on the bench and I'll get it all wiped down and put away."

"No problem." I watched him walk to the front before I looked back at Nora. She looked . . . lighter. "You okay?" I asked.

A smile still played on her lips. "Yeah. This was . . . *very* therapeutic."

I shook my head. "I admit, I didn't expect it to get *that* heavy. But I hope it helped?"

She beamed. "More than you know."

I dipped my head, finding reprieve from the chaos of my heart as I looked at the ground between us. I took a deep breath, then stepped toward her. "Let's get those gloves off, yeah?"

Chapter Fourteen

NORA

For the first time in my entire life, I had a place all to myself. I had keys to my *own* apartment. And while that might've seemed depressing after living with a man I'd thought was going to be my forever, it actually felt unbelievably right.

I was also the proud new owner of a job—something I hadn't had in over three years—which I was due to start on Tuesday, and I was *elated*. I would train with Mara behind the bar on Tuesday and Friday nights, and then I'd work as a cocktail server on Wednesday, Thursday, and Saturday nights. Once she felt I was ready, I'd start bartending all of my shifts. Seeing Mara in action on Friday had made me want a good rush of my own, and I looked forward to being thrown into it.

I was thoroughly enjoying the thrill of rebuilding my life—and I'd been back in Denver for only a week. I felt like I was kicking ass and taking names on all of my goals, but I also knew I had to give credit to the friends who surrounded me.

Andre had helped me beyond belief, from trading in the Range Rover to working me out at the gym. Mackenzie had spent an entire day with me apartment hunting, and if Amelia hadn't asked Mara about an opportunity at the bar, I never would have thought to ask. For as much as I was craving my newfound independence, I was learning to accept the help being tossed at me.

I was pulled out of my thoughts at the sound of the doorknob twisting on the front door, as if someone were trying to walk into my apartment. I looked around my small living room and then froze. It was late. *Why would anyone be at my door right now?* No one except Mackenzie and Andre knew where I lived, and they would've called me if they were dropping by for any reason. Plus, Mackenzie had already stopped in hours ago to see the place and congratulate me, and Andre said he would come by tomorrow.

Maybe someone had the wrong apartment? Or they were looking for the previous tenant? As the doorknob continued to rattle despite whoever it was being met by an obviously locked door, real fear started creeping up my spine.

I quietly got up from where I was unpacking a box of bathroom items and bolted to the kitchen to grab a pair of scissors from a drawer. I noticed my phone on the counter as well, next to the bag of gummy bears I'd been snacking on all night for fuel, and reached to pick it up. The clock on my home screen showed that it was just past midnight—*way* too late for anyone to be here for good reason.

While I was proud of my new place, I knew that it was far from a luxury apartment. The building was *not* in a great part of town. Maybe someone noticed me hauling things up from my car today and saw something they liked, and now they wanted to steal from me? My eyes swept around the apartment —there really wasn't anything of value for them to take.

Without a second thought, I sent off a panicked text, but then realized the sound from the door had stopped just as suddenly as it started. I stood like a statue, waiting for any sign that the possible intruder was still outside my door—but I was only met with silence.

Sighing, exhausted, I turned the lamp off in the living room and made my way into my bedroom. I set the scissors on my nightstand and quickly changed into pajamas, crawling into bed and pulling my comforter up like a shield. Staring wide-eyed at the ceiling, I willed my body and mind to relax.

A ROUGH POUNDING at the door had me flying back out of bed, fear rattling right through me again. I checked my phone and saw that only twenty minutes had passed; I must have fallen asleep. Was it the same person as before, or was this a whole new problem to deal with? The knocking was vicious and loud.

With my trusty scissors in hand, I took hesitant steps toward the front entryway, keeping my feet light and quiet so as not to give any indication that I was inside. I wanted to peek through the peephole and get a good look at whoever might be trying to mess with me.

"Nora, it's me!"

My shoulders relaxed at the sound of Andre's voice coming through the door. I let out a long sigh, feeling the adrenaline flowing rampant through my shaky limbs. I twisted the deadbolt on the lock and opened the door to see a wild-eyed Andre staring back at me. As soon as his eyes caught mine, he slumped forward and braced a palm on my door frame, dropping his head.

"What are you doing here?" I asked, moving out of the way for him to come inside. It wasn't until I'd shut the door behind him and turned around that I noticed a long, silver pipe hanging from his hand. "What is *that*?"

Andre's face was hard and he was breathing heavily. "You said someone was trying to get in your door."

I felt a nervous bark of laughter squeak from my throat. "So you came over with a *pipe*?"

His eyes narrowed as his jaw clenched. "Yes, Nora. I came here to make sure you were okay."

My mouth hung open as my brain flicked through potential scenarios, all of which had Andre showing up to find someone still here, still messing with the outside of my door. "You could have hurt somebody with that, Andre." It was a statement of surprise, more than anything.

"Yeah." He nodded his head. Like the promise of blood and broken bones should have been obvious. As if to say, *Of course, Nora, what did you expect?*

My stomach did a flip, then another.

As my thoughts bounced around the edges of his words, he turned toward the front entryway like he might leave. He paused at the doorway though, and after leaning the pipe (pipe!) on the ground against the door jamb, he bent down to inspect my locks.

I realized I was staring at the ass that presented itself to me through black sweatpants when he began speaking. "Nora," he grumbled, "these locks are shit." Standing up straight, he turned to face me with a murderous determination set in his brow. He looked . . . *scary* when he was angry. His tall, dark form and the tattoos crawling all over his skin certainly made for a menacing presence. "I need to install something more efficient. Something much stronger. I'll do it tomorrow. You can't stay here with that flimsy-ass hardware." He looked back at the door, eyes tracking up the length of it as his mouth pressed together in disapproval. "We should honestly consider a whole new door . . ."

We. "Andre," I interrupted him. "I'm not sure the landlord would love for us to tear apart the doorway. I literally *just* moved in here."

The look he threw back at me was thunderous. "I don't give a shit," he spat. I could see a vein popping from his neck as his jaw worked. "This isn't safe. You being here isn't safe."

My thoughts unraveled. I knew that being in this building wasn't exactly cushy living, but it was what I could afford. And I was *proud* that I could at least afford it on my own. Still, seeing Andre so visibly affected by the perceived danger was . . .

Truthfully? *Hot.*

"You can install new locks, okay?" I encouraged. "And then we'll see how it goes before we jump into anything else."

His gaze sunk into me like an arrow as he considered.

"I'll be okay until tomorrow," I continued, ignoring the rush through my chest that rose from that look. "It's late, and I feel terrible that you came all the way over here in the middle of the night. I'm sorry for texting you. I'll be okay, Andre. You can go home, okay?"

Immediately, he was shaking his head. "No, Nora, I'm not

going anywhere. Not until those locks are replaced. I'll sleep on the couch."

I felt a little breathless as I looked around the apartment, where clearly no furniture existed. "I . . . I don't have a couch." My focus shifted back to Andre who was also realizing his mistake.

He shrugged. "Then I'll sleep on the floor." And just like that, he was taking his phone and keys and wallet out of his pockets, piling them onto the counter that separated the entryway from the kitchen, and then he moved into the small living room where he sat down onto the carpeted floor against a wall.

"You can't just sleep on my floor, Andre."

"Watch me," he said with a look that dared me to argue. And then his eyes softened and he took in a deep breath, pushing it out through his nose a moment later. "I'm not going anywhere, Nora. Go to bed, get some sleep, and we'll sort this out in the morning, yeah?"

I stared at him for a moment, the tight coiling in my stomach constricting me like a vice until I conceded. "Fine." Walking back to my room, I grabbed a pillow off my bed and the extra blanket that lay folded and brought them both back out to him.

His eyes bounced from my eyes to the limp pillow in my hand and back up to eyes again before he took the offering. "Thanks."

"No problem," I huffed, then retreated back into my room, softly shutting the door behind me. I crawled back into my bed and shut the lamp off on the nightstand, pulling the covers straight up to my chin once more. Staring at the dark ceiling, my head was swirling with so many thoughts.

Andre was *here.*

He was just on the other side of that door, sleeping on my floor.

To make sure I was . . . safe.

I didn't know what to make of that. I honestly had no grasp on the completely unconventional trajectory of this friendship. Days ago, I thought that rogue kiss at Jackson's would have permanently scared him away, but it hadn't sent him running at all. If anything, he continued to drive himself closer to me, wedging himself into the cracks I left open in my vulnerability to secure a place next to me. He was determined to be there for me, just as he had at Larkspur, and just as he had at the gym yesterday. The continued proof was on the other side of my bedroom wall.

Closing my eyes tight, I begged for sleep to claim me—but instead found myself locked in hazy visions of neon lights and a warm hand around the nape of my neck as hungry lips pressed against mine, of a violently swinging pipe against anyone who wanted to hurt me, of skull tattoos with wings that fluttered against my heart.

THE NEXT MORNING, I woke up sweating.

The sun was glaringly bright through my small window, and a toasty patch of sunlight was outright smothering me. I pushed my pink comforter off my body and pulled my legs out from under the sheets.

My head pounded and I felt exhausted, having gotten barely any sleep from the night before with all of the—

I shot up as memories came flooding back to me. *Holy shit.* Andre was here! I jumped out of bed, and after taking inventory of my pajamas to make sure everything was as it should be, I crept toward my bedroom door.

Opening it a few inches, I peered out and found Andre's sleeping body spread out like a behemoth on the floor against the wall. He was lying on his back, his head on the pillow I'd brought him and the small, yellow throw blanket covering his legs.

It was almost laughable, the size of the blanket against the full length of his body. It definitely hadn't been enough to cover him or keep him warm. Though he must not have been cold, because he'd taken his shirt off at some point during the night—an observation that both delighted and terrified me. I was entranced by the hard planes of his chest, tracing my eyes along the tattoos that covered them, following the art as it meandered down to his stomach. His entire chest and torso were covered in an incredibly intricate design of what looked to be some sort of masked face, complete with large horns that trailed up his pecs.

"See something you like?" Andre's voice filled the air, startling me so deeply that I yelped as I jumped backward into my room. A rumbling chuckle sounded from where he lay before I heard the unmistakable shuffling of him getting up from his makeshift bed.

I poked my head back through the doorway and peered at him, catching sight of his tall form, his outright *chiseled* muscles. I felt a blush wriggle up my neck at the prospect of him thinking I was so brazenly lusting after him. But honestly,

Andre without a shirt bordered on the line of obscene. "I wasn't staring, for the record." I threw out in my best a matter-of-fact tone.

A grin bloomed on his face, and the tension in my chest cavity pulled taut. After seeing his frustration and worry last night, I was thankful to find an easy expression now held in his dark features. I had no doubt that spending the night on the floor had been uncomfortable, but he still somehow looked rather . . . rested. "Sure," he said, nodding once, "okay." His voice was thick and raspy with sleep.

I scoffed. "I wasn't! I mean, maybe I was *looking*. But I was just . . . trying to see what your tattoo is of." My eyes fell to the angry face roaring at me from his stomach. "What is it?" I asked.

He reached down to pick up the blanket from the floor, folding it in front of him as he continued to grin. "It's an oni mask."

"What does it mean?"

"It can mean a lot of things in Japanese folklore," he said with a small shrug. "But this one is for protection against my enemies. It's meant to ward off bad energy and bad omens."

I stayed quiet for a moment, watching him stack the now-folded blanket onto the pillow, setting both neatly against the wall. As if he might be back to use them again. "Do you believe in it?"

His eyes flicked up to mine, his expression morphing into something a smidge heavier. "I do. I . . . I got it after my brother passed away. There was a lot of evil in our lives back then, and after he died, I felt . . . scared. Without Gabriel around, Marisela and I were vulnerable. He'd always been our protector. So I wanted to get something that would help us, in case we needed it. And I believe that it's helped." He regarded me for a moment before adding, "When we believe in something, we give power to it. We give energy to it—love and fear, remember?"

Smiling back at him, I nodded toward his hands. "You have it written on your fingers. How could I forget?"

He looked down at the tattoos on his fingers and grinned. "I do. It's a good reminder." His eyes moved to my bare legs before they rose to my face. He swallowed hard. "I'm going to give you some space and head to the hardware store for supplies. Do you need anything?"

I shook my head. "No, thank you."

He picked up his black T-shirt from where it lay folded on the floor, and I wondered if he was always so neat about things. Folding his shirt, folding the blanket . . . he kept his environment organized. A man of structure. I watched him tug the shirt over his head as he moved to grab his things from the counter. "I won't be long," he called back to me. His lips pressed into a hard line before he added, "Call me right away if someone touches your door, yeah?"

"Yeah." I nodded. "I will. I promise."

Seemingly satisfied, he unbolted the door and walked out, shutting it softly behind him as he left.

I got to showering and threw on an old college T-shirt and athletic shorts, knowing I was in for a morning of unpacking. I really didn't have much left, but I also planned on hitting up a few stores to get some furniture for the living room. Thankfully, with a job already secured, I had a little bit more wiggle room to spend the money from the Range Rover.

It was about another hour before Andre returned, wielding multiple bags in both arms—one of which looked and smelled like a pastry bag, which piqued my curiosity. He set everything down on the kitchen counter, then grabbed something out of one of the plastic grocery bags and turned around.

He held up a bottle of white wine, his eyes eager as they found mine. "For you," he said simply. As if it wasn't the sweetest of gestures.

A smile crept up along my cheeks. "You didn't have to do that." My eyes bounced from the bottle in his hands to his face, watching as he waited patiently for my reaction. "That was really sweet, Andre. Thank you."

He shrugged. "Happy new apartment."

My smile grew wider. "Happy new apartment, indeed."

He turned to put the bottle down on the counter and grabbed a white paper bag. "I also got you a muffin."

My heart soared. "I love muffins."

He nodded. "I was hoping you did. Mind if I get to work on your door?"

"Not at all. Thank you so much for doing all of this." I sashayed into the kitchen, itching to get my greedy hands on the baked prize.

"It's all good, I'll feel better knowing you have stronger locks." He picked up a couple of bags from the home improvement store and set up by the door.

I watched him work as I ate the heavenly blueberry muffin directly from the bag. A groan escaped me, and I felt Andre's gaze snap to me. "This is seriously amazing."

His eyes were dark as he watched me. Clearing his throat, he turned back to his work of unscrewing the current locks from where they were fastened on the door.

"Hey, can I ask you a favor?"

He looked back at me again. "Anything." He said it so earnestly it made my stomach roll.

"I want to get a tattoo." I looked down at the dragon that wrapped around his arm. "And I was hoping you could take me?"

A grin splayed out over his lips as his eyes flashed in surprise. "You want to get a tattoo?"

"Yes."

His grin widened. "Hell yeah, I'll take you." He was . . . *excited*. "I can call my tattoo artist and see if she's available. Or . . ." He hesitated. "Do you have a place in mind already?"

"No, no. That would be great. I was hoping you would bring me to wherever it is that you go." As soon as the words left my mouth, I heard the blatant eagerness of them. The spark of desire for Andre to bring me further still into his life. The gym was one thing, but tattoos were clearly a big deal for him, and his shop was probably a personal place.

He nodded his head once, dispelling my overcooked thoughts. "Cool. I'll make a call and find out when she can take you, okay?"

I smiled. "Okay."

He went back to work, and I took another big bite of muffin. Eventually, I felt him turn to face me again. "What do you want to get?"

I smiled. "You'll see."

Chapter Fifteen

ANDRE

peeled the wet label from the bottle between my hands—I couldn't help it. She looked like a ray of sunlight in this dark and dingy club, like the brightest star in the night's sky. Beckoning me, as if she'd lead me home.

It was her first shift at Larkspur, and she was training behind the bar with Mara, the bar manager. Nora was dressed a little more conservatively than Mara, who showed off her form in spandex bottoms and a tight, white tank top. Nora had opted for denim cutoffs and a loose-fitting black T-shirt with the Larkspur logo printed on it. Her long, blonde hair was pulled in a loose braid that trailed down her back.

I'd gotten here only twenty minutes ago, taking up a lone spot at the end of the half-occupied bar, and found myself completely invested in her movements as she learned the ropes of bartending. From where I sat, I could see that she was a little nervous—her eyes were constantly assessing the environment around her, eager to perform well and anticipate the needs of those who sat before her. But her smile radiated as she chatted with the patrons.

The bar wasn't very busy—it was only Tuesday. But there was still more people here than I would have expected to see for a weeknight. Mara and Nora were the only ones working behind the bar, while another short brunette served cocktails on the floor. There was a bouncer at the door—a sight that made me happy, knowing Nora was that much safer for it.

On more occasions than would have been deemed appropriate, she caught me staring at her. I should have felt embarrassed by it, the utter fool that I was. But something about the way she looked back at me, with a curious glint in her eye, made me think that she was feeling the same impulse. The same gravitational pull.

If she was a star, I was her moon, orbiting around her with zero regard for anything else.

Get a fucking grip. I shook my head and pulled my gaze away from her, taking a long sip of my beer and relishing the burn of icy carbonation as it slid down my throat. A small distraction from the churning in my chest.

Within mere seconds, my eyes were on her again. I watched her turn to pull on a tap, filling a pint of beer as an unfamiliar voice came into focus. "Whatever bro, twenty bucks says you can't get her number."

Something about those words caught my interest. I felt my attention snare on them as I tried to piece together what they meant. Who they were in regards to. I peeled my eyes away from Nora to glance at the three guys seated closest to me at the bar—preppy looking rich boys.

All of them were practically gaping at Nora. I turned back

to look at her, seeing her from their point of view—the v-neck of her shirt revealing the skin of her chest, her long gorgeous legs on display. It was all I could do not to jump over this fucking bar and wring their weak little necks for ogling at her like she was ripe for the taking.

I tried to calm the surge of cold rage that flooded through my veins, tried talking myself down. Who was I to say they couldn't look at her? I mean . . . I knew damn well how beautiful she was. And these guys looked like they'd probably be her type. Fuck, her ex was a damn LA model. Who was I to compete with something like that?

Still, I couldn't help the territorial urge to knock their asses out for looking at her the way that they were. Like she was a commodity. Something to be had.

The one closest to me shook his head, his outgrown, curly brown hair flopping as he did. In a voice deeper than the first, I leaned in to hear him say, "Dude, she's way too hot for you. Out of your league."

I snorted. Had that right.

The one in the middle looked back and forth between both of his friends. "Oh ye brothers of little faith." He scoffed. "I could have that bitch in my bed tonight if I wanted to. And she'd be moaning my name like a good little slut." He let out a cocky laugh.

My body moved before my brain could produce a single thought, bursting out of the stool to stand up and take a heavy step toward the little trio of dumbfucks. The leg of the stool squeaked as it slid backward on the concrete ground, and all three of them looked over at me, obviously startled.

I knew the effect I had on people. With my dark clothes and tattoos and the heated glare that was so damn easy for me to muster, I'd seen enough people look at me and look away *just* as quickly. As if not giving me more than a hair's breadth of acknowledgment could lessen any threat that I might pose.

The curly haired one looked away first, finding great interest in the straw of his stupid, red cocktail. His drink matched the color of his ears—no doubt feeling fear. The furthest one, the one who I'd heard speak first, looked around to see if anyone else could help them if this went south. Good. They'd need it.

But the middle one, the cocky fucker, he kept his icy, blue eyes right on mine. He didn't seem to want to back down as easily—had to give him that.

"What the fuck did you just say about my friend?" I asked, my voice low and dangerous. My fists were closed tight on either side of me, ready for anything.

His eyes widened slightly at the word 'friend', quickly realizing his mistake. I saw Nora approaching us through my peripheral vision, but I kept my gaze firm. "Everything okay here?" she asked, concern lacing her voice.

The little cockroach put his hands up. "Whoa, no need for all this. I didn't know she was taken. My bad."

"Your *bad*?" I spit out, taking another step forward. My shoulder nudged into the chest of the closest one while my eyes stayed firm on the middle one. "Tell me, do you talk about all females that way? You think you're the fucking *man*, that you can just have any one that you want?" I felt the weight of Nora's gaze on me, but I didn't break my eye contact from my opponent. I briefly wondered if she noticed that I didn't correct him.

"Dude, I was just talking shit with my friends. It's not a big deal." He nervously ran a hand through his dirty blonde hair.

"I disagree. I think you need to apologize for the foul disrespect," I seethed. "*Now.*"

Finally, his stare broke away from mine as he looked to Nora, who was trying to get my attention. "Andre . . . " she said.

But I didn't look at her. Not yet. Not until he fucking apologized to her. He had three fucking seconds, or else—

"Look, I'm sorry," he muttered, cutting through my train of thought. He looked back at me and raised his eyebrows, annoyance flaring through his features. "I'm sorry, okay? Christ."

"You good over here, Nora?" Mara asked, approaching our end of the bar as she realized the contention brewing.

I finally broke my glare on the trio in front of me and let my gaze slide to Nora. Her eyes were wide as they bore into mine. *Shit*, I thought—I hoped I didn't scare her. She kept her focus on me as she answered Mara. "Yeah, I'm okay."

"Well boys," the little prick said as he dropped a twenty dollar bill on the bar, "It doesn't feel like we're very welcome here. Let's go somewhere more fun." His eyes flicked back up to mine as he stood, and then he turned and walked towards the door. His friends stood up to follow him, the one closest to me muttering an apology under his breath as they, too, made their way towards the exit.

I let myself exhale, and turned back to Nora. "I'm sorry, Nora. They were saying terrible things about you, and I just couldn't . . ." I swallowed, hard.

Her eyes softened. "It's okay." She tucked a falling strand of hair behind her ear. "I appreciate you sticking up for me."

I looked at Mara. "I'm sorry, Mara. I didn't mean to cause a scene—it wasn't Nora's fault at all, she didn't know what was going on."

Mara put a hand up to stop me. "Hey, no complaints from me." Her eyes moved to Nora and then back to me. "There's a lot of vermin that come in here, thinking they own the place, that they own *us*. It's unfortunately just part of the gig. Honestly, I'm glad you called them out. I don't care about their money being spent in this bar if it means our staff is disrespected in the process." Her voice had a slightly hard edge to it, like this was something she dealt with often. She shrugged, "As far as I'm concerned, you did us a favor."

I mean, it was a fucking *bar*. Of course there was going to be a little drama now and then—but I hated knowing Nora could get mixed up in it. Mara turned to help a customer that had just approached, and I took the opportunity to face Nora again.

There was a ghost of a smile on her face, and relief poured through me. "Seriously, Nora—I didn't mean to cause any issues for you."

She shook her head. "There's no reason for you to apologize, Andre. Seriously, thank you for sticking up for me. I don't know what they said, but I can only imagine based on your reaction."

I ground my teeth. "It's not worth repeating, trust me."

Her eyes danced at my hard edges, grounding me. She reached a hand over the bar and pressed it to my arm. "Thanks for being here—your support means a lot to me. I know you probably don't normally spend Tuesday nights at downtown clubs, but I like having you here."

"It's your first shift, girl. I wouldn't miss it." She smiled as she pulled her hand away, rocking back on the heels of her converse. "Hey, by the way—my tattoo artist has a bit of free time in the morning if you're game. She only has a couple hours . . . I don't know how big you want this mystery tattoo of yours, but it should be enough time to at least start with."

Her eyes lit up. "Oh, that's perfect! And it's super small, I think that's more than enough time. You'll take me?"

My chest squeezed at her eagerness—her desire for me to take her made me feel *good*. "Of course. As long as you want me, I'm there." And I meant it, even beyond the tattoo appointment. Nora was slowly but surely wrapping me around her finger, and I wasn't at all interested in putting up a fight against it. "I'll pick you up at eight, if that works? Her availability starts at nine-thirty, but you need to eat something before hand. I was thinking we could pick up some breakfast."

A couple approached the bar to my right, replacing the space where the three douchebags had just been sitting. Nora eyed them quickly before looking back at me. "That sounds perfect, it's a date." Her eyes widened at the word. "I mean . . ."

I chuckled. "I know what you mean." She looked relieved, and an unexpected jolt of disappointment pierced me. Would a date with me be so bad?

I nodded my head towards the couple, letting her know that I was okay, that I'd keep myself in check so she could get back to work. She gave me a quick smile before she turned her attention to them both. "Hey guys! Welcome in. What can I get ya?"

I turned to sit back in my stool, taking a heavy swig from the bottle that awaited me.

THE NEXT MORNING, I pulled into the parking lot in front of Nora's building a few minutes before eight to pick her up for breakfast. We'd have about an hour to get food and eat before we'd need to make our way to the tattoo shop for her appointment. I'd woken up early this morning, eager to get the day started so that I could see her again. It was my first day off in a long time and I couldn't think of a better way to spend it.

In the few weeks that had passed since she first walked into the shop, I'd seen her more days than I hadn't. In the beginning, I just wanted to find ways to support her through this big transition in her life—but as time went on I could feel her rooting deeper and deeper into my mind, carving out space that could only be filled by *more* of her.

Shifting the car into park, I inhaled a deep breath and looked around. It wasn't likely that I'd find anyone shady hanging around outside of the building during this bright, morning hour, but still—it was worth it to take a second to make sure. Nora still didn't know who had been messing with her door the other night, and I hated knowing she was alone in her apartment.

I'd replaced her lock with something a bit more industrial, but I still found myself constantly worrying about her safety here. It was a tough balance of supporting her need for independence and my selfish desire to wrap her up in my arms and shield her from a world that I knew could be so damn cruel.

If anything ever happened to her . . .

I shut the thought down as I got out of my mustang and

headed towards the front entrance. I took the stairs inside two at a time as I bounded my way up to the third floor where her apartment was. When I reached her door, I rapped lightly against it and called out, "Nora, it's me!" I didn't want her to have to worry for even a second about who could be on the other side of her safety bubble.

"Just a second!" I heard her call back as the undeniable sound of feet pounding along the floor edged closer from wherever she'd been.

The door opened, and she gave me a thousand-watt smile. "Hey!"

I was literally struck stupid at the sight of her, eyes glued to her long body as she came out of her apartment door. She wore a pale yellow tank top that hugged all of her soft curves and sharp angles, and denim shorts that only barely covered her . . . assets. They looked shorter than the ones she'd worn last night at the bar. Her white, high-top converse were stark against the smooth, tan slope of her calves, and her hair draped down her back like sunshine, long enough to reach her waist.

As she turned away from me to lock her door, I caught a whiff of her shampoo and I had to force my eyes up to the corner of the door jamb to take deep, steadying breaths.

Those damn shorts were going to be the death of me.

After locking up, she turned back to face me. "So, what's for breakfast?"

I was still a little star-struck, now distracted by those deep, brown eyes. I cleared my throat and forced myself to focus. "You like breakfast burritos?" I asked.

She scoffed. "Who doesn't?"

And without a need for any more details, she turned on her heels. I wordlessly followed behind her as she moved towards to the stairs. As we exited the building, I heard a small gasp as she looked to the sky. "Do you smell that?"

I looked up, but didn't see anything unusual. "Smell what?"

She looked at me, smiling. "Rain."

Sure enough, there was a hint of rain in the air despite the bright, blue sky spread wide above us. Rain wasn't uncommon during the summer months, usually manifesting in the late afternoons and lasting for only a couple of hours, but it had been so hot and dry lately that we hadn't seen any rain in at least three weeks. "You like rain." It wasn't a question—the proof was evident in the wide smile still plastered on her face.

"I *love* rain. And it hardly ever rained in LA—I've missed normal weather. The endless sunshine in California can sometimes be a little daunting."

"Oh yeah? How so?"

I watched her shoulders lift in a small shrug as we continued walking towards the car. "It doesn't feel real. It's unnatural for things to appear so perfect all the time."

I hummed, considering, as I adjusted the hat on my head. There was a definite weight of humidity in the air, and despite the cool temperature, I could feel sweat beginning to cling to the stiff fabric against my forehead.

Her face turned up to mine, teeth scraping against her bottom lip. "What about you?"

I propelled myself forward, stepping in front of her just before she could reach the handle of the car door, herself. I pulled it open for her instead, stepping out of the way to let her in. She flashed a grin at me and I could feel it in my throat. "I like rain," I finally answered, before shutting the car door and rounding to the other side.

"Okay, but you don't love it?" she asked as I opened the door on the other side and fell into the driver's seat.

Pulling the seatbelt down in front of me, I chanced another quick glance at her. It was hard to keep my eyes trained forward when I knew she was next to me. "People drive like shit in the rain, and I don't like that I have to wash the car afterwards. But I don't have anything against it. It's just . . .weather."

She let out another gasp and *damn it* if my pulse didn't skip at the sound. "Well, I feel sad for you, Andre, because clearly you haven't let yourself be really, truly swept away by the romance of rain before."

I started the ignition, smirking at her. "Romance isn't really something I know well, Nora."

She didn't say anything for the whole drive to Fernando's.

Chapter Sixteen

NORA

I let Andre order for me at Fernando's—the sparkle in his eye as he did was confirmation that he knew his way around a good breakfast. We sat in a small corner booth, the table lined with floral vinyl that was firmly stapled in place underneath, the biggest burrito I'd ever seen sitting on a paper plate in front of me. "I hope you like chorizo," he said, nodding to the tortilla-wrapped monstrosity that I was studying as he picked up his own.

"I love chorizo." I sighed. "I just have no idea how to pick this up. It's too big for my hands, let alone my mouth."

He choked on his first bite.

I narrowed my eyes at him. "Something funny?"

His face immediately went serious. "Not at all."

Cracking a smile, I relented. "Just kidding. I walked into that one." Relief flashed across his face, and I looked back down at the burrito baby in front of me.

As it turned out, I *could* pick it up. I could also eat the entire thing—a feat that surprised and impressed us both. "That was, without a doubt, one of the best burritos I've ever had," I said as I tossed a fallen piece of potato in my mouth, feeling gloriously stuffed.

Andre smiled. "It's one of my favorite places," he said. The statement made my face feel warm. Something prickled under the surface, an instinct that told me he didn't bring *all* the girls to his favorite hole-in-the-wall eatery . . . *or* into his gym, or his tattoo shop.

"So, on a scale of one-to-death, how painful are tattoos?" I asked, suddenly nervous. "And don't lie to me," I added, pointedly.

He grinned, wiping his hands on a napkin and adjusting his hat again. I liked him in a hat. It suited his edgy, bad boy image. "A scale of one-to-death is a pretty wide scale. I'd say somewhere in the middle."

I dropped my head back onto the vinyl cushion behind me. "That's not helpful."

Smoky gray eyes crinkled as he gathered our trash from the table. "You'll be fine. You said it was small, right?" I nodded, and he shrugged. "It's like being scratched with a toothpick over sunburned skin. It can be annoying during an hours-long session, but you'll handle it just fine with something small. Even if it sucks and you hate it, it'll be over before you know it. And plus"—his gaze landed on me with a small amount of heat —"I'll be there with you."

I felt his assurance in the pit of my stomach, like a warm current of light winding its way through me.

A half hour later, Andre parked his Mustang along the sidewalk in the lower downtown district. He led me to a corner suite with purple brick walls and a bright neon sign that read

TATTOO above the glass doors. Inside, the walls were black and covered in vibrant illustrations, and it smelled like someone had recently smudged with a sage wand. A beautiful Hispanic woman with mauve-painted lips stood behind the reception desk, her hair wound above her head in glorious victory rolls. "*Hola, mijo!*" she exclaimed, pressing off the desk to walk around it and hug Andre.

"Hi, Myrna, how are you?"

"Good, baby, thank you. It's been a busy summer." She released him from her embrace, her white-and-red checkered halter dress swaying from the movement, and looked at me. "You must be Nora?"

"Yes," I said.

I felt the sweeping weight of her gaze as she looked me up and down. "I'm assuming this is your first tattoo?" she asked, kindly.

I smiled. "Is it that obvious?"

Her cat-lined eyes were warm as she looked back at Andre. "Did you get her something to eat before you got here?"

"Yes, ma'am."

"Good. All right, sweetheart. What are we drawing on you, today?"

I flicked my gaze at Andre, suddenly hesitant. He nodded at me in assurance, and then turned to take a seat on a black leather sofa that rested against the front wall—giving me the space to reveal my plans with Myrna without forcing himself in the know.

Myrna excused herself to draw something up in the back once I shared what I wanted, and I took a seat next to Andre on the small sofa.

"You good?" he asked.

"Yep. Are all of these drawings Myrna's? They're amazing." My eyes roamed the vibrant colors along the walls. I could see the resemblance in the style of art to what existed all over Andre's skin.

"Most of them. She owns the shop and has been here for decades—but there's a few other artists who work here, too."

"How long have you been coming here?"

He smirked. "Since I was sixteen. I used my brother's license to get around needing a guardian's signature the first time—Gabriel *was* my guardian at that point, but I knew he'd try and stop me, so I stole his ID out of his wallet." I watched as his eyes became a bit wistful at the memory.

"And you got away with it?" I asked, encouraging more of the story.

"Yeah." He chuckled. "Except I realized much later that Myrna was his artist, too—she'd been tattooing him for a couple years before I ever came in here—so she had to have known that I wasn't him when I gave her his license. I really thought I'd fooled her."

A laugh burst out of me. "Didn't think that through, did you?"

He shook his head. "Definitely did not. Myrna never ratted me out, though. She's cool—she took Gabriel's death really hard. It was nice to come here . . . after . . . and talk to someone else who knew him." His gaze moved around the shop, as if lost in memory. "I was terrified of her the first time I sat in her chair, but she's one of the best people I know. You're in good hands."

Just then, Myrna reappeared from her back office, waving me over. "Nora, come take a look."

I shot Andre a quick look, shimmying my shoulders. The

side of my knee brushed against his as I stood, and I could have sworn I saw his brow furrow as he looked at where the contact had been made on his own leg, as if my skin had burned him.

On the other side of the shop, Myrna held out an iPad for me to see what she'd just drawn, and I gasped as soon as I saw it. There, as if smiling back at me from the screen, was a beautiful and dainty butterfly—only an inch or so in both length and height. Despite its delicate size, Myrna included intrinsic patterns on the wings that I hadn't expected would be able to fit in something so small. It was better than I imagined. "It's perfect," I whispered.

She smiled. "Let me get it transferred to stencil paper and we'll get it fitted on you. Give me another moment, you can wait here in the chair." She nodded toward the black chair with wooden legs that sat in front of a full-length mirror. I smiled, taking a seat, and watched her disappear back in her office.

FIVE MINUTES LATER, I was looking in the mirror at the butterfly design stamped on the back of my arm, just above my left elbow. My chest tightened in pure joy at the sight—it really was perfect, and it fit my arm beautifully. I excused myself from Myrna for a moment, walking back to Andre who was still seated at the front. He grinned when he looked up at me. "How's it going?" he asked.

I turned my body to the side and stuck out my elbow, showing him the purple stencil lines on my skin. "Do you like it?"

His returning smile was wide, wrapping around my heart. "*Una mariposa*," he said, nodding. "It suits you."

And just like that, I knew he understood what it meant. That he knew how hard I was willing to work to transform my life into something beautiful, something . . . happy. "Will you come back there with me while she tattoos it?" I asked. My nerves began to tangle inside of my throat.

"Of course," he said, instantly rising to his feet. He followed me back to the chair where Myrna had me prop my arm out behind me so that she could easily access the back of my elbow. As soon as the whirr of the tattoo gun started, she said, "Okay, Nora. This should only take a few minutes. Let me know if you need me to stop for any reason, okay?"

I nodded, and looked up at Andre. My face must have revealed just how scared I suddenly was, because he stepped forward and laid a big, warm hand on my thigh. "You're all right, Nora." His low voice motored through me. "Take a deep breath."

I inhaled a long breath through my nose just as I felt the bite of the needle on my skin, and let out a small, pain-seared groan on the exhale. "Whoaaaa . . ."

His hand gripped my thigh a little tighter. "You okay?"

Another deep breath, and I forced myself to adjust to the ongoing sensation. "I'm okay," I muttered through a clenched jaw. I was tough . . . I was *strong*. I could handle this.

His eyes danced, shining down on me like moonbeams underneath a fan of dark eyelashes. "That's my girl," he murmured, his voice low.

Suddenly, I didn't feel anything at all except for the way those words penetrated through my skin with more force than the needle of the tattoo gun behind me. My mouth parted open in surprise, and I watched those silver eyes catch the movement and then darken into hazy smoke.

"Almost done!" Myrna chirped from behind me. "Just another minute or so—you're doing great."

"Okay," I breathed out, but I hardly remembered what was even happening, because Andre had just called me *his* girl. I was locked in the onslaught of his gaze . . . in the pressure of his thumb on the outside of my thigh as it stroked over my skin. His touch was reassuring. But also . . . exploring.

After what felt like only seconds, the whirr of the gun stopped, and the ensuing silence finally broke through our trance. Andre pulled his hand back to his side, the loss of its warmth more shocking than the sting on the back of my arm as Myrna wiped the area down with something cold. "Are you ready to take a look, Nora?" she asked brightly.

"Yes, please," I rasped, forcing my eyes away from Andre's and eagerly looking at her over my shoulder. After she gave me the go-ahead, I stood up and faced the mirror behind the chair, twisting my arm to get a good view of the butterfly that now adorned my skin just above my elbow.

I couldn't help the happiness that flowed through me. "It's stunning." My eyes found Andre's, looking at me though the mirror from where he stood behind me. The raw tenderness and traces of hunger from a few moments ago were no longer present, but his stare felt loaded all the same.

I turned back to Myrna who'd started to clean up her supplies. "Thank you so much, it's . . . it's exactly what I wanted."

Her dark brown eyes were warm as her full lips twisted into a smile. "I'm going to wrap it with some plastic to keep bacteria from getting around the area, but you should wash it with warm water and fragrance-free soap in a few hours. I'll give you a pamphlet with all the after-care instructions. Andre knows it all well, so I'm sure he can help you, too." She winked at me, as if she fully knew the moment that had just fired between us.

Myrna wrapped my arm and led me to the front desk where I paid and gave her a generous tip. While Andre and I said our goodbyes to her and walked out of the shop—my arm only mildly burning beneath the plastic wrap—I felt his hand press to the small of my back as he let me step through the shop's door first. The pressure of his fingertips was light as they grazed down the fabric of my shirt, across the ridges of my spine. It was a touch that felt on the cusp of something severely intimate.

"How do you feel?" he asked, looking down at me from where we stood on the sidewalk, dark shadows cast all around us. In the forty-five minutes that we were inside the shop, storm clouds had rolled in over the city. The scent of rain was stronger now—it was only a matter of time before the down-pour hit.

His gray eyes mirrored the sky above. "I feel alive," I said, then laughed at myself. It sounded so dramatic, but I could honestly say it was the truth. I felt more alive in the doorway of this tattoo parlor than I had in months. *Years*, even.

A ghost of a smile played on his lips, but there was also an evident restraint in his features, and I knew it for what it was. He wanted to stay on the safe side of the line that we were toeing—the side that definitely did *not* include him backing me up and pressing me against the purple-painted bricks of the building like I wanted him to, our breaths mingling together as he leaned down toward my mouth. "Good." He nodded, looking down at the two feet of concrete between our toes. At all the space he was keeping, instead.

I wasn't ready to go home yet, not ready for this to be over. But I wanted to respect his restraint—respect his boundaries. I'd already thrown myself at him once, and we'd been hanging out so much lately that my comfort level with him was becoming pretty rock-solid. I didn't trust myself not to make another move when I was feeling so good, so euphoric. Not when I'd been taking his advice and making decisions based solely on what made me happy—like this tattoo now on my arm.

Because the reality was that Andre had been absorbing a hefty space inside of the category of "things that make me happy" too, and based on the swirling feelings currently threatening to tornado out of me, it was probably a good idea to put a little distance between us so I didn't mess it up again.

"Thank you for coming with me today," I offered.

"Of course, Nora. I was happy to be a part of it."

THE DRIVE back to my apartment was mostly silent, save for the Spanish music that played through the speakers. I loved hearing it—it'd made me smile from the moment he started the car.

It seemed the citizens of Denver were hunkering down in anticipation of the oncoming storm, because the streets were mostly empty. We made it back to my building in record time, and as we pulled into the parking lot, I once again felt the disappointment of not wanting this time with Andre to end. Although I *did* have to work another shift at Larkspur in just a couple of hours.

I chanced a quick glance over at him and found his eyes focused on the row of parking spaces in front of us. His brow was slightly furrowed, his jaw clenched tight. He'd tipped the bill of his hat down behind his head so that it didn't hit the headrest behind him, and the sight of it sent that tornado roaring to life again.

He parked close to the building's entrance, and in a flash was out of his seat to open my door for me. The ignition was still running, though—an indication that he wouldn't be coming up.

Stepping onto the pavement, I slipped both hands into the pockets of my shorts and tilted back on my heels. "Thank you again for everything—Myrna was incredible. It . . . it means a lot that you let me into such a personal space."

To my delight, I watched the firm lines of his schooled neutrality fall away, revealing a much lighter expression that warmed me from the inside out. The cherry on top was a wide grin that spread across his beautiful face. "I really liked taking you there."

I felt myself beaming, and tried to tamp the emotion down.

He nodded toward the plastic wrap on my arm. "I have something for you," he said, then turned back to the still-open door and reached into the back seat. I heard the crinkle of a plastic bag in his hands as he pushed himself up to his full height and turned toward me. "Here, this should have everything you need to take care of the tattoo." He held out the bag with a drugstore logo on it.

I looked inside to find fragrance-free soap, healing ointment in tube-form as well as spray-form, and a bag of gummy bears. I giggled at the sight. "Gummy bears?"

He smiled. "Essential to proper tattoo after-care."

My mind flitted back to the bag of gummy bears I'd devoured while moving into my apartment. He must have seen them on the counter when he came over that night. "Very thoughtful of you."

He looked down at his feet for a moment, as if considering, before he spoke again. "I'm not sure what time you get off work tonight, but my sister's cooking dinner and Chino and his family are coming over. Just . . . if you're hungry. You're more than welcome."

My heart tripped over itself. "Really?"

He grinned. "Yeah. No pressure though."

Does this make me happy? I nodded. "Okay. I'll let you know when I'm off."

Chapter Seventeen

ANDRE

THE SKIES HAD BROKEN OPEN AND ALL HELL WAS raining down on the city as Marisela moved confidently around the kitchen. With the storm in progress, we were forced to hang out inside the house with Chino's family—not that it was a problem to host them inside, there just wasn't a whole lot of space. Our house was small, but we lived on a corner lot so our backyard was spacious, and we usually used it to entertain guests.

Despite the lack of space, it was hard to feel anything but comfortable with Chino's family here. His mother, Gloria, shadowed Marisela as she worked to cook dinner for us all—tonight's menu included birria tacos with homemade tortillas and a side of Spanish rice. My mouth was already watering from the incredible smells permeating through the house.

Chino sat on our small couch with his wife, Frances, watching TV while his little sister, Mary, sat on the floor with his two children as they played a game of Uno. Marisela and I had known Chino and Mary since we were kids, after Gabriel met Chino at a high school party. We'd been living with El Viejo at the time—the longest state-appointed guardian that we'd had growing up. His real name was Raúl Mendoza, but we only ever called him "El Viejo." He was a kind but extremely strict man who had lost his wife in his late fifties and wanted to open his home to children in need. He was appointed guardianship over us through the foster system when I was thirteen.

He gave us everything we needed to make it in the world— but we'd still never experienced a full, healthy family dynamic until we met Chino and his family. It wasn't long before Gloria was inviting all of us over for weekly dinners, providing us with a much-needed mother's touch while giving El Viejo a break.

Gloria was the reason Marisela had even learned how to cook in the first place—and to see them in the kitchen together now, after all these years, felt like the biggest full-circle blessing. It was because of Gloria that Marisela had the confidence to chase her dreams of opening her own restaurant.

"So, Andre," Chino said above his children's giggles, looking at me with a smirk, "tell us about Nora."

I let out an audible breath from where I stood between the kitchen and living room. I knew this was coming; I'd never asked Chino to save the ring for me at the gym before, *especially* not for a girl. But I'd also invited Nora over tonight— another thing I never did—so I'd have to address this eventually. Frances scooted forward on the couch to look at me over Chino's head, also eager for more details. Chino must have told her about it already.

"She's a friend. She knows Logan from the shop, and she

came in needing some help with her ride. She's . . . she's going through some shit and I've been helping her out."

Chino gave me a knowing look. "Just a friend, huh?"

I felt Mary's eyes slide to me from where she sat on the floor. *Shit*. I'd dated Mary's best friend, Leticia, for a little while a couple of years ago. Even after all this time, Letty was still hell-bent on us getting back together—something I had zero interest in doing. It was my fault for dating someone so close to the family, the breakup had been messy when Letty refused to accept that I was done with the relationship. I hoped that Mary would keep anything I said about Nora to herself.

I let my eyes fall directly on her now, a small plea. "Just a friend," I confirmed. She looked back down at the cards in her hand, and I hoped she'd picked up on the silent communication. I looked back to Chino. "She may come by tonight, actually."

Chino's eyes danced. "Just a friend—and you invited her to family dinner?"

I rolled my eyes. "Just be cool, please."

Nora's ears must have been ringing from across the city at Larkspur, because I felt my phone buzz with an incoming text message and looked down to see her name flash across the screen.

NORA

So about that dinner...

I couldn't help but smile . . . a thrill jolted through me at the vision of her inside this house.

I gave Marisela a heads-up about the possible additional guest earlier before the other's arrived, and even though she didn't ask any questions, I could see the curiosity in her expression. Walking into the kitchen now, I asked her how long we had until the food was ready. She nodded toward Gloria at the stove, and said, "We've got the tortillas warming now, the birria is done and the rice is close. Maybe fifteen minutes?"

"Perfect," I said, looking back down at my phone as I began typing, "thanks, Sela."

> Marisela says we'll be ready in fifteen minutes—and it smells delicious. You coming?

NORA

> Sounds amazing. Leaving work now!

I sent her my address, and then tucked my phone into my pocket. "Is there anything I can help you with here?"

Marisela shook her head, her brown hair swinging from where it was clipped on the top of her head. "I think we got it," she said, grabbing a paper towel to wipe down the counters. She looked at me from under an arched eyebrow. "Is Nora coming?"

"Yeah, she's on her way here now."

She smiled. "I look forward to meeting her."

Gloria looked over her shoulder at me from the stove. "You have a girlfriend, *mijo*?" she asked.

"No, no. Just a friend."

Gloria and Sela exchanged glances before they both looked back at me again.

I sighed, praying like hell this wasn't going to be as awkward as it was already feeling. I didn't want Nora to be uncomfortable—maybe it had been a bad idea to invite her over in the first place. Family night was sacred to me, was this really the best idea?

Truthfully, I was already feeling a little torn up about the things I was beginning to feel around her. This morning at the tattoo shop, I'd started imagining what it would be like to truly call her mine. I even called her *my* girl . . . I hadn't meant for it to slip out like that, but it did. And the way she reacted to the words—the flush in her cheeks, how her eyes had locked on mine—I wondered if she was starting to feel it too.

I told her I would be there for her through anything she needed, and I meant it. I didn't want to jeopardize the friendship we had or the trust she was giving me. But it was so damn easy to be around her, and I selfishly wanted more and more of her.

But if she *was* feeling it too . . .

No. I needed to cool it. She would have to make the first move toward something more than friendship. But until then, she needed me to be her friend, and I'd be sticking to that.

NORA ARRIVED A HALF HOUR LATER, soaking wet from the storm. Strands of her hair were plastered to her cheek, her makeup from her bar shift was running down underneath her eyes, and her cheeks were rosy from running from her car to the front door. But as soon as I saw her bright, smiling face, it was like all of my nerves about her being here instantly evaporated. Just seeing her in my doorway solidified that I didn't care what anyone else thought, I was just glad that she'd made it here.

I gave her a fresh towel from the linen closet in the hallway to dry herself off with, and then walked her through a quick tour of the house, introducing her to everyone along the way. As soon as we got into the kitchen, she was putting down her purse and jumping in to help Marisela set the table. There were way too many of us to fit at our small kitchen table, and the outside patio table was still out of commission, so Nora and Sela placed settings on the kitchen island as well.

Gloria made Nora one of her famous—and extremely strong—margaritas, and the two women chatted like old friends as the rest of us started serving ourselves. I made Nora a plate and set it next to mine at the island, and as we ate, she practically moaned over the tacos, begging Marisela to teach her how to make them.

After dinner, Nora and I helped Gloria and Marisela clean up while Chino and Frances started a movie for the kids. Normally when they came over, we let the kids have a movie after dinner so that the adults could hang out in the back—and tonight was no exception. The rain had even stopped, and though everything was wet and humid, we still found ourselves laying towels down on the wooden patio furniture so that we could enjoy the remnants of the storm.

The way Nora moved around so comfortably and confidently with everyone here made it hard for me to look away. Everyone seemed to welcome her with open arms, even Mary. And Nora—

She was incredible. The ease with which she adapted to our loud and chaotic environment was something else entirely. Over and over again, I felt a stab of awe in my chest that I tried like hell to push down and ignore. She didn't just sit quietly or stay by my side—she infiltrated right into the heart of the family with such an ease that I couldn't imagine her *not* being here every week.

Gloria kept the margaritas flowing, and by the time the kids' movie ended, Nora, Marisela, Mary, and Gloria were all well beyond tipsy as they laughed and told stories about us all when we were younger. There were a few moments when Nora and I looked at each other in the midst of the loud conversation, and she radiated joy.

It resembled the way she'd looked when she had the keys to her new car in hand, or the way she looked this morning with her new tattoo. She was *happy*—it was undeniable. And it shook me.

Later, after Chino piled his whole family into his Suburban and took them home, Marisela, Nora, and I hunkered down on the couch and put on a movie for ourselves. There was no way Nora was driving home tonight, and she fell asleep within fifteen minutes of the movie starting, anyway.

"I like her," Sela whispered from where she sat on my left, looking at Nora on the other side of me.

I smiled. "She's great, right?"

Sela nodded, patting me on the shoulder. "She really is. I'm happy you found her, she's good for you, Andre."

"What do you mean?" I asked, hungry to know what she saw. Marisela knew me most in the world, so her opinion meant everything to me.

"You've smiled more tonight than I've seen you smile in the last few years."

"We're just friends," I stated bluntly. I didn't know if it was for her or a reminder to myself.

"If you say so," she said, grinning. "I'm going to bed; those margaritas made me sleepy."

"Good night," I said, watching her peel herself off of the couch and walk down the hall.

The soft sounds of Nora's snores came from my right, where she was fast asleep. She looked so peaceful—her head tilted back against the couch, her mouth slightly open as she sucked in air. A rogue strand of blonde hair fell into her face, covering one of her eyes, and I held back the urge to move it away.

I didn't want to admit that seeing her this way, vulnerable and unguarded, stirred that familiar need to protect her that had been rising inside of me for weeks. I shifted in my seat and attempted to focus back on the movie.

My focus didn't last long before I felt my eyes slip back to the beautiful girl sleeping next to me. The fact that she was here, sleeping on *this* couch in *this* living room, was almost shocking.

Agonizing longing flared in my chest then, and I wished Gabriel were here.

I yearned for his guidance as I wrestled with the feelings that Nora was bringing out of me. He would know how to handle this, whether staying safe in the friend-zone or being honest about wanting more would be the right thing to do. Tension I was used to feeling crept its way into my jaw, into my shoulders. I was so . . . *angry* that he wasn't here for this, that he wasn't here when I needed him. But he was gone—taken from us way too fucking soon from an addiction that never should have started. We were three kids just trying to survive with what little we had.

How quickly things could slip away, despite all the fucking effort.

Nora murmured something soft and unintelligible as she wrapped her arms around herself. Without a second thought, I shook the memories and pain away and looked back at her sleeping form. I carefully reached over her to pull up the blanket that lay across her lap so that it covered her chest and arms. She let out a low hum in response, and the sound jarred me.

Fuck. Whether Gabriel was here to tell me the truth or not—I knew this was dangerous. I could not afford to be distracted from the finish line. Marisela and I had worked so hard, and letting this girl get too deep inside my mind that it led me off course wasn't an option. I needed to be more careful.

The wildfire under my skin was undeniable, and I needed to find a way to extinguish it before things got too messy.

I knew the right thing to do was to create firmer boundaries between us, but I'd already proved to myself that it was difficult to stay away. I took a swig of my beer, continuing to stare at her face as I settled into the rhythmic rise and fall of her breathing.

Chapter Eighteen

NORA

The first thought I had waking up was *What in the ever-loving hell is that gross, sour taste in my mouth?* followed by the familiar pounding in my head that only meant one thing —I'd had too much to drink last night. Before I even opened my eyes, I tried to remember exactly *how* I'd gotten back to this terrible morning-after feeling after swearing to myself last time (and the time before that) that I would never drink again.

Flashes of a frozen, lime-green drink swirling around in a large blender popped into my head, and it was then that I remembered—margaritas. Gloria's ridiculously delicious but insanely strong margaritas. *Shit.* How many of them did I have? Three? Maybe four?

I groaned as I tried like hell to avoid consciousness, keeping my eyes sealed shut—as if that would prevent me from having to wake up and face this hangover. Shifting on the soft, warm bed, I pulled the comforter up high and over my head and found a glorious reprieve in the heavier darkness. I wasn't ready to face the light of morning, and based on the state of my head, I wouldn't be for some time. Maybe I could just fall back asleep for a little while and try to face the day later, when the pounding in my head wasn't as incessant.

Under the blanket, the smell of clean soap and spice wrapped itself around me, and I almost moaned . . . it was such a nice scent. So warm and inviting. A certain tattooed man came to mind—it smelled just like him.

Oh fuck.

I bolted upright, tearing the comforter back off me, and looked around at unfamiliar gray walls and dark, wooden furniture that looked like it had been pieced together from various yard sales. Nothing quite matched, but there was an unmistakable male charm that tied it all together.

Andre.

I was in his room.

I was in his *bed*!

Oh god, oh god, oh god. I squeezed my eyes shut again and rubbed my face with my hands. How did this happen? I mean —I knew without a doubt that Gloria and her lethal margarita recipe had gotten me past the point of tipsy, so it wasn't like I would have been able to drive myself home. *Everyone* had been drinking last night . . .

But what happened after that?

Vague memories of a movie, of curling up on the couch as my bare feet grazed against Andre's leg—I must have fallen asleep. *Did Andre carry me in here?* I groaned. It wouldn't be the first time he'd carried me to bed.

I hoped to god that I didn't throw myself at him again.

I'd woken from the center of the double bed, leaving very little room for anyone else to have slept next to me. Feeling the sides of the mattress around me, I found it to be cold. I was fairly certain that I'd slept in here alone. And, *most* importantly, I was still wearing my work uniform from last night, which meant that no clothing had been removed.

Taking in a deep breath, I put on a brave face. I couldn't let myself go back to sleep now, not after knowing where I was. I'd have to face the hangover . . . and whatever else lay outside of this room.

The door to the bedroom was shut, and I didn't hear anything from the other side. *What time is it?* I wondered, before looking down at the nightstand and spotting my phone resting atop the wooden surface, plugged into a long cord that disappeared between the bed frame and the wall. Next to the phone was a glass of water and a bottle of ibuprofen.

I tapped my phone's screen and sighed, my stiff shoulders loosening. Seven thirty—still pretty early. There were also two new text messages from Andre from an hour ago.

ANDRE

You fell asleep during the movie, but I figured you'd be more comfortable in my bed. I hope that's okay—I slept on the couch. I have work at eight, but make yourself comfortable and stay as long as you want.

Thanks for coming over last night. I really enjoyed having you.

Heat bloomed on my cheeks, and any anxiety that I felt dissipated in an instant. A thought hit me with the force of a freight train as I read his texts again: I'd never felt more respected by a man for being unabashedly myself in my entire life. He wasn't judging me for how many margaritas I'd had. He didn't care that I'd fallen asleep on his couch and accidentally spent the night. And after witnessing a new side of *him* last night—wide open, laughing freely, completely at ease—I had a feeling that I wasn't the only one learning how to feel good in my vulnerability.

I unplugged my phone and stuffed it into the back pocket of my black shorts before making my way out of his bedroom, hoping he hadn't left for work yet. The hallway was short, leading to only one other bedroom and a bathroom and then opening up to the main living room and kitchen.

To my delight, I found Andre sitting at the round kitchen table, hunched over a bowl of cereal. Lucky Charms, I noticed with a smile—Andre started his morning with a bowl of freaking Lucky Charms. The box sat proudly on the table in front of him, as if he might wiggle out more cereal into his bowl at any moment.

"Good morning," I said from behind him.

He sat up straight and whipped his head around, chewing on a bite that he'd just put into his mouth. After taking a minute to swallow, he grinned at me, and I felt it like a caress across my face. "Hey, Nora," he said, keeping his voice low. Marisela must still be sleeping. "How'd you sleep?"

I scoffed, moving to sit in the chair next to him. "I slept like the dead. Thank you for letting me stay the night. Gloria's margaritas got me."

He nodded, smiling. "Yeah, sorry, she puts a *lot* of tequila in that damn blender. Everyone knows to only have one or two of them—I should have warned you." I watched as he dropped his spoon into the milk before bringing it back up to his mouth again. The way his mouth so casually covered the entire space of the spoon's ladle and sucked the contents of the cereal into his mouth was ob*scene*.

With a lot of effort, I forced my attention away from his mouth and back up to his eyes—finding, to my utter horror, amusement dancing on his face. He'd known exactly what I was watching.

"Do you want some cereal?" he asked through his smirk.

I felt the rush of pure heat on my neck and cheeks. "No, thank you." I shuffled back out of the chair. "I'm actually going to head home, but I wanted to thank you for inviting me over. The food was incredible and your family—they're *so* nice." I didn't know what I'd been expecting when I accepted the invitation, but I definitely didn't anticipate being so comfortable amongst strangers. "I had a lot of fun."

Andre stood up, dropping his spoon in the bowl and pushing his chair back on the linoleum floors with the force of his movement. "Do you work tonight?" he asked as he walked me toward his front door.

"Yeah, another early shift. I think I'm going to invite some of the girls over after . . . break in the apartment with a good, old-fashioned girls' night."

He grunted. "What do women actually *do* during a 'girls' night'?"

I shrugged. "Cast spells on the men in our lives, stab a lot of voodoo dolls. There's always a few tears shed. And wine . . . wine by the buckets."

A laugh burst out of him, and he shook his head. "I'm not sure if that makes me more intrigued or more afraid."

"That's the way we like it." I winked. We reached his door and I hesitated, feeling the same layers of complex emotion that I'd felt yesterday morning—a resistance to leave, to end this time with him, even though we both had our own lives to live and this friendship to protect.

There were moments that I wanted to throw caution to the wind and press myself up against him to see if it'd be worth it— but I knew that was a dangerous impulse.

Andre cleared his throat. "Be safe tonight, yeah? And don't forget to moisturize that tattoo."

I felt my throat tighten. "I will. Promise."

He nodded and reached to open the door for me. "Be happy out there, *mariposa*."

"Oh, thank god—you have snacks." Mackenzie beelined to the kitchen where a charcuterie board was surrounded by bowls of chips and candy and popcorn. When I'd texted Mackenzie and Amelia this morning about a girls' night, they'd both immediately confirmed that they'd be here. Amelia brought Rachel as well, and I was looking forward to getting to know Adam's girlfriend. I'd also taken a chance at work earlier and invited Mara—and though she looked genuinely touched at the offer, she was forced to decline so that she could close the bar tonight.

In the days since moving into the apartment, I'd purchased a gray sectional and coffee table for the living room that helped make it feel more like a home. I also found some high stools that were perfect for the built-in breakfast bar, as well as a few houseplants that added life to the small space.

"Of course I have snacks," I stated. "There's also a scary

amount of rosé in the fridge for just the four of us. And honestly, after last night, I don't know that I'll be drinking much."

Three faces turned toward me. It was Amelia who asked, "Last night?"

"Yeah." I swallowed, realizing what I'd inadvertently opened myself up to. "I had one or two too many margaritas at Andre's house and—"

"You were at that beautiful man's *house*?" Mackenzie's blurted, both palms slamming down on the counter.

"How did that happen?" Amelia chimed in from where she stood next to Mackenzie in the kitchen.

Rachel's bemused expression came into focus. "Wait, is this the guy from the bar the other night? The tall one with the tattoos?"

Amelia turned to her, exclaiming, "*Yes!*"

Rachel nodded. "He was hot."

"Okay, okay," I interjected. "While that may be true . . . we're just friends."

Amelia scoffed. "Nora. I've known that man for well over a year now. He doesn't just invite girls to his house."

"What do you mean?" I asked.

"He's really quiet and intensely focused. He doesn't have much of a social life. And he definitely doesn't date. Logan's been able to drag him out a couple of times, but the way he acted at Larkspur the other night—quiet and brooding and a bit terrifying—that's how he normally is. I was actually surprised he even came, but now I think it was because he knew you'd be there." Her eyes flashed with excitement.

I frowned. "We're not dating. And just because he may not have a lot of friends doesn't mean I can't be one."

Mackenzie rolled her eyes. "Nora, I watched that fine man carry you into my house like you were his long-lost treasure."

Amelia's focus snapped to Mackenzie. "*What*?!"

"Yeah"—Mack looked at me with smug satisfaction before her gaze jumped back to Amelia—"after he helped her with her SUV when she first got to Denver, they went out to a bar. He drove her home *late* that night and carried her inside because she'd fallen asleep in the car. He even tucked the blanket up over her shoulders and moved her hair out of her face like he'd crawled right out of a fucking romance novel."

Amelia faced me again. "Nora. Mark my words—that man wants you. There's no way he'd have you over at his house otherwise. He's super private. How late did you stay? Was anyone else there?"

I felt heat prickling at my hairline, threatening to reach my face. "His sister was there, and their family friends. And, because of the margaritas, I fell asleep during a movie and sort of spent the night."

Amelia whooped while Mackenzie twirled in a circle—some lunatic attempt at a celebratory dance. I wondered, for a moment, what they might do if I revealed that Andre had spent the night *here* first, swooping through my front door like a bat out of hell ready to slay my enemies. The pipe he'd brought was still propped up against my doorjamb—my newly minted home security system.

It was Rachel who asked probably the most important question. "Are you into him?"

If there was one thing Mackenzie and Amelia knew about me as two of my best friends, it was that I was a terrible liar. I always had been. As soon as a lie formed in my mouth, it never failed that my breathing would falter and my skin would transition to the brightest shade of red. So I took a deep, steadying breath before I answered, hoping I had more control over myself now that I was a grown adult. "No."

Even I could hear the blatant tremble in my voice, my tone far from casual.

Mackenzie blinked once before she burst out laughing.

Amelia just shook her head. "You're screwed."

"Or, she'll be screwed soon," Rachel let out with a giggle.

Amelia threw a piece of popcorn at her. "Okay, Rachel with the dirty jokes—I see you!"

"You should bring him to the wedding," Mackenzie exclaimed. "As your date!"

If I dared to be honest, I would admit that I'd already been thinking about doing just that. It wasn't like there was anyone else that I was remotely interested in bringing—I'd been planning on just going solo. But the idea of having Andre there . . . a friend to enjoy it with. "It's not the worst idea." It was all I allowed myself to say.

"Speaking of the wedding," Amelia said, grabbing a bottle of wine from the fridge and four glasses from the cabinet, "I had the *best* idea. Why don't we take a little pre-wedding trip to my parents' house in Breckenridge before we head up to Wyoming for the wedding?"

Mackenzie and Eric were getting married south of Cheyenne where Eric's aunt had a beautiful property that overlooked a meadow—just over an hour's drive from Denver. Mackenzie had sent all of her bridesmaids pictures months ago. It was the perfect place for a sunset ceremony.

"Oh my god, I've been dying to finally see that house." Mackenzie's eyes were wide and bright.

Amelia shrugged. "It's the perfect place for one last hurrah, and it's gorgeous this time of year—my mom has been going non-stop with her gardening." She handed each of us a glass of wine and held hers out between us. "Let's spend a couple nights in Breckenridge together, and then caravan up to Wyoming from there."

"Your parents wouldn't mind?" Mackenzie asked.

"Not at all. They'll be in Boulder for a surgical conference, anyway. That's why they can't make it to your wedding, remember?"

Mackenzie nodded, buzzing with excitement. "I'm so down. And Eric will already be off work; we planned to spend a couple of quiet days together before heading to his aunt's house. But this is *so* much better! Rachel, bring Adam—I mean, obviously. It's his house, too. Nora"—she turned to face me—"bring Andre." A statement. There was no question in her tone. "This is going to be epic, a joint bachelor/bache-lorette vacation!"

Amelia nodded. "There's plenty of space for all of us. And I'll tell Logan to give Andre the time off or I won't put out for a month."

I squeezed my eyes shut as I tried to hold in my laughter. "I haven't even said that I'm going to invite him!"

Mackenzie rolled her eyes. "Come on, Nora. It's practically inevitable at this point. Just do yourself a favor and bring that gorgeous man to my wedding."

Amelia threw her pointer finger in the air. "And Breck-enridge!"

I shook my head, grinning. "You guys really know how to lay on the pressure."

Chapter Nineteen

ANDRE

Distant, incessant pounding rapped at the dregs of my post-sleep fog. It took a full three minutes before I realized the pounding wasn't coming from inside of my dream, but from somewhere outside of my body.

Peeling one eye open, I saw that it was still dark—way too early for Sela to be up. I lifted my head to see the time on the small clock that sat on my nightstand and saw that it was just past two-thirty in the morning. What the fuck? Another round of hard pounding, and I understood that it was coming from the front door—this time alarm bells started blaring inside my mind and I flew out of bed. Whoever was outside that door was about to catch a fucking ass whooping.

I stormed out of my room and found Sela in the hallway, her face still swollen with sleep. "What's happening, Andre?" she asked nervously as she eyed the front door.

"I don't know, but I'll find out. Go back to your room and lock the door." I didn't know who was outside, but it couldn't be

for anything good and I didn't want Marisela near it. She looked at me for a long moment before she turned and quickly shut herself in her room. I heard the click of the lock on her door-knob—it wasn't much as far as security went, but anything was better than nothing.

With my sister out of the line of sight, I focused my attention back on the pounding. As I walked toward the front entryway, I mustered as much fucking rage as I could, bringing the heat of it right to the surface of my body. We kept a long, metal pipe next to the door jamb for moments like this, and I picked it up and clutched it tightly in my hand before unlocking the deadbolt of the door and opening it an inch to peer outside.

Fuck. "Gabriel?!" I hissed out his name in a hard breath between my teeth.

We hadn't seen our older brother in months, not since he started using drugs again. He'd been clean for almost two years before his old dealer found him at a party and wrapped him back up in the bullshit. I'd heard from a few people that Gabriel had started dealing again, too, and it'd devastated me. I honestly thought he was done with all that shit.

Years ago, after Gabriel turned eighteen and took over guardianship of Sela and I when El Viejo passed away, he'd gotten involved with a neighborhood street gang as a way to make extra cash for us—to ensure we could make it on our own. It wasn't long before he started using some of his own product, and things went downhill really fast after that.

An eventual deal-gone-wrong led to Gabriel being shot at, and he swore off the life and promised us that he'd get straight. And he did. He'd been working day shifts at a home improve-ment store and night shifts stocking shelves at a big retail outlet, and he'd gotten himself clean. I'd worked when I could, too—

Gabriel never let me quit going to school, but I'd been able to find small jobs at local restaurants to help ease some of the burden.

We'd been doing so good for such a long time, until earlier this year when Gabriel's old street boss found him at that party and threatened his family to get him working again. Apparently, it wasn't so easy to just "quit" gangs.

Gabriel didn't tell us about it, but I figured it out soon enough. He'd stopped coming home between his shifts at both jobs, stopped texting to check in with us throughout the day, and eventually the notices for unpaid bills started coming in. It was only a month or two before things got so bad again that I knew for sure he lost his purpose to the needle. He loved Sela and I, but his love for being high skewed his vision, made him forget. Being an addict was all-encompassing, rearranging every priority into a new hierarchy where drugs sat at the top of the list.

I caught him coming home one day and blocked him from getting into the house. I told him we were done putting up with his shit. When he wanted to get clean and be part of this family, he could come back home—but until then . . .

Now, he was standing at our door in the middle of the night. It had been over six months since I'd seen him—he looked like shit. He'd lost weight, his cheeks were hollowing out, and even in the dead of night I could see the shadows around his eyes.

He grinned at me, but his eyes were void of any emotion. It was obvious he was nowhere near being clean. I braced myself for whatever he was about to say, ready to protect my sister above anything else. "Hola, hermanito." His voice was like sandpaper, like he hadn't had water in days. I watched as he looked me up and down. "You're looking more and more like a man. How have you been?"

I shot him a glare. "You would know, hermano, if you were

home with us . . . if you weren't running around the streets like a fucking thug."

Gabriel's face fell, immediately shifting to the defensive. "You disrespect me? Everything I've done was for you and Sela. I busted my ass our whole lives to keep you both safe."

I scoffed. "Maybe back then it was for us. But not anymore. Everything you do now is for that fucking crystal. What are you even doing here, Gabriel? You're not clean. I told you not to come back until you were."

He looked at me for a long moment before he sighed. "I need some money, Andre. Just a little bit. Just enough to get better. I— I'm sick."

I felt a cold laugh rumble through my tightening chest. "You want to get better? Check into a rehab center and I'll find a way to pay them. But I'm not giving you any money. My money goes to this house. It goes to our sister. It sure as fuck *doesn't go to you and your fucking demons."*

Pain flashed in Gabriel's eyes, and my chest squeezed. I loved my brother more than anything, wanted nothing more than to pull him in and save him from himself. But I couldn't—we'd been down this road before, and the only way to help him was to convince him to help himself. As much as I wanted to, I couldn't be the one to make the choice that saved his life.

"Gabriel, listen to me." I looked him right in the eye, desperate to reach the man under the high. Desperate for my brother. "It doesn't have to be like this. If you're scared of getting out or scared of retaliation, we'll figure it out. We'll get out of this city and go somewhere where we can start fresh. Together—you, me, and Marisela. I will help *you, I swear I will. We can do it.*

"When you're ready for that, when you're ready to leave all this behind, come back and we'll go. But until then . . ." I shook

my head. "Until then, I have nothing for you, hermano. *Nothing."*

Before Gabriel could answer, I stepped backward into the house and shut the door, quickly locking the deadbolt. It was only a moment before the pounding started again.

"Andre!" His voice pierced through the door. "Andre, open the fucking door! Open the fucking door, you ungrateful little shit! Fuck you, Andre! Open this fucking door!"

Still holding the pipe in my hands, the metal slickening with the cold sweat from my palms, I sat on the ground with my back against the door and listened as my brother—my hero, my best friend—relentlessly banged against the other side.

He didn't let up for almost an hour. Eventually, though, the pounding stopped.

For a while, I could still hear him talking to me out there— talking to himself, talking to god. I knew that he was tired, that he wanted to come home. The drugs were robbing him of everything good in his life, and I knew he hated himself for letting it get so bad. But he had to battle this monster. He had to prove to himself that he wanted to live, and as hard as I prayed for him to see that there was always an opportunity to come home, always a light to be found in his nightmare—he had to be willing to open his eyes and see it.

IT HAD BEEN A LONG WEEK. Hell, it had been a long few years.

Today was a day that I dreaded—the worst kind of anniversary. I'd been having more and more dreams these last few days as I readied myself for the blow that today would undoubtedly yield. The worst kind of impact. Even Marisela looked rough this morning when she finally came out of her room at ten— much later than normal. Her eyes were almost swollen shut, as if she'd sobbed into her pillow all night. I wondered if she'd heard me talking. If I'd yelled at my brother aloud from where I faced him in my sleep.

Gabriel had been gone for four fucking years.

I pushed the lawn mower through the grass of our front yard as memories of my brother coursed through my mind. The waves of guilt and devastation I knew too well tore through me as sweat dripped down my face. Self-deprecation swallowed up my insides and left me empty—void of any semblance of joy or peace.

Gabriel. *Mi hermano de sangre. Mi familia.* Gone.

And I didn't do anything to help him. Worse, I slammed the door in his face.

It had only been two weeks later that Gabriel left this world —left us behind forever.

He was sitting in the driver's seat of his little beater car in front of the apartment building we'd lived in at the time, just two weeks after that middle-of-the-night visit. Seeing him there, waiting in his car during the daylight hours, had sent a jolt of hope so fierce through me that I nearly crashed into a parking barricade.

He'd come back. He was ready to fight his demons. I could finally do something to help him.

I could see Gabriel's head tilted back, leaning against his headrest. It looked like he was sleeping, taking a moment of reprieve as he waited for me to get home from work. I thought about how tired he must have been, and I'd felt *grateful* for it. If he was tired enough to give up the poison he was putting into his body, it would be worth it.

I approached his faded blue car, noticing the rust that was accumulating along the door's edges, and knocked on the window to wake him up. But he didn't move. I tried the handle, but the door was locked—so I knocked harder to try to wake him. To get him to hear me.

It was a full minute before I noticed the needle still hanging from the crook of his arm.

To this day, I still didn't understand it. I didn't know if he thought he needed one last high before he flung himself back into sobriety with nothing but a shred of hope—or if it had been revenge, a big "fuck you" to a family that he felt had left him behind. I knew the Gabriel I loved would never hurt us so deeply. But it wasn't Gabriel who'd shown up in the middle of the night to demand money. It wasn't Gabriel who prioritized a high above his family. He hadn't been our Gabriel in quite some time.

Marisela and I were devastated. The world was a cruel, nasty bitch, and the darkness that enveloped us was unconquerable for a long, long time. We retreated back into ourselves, keeping a firm distance between us and the rest of the world. But such thick walls were hard for Marisela. As the youngest, she was our dreamer. She ached to experience the world, to belong to it in a way that I never understood . . . still didn't understand. But I couldn't bring myself to snuff out her hope.

And so I worked really fucking hard to try to piece my life back together. We both did.

She began taking college classes around the same time I started working at Logan's shop, and we both fell into new routines. A new life in a world that no longer held our big brother in it.

Eventually, the day-to-day routine became easier. It no longer took every ounce of energy to peel myself out of bed and get myself into the shower before work. And Marisela was thriving in school, even getting herself on the dean's list for a straight-A semester.

We established a finish line, a new dream for ourselves—Marisela's restaurant. A place where she could cook. Our own business that no one could ever take away from us. We'd pay off our house and finally have something to the Vasquez name that wasn't full of heartache. It was a dream that'd put the ground beneath my feet again, one that gave me a lasting purpose. I had to get us there—I promised my brother that I'd get Marisela anything she needed, and I had no intention of failing this family again. Not with her.

We worked to save as much money as possible, and Marisela had eventually transferred to an online university where she could finish out her Bachelor's program for a business degree. She worked part-time at the nearby market, stocking shelves and ringing up customers at the cash register. Eventually, I became a manager at Logan's shop.

The days turned lighter. Brighter, even. We still missed Gabriel with every breath we took, never able to overcome the pain of his loss—but the pain did become more bearable. Still, the anniversary of his death reopened all the jagged wounds that we worked so hard to heal.

And yet, it also felt like a reminder. A reminder of everything Marisela and I had faced, everything we'd conquered. There was a fight in us so strong that the only possible outcome was to succeed. To win.

In the past few weeks, I'd even let myself start to believe there could be more that life had to offer a young orphan from the streets than just financial security. More to the finish line than originally anticipated. Maybe . . . maybe there was also a girl. A girl made just for me. A girl who I would honor and protect just as fiercely as my sister. A girl I could give a home to, who could give me one right back.

Even through all the pain and despair, even as I stood under the dark cloud that hung above me on this worst day—a shudder zipped down my spine at the thought of her.

Chapter Twenty

NORA

For as long as I could remember, my birthday was the most sacred of all holidays. It was the one day of the year that my mother and I dropped *everything*—school, work, any responsibility that we could've possibly been bound to—and spent the entire day together, from sunup to sun down.

It did not matter what else was going on in our lives. We could have been in the middle of a big fight—something as trivial as me stealing her clothes, or as big as me stealing her car for a night out with friends—and still, the morning of my birthday wiped away any traces of frustration or stress or guilt. We'd laugh so hard our ribs hurt, eat so much sugar our stomachs hurt, and talk about everything. Our past. Our future. Our dreams. After all, we were celebrating not only my life, but *our* lives. Together.

My mother became pregnant with me when she was only twenty years old. She'd been casually dating a football player from the college she attended to earn her degree in education, and though she always assured me that their relationship had never been anything more than a casual fling, I could see the pain in her eyes when she talked about him. I believed that, despite her version of the story, she may have actually loved him quite fiercely.

Nevertheless, when she became pregnant, he became distant. He wasn't ready to have a family, he'd said. He had a future to look forward to, so much life to live. He knew that accepting the pregnancy would more than likely mean the end of his football career, and he'd loved football more than anything or anyone. His dream was to go pro. So, my mother let him off the hook, allowing him to pretend that it'd never happened.

But it did.

From the moment she knew I existed, my mother said she couldn't imagine a version of life where I wasn't hers. I felt her love every single day of my life—even through the hard days, when her meager teacher salary had barely been enough for us to survive on. She always found a way to keep us happy and safe. She loved me so completely that I never even thought to miss my father. I was perfectly content to be all hers, for her to be all mine.

Now that she was gone, I didn't know how to handle the emotion that hit me on my birthday. And three years later, this one was no exception.

I'd awoken just before the sunrise, as I'd somehow done every year growing up—usually in anticipation for some big, cavity-inducing breakfast of pancakes with sprinkles and ice cream and bacon constructed into a smiling face. Today, I spent the morning curled up on the couch staring at the blank wall in my living room, my mind reeling and aching with so many memories, so many happy moments that would never exist again.

Since she'd passed, I chose to spend my birthdays alone. I needed the space on this day to allow myself to grieve. Thankfully, Parker had always granted me this—never fighting me when I insisted that I had no interest in celebrating another year around the sun without my best friend in the entire world.

This was the first birthday I would spend *alone* alone. There was no Parker hiding out downstairs in his office, no staff running a too-big house. It was just me and this apartment that was much too small to possibly hold in so much feeling.

When a knock sounded at my front door at eight-thirty, I chose to ignore it. I wasn't expecting anyone, and didn't want to deal with anything right now. But when the knocking persisted, I let out a huff and peeled myself off the gray cushions of my couch, taking the steps to the front door.

I was surprised to find Andre on the other side.

"Good morning, Nora," he said, cheerful as all hell. Even in my numb and distant state of mind, I looked him up and down. *Of course* I did. He wore a gray, short-sleeved shirt that matched his eyes; black athletic shorts that exposed his long, tattooed, muscled legs; and black running shoes. His white crew socks were pulled up high around his calves—the same way he'd worn them to the gym.

I frowned as my eyes moved back up to his face. "Hi."

It was rude of me to not offer him a happier greeting, but I wasn't expecting company—nor did I want any. I wasn't sure how to handle this.

My lack of manners didn't seem to faze him, though. His grin was wide and his eyes danced as he took in my crumpled hair and baggy pajama shirt that hung down mid-thigh. "Do you know what today is?" he asked, and I internally groaned. Someone must have told him.

"Look," I started, "I don't normally—"

"It's National Gummy Worm Day," he exclaimed, his face bright and expectant as he delivered this strange new update like it might have me dancing with joy.

"What?" I asked, deadpan. *Am I missing something?*

"Swear." He crossed an X down his front. Over his heart, as if we were kids swearing to wild oaths.

And it got me, like a beacon of light breaking through the heavy, dark clouds. I couldn't help it. I smiled. "National Gummy Worm Day, huh?" I said, entertaining this bizarre conversation.

He nodded enthusiastically. "Yes. Go shower and get dressed. I'll wait for as long as you need."

Wait a second. "Wait for what?"

The wink he shot at me sent a rattle right to my core. "For you."

"For me? For what?"

"You'll see."

"Andre . . ." I began, but he wasn't having it. He threw his hands up in the air between us.

"Nora, trust me. Okay?" His silver eyes gleamed. I swore I saw one legitimately twinkle.

I let out a long breath as I stared at him, utterly baffled. It was a full minute before I responded. "You can wait on the couch."

AN HOUR LATER—I made sure to take my time, half-believing during my shower that my mind was playing tricks on me and he wasn't actually waiting for me in my living room—I sat in the front seat of Andre's Mustang as he maneuvered us down city streets.

"Where are we going?" I asked again, for probably the twelfth time.

Just like he did three minutes ago, he shook his head. "Patience. It'll be worth it, I promise."

I sighed, leaning back against the headrest and staring out the window as tall buildings and meandering pedestrians whirled past us.

After twenty minutes of driving, I realized we were headed *out* of the city, the main road transitioning into a two-lane highway with farms and plots of empty land on either side. It was another fifteen minutes before he finally slowed down, flipping on his blinker to turn right onto a narrow dirt road. I scrunched my eyebrows as I studied the view, searching for signs that might give away where we could be going. "Andre, what're we . . ."

And then I saw it.

Just up ahead, cresting into view from the other side of a steep hill, was a giant Ferris wheel. As we continued our ascent, more rides came into few.

"A carnival?" I asked, incredulously. Turning my head to Andre, I found him smiling from ear to ear.

"The county fair," he confirmed. He pulled the car into a

fenced-off dirt lot that was already almost full of vehicles from other fairgoers, then parked and turned off the ignition. I must have been showing my hesitation because he turned to face me and murmured softly, "Nora, come on—it's to celebrate the gummy worms. You love gummy worms."

A laugh burst out of me at the sheer absurdity of the situation, and Andre peered out toward the colorful rides spread out in front of us, smiling to himself. His curved lips revealed a flash of teeth that made me feel like I was floating.

He looked back at me, the humor from his face dissipating as his expression grew more serious. He focused on my face, as if to assess my emotions. "Give me an hour of trying, and if you hate it, I'll take you home, okay?" His voice was low and full of sincerity and it almost made my heart break. I didn't know how he knew it was my birthday, or how he knew how hard this day was for me . . . but here he was, showing up for me in the midst of heartache yet again, making sure I didn't feel alone.

The burn of tears in my eyes made me waver. Grief was like a heavy blanket that was so damn hard to peel off. It was an isolating experience, and deeply suffocating. I didn't think I'd ever stop grieving my mother. Years later, I could still feel the aching tug from the deepest depths of despair. It was so damn easy to slip back into that broken place.

But . . . maybe it was time to start learning how to cut the ties to some of that pain. Even if it scared me. The least I could do was try—I knew my mother wouldn't want me to suffer like this for the rest of my life.

I looked up at Andre and nodded as a tear slipped down my cheek. "Okay," I said, my voice full of raw emotion. "Okay, let's go."

Andre raised his hand to my face, softly brushing the tear away with the pad of his thumb. His touch lingered for a moment. "You got this." It was almost a whisper. "I'm right here with you." I nodded again as I felt my defenses splintering along their edges. And then I let him lead me into the fairgrounds.

There was something about the way his hand slid down my back to rest firmly at the base of my spine as we walked through the entrance gates that felt . . . soothing. Protective. And maybe even a little possessive. And I happened to like all of those things very much.

It occurred to me that I might have been slightly miscalculating my ability to keep control of this friendship's boundaries. It wouldn't take a whole lot for him to pull me under, and if he figured that out—I was done for.

We spent the next half hour walking the grounds, taking in everything the fair had to offer. The screams and wild laughter coming from the various rides filled the air around us, as smells of freshly-baked funnel cake and fried Oreos wafted through our noses. It was a beautiful day—the heat of the sun along my skin felt like a warm embrace, and I wondered if my mom was here, seeing this too. I was desperate for her.

Eventually, we decided to ride the giant Ferris wheel. I followed Andre to the back of the line, and as we waited, we were content to just stand near each other, watching the excitement of the people around us.

He was notably not pushing me into any lengthy conversations, allowing me to work through my feelings with minimal pressure. It floored me, his ability to intuit my needs. It was like he knew the complex layers of everything I was fighting my way through.

But then . . . he *did* know it. He went through it too, after losing his brother.

When it was our turn to enter one of the many gondolas, Andre followed me inside the cramped, yellow-painted interior and sat next to me instead of on the other side. There was just enough room for two people on the single bench, but we were still sitting snugly enough together that I could feel warmth spilling out of his body and into mine, lighting up my nerve endings.

I looked up to find his eyes already on me, their silver hues shining like the blade of a knife in the sunlight. The dark lashes surrounding them were a stark contrast—he was, without a doubt, the most attractive man I'd ever known. And not in a perfectly groomed, pretty-boy way. He was nothing like Parker. Andre's presence alone was toe-curling.

We stared at each other for another long moment, even as the ride attendant shut the gate of our gondola and the large wheel lurched us forward. Eventually, his face stretched into a lazy grin, eyes crinkling and head tipping back, and it tightened something low in my stomach.

"What?" I asked, failing to keep my own small smile from spreading across my face.

His eyes sparkled in the sunlight snaking through the metal bars. "Sometimes you look at me like you want to eat me."

I huffed out a laugh as my cheeks flushed with heat, but we never broke our eye contact. "Sometimes," I responded, a bit breathy, "you look at me the same way."

I watched as Andre's smile disappeared, his features transforming into a gentle curiosity as he scanned my face. Every ounce of that dangerously intense focus was fixed on me. "Give me one honest truth," he murmured.

Nerves uncoiled from inside my stomach and spooled out across my limbs. I felt like I could give him so many raw truths right now: my debilitating grief and pain over missing my mother, the disbelief that I was sitting in this Ferris wheel with him right now, the way I ached to touch and feel him.

But instead, I settled on something safer. "You first."

His gaze hung heavy on me for a moment before he blew out a quick breath, nodding in agreement. His voice was gritty as he spoke. "The anniversary of Gabriel's death was two days ago, and as much as I try to prepare myself each year, there's nothing like that pain. It's damn near impossible to anticipate how much it's going to hurt." Emotion shimmered in his eyes, but he didn't hide a single ounce of it from me, and my heart pounded furiously at the gift that it was. That, by him expressing the feelings that were too hard for me to say out loud, he knew I wouldn't have to. And I would still know that he understood. That he was here to sit with me in it.

"I'm so sorry," I whispered.

He grabbed my hand, squeezing it tight. "Me too."

I brushed away a tear that'd escaped, taking a second to look out at the sky before I offered him a truth of my own. "I want you to come to Mackenzie's wedding with me. As . . . my date."

Surprise flashed across his face. "You do?"

I nodded. "Yeah. But you should know it's, like, a *whole* thing. The wedding is across state lines in Wyoming, so we'd have to stay there for a night—and there's also a pre-wedding hurrah in Breckenridge for two nights before that I also want you to go with me to. So . . ." I paused, searching his eyes for any hesitance, knowing how much I was asking of him, "it's like, a four-day commitment. And I know that I'm asking a lot

. . . and I would be completely okay if you don't want to commit to all that. But yeah, if by some miraculous chance you're up for it, I'd really like for you to go with me."

The corners of his mouth raised, and I felt relieved that I wasn't making him uncomfortable. "What, exactly, is a 'pre-wedding hurrah in Breckenridge'?"

I smiled, shrugging. "I honestly don't know. Amelia is planning it, I think it's like a joint bachelor/bachelorette party slash vacation?"

Andre chuckled, finally breaking our eye contact as he looked out at the view in front of us. I did the same, and saw we were almost at the top of the wheel.

"I'll have to see if I can get the time off," Andre said from beside me, his voice a little husky, "but if Logan's cool with it and we can find coverage for the shop, then I'll be there, *mariposa*."

I turned my head to face him again and found his eyes blazing with emotion. *Mariposa*. It was such an intimate nickname that he'd given me.

"A little birdie told me you'll have no problem getting the time off," I said, my own voice wavering. It wasn't until his brows narrowed that I realized the admission I'd inadvertently given him—that I'd told others about wanting to ask him to the wedding. That I'd wanted him with me.

His eyes gleamed in the afternoon sunlight as the Ferris wheel brought us back down. "Is that right?" he asked. I watched intently as his top teeth raked over his bottom lip.

"Yep." I felt the pop of the P from my lips as I forced my gaze away from Andre, instead studying the frame of the giant wheel as we moved back through the platform at the bottom for another rotation. Insecurity ripped through me at how much I was letting myself admit.

"Nora," he murmured. Gentle but commanding. "Nora. Look at me." And despite myself, despite the stubborn reluctancy to let him see me so vulnerable, my eyes outright betrayed me as I met his eyes. His expression was soft and warm. He reached out to put a hand on my knee, and I exhaled at the comfort of his calloused fingers against my bare skin. "Thank you for your honest truth. Don't shy away from asking for the things that make you happy. Especially not from me. Okay?"

I looked down at the large palm covering most of my knee, my eyes tracing along the curves of ink on his hand, at the letters on his fingers spelling out the word *LOVE*. Such a contrast from the word tattooed on the fingers of his other hand—*FEAR*. And I thought, *That's all it really comes down to, isn't it?*

I didn't want to play things safe anymore. If today was a reminder of anything, it was that life was way too short. And I knew fear had no place in the future I was ready to build. But love . . .

There was definitely room for love. A *real* love—the kind that hurt. The kind that could cleave your soul in two and ruin you if things went wrong . . . but the kind that could light your soul on fire if you got it right.

My eyes found Andre's again as I placed my own hand on top of his. "Okay." I smiled, feeling some of the day's anguish begin to release from where I'd been holding it so tightly in my shoulders. Leaning back into the bench seat, my shoulder settling into Andre's beside me, I took a deep breath and let myself feel gratitude for another year around the sun . . . for another chance to get things right.

Chapter Twenty-One

ANDRE

To my relief, things were beginning to take a turn for the better. I wasn't sure that I'd be able to break through the walls Nora had built around herself when I got to her apartment this morning. They were hard and impenetrable —and I couldn't blame her for it.

I knew what those walls felt like . . . knew the kind of heartache that they helped guard against.

But when Logan pulled me aside yesterday, looking slightly uncomfortable as he explained that Amelia was worried about Nora facing her birthday alone after an especially hard few weeks, I couldn't just let her spend the day by herself, holed up in that tiny-ass apartment. Apparently, Nora had spent every birthday since her mother died on her own, unwilling to celebrate another year without the beloved matriarch of her life. And—according to Logan—Amelia seemed to think that I'd have the best chance to help her through the torment of her grief. Nora's friends had tried in the past. Tried and ultimately failed to break through.

While I took Nora's pain seriously, I couldn't help but feel a smidge of pride that Amelia thought I could be the one to help. That she thought my relationship with Nora was powerful enough to break through her walls. It stroked something deep within me, made me feel like . . . like a man. Like I *could* take care of her the way I wanted to.

When I got her into the car with me this morning, I almost kissed the ground at her feet in thanks. And when she didn't immediately demand I turn around and head back home after she saw where I was taking her, I knew the day could only go up from there.

After all, it was her birthday. And she deserved to celebrate herself. To celebrate her *life*.

If I'd learned anything over the last few years, it was the importance of celebrating the good shit. El Viejo always told us: *Donde el diablo puso la mano, queda huella para rato.* Where the devil put his hand, it would leave a mark. After losing Gabriel, I understood exactly what he meant by that.

Pain was inevitable, and it left traces within us. It was easy to stare at those scars, to hate them, to get so angry that anger and heartache were the only driving forces in life . . . I knew all about it, and it seemed that Nora did too. But the sooner she could find something else to focus on—something good and light and worthy—the sooner those scars would cease to dictate her every move. I wanted Nora to see the light that was all around her. I wanted her to see herself the way I did—shimmering, whole, *perfect*.

We were sitting next to each other on the Ferris wheel, making another slow ascent to the top as my hand rested over her knee, and I was finally starting to see her open up. And I still felt like I was floating after she asked me to be her date at her friends' wedding.

She wanted *me* to be there with her. And it wasn't just for a night—it was a whole three-night ordeal. I hoped like hell I could get the time off. I was sure Logan was also going—this was his friend group, too. For both of us to be out that long wouldn't be easy. But Manny had been asking for more responsibility, and he was definitely a rising leader amongst the crew in the shop. Maybe we could pull it off.

It was unlike me to even contemplate taking time off at the same time Logan did. That was typically a no-brainer decision —I was needed at the shop. But my priorities were clearly shifting when it came to Nora. There were so many things I wanted to do for her. Do *with* her. But more than anything, I wanted her to find real happiness for herself. And if I could help nudge her along the way to find the confidence to demand it, to find the courage and conviction to put herself and her desires above anything else, I would do it.

As if she knew what I was thinking, her fingers began to lazily stroke the back of my hand, making me wonder if what she wanted was right here in this gondola. I was pretty sure she was aware of this *thing* between us. This thing that had the makings of being so much more than friendship. But if that was something she wanted to pursue, she was going to have to make it known. After everything she'd been going through, I wasn't going to ask for something just because I wanted it— not when it was her time to be selfish.

I let myself give in to just one urge, one burning temptation to wind my fingers through her hair with my free hand as her head rested on my shoulder, to smooth it back and gently tuck it behind her ear. It was a risky move. I lost momentary control of my fingers, watching as they skated down the side of her neck before I realized what I was doing and pulled my hand back.

I felt her shift in response to my touch—shift *closer* to me as her hand gripped the one I still had on her knee. And I couldn't help the smile that grew on my face. Luckily, she was facing away from me.

We stayed like that, curled into each other on the bench seat of the gondola, for the rest of the ride. After a second full rotation it was time for us to get off to let an eager couple get on and take our place. I followed Nora as she meandered away from the Ferris wheel, looking lighter and more at ease than she had all day.

"Nora," I called out, stopping her movement. She turned to look at me with those beautiful brown eyes of hers—a lighter, golden chestnut in the sunlight. My eyes fell to the ground, searching for the words I wanted to say, before I lifted them back up to meet hers. "I'm not going anywhere. Okay?"

Her eyes widened—just millimeters, but I still caught the change. Her head dipped in the slightest nod. "I know," she breathed.

And dammit if my heart didn't falter at the words. Was it obvious, her effect on me? And yet, I knew the right thing to do was to keep my feelings for her as platonic as possible. I'd stay firmly rooted in the friend-zone forever if it meant her happiness.

She gave me a soft smile before a playful glee fell over her face. "So," she said, narrowing her eyes at me, "you dragged me off my couch and out of my pajamas with some tease about gummy worms. I'm ready for my sweet treat now,

Andre." She shifted her weight to one foot, tilting her head at me in jest.

I grinned, eating her banter from the palm of her hand like the greedy man that I was. "If there's one thing you should know about me, *mariposa*, it's that I don't tease."

Her eyes flashed at my words, but she kept her face schooled with that cool expression. "Well then?"

Shaking my head, I nodded toward a food truck that was advertising all types of sweets—giant blobs of cotton candy, ice cream sundaes, and funnel cake. "Let's get you sugared up, yeah?"

Her smile was bright and wide open, further erasing the shadows of pain that had been present all morning. "Yes, please."

WE SPENT the rest of the afternoon roaming the fairgrounds, hopping from one ride to another. Some of them were so intense they shot my stomach into my throat and I felt like I could hurl—but I kept myself composed. It was worth it to see Nora open up. We gorged ourselves on random fried foods, shared a huge cone of bright pink cotton candy, and even found a bag of gummy worms I'd proudly bestowed on her after over an hour of searching.

It was a great fucking day—a day I knew we both needed.

As the sun dipped toward the horizon, the crowd around us began to look a little rougher. I knew from experience that the fairgrounds were a hot spot for criminal activity at night, and I wanted to make sure Nora was far away from any of that bullshit. After ending the day with another ride on the Ferris wheel—again sitting pressed together on the same bench seat—we made our way back to where the car was parked in the large dirt lot outside the grounds.

Just as it was this morning, the ride home was quiet. Except this time, it was a comfortable silence—the easy contentment between us was back, and I was grateful for it. It was her birthday, after all, and she deserved to hold some peace with it. But when we pulled up to her apartment, I sensed her stiffen next to me. It was something I'd noticed the last few times we'd hung out, as if she wasn't ready to be alone again.

I knew just how she felt.

I turned the ignition off and faced her. "I'll walk you up?"

She nodded. "Yeah, that sounds great."

"Hang tight," I said, before I pushed the door open. I jogged over to her side of the car to open her door, offering my hand to help her out.

When she stood at her full height, just inches in front of me, it was hard not to imagine kissing her. But I had to be careful, so I forced my gaze away from hers, shutting her door and moving toward the main entrance of her building. Her sneakers crunched against the cracked asphalt behind me as she quietly followed me in.

When we made it up to her apartment, I could still feel her hesitance to say goodbye. She pressed her back against her front door as she let out a sigh. Her eyes were full of something I hadn't seen before—it looked a lot like longing.

Her brown eyes were wide as she rasped the words, "Stay with me."

My pulse tripped as I scanned her face, watching her

vulnerability flare as she realized the words that left her mouth. Stay with her? What did she mean? "What?"

She sighed again, shrugging. "Stay," she repeated. Like it was a simple request. "It's not like we haven't done it before. Let's have a drink."

I was instantly leaning over the edge of a cliff, and I knew that if I made any sudden movements, I'd fall down into a deep chasm that I wouldn't be able to crawl back out of. It was thrilling and terrifying all at once. I'd never felt this way about anything before, and certainly not about any*one*—I didn't know that I could.

For a moment I let my gaze drop to her mouth, and I again imagined kissing her, pressing my body against hers and claiming her. Marking her with my teeth. Getting her into that apartment and finally showing her just how badly I was starting to *need* her. But again, I stopped myself, mustering up whatever restraint I had in my arsenal. Forcing my eyes back up to hers while simultaneously forcing down that lust.

Staying was a bad idea—I knew I was only a hair-trigger away from crossing a line that I'd worked so hard to respect. But after seeing the pain in her eyes this morning, and then the smile on her face . . . I couldn't say no to her now. I told her I was here for anything. So before I could second-guess myself, I nodded my head, readying my mind to conquer any tugs off the deep end. "Okay," I said, my mouth full of cotton.

Nora's eyes lit up instantly, all traces of anxiousness gone in seconds. She turned around to unlock the door, pushing it wide open. "I hope you're okay with wine," she said as she crossed the threshold and made her way into the kitchen. "That's all I have right now."

"Sounds great." I stepped in to the apartment after her, right into the pit of temptation.

As she grabbed two wineglasses from her cupboard, I pulled my wallet, keys, and phone from my pockets, setting them down on the high counter that separated the kitchen from the living room. It felt too intimate, to leave my stuff there like this was my space—just like it had the first night I'd stayed here.

Triggered by the memory, I did a quick inspection of her locks, ensuring that everything was as it should be. There were no signs of any attempt to break in, although I still didn't trust the cheap-ass door. I again found myself wishing she didn't live in a place like this, especially alone.

I heard the pop of a cork and the sound of wine being poured into glasses, so I made my way into the living room. Just as I sat down on her couch, she came in from the kitchen holding two glasses of red wine, her long hair draped down her chest, and handed me one. When she flopped down beside me, my veins buzzed with her nearness.

"Thank you, Andre," she started, her voice full of emotion, "for making this day—"

"National Gummy Worm Day," I interjected, keeping up with the silly ruse.

I didn't plan on the joke, but I knew Nora wouldn't have wanted to acknowledge her birthday when I'd knocked on her door this morning, so I came up with some lame bullshit on the spot as soon as she opened her door. And as truly lame as it was, I was thankful that it worked—at least well enough to throw a wrench in her plans of sending me right back home.

She smiled so wide her mouth nearly reached her ears, and it provoked an aching desire to coax even more out of her.

"Yes," she said, giggling as she shook her head, "National Gummy Worm Day. Thank you for making such an *important* holiday so special for me. I didn't expect anything like this to happen, and I know I was a terrible brat this morning, but . . ." She paused, the shine of tears cloaking her eyes despite the smile still on her face. "Today is just pretty hard for me in general—no offense to the gummy worms. I'm not sure which one of my friends sold me out to tell you about it, but I'm really thankful all the same."

My self-control was faltering as I reached out a hand to rest on her leg, just as I'd done on the Ferris wheel. I was finding the smallest of excuses to touch her. "You weren't a brat, Nora. Being emotional isn't a bad thing—you're entitled to your feelings."

She tilted her head as she considered my words, strands of her long hair falling against her cheek. I resisted the urge to touch her more, to move them away. I wondered if she knew how that golden hair had taken up residence in my daydreams. If she had any indication of how often I thought of her.

I took a long sip of the red wine. It was dry and strong—much better than the sweet shit my sister liked to drink. "This is good."

"Thank you. It's nothing fancy—I tend to like the seven-dollar bottles best."

"Hm." I watched as she took a sip from her own glass, my eyes tracing her movements as she swallowed and then licked her lips. My pulse spiked, sending blood flow straight to my dick.

I cleared my throat, ripping my gaze away from her face. "I uh . . . I like the furniture." I looked around the room, taking it all in as if I hadn't scrutinized it all already this morning while I waited for her to shower. "It's nice."

"Thanks. Most of it was on sale, actually. I lucked out."

"It's nicer than anything we have. Sela likes to find furniture at flea markets and yard sales." I smiled. "Old habits, I guess."

"Did you go to them a lot as kids?"

I nodded. "Yeah, our foster father—we called him El Viejo —he refused to ever buy anything new. He was old enough to be our grandfather, and he was cheap as hell. He taught us how to be frugal, though, how to make money last. It stuck.

"Sela and I have been saving like crazy for a while now. She wants to open her own restaurant—she loves cooking. Gloria taught her, actually." Nora smiled at the mention of the Margarita Queen. "Anyway . . . we're close to her dream, I think."

"Yeah?" Her tone held a dizzying level of excitement.

"Yeah. I mean . . . I think. Honestly, owning a business scares me to death, so I keep raising the savings goal. But it's been our dream for a long time—our finish line, as I like to think of it."

"Would you leave the shop, then?"

I hesitated. That was a hard question to answer. It was something that had been weighing on me for a long time. "I'm not sure. I love the shop and I love the team. I'd hate to leave it all behind, but Marisela is number one. I don't know anything about running a restaurant, but I'll learn whatever I need to if she needs me there. We haven't really talked about my role in it yet, other than my investing in it."

"Sounds like a pretty big decision to make for someone else."

Her words wrapped around my mind, brushing against an insecurity that I'd been trying to ignore. "It's my sister. After the life we've had, I'd do anything to help her make her dreams come true. Any sacrifice is worth her happiness."

She nodded, a polite smile curving from her lips, but it didn't hide the disappointment I could feel radiating from her. And I knew it was well-intended, but it wasn't something I wanted to argue about right now. I took another sip of the wine, searching for a subject change. "How's the bar?"

Her eyes lit up. "Really good, actually! It gets so busy sometimes that I feel like I can't think straight, and sometimes customers get a little rowdy, but it's such a fun high to work through. And the tips are *nice*."

I laughed, though my mind snagged on her words about rowdy customers. "Have you had any trouble with anyone?"

"Nothing I can't handle." She eyed me playfully, but still my blood simmered, gathering in my ears.

"Nora."

"Don't worry about me, Andre. While I appreciated your display of macho-protector my first night, I can handle myself. And Mara—she's pretty badass. Did you know she keeps a bat behind the bar?"

I closed my eyes, dropping my head. The thought of *anyone* disrespecting Nora made me fucking crazy. "Nora . . ."

I felt her hand on my arm, and I opened my eyes to find hers watching me, that playfulness still dancing in them. "Andre. I promise I'm safe there. Okay? Trust me. Working there . . . it makes me happy."

She knew the magic words that would force me to stand down. Her happiness was her finish line. I swallowed down the anger and frustration and blew out a breath. "Just—tell me if anything ever goes too far. Okay? I can be there really fucking fast if you ever need me."

Her mouth tugged up on the side and I wanted to press my thumb into her lip. She finished off her glass of wine and set it on the coffee table. "I'm exhausted. I think I'll get ready for bed, if that's okay."

I nodded. "Yeah, of course. I'll sleep out here—the couch will be a nice upgrade from the floor."

She smiled before standing up and walking toward her bedroom door. My eyes grazed down her legs, unable to resist the perfect curve of her calves. When she reached her door, she stopped, seeming to consider, then looked over her shoulder at me with a worried expression. "Just . . . sleep with me?" The words came out in a rush, her voice barely there. "I . . . I don't mean like *that*. I just . . . I don't want to be alone."

Her mouth pressed together as she waited for my response, hope and vulnerability swirling around her. And despite knowing it was a *terrible* fucking idea, despite knowing sleeping next to her in her bed would undoubtedly be the final shove off the ledge of no return, I knew she already had me. I was incapable of denying her.

"Okay." And then I nodded, my body tipping weightlessly into the abyss.

Chapter Twenty-Two

NORA

"Okay," he said, almost breathless. I didn't blame him; I was feeling a lack of oxygen myself.

Andre's eyes stayed firmly planted on mine as he set his wineglass down on the table and stood up, making his way toward me with a predatory grace. The hunger in his eyes had returned in full force.

A shudder gathered at the slope of my neck. When I asked him to stay the night, I hadn't at all meant for him to actually sleep with me, to invite him into my room, much less into my bed. But his presence was intoxicating, and I couldn't disentangle myself from it.

And, bottom line, I didn't want to be alone.

As he prowled toward me, I turned to push open my bedroom door, the lure of strong, tattooed hands on my skin making my breath catch. I hadn't made my bed this morning—the covers were hanging off the side, the sheets crumpled from where I'd tossed and turned the previous night.

I struggled to decide if I should turn my bedroom light on or keep it off. If I turned it on, it would feel like shining a beacon on what we were doing, giving us both more visibility as we inevitably settled in for bed. And then a thought lodged front and center in my mind—Andre didn't have anything to change into, and I didn't have anything to offer him.

Lights off, then. Better to keep some semblance of privacy.

God, was I selfish for asking him to stay with me tonight? I should tell him I was just kidding—I could still call the whole thing off, right? He probably only said yes to this dumpster fire of an idea because I was a sad girl who missed her mom.

I mean, what kind of girl asks a man to join her in bed for nothing but some casual, emotional co-dependency? It was probably his worst nightmare. He was way too cool and, well, *normal* for something like this.

But, then again, I'd seen the way he looked at me when I asked. I knew it wasn't pity that drove him to say yes.

"I'm going to brush my teeth and change into pajamas." I could feel Andre still behind me. "I have an extra toothbrush you can use . . . mine came in a pack of two."

I turned to find him nodding, his throat working as his eyes swept the room. "Sounds good." He sounded like he was swallowing rocks.

I grabbed a pair of pajamas—a full-length, heavy cotton pants and shirt set—and ducked into the en suite, softly shutting the door behind me.

Looking into the mirror, I allowed myself one deep breath before making quick work of changing and brushing my teeth. I tucked my clothes in the hamper that I kept in the bathroom and rinsed my mouth a second time with mouthwash.

Not that he'd be close enough to know what my mouth smelled like. Unless . . .

No, Nora.

Right. I gargled and spit out the bright blue liquid, then wiped my mouth on a towel and opened the door to step back into my room. Andre was sitting on the foot of the bed, his back straight and his body stiff as he stared at the floor. "All yours," I said, forcing the sound into my words.

His eyes flashed to me before quickly finding the floor again. "Great. Thank you." He stood, long form in tow and perfectly sculpted arms firmly at his sides as he turned toward the bathroom. His eyes flicked to me again when he passed by, taking in the pajamas I was wearing, and I swore I saw a flicker of amusement.

"What?" I asked.

"Nothing," he said, his tone an octave higher, and stepped into the bathroom, the door snicking shut behind him.

"The toothbrush is in the package on the counter!" I called from where I was frozen in place.

"Thanks," I heard him say.

I stared at the door for a full minute before I forced myself to the bed, crawling into the cool blankets and pulling the covers up high around me. I left plenty of room on the other side for him—it was a queen bed, just big enough for two people to sleep without touching each other.

It became apparent that the thick pajama set was a foolish mistake. It was the middle of summer, and though the air conditioning was on, I was already sweating. I normally slept in an oversized T-shirt and nothing underneath, but that wasn't an option. This was nothing more than a platonic, emotional-support sleepover.

That was acceptable, right? Mackenzie and I had done it all the time before I moved to L.A., after some asshole inevitably broke my heart or one of us had failed an important assignment in school. But Mackenzie wasn't a tall, tattooed heartthrob. So maybe it was different.

I heard the knob of the bathroom door twist and schooled my face into a casual, easy-going expression. When Andre stepped back into the room, I asked, "You good? Need anything else?"

He shook his head twice as his eyes traced the outline of my body under the comforter. "I, uh . . . I normally only sleep in boxers." He glanced down at himself, at the nice pair of shorts he'd worn today. Although they were baggy, they didn't look comfortable enough to sleep in.

"That's all right. Boxers are . . . *like* shorts. So it's not a big deal." I made a show of shrugging to emphasize how much it wasn't a big deal, but I doubt he noticed it under the covers.

His eyes rose to mine, narrowing slightly. As if looking for any indication of my discomfort. I hoped he couldn't hear how loud my blood was pounding through my body.

If he was suspicious, he didn't show it, moving instead through the dark to the far side of the bed. Facing the wall on the other side of the room, he unfastened his shorts, the zipper sounding off alarm bells inside of my head. And then, in one swift motion, he slid his shorts right down his legs, leaving behind a pair of blue-and-white plaid boxers.

The sight of the loose cotton around his dark, muscular thighs shouldn't have been erotic. But alas, here we were, and the fact that there was nothing more separating the cotton from the slopes and curves of his body surged through me, upping my blood pressure even more.

Andre sat on the bed, turning and sliding his legs into the covers.

"You're sleeping with your socks on?" I didn't even realize I'd asked the question out loud until he looked at me.

"Yeah, why?"

"Do you always sleep with your socks on?"

"No, not usually."

"Oh," I said. "Are you cold?"

"No."

I blinked. "Am I a threat to your feet?"

"Nora, bare feet is like the ultimate exposure."

"You're lying next to me in my bed in your *boxers*, and it's your feet you're worried about?"

Andre let out a grunt, and I couldn't help the wild, nervous giggle that escaped from my mouth.

"Go to sleep." His voice was laced with an irritation that only had me giggling harder. He turned to face me, his expression light. My laughter died in my throat, and for a handful of long moments we simply stared at each other.

Shadows caressed his face, his tattoos like dark whorls charting over the skin on his neck and chest and arms. The air around us grew thick as a fire ignited inside of me, a deep source of heat unfurling and warming me from the inside out.

"Thank you for staying with me," I whispered, watching his eyelashes dip with a blink. I wanted to feel one between my fingertips, to wish upon it.

He reached a hand out and traced a light, lazy trail down my cheek. "Thank you for giving me an excuse to be near you." I smiled, closing my eyes at his touch, relaxing deeper into my pillow. I felt goose bumps break out over my arms beneath the sheets as his fingers reached my chin, curving around my jaw and continuing down my neck. "Good night, *mariposa*."

His voice was like gauze, swathing me in the dark and bringing me comfort in a way I'd never felt before—certainly not from a man in my bed. I couldn't even find the motivation to open my eyes as I melted right into the sheets. "Good night, Andre," I managed, my entire body focused on the fingers still grazing up and down my neck and face.

It didn't take me long to fall asleep.

THE FIRST THING I came to consciously understand was how *hot* it was—as if I were lying inside of a sleeping bag on a lounge chair in the sun. There was a heavy weight across my body, pressing me deeper into the bed, and I wondered if I might be hungover again.

But no, I felt . . . clearheaded. Actually, I felt more rested than I had in weeks, my body thrumming with a renewed, electric energy. I shifted my hips, snuggling deeper into the soft bed, and felt something press firmly along my backside. Something hard and warm squeezed against me with a delightful pressure, a steadying, grounding force.

It was *moving*, a long rhythm of motion that felt a lot like . . . breathing.

Andre.

Along the fringes of my dreamy haze, I realized it was *Andre* pressed against me. A big warm spoon to my little one, his body bowed around mine. The awareness of him prickled along my skin as I took inventory of our positions. He was fully cuddling me, his heavy arm wrapped around my middle, holding me close to his chest. His face was somewhere in my hair, warm breaths skating along my neck as he breathed deeply, still very much asleep. Another quiet shift of my hips, and I could feel his strong thighs behind the curve of my ass.

But there was something else—something pressing into the small of my back that had my cheeks instantly heating.

He must have been on the verge of waking, too, because in my shifting I felt him flinch—his arm tightening around me as his hips tilted in a reflex, thrusting against me. The hard length at my back drove its way deeper into my spine.

We both completely stilled, neither of us daring to move. The room was quiet, nothing but the pounding of my heart between us. The right thing to do would be to disentangle myself from him as gently as I could so that we could both escape relatively unscathed. I could even pretend like I was still asleep.

That was really what I *should* do.

But instead, a burning curiosity had me shifting my hips again—the barest of movements, but enough to move my body further into him.

Andre groaned behind me, a low and throaty sound, as he again met me with his own lazy thrust.

I let out a slow breath.

Curving my back, I drove my ass deep into his thighs. I wanted to arch into his length, but we weren't quite positioned in the way I wanted to be, with that length between my legs where I could grind into it as I sought friction.

Andre's arm peeled away from the front of my body, and I was mortified that he was doing what I'd failed to do by removing himself from this dangerous game—but instead of pulling his arm completely away, he merely raised his hand to my chest, grazing his fingers down the front of my pajama shirt along the trail of small buttons, following them down between my breasts.

Fiercely regretting my choice of pajamas, I yearned for that touch along my bare skin. I wanted the feel of those roughened fingers on my softest places. His hand trailed all the way down to the hem of my shirt, hovering as if in question. I arched again, and felt his hips grind against me in response before he slipped his hand beneath the fabric of my shirt and dragged his fingers back up along my belly.

I gasped at the sensation, closing my eyes as I concentrated on those fingertips against my ribs. They rose higher and higher, this game becoming much more than innocent play. I was burning with a need for more—more of his touch, more of the delicious pressure of his body against mine, more of anything that would help to drive me toward the release that I was aching for.

As his fingers reached the curve beneath my breast, he began to tease me with his thumb, stroking against my ribs when he knew damn well that I wanted him *higher*. My nipples peaked, desperate for him.

Suddenly, his mouth pressed against the top of my shoulder at the neckline of my shirt. It was nothing more than lips on skin, but it was so unexpected and hot that I couldn't keep my head from tipping back and resting on his naked chest. Another groan escaped his mouth, reverberating into goose bumps that spread across my skin like wildfire.

His hand rose to fully cup my breast, and the feel of his large palm wrapped around me was unbelievable. His mouth skated up my neck, leaving an inferno in its wake, and I ground myself against him again, seeking the friction I so desperately needed. His breath fluttered along the shell of my ear as he whispered roughly, "Nora . . ."

And then, in a single fluid movement, he used the hand on my chest to press my shoulder down into the bed as he rotated himself on top of me, settling the weight of his hips between my thighs. Now that impressive length of his was positioned exactly where I wanted it, and as if he could read my thoughts, he curled a slow thrust right into me, his boxers and my pajama pants the only barriers stopping him from driving home.

His mouth found my neck again, and he pressed languorous kisses up my throat to the edge of my chin. Just as he was about to reach my mouth, just as I was about to devour him, a loud knock sounded at my front door.

We both stilled, near panting with the effort of our terrible, trembling resistance.

"Are you expecting someone?" he asked roughly, his thumb drawing small circles against my cheek.

"No," I whispered, wrapping my arms around his back. "Let's just ignore it."

He groaned, pressing his forehead against mine as he considered. A glazed look pierced me from his pretty gray eyes. But when the knocking sounded once more, I knew our heated game was over.

I wondered if someone was messing with me again, and I could tell he was anticipating the same thing as his eyes hardened. He shifted his weight off me and moved back to his side of the bed. I turned to look at him when he stood, my eyes locked on the bulge tenting his cotton boxers.

Instantly, my mouth went dry.

He hurriedly pulled his shorts back on and fastened the button, then strode toward the bedroom door and out into the living room.

I sighed, frustrated with the interruption and the incoming anxiety of how to navigate the *after* of what just happened. I reluctantly threw the covers off my legs and went to meet Andre at the front door.

He picked up the pipe and unlatched the deadbolt before swinging open the door with a menacing growl.

"Hey! Oh—I wasn't expecting *you*," Mackenzie said, holding a bag of food as her eyes skimmed along his bare chest.

Andre grunted in response.

"Mackenzie? What are you doing here?"

She put a hand on her hip, looking Andre up and down with a spark of gleeful interest in her eyes. "I should ask the same thing of your friend. Did you guys have another sleep-over?" Her eyes fell to the object in his hand hanging loosely at his side. "Oh my god, is that a *pipe*?"

"Okay, Mackenzie, it's like"—I cranked my head backward to find the digital clock on the microwave, squinting my eyes to read the blue numbers before turning back to face my friend—"seven thirty in the morning, and I don't remember making any plans with you today. So please, spill it. What are you doing here?"

I couldn't prevent the irritation from breaking loose, but if she only knew what she'd just interrupted . . .

A flash of hurt crossed over her features, and I instantly regretted the harshness of my words. "I just wanted to check on you—you know, after yesterday." She held the pastry bag up, as if in proof. "I brought doughnuts. For your birthday."

A huff of dramatic surprise sounded from the gorgeous

man next to me. "Why didn't you tell me it was your *birthday*?" Andre nudged my shoulder, and I rolled my eyes at him in response. He chuckled darkly, throwing me a devilish wink that nearly buckled my knees. He put the pipe down where it now belonged and grabbed his stuff from the countertop beside us. "I'll let you two have some time. Text me later?"

The last thing I wanted was for him to leave, but it *would* give me some time to figure out how to handle this morning's . . . activities . . . before we were forced to discuss it. "Yeah, okay," I rebounded as casually as I could, "that sounds good." I watched him step into the hallway, and then jolted from my trance. "Wait," I yelped, grabbing his arm, "your shirt."

He turned around, leaning in to press a quick kiss against my cheek before whispering, "Keep it."

Mackenzie took his place inside the apartment, joining me as I watched him walk away. "That is one good-looking motherfucker," she whispered.

I didn't even bother to lasso the giggle that released from me.

Chapter Twenty-Three

ANDRE

As it turned out, Nora was right. Logan had been expecting a conversation about time off for the upcoming wedding, and had already made a plan for coverage for the shop. Manny, he explained, would take charge, with Ernesto providing backup as needed. Manny was a bit of a goof, but he took his job as seriously as I did. I knew he'd step up for this opportunity.

I was shocked that Logan approved the time off so easily, but he'd grumbled something about making Amelia happy under his breath and I knew it was a battle that didn't actually have anything to do with me. I was just the lucky bastard who benefited.

Of course, the benefit didn't come without its share of guilt. I'd been busting my ass at Logan's shop for years, working hard to earn trust in my leadership from him and from the team. I was Logan's right hand, and when he was out, I was in charge. For both of us to be out—and for four days—it worried me that I might be failing Logan in wanting to do this for Nora.

But I *did* want to do this for Nora. There was no doubt that I would do just about anything for that girl. Ever since the other morning in her bed, I'd been grappling with the wicked and dangerous thoughts plaguing my mind. The feel of her body against mine, of her soft and delicate skin beneath my hands, and the breathy sounds she made when I teased her with my fingertips—it was my undoing. I'd never been so invested in something like that before.

Usually, with girls, I was just in it for the sex. To burn off some steam and chase a quick release. I'd had a handful of girlfriends here and there over the years, but I never really understood the appeal of a long-term relationship. Most recently, with Leticia, I'd been unable to give her everything she wanted—a proposal and a happily ever after. Things quickly got out of hand when she realized I wasn't as committed as she was, and she started some weird, territorial bullshit that had me ending things pretty quickly.

But Nora . . . it was like my entire heart was made for her. Like she was changing the very composition of my DNA to make my body respond to her so wholly. I was constantly thinking about her, constantly worried about her, and I didn't know what to make of it.

I hadn't heard much from her since the other morning— only exchanging a few sporadic texts to make plans for today's drive to Breckenridge—so as I turned my Mustang into her parking lot and found her waiting for me on the curb, it was like my chest expanded with its first full breath in three days.

She was wearing a pale pink sundress that flowed around her legs in the breeze, her golden hair trailing down her back in a long braid. Three bags were at her feet—everything she'd need for both Breckenridge and the wedding in Wyoming after —and the sight of them, the proof that this days-long trip was *actually* happening and that I would be with Nora through it all . . . it sent my heart pounding in my chest.

I parked and jumped out to help with her bags. "You should have waited for me—I would have carried all of this down for you," I said, reaching for the straps to pull them into my trunk.

"I know, but I had it," she responded, her sweet voice momentarily distracting me. "Good morning."

I grinned. "Good morning." Dropping her bags into the trunk next to mine, I closed the hatch and moved to open her door. Just as she was about to step in, my eyes locked on the butterfly tattoo just above her elbow and I caught her arm. "Pretty," I murmured, tracing the mostly healed lines with my thumb.

My eyes moved to her face, where I found the brightest, most blinding smile I'd ever seen. It was like an arrow being shot at me—a bull's-eye to my heart. Releasing her arm, I watched as she tucked herself into the black leather seat. After settling into my own and reaching for my seat belt, I was a bit nervous to look at her. "We're still meeting at Mackenzie's house, right?"

"Yeah," she replied. "Logan, Amelia, Adam, and Rachel are all meeting us there.

I nodded, shifting the car into gear before taking off. It took us about twenty minutes to get to the quaint neighborhood where Mackenzie and Eric lived. Seeing the house triggered the memory of carrying Nora into it after that late night at Jackson's. She pushed out a breath as I parked, and I wondered if she was thinking of that night, too.

Logan's Bronco was already parked along the curb, and I saw him and Adam leaned against it as their women huddled around Mackenzie in the center of the lawn. Nora and I got out of the Mustang, and at the sound of our car doors closing, Adam turned his head to see us.

"Well, if it isn't Andre joining us on this adventure!" he quipped. He was wearing old Vans and a T-shirt that looked like it'd been pressed.

I smiled a hello, turning to Logan beside him and giving him a nod as well. "Hey, boss. Hey, Adam. What's good?"

Adam waved a hand at the group of girls, which now included Nora. "Oh, we're just waiting while they compare notes on what they packed to make sure no one forgot anything."

Logan shook his head, one hand coming up to flip his worn Rockies hat around. "Amelia packed her entire closet. I don't know how she could have possibly missed anything."

Adam chuckled. "See, that's why I found a woman who's a *smart* packer. Rachel only has one bag. I brought more than she did."

Logan turned to him. "That's because you're the biggest diva of them all."

Adam punched him in the arm. "Am *not*."

A gray form stirred inside Logan's Bronco, crashing from the back seat to the front and whimpering, its wet snout pressed through the open gap of the partially rolled-down window.

Logan turned back to face his dog—a three-legged pitbull named Hook that had made frequent visits to the shop over the years—and in a firm voice commanded, "Hook, sit." The whining stopped as his snout disappeared from the window. "Good boy."

Eric made his way down the driveway after loading his car with his and Mackenzie's bags. "You boys ready for this?"

Adam nodded eagerly. "Yeah, dude, we're going to have a blast and send you and Mack into marriage with a *bang*." He slapped Eric on the shoulder for emphasis. "Well, you two will send yourselves off with a bang, I guess, but you know what I mean . . ."

Eric laughed as the girls headed toward us. I couldn't help but study Nora's smiling face—her brown eyes almost golden in the sun, little laugh lines already etching around her mouth. She looked happy. And I knew somewhere in that smile that my being here was part of it. The thought almost drove me out of my mind.

She nudged her arm against mine when she reached me. "You're awfully quiet this morning, mister. You okay?"

I leaned in and grinned, keeping my voice low. "I'm good. Just taking it all in, *mariposa*." She smiled wider.

"All right, everyone. Listen up," Amelia called out, getting everyone's attention. "We're all going to stick together on the drive out so that no one gets lost—Logan will take the lead, and Eric and Andre can follow him. It's only an hour and a half from here, so we should get there by ten thirty.

"I hope you all are ready for the next two days. A lot of planning went into this little pre-wedding bash, so get excited for some fun and games as we celebrate the last two days of single life for two of our best friends!"

Everyone whooped and cheered, and I found myself *really* taking it all in. I'd never experienced anything like this—a group of friends who vacationed together, the closeness they all shared. It was cool to witness, but I felt a little like a fish out of water. No one I knew would ever plan a two-day party like this. We just got together and drank beer until everyone more or less tapped out or passed out.

"All right," Logan said, pushing off his Bronco. "Let's go."

I waited for Nora to say her goodbyes to the other women—I had to squash my desire to laugh, we were literally all going to the same place—and then led her back to the Mustang. In a spur-of-the-moment decision, I asked, "You okay if I take the top down?"

Her eyes flashed. "*Yes*!"

I laughed as I unfastened the fabric top from the frame, pulling the entire thing back. She sat comfortably in her seat, pulling a pair of sunglasses out of her purse. "Ready?" I asked as I got in next to her.

"Yep."

I nodded toward Logan who was watching us from his rearview, and we all set off.

THE HOUSE—IF you could call it that—was nestled in the mountains of Breckenridge. It sat on a foothill, large evergreen trees spread out all around it. The exterior was all dark wooden planks and cobblestone pillars, and tall windows made up most of the walls. I could only imagine the view from the inside.

"Damn," Nora whispered beside me. She'd never been here before, either.

"Yeah." I nodded. "This is a nice place." I pulled into the long driveway behind Eric and Logan. With the top down, the smell of pine needles and fresh, mossy air was all around us. Everyone got out of their respective cars, and the same mirrored look of wonder could be seen all around. I looked at Nora, whose loose strands were spilling this way and that from her braid, and said, "I'll grab our bags, okay?"

She pivoted in my direction, smoothing her hair behind her ears. "I can help!"

I shook my head. "Nah, I got it. Go ahead, I'll meet you up there." I watched her hesitate for a moment before she nodded and began the hike up the gravel driveway.

As soon as I had all the bags in hand, I started my own climb. I only made it five or six steps before I heard Logan call down, "Shit—Andre, incoming!" I looked up and found Hook barreling down the driveway with as much power as his three legs could muster. I planted my feet firmly in the ground and prepared to take on the impact of his body, and sure enough, he plummeted right into my shins.

I chuckled. "Hey, *tonto*, you causing problems already?" Hook let out a single, celebratory bark. Grinning, I tilted my chin. "*Vamos.*"

Hook followed me up to the front walkway where the group was gathered before prancing back to Logan, satisfied. Adam unlocked the massive front door and opened it wide to let everyone in.

Amelia's voice sounded over the group. "We'll get everyone to their rooms so we can get settled in. Adam will give a little tour after for those who haven't been here yet." She motioned for Nora, Mackenzie, Eric, and me to follow her up the stairs. On the second floor, Amelia showed Eric and Mackenzie to their room first, and we watched them disappear into their doorway. When we stopped a little farther down the hall, Amelia turned around.

"I wasn't sure if you guys would want a room together or separate, but there's two rooms down the hall." She pointed between the two doors that stood opposite each other at the very end. "There's also a bathroom down there on the left. Let me know if you need anything?"

Nora nodded. "Yeah, this is great, Amelia. The house is gorgeous. Thank you."

"Yeah, it's great to be here—thank you," I added, once again feeling like a fish gasping for air. I was still wearing my shoes, for fuck's sake, and this didn't seem like the kind of home you wore shoes in. *Dammit.* Marisela would've had my ass for something like that. I looked down, seeing that both Amelia and Nora were still wearing their shoes, and breathed a small sigh out through my nose.

I looked up again and caught Amelia throwing Nora a sneaky wink before turning on her heel and heading back down the stairs. Nora turned to face me as if nothing'd happened, and I gave her a knowing look.

She cleared her throat. "You can totally have your own room," she said with a breezy tone. "Take whichever one you'd like."

I adjusted the straps on my shoulder, feeling a sharpness clang in my chest that she'd elected for separate rooms—even though I knew that feeling was bullshit. Nora didn't owe me anything, especially not here on a vacation with a bunch of her friends. We still hadn't even talked about the other morning, so who was to say it wasn't just a one-time moment of weakness? I shook my head. "No, I'm not picking. You pick where you sleep."

I saw the slightest flinch in her eyes, though she kept her face neutral. "Okay." She let out a breath, folding her hair behind her ears again. "I'll take the one on the right."

"You sure? You didn't even look."

She nodded. "Yeah, it doesn't matter what it looks like. I'm sure they're both nice."

I searched her eyes for clues, for a way to read this right. I didn't like that flinch, and I wondered if I'd been too blunt with my response.

Before I could find the words to ease her mind, she spoke again. "Look, I know we haven't talked about the other morning. And I don't want to put any pressure on either of us by putting us in a room together. But that doesn't mean I don't *want* a room together—"

"Nora," I cut in gently. "Don't worry about it. The other morning was . . . unexpected. But this isn't the place to hash any of it out. This is about you and your friends and this wedding. Just focus on having fun and enjoy your time with them. We can talk shit through when we get back home. There's no pressure here, okay?"

She stared at me, eyebrows furrowed and deep lines etching her forehead. Like she wasn't sure how to take my words. But then she nodded and wiped the expression, her big brown eyes calm and trusting. "Okay."

Chapter Twenty-Four

NORA

I couldn't shake the feeling that I might have offended Andre by suggesting we sleep in separate rooms. Although he said he was supportive of it, the disappointment in his eyes was hard to miss, the glittering gray I'd come to know so well dulling in seconds. I meant what I said . . . it wasn't at all that I didn't *want* it. I actually couldn't think of a better way to start and end each day of this vacation than having his large body curled around mine, the weight of his arm around my middle like a heated security blanket. But I knew my nosy friends, and while their inevitable harassment would be innocent and well-intended, the last thing I wanted was for Andre to feel like a circus animal.

Whatever was going on between us—it didn't feel like something to joke about, and I didn't want to open it up for scrutiny like that. Luckily, by the time we'd put our stuff down in our respective rooms and met back downstairs for Adam's tour, Andre looked like he was back to his usual untroubled and easygoing self.

During the tour of the house, I'd made the mistake of breathing next to him. He smelled incredible, like spice and sin and bad decisions, and it made me dizzy as I tried to listen to Adam's long-winded description of the basement and all its finery. I tried to focus, to *listen* to what Adam was saying, but by the time the tour was over, I'd barely heard a word of it.

Back on the main landing of the house, the tour group met the others in the kitchen, where a large CONGRATULA-TIONS ERIC & MACKENZIE sign hung along the wall. A big bouquet of fresh flowers served as the centerpiece on the kitchen island, and Amelia was working on setting out an assortment of snacks. Logan was emptying cases of beer into the fridge while Rachel cut a sheet of what looked like fresh-baked brownies. She looked up at us as we all came in and said, "I will warn you all right now, these brownies are not for the faint of heart."

Adam moved around the island toward his girlfriend with a gleam in his eye, kissing her on the cheek when he reached her. "These, my friends," he said, turning to where Andre, Macken-zie, Eric, and I stood, "are my famous Magic Brownies."

Beside me, Andre laughed softly. "Magic brownies? As in . . . ?"

Adam nodded mischievously. "Yes, my tattooed brother from another mother—pot brownies."

"*What*?!" Mackenzie chirped from where she stood next to Eric, who'd moved to help Logan with the beer but was now intently focused on Adam, too.

"Oh, yes." Amelia looked up from the sliced cheese and salami she was laying out and shot a look at Adam. "My brother has been working on perfecting his little *magic* recipe for a while now."

"Isn't it, like, illegal for a doctor to get high?"

Adam feigned confusion. "Weed is legal in Colorado, for *all* its wonderful citizens."

Mackenzie and Amelia caught each other's eyes, Amelia's widening as if to telepathically communicate, *He can't be stopped*. Mackenzie burst out in a giggle. "This is already the best vacation ever."

Adam looked pleased. Logan closed the fridge and shook his head.

"It's not even noon yet," Eric chimed in from his place beside Mackenzie, pointing to the casserole dish filled with chocolate drugs. "Are we eating those now?"

We. I hadn't been high since college, back when I was still dating random frat boys in two- or three-month spurts and joints were passed around in backyard parties like they were candy.

Before my mother had gotten sick.

I looked around the room, wondering what everyone else thought of this. It should feel irresponsible . . . Adam was a neurosurgeon, for goodness' sake.

And yet, I was thrilled.

Turning to look at Andre, I found a similar excitement in his smoky eyes, as well as a question meant for me: *Should we?*

He'd be taking my lead with this, then. Asking myself my new favorite question—*Does this make me happy?*—I shrugged in response to him, as if to say *Why not?*

He smirked, turning to look back at Adam. "I didn't know you had it in you, Doc."

Adam placed his hand over his heart, his face filled with an absurd pride. "Is this the moment I become 'cool' . . . to *Andre*?"

Everyone burst out laughing. Rachel tucked herself under Adam's arm, like she couldn't get enough of his humor. "In all seriousness"—Adam looked around the room—"we're just about due to start our first big adventure of this little vacay—it was the one thing Amelia let Logan and me plan. And I'm gonna be honest—we fucking nailed it."

Amelia made a show of rolling her eyes from where she was setting out hummus and vegetables.

"So take a little breather," Adam continued, "have a little snack, because you're going to need it. And if you're feeling up to it, please enjoy one of my magic brownies. You all have thirty minutes before you're expected in the backyard with sneakers and game faces on. Any questions?"

"Sneakers?" Eric asked. "Are you asking us to get high before we exercise?"

"Yeah, wait, what are we doing outside, exactly?" Mackenzie narrowed her eyes.

"Just trust me, okay?" Adam's eyes danced." It's gonna be a blast. Logan—" His head turned to where Logan was leaning against the kitchen wall with his arms crossed over his chest. "Let's go set up."

Logan followed him out the back door, and everyone stood silently around the kitchen, staring at the now-plated pile of magic brownies.

"Fuck it," Eric said, grabbing one off the counter. We all watched as he shoved the chocolate square into his mouth and chewed.

"Babe, aren't you supposed to, like, eat a bite at a time?"

"Yeah." Amelia laughed. "You don't even know how much is in there."

Rachel spoke up, a smile wide on her face. "They're not *that* strong. Although—I didn't actually witness Adam making these ones, so I'm also not liable if I'm wrong."

"I don't think anyone can be *liable* for a group of grown-ass adults choosing to eat magic brownies," Amelia countered.

"Good point." Rachel nodded.

"Just eat a brownie, honey. Come on, we're celebrating." Eric's persuasion worked, because not a moment later, Mackenzie picked up her own square and ate it.

"We have a dinner reservation later tonight, but it's not until seven. So that gives us eight hours to get sober," Amelia stated matter-of-factly before she, too, shoved a piece of brownie in her mouth.

That just left Rachel, Andre, and me. Briefly glancing at Andre, I saw traces of amusement in his otherwise neutral expression. He looked at me and raised his eyebrow as if in a dare. So I pinched a chocolate square and, after a brief moment of examining it, put it into my mouth.

It was actually, all things considered, a very good brownie. There was something a bit earthy about it, but I never would have guessed it to be weed. It was sweet and gooey and practically melted in my mouth as I chewed—I wanted another one, though I knew that would be a bad idea. I looked back at Andre, throwing him a dare of my own. He, too, silently picked up a square and ate it.

A HALF HOUR LATER, no one felt anything.

Rachel abstained from partaking, saying that it would make her feel better to stay sober "just in case"—which, honestly, made me feel better, too. Adam and Logan set up whatever they needed for our upcoming game, and then returned to the house to eat squares of their own. The whole group now stood around the kitchen island, nibbling on the snacks Amelia had set out, waiting for *something* to kick in.

"I think your recipe wasn't strong enough," Eric said before stuffing a cheese-and-salami cracker in his mouth.

"Dude," Adam retorted, "trust me. They work just fine."

Eventually, we threw on our sneakers and ambled out to the backyard. Gathered on the lush green lawn, Logan and Adam took their places at the head of the group to issue instructions. I heard the words "woods" and "laser tag" before I felt Andre move to stand close to me, his arm brushing against mine.

Suddenly, all I could think about was that arm, about the tattoos that covered it. About what he looked like shirtless, climbing on top of me in my bed, his muscles moving underneath hot skin.

All sense of reality around me went out the window when he leaned his head down low and whispered in my ear, "I guess that makes us partners, then?" His breath curled around my neck just like it had the other morning, and I shivered at the memory.

"Hm?" I asked, my knees practically wobbling.

"For laser tag."

I stared blankly at him. "What?"

He looked at me like I was growing another head before Adam's voice finally penetrated through my thick skull. "The laser guns are in colored pairs, and each pair is spread out around the property—which is essentially a quarter mile around the house in every direction. You and your partner have to first find your guns and then hunt everyone else down." Eric whistled in excitement. "We'll wear vests that read the laser lights from the guns, so if you get a kill-shot to the back or chest, the light on your vest will turn red. The last pair with a team member still standing wins."

Logan moved around the group to hand out black Velcro vests to everyone. Mackenzie held hers up and examined it. "This tag says for ages six and up."

Adam's mouth curved up into a charming smile. "Good thing that includes you, buttercup." He swept a firm look at everyone. "Please, nobody get hurt out there. I just ate two squares—your doctor is about to be on the fucking moon."

Amelia snorted.

Logan made it to where Andre and I stood, and Andre reached out to take two vests from him. He tucked one between his knees and unfastened the Velcro straps on the second one, reaching to place it over my head. He gently slid the thick, nylon material around my ears and down to my neck, then pulled the straps on the sides to fasten me in, his fingers brushing against my ribs over my dress. I watched the curve of an eyebrow raise as he pulled his hands back and asked, "Is that too tight?"

I shook my head, struggling to find the voice that was caught in my throat.

He threw me a sly grin and pulled his own vest over his head.

When everyone was strapped in, we migrated toward the edge of the clearing in the backyard, where giant spruce and fir trees touched the sky. Andre stepped to my side, leaning down so that his mouth skated along the tip of my ear. "You ready?" he asked, his voice a dangerous whisper.

I nodded, but then urgency tracked down my spine. "Wait—what do we do?"

A loud clap sounded from somewhere to my left, and Andre's voice slithered through me. "*Run*."

And it was *then* that I felt it.

Chapter Twenty-Five

ANDRE

Nora took off at the speed of light, sprinting right into the trees. The hem of her pink cotton dress whipped left and right as she moved, exposing the steep slope of her calves that always made me a little bit crazy.

I followed closely behind her, keeping with her pace and trying really hard to pry my eyes away from the hypnotic movement of her dress and legs so that I could look for any signs of the hidden laser guns around us. The vest strapped to my body was way too tight, clearly meant for bodies half my size and age, but I had to admit—the thrill of a game like this was undeniable.

Mostly because it meant Nora and I would be alone together as we hunted for the others.

Logan and Amelia had taken off somewhere to the right of us, and Eric and Mackenzie were somewhere on our left. I didn't see where Adam and Rachel had gone, although Rachel hadn't opted for sneakers and by the looks of her strappy sandals, I couldn't imagine they were headed anywhere fast. Apparently, Adam hadn't clued her in on the right shoes needed for this week's adventures. I found it highly unlikely that he had clued *anyone* in—it was pure luck that the rest of us had something decent enough to work with.

As Nora veered off to the right to avoid a thick cluster of trees, I saw a sudden flash of orange to my left. "Nora," I breathed out, already winded—the air was much thinner up in these mountains.

She halted, spinning to look back at me with a huge smile on her face. "Andre!" The way she said my name . . . it was like she'd forgotten I was behind her.

I chuckled—it seemed the brownie was kicking in. "I think I found something," I said, nodding to the left.

Her eyes trailed to where I'd indicated and widened in delight. "Oh, yes!" She flounced to where two orange laser guns were tucked haphazardly beneath some shrubs and pulled them out. She held them both up, one in each hand, with a wicked light in her eyes. "Would the gentleman care to go hunting with the lady?"

Grinning, I took a gun from her, reaching out to tug on the braid that hung down the front of her chest. She giggled, and it was the best sound in the world.

"I feel like I'm floating," she whispered.

"Yeah," I said, lost somewhere in the brown of her eyes. "I do, too."

We decided to take our chances by heading right to look for Logan and Amelia. Our steps were careful on the forest floor as we did our best to avoid making too much noise. Which was an effort continuously compromised by Nora's giggling.

"Could you imagine?" she turned around to ask me.

"Imagine what?"

"Being assassins."

I looked up at the sun winking down through the foliage, at the canopy of leaves casting a kaleidoscope of green. And I wondered, for a moment, how I'd gotten here. How my life had shifted so radically that I was scampering around the mountains with a beautiful girl and a couple of toy guns. It was like my life was . . . changed. New.

And I was scared to death of going back.

"You'd be a terrible assassin," I said.

She scoffed, straightening and turning around to face me. "Excuse me?!"

"Okay, I'm sorry"—I threw my hands up in the air—"you'd make a great assassin. The *noisiest* assassin to ever live, but it could work for you."

She nodded once. "Thank you very much." She stepped into the sunlight, and golden flecks infused her eyes. "You're probably a real assassin."

I smiled, but the question was like a poison dart. If she only knew the things I'd seen, the pain and sorrow of a life in the streets. I didn't want her to ever know a single thing about that. She was too good. Too pure. She shifted her weight back to lean on the tree behind her, pulling her bottom lip between her teeth as she looked up at me. My eyes fell to her mouth and my mind went blank.

I reached out to tug on her braid again, feeling the soft plaits lighting up the nerve endings in my hands, in my face, and I swore I could even feel it across the scar tissue on my heart. "Give me one honest truth," she breathed out, calling to mind the question I'd asked her on the Ferris wheel.

I felt dizzy. Spinning and weightless, like I'd just jumped

from a cloud and was aiming right for her. I wanted to wrap myself around her and never let her go. "You"—I leaned in, dusting my nose against hers—"are sexy as hell, Nora."

I felt her breath hitch, a lapse in all movement. A pause in time. And then a shaky exhale that warmed my cheek.

God, I wanted to bury my heart inside of her, to give it to her for safekeeping. She could have it forever. It was already hers.

I'd already tasted her mouth, her neck, the soft lobe of her ear—but it wasn't enough. It would never be enough. I was greedy for all of her. Every gorgeous limb. Every inch of skin. I needed to know the depth of every groove. To know how soft her stomach would feel beneath my tongue. I wanted to brand her with my teeth.

Clearing my throat, I tried like hell to clear my mind. Tried to stay focused on my feet rooted to the ground. The pine-scented air in my lungs. But my mind was on a loop, like a scratch on an old CD, stuck on her her her her *her*.

My *mariposa*.

"Do you think the others are on to us?"

I didn't know whether she meant the game or the way my heart pounded in my throat when I was close to her like this. I pulled my face away from hers and found her looking at me with adoration in her eyes, like I was . . . was something to look at that way. I was nobody. I did nothing to deserve that look. "Nah," I replied, my voice low. "You're too good of an assassin."

"You said I was noisy."

"Yeah, but in a good way."

Her eyes flicked down to my mouth. "I could be, I think. With you."

My mind spun faster. "What do you mean, Nora?"

She swallowed, and I wanted to taste it. Allowing myself only millimeters at a time—so slowly that I convinced myself I wasn't really moving at all because I swore I wouldn't be the one to make a move—I pushed my mouth down, seeking hers. Feeling the faintest brush of her lips against mine, a whisper of a kiss. Only barely there. Like if you didn't look just right, or just in time, you wouldn't have seen it. Wouldn't have known.

When I pulled back, she kicked herself off of the tree with the sole of her muddied sneaker, chasing my mouth with hers. But I didn't let her catch me. "Nora," I hissed, gripping her hip to hold her in place, "I won't be able to control myself—"

The crunch of sticks and dried leaves somewhere in the distance pierced through the haze, and I let out a frustrated breath. Frustrated with all this goddamn *want*. Nora blinked and sighed, like she felt the frustration, too. But this wasn't the place, especially not after the brownies.

Magic. Maybe it did exist.

If and when we finally did this, though, I swore I'd make it good for her. I'd make up for all of this need and longing for the both of us, that was for damn sure.

She nodded and took a step backward, sidestepping the orange gun lying at her feet that she must've dropped at some point. I reached down to pick it up for her, and heard what sounded like a bomb detonating through a little speaker inside my vest.

"HA! Got ya!" Eric's eyes were manic as he tumbled through the brush. He swiftly looked at Nora and pointed a lime green gun at her chest, the same bomb going off within her.

Her face crumpled. "Dammit."

I couldn't help the laugh that spilled out of me.

The cracking of branches underfoot sounded and Mackenzie appeared from behind a tree twenty feet away. "Did you get 'em, babe?" she called out.

Eric looked back at his bride-to-be. "Shot 'em down like pheasants!"

Mackenzie gingerly tiptoed through the copse of trees, quiet as a mouse even though we'd already been had. She looked at Nora's scrunched-up face and loosed out a maniacal laugh. "Nor, I am *so* fucking high."

Nora's face morphed into pure joy, her eyes flicking to me for just a heartbeat before moving back to her friend. "I think I'm *literally* a kite."

Something solid stirred within my bones—a sharp realization that I could spend the rest of my life finding ways to make Nora smile like that. *Would*, in fact. Happily. I'd draw those beaming smiles out of her every chance I got. Every single day, no matter the effort required.

It would be worth it.

"Come on, I lost Logan about ten minutes ago somewhere over that hill. Let's go get the smug bastard."

"I think you're taking this a little too seriously, honey." Mackenzie rolled her eyes.

Eric shushed her and prowled forward, sweat gleaming on his forehead.

Nora tucked her arm into Mackenzie's and they watched him move, together. "He's a much better assassin than me."

Mackenzie chortled. "Please don't tell him that."

We followed Eric as he hunted Logan, eventually finding him and Amelia sitting along the edge of a creek. She was in his lap and they were making out like horny teenagers, Logan's

Rockies hat on Amelia's head. I averted my eyes. I guess there was just something about being high in the woods that made a man want to imprint on his lady.

When he heard us, Logan maneuvered Amelia off of him and dodged Eric's laser assault. After a minute-long standoff, Logan got the kill shot on Eric's back with his blue gun just as Eric bolted for cover behind a tree.

Amelia jumped into Logan's arms, kissing him aggressively. "You're so hot."

Logan chuckled. "Amelia, behave."

He set her back down and we meandered back toward the house. "Has anyone seen Adam or Rachel?" Logan asked, looking around. As if he'd only just remembered his best friend.

"No, but Rachel's got him. She didn't partake in the magic."

Mackenzie started intently at a tree. "What a shame."

Logan looked between both women, and then turned his gaze to me in question. I shrugged, smiling. "They're flying."

Hilarity flickered in his face. "Dude, your eyes are barely open. You're flying, too."

I felt my eyebrows scrunch together as Nora giggled, pulling her arm out of Mackenzie's and moving to stand beside me. She looked up at me, her eyes full of wonder. She smelled so good—how did she do that? "Fly with me?"

I wrapped an arm around her and gently pushed us forward, continuing in the direction of the house. "Always."

It was only a few minutes before we were back in the clearing, finding Adam lying on his back in the middle of the lawn. He wasn't wearing a shirt, and his shoes were discarded around him. His tiny black vest was strapped tightly around his bare chest and his arms and legs were splayed out around him. He looked like a fallen soldier, as if he'd been shot for real.

"Is he okay?" Logan called out to where Rachel was sitting on a patio chair, reading a book.

Rachel put her book down and smiled at us. "Yeah, he's fine. He's a little tuckered out from all his wizarding. Didn't even make it out of the backyard."

Logan nodded, as if that made sense.

I laughed, dumbfounded. It hit me again, clear as day, that I'd never, in my entire life, been a part of anything like this.

Suddenly, in a move so abrupt it took me a solid five seconds to realize what was even happening, Mackenzie jumped in front of all of us, turning to face Logan and Amelia with a wild look in her eyes. She shot her laser gun at both of their chests, detonating the same, faraway bomb in both of them. "Aha! Fuckers!" she exclaimed.

Logan stared at her blankly. "What?"

Mackenzie stood proud. "You never got me! You only got Eric!"

Eric's eyes went wide as he stepped forward. "You've been a live enemy to them this whole time?"

Mackenzie winked at him. "Yeah, babe."

Nora gaped. "Holy shit. You're the *real* assassin."

Amelia scoffed. Mackenzie looked smug as she turned on her heel, walked up to Adam with her gun pointed at where he lay on the ground, and shot him like a goddamn warrior.

Chapter Twenty-Six

NORA

It took almost the entire afternoon for the high of Adam's brownies to subside. After we made it back to the house, the group worked together to move the snacks outside to the backyard patio table—though it was a pretty uncoordinated and chaotic transfer, as we were still overstimulated and distracted from all the magic.

Adam laid out in the lawn for hours, basking in the sun like a cold-blooded desert lizard. But he eventually rose and migrated over to the rest of the group, his face swollen with sleep and the sheen of a fresh sunburn on his skin. He tucked himself into a chair next to Rachel, who put an arm around him and snuggled in.

Eric continued to burst with pride about Mackenzie's sneaky killer prowess during our laser tag game while Logan and Amelia touched each other very obviously under the table. There was an undeniable contentment amongst us, a lazy comfort that was only built through years-long friendship. I'd missed this so much that it made my heart ache thinking about all the time I'd missed out on while in L.A. Everyone who mattered most to me was right here at this table.

Except Andre.

Andre had spent the majority of the afternoon shut up in his room, and the longer he stayed in there, the more anxious I felt about his absence. It wasn't like me to be this emotionally bound to another person—as if he'd become my center of gravity—but I'd also never felt a connection like this before. It was both thrilling and daunting to know he had this type of power over me.

It didn't take me long to realize that Andre was . . . *different* with a group of people around him—especially people he didn't know well. Not that I expected him to be animated or outgoing on this vacation—and to be fair, it was only the first day. But I was used to having him all to myself, spending time alone with him, and this change in his demeanor felt like a shifting of the tides. I felt caught up in that shift as I tripped harder into this swarm of feelings for him.

Maybe it was just hard to be so close to him without the freedom of expressing all of these feelings. If today in the woods was any indication, Andre was feeling them too.

I won't be able to control myself.

God, I hadn't wanted him to. I'd wanted to feel his trembling hands as they pulled me in closer, to feel his mouth on me in all of my favorite places, to settle these nerves that were wound so tightly around him.

If I were to peel back the layers of this thing between us, I'd find at the core a man who is good and solid, a real friend, and a hell of a support system. But I'd begun to allow myself to fantasize what it would be like to have both: the man who was my friend *and* the man who twisted my insides into a beautiful mess of sparkling anticipation.

As the sun dipped lower in the sky, I decided to head back inside to get ready for our evening out. Excusing myself from the others, I walked toward the house, still feeling like I was floating as I moved my limbs. Like the world beneath me was as soft as cotton candy and if I didn't find something to hold on to, I might drift away.

Those damn brownies.

I opened the back door and stepped inside the house, and —to my delight—found Andre grabbing a soda out of the fridge. When he turned around and found me standing there, all of those delicious and familiar signs of joy flooded to his face, and I realized that I had absolutely nothing to worry about.

This man was solid in the way he grounded me.

As I moved toward him, my eyes caught on the way that his glittered, the way his mouth crawled up at the corners as he watched me move closer. He gave me a look that I knew was made just for me—just like the one in the woods. And it was a gift to know that these moments were ours. That there was even an *ours* to exist.

I moved until I was standing right in front of him, looking up into those swirls of sparkling gray. From this angle, the light of the sun through the kitchen window cast a shadow across the side of his face. He set the soda down on the counter, and just looked at me.

"What?" I asked with a shaky breath.

"Nothing," he said softly. But he didn't look away, and it didn't feel like nothing.

There was a dark flicker of hunger in his gaze, just as there had been earlier when he'd pressed me up against that tree. I could almost still feel the bite of the bark against the back of my arm.

He must have felt it too, because he took a quiet step toward me, until he was standing so close to me that our bodies nearly touched. And it felt like a relief, to be this close to him. Even my lungs produced an audible exhale—which caught his attention, his eyes moving to my mouth at the sound. The smoky gray of them seemed to be alive, moving like the morning mist after a heavy night of rain.

I wanted to dive right into that mist. Wanted to be consumed by him.

As if he could read my thoughts, he reached a hand up to slide one calloused finger along my jaw, sending a violent shiver down my spine. His eyes were dark as they looked into mine. That finger made a second sweep across my jaw, and this time his thumb ran down the column of my throat, until his palm lightly rested between my heart and my collarbone. He held it there, as if in claiming.

"Nora." It was barely more than a whisper. Laughter boomed from the backyard, the baritone of Adam's voice seeping through the walls of this house. A reminder that we weren't alone.

"I thought you were avoiding me," I breathed, instantly regretting the words. Regretting the vulnerability and desperation of them. I didn't want to look like a desperate fool. Not to him.

A deep line etched between his brows.

Suddenly, the back door opened, and Amelia's voice filled the air. "Oh . . . sorry . . ."

Andre's hand dropped from my chest as he took a firm step

backward. I turned to my friend, seeing the flash of surprise across her face as she looked back and forth between us. I cleared my throat, straightening my posture.

"We've got to leave in a half hour to make it to dinner on time," was all she said before she moved again, retreating up the stairs. I could see through the windows that the others were making their way inside, too.

I gave Andre a soft smile before I turned to head up those stairs, myself.

Thirty minutes later, the group split into two cars for the drive to dinner. Rachel drove Logan's Bronco, and Andre—who insisted that his afternoon nap overcame any lingering high—drove Eric's car, since it had a back seat that was roomier than his Mustang. After we'd parked and the group got out, Andre caught my arm and held me back.

"Nora," he said, keeping his voice low so that only I could hear, "what you said earlier, about me avoiding you . . . I'm not."

"You're not?"

"No. I'm not."

"Okay," I husked. "You just . . . you felt so far away from me, after the woods."

He reached a hand out to tuck a strand of hair behind my ear, briefly holding my chin between his finger and thumb before dropping his arm back to his side. "It's really hard to be so close to you in front of the others. I don't know how to act. How to hold back from touching you. But I'm not avoiding you. I'm not going anywhere. No matter what, remember?"

I stared at him for a long moment, my eyes drifting from the slight flush on his cheeks to the pulsing artery pumping along the curve of his neck. My own pulse tripped as my eyes darted further down to the broad slope of his shoulder, to the obscene bulge of his bicep despite the lankiness of his arms. "Why?" I asked, forcing my eyes back up to his.

He seemed to assess me with the same pull that was so familiar to me, his eyes drifting somewhere near my mouth, my neck. "You know why," he answered. His voice was pure grit, and it ignited such a riot in my chest that I may have gasped.

His eyes darkened to hazy storms for just the smallest of moments before he cleared his throat and nodded his head toward the rest of the group, who were now stalling to wait for us. "Come on."

I followed him into the restaurant, my heart pounding hard in my chest.

LATER, after a perfect evening out with everyone I loved—my heart so full of gratitude and contentment filling me to the brim—we made it back home and decided to head to bed. Everyone agreed to get a good night's rest for the actual pre-wedding bash set to take place at the house the next day.

Andre followed me up the stairs, and an electric energy zipped down my spine. We took quiet steps to the end of the hallway we shared, and when there was nowhere else to go but to our own rooms, we turned to look at each other.

As my eyes traced the features of his face, there was nothing significant occurring between us, nothing to grab a hold of besides the rhythm of his chest rising and falling, the way his eyes danced in the light of the wall sconce that hung next to his head. It was just another moment . . . another heated moment that looked like so many others between us.

Except, this was the first time I fully dove in, the first time I really let myself feel it.

I want you.

And I did. I wanted him badly.

Not just in the physical ways, although the memory of his mouth setting a path along my neck was like a tangle of silly string in my heart, unleashing me from the inside out. But I wanted him in all the intangible ways, too. I wanted to be who he thought of when something good happened. Or even something bad. I wanted to sooth his sharp edges, quiet his nerves. To be who lit the fire inside of his chest, the way he lit mine. I wanted to have him in every way that I could. In every way that he would let me.

My tongue felt thick in my mouth, heavy with all the things I wanted to say. But instead, I held back, settling on, "Good night, Andre."

The right corner of his mouth lifted, cutting out a dimple that made me feel dizzy. I wanted to push my finger into it. My tongue. "Good night, Nora," he rasped, flipping off the hallway light as he still looked at me.

He waited until I was inside my room, door swinging shut, before he turned around toward his.

At the last second, I changed my mind and flung my door open wide. "Wait—"

His door opened too, his face twisted in question.

I want you.

I love *you.*

Does this make me happy?

The hell with it.

I stalked toward him, mesmerized by the dark charcoal of his eyes in the unlit hallway. I didn't hesitate as I pressed my mouth up to his, catching his gasp in my mouth, making it my own.

It was a delicate slow dance of a kiss, warm and soft and comfortable—all of the things that he was. So different from the first time I'd kissed him. It was a gentle dance that I was leading until I felt his warm palm press against my waist, sliding to my back, pressing me closer to him. When his other hand moved to cradle my cheek, he took the lead with his tongue sweeping along my bottom lip in torment.

In all, it only lasted ten seconds. Fifteen tops.

But it was enough to cement what I already knew.

"I want you," I said on an exhale as our lips parted. It felt like a relief. It's one thing to say something like that with your hands, with your mouth. But it's quite another to say it with your heart.

His eyes flashed before they darkened even more, as if the shadows of the night were converging within him. "Nora . . ." he started.

Before he could say anything else, I pressed another chaste kiss to his lips, catching on his cupid's bow with the swift movement, and turned around to walk back to my room. I shut the door softly behind me, the phantom brush of his lips still whispering on my skin.

Chapter Twenty-Seven

ANDRE

I HARDLY SLEPT. MY MIND RACED ALL NIGHT AS I replayed Nora's words over and over again.

I want you.

I couldn't stop myself from imagining her curled up next to me, her warmth spreading across this bed like sunlight. To feel her, to breathe her in with every breath. To chase her in my dreams. But she was all the way across the hall, where she'd shut herself in for the night.

The morning I'd woken up in her bed had been fucking incredible. To feel the way her body responded to my touch was as close to heaven as I imagined I'd ever get.

But last night Nora finally admitted that she wanted me. The words were an echo of the thought that replayed in my head over and over again, every single day. Because fuck if I didn't want her too. And now that I had real, solid permission —it was like my body was on fire and I couldn't settle myself down.

I was out of my damn mind for her.

The chains buried deep inside of me that had been holding my feelings captive finally broke, and as those desires rose to the surface in a maddening fury, they hit me stronger than anticipated. The truth of them knocked me sideways.

I *loved* this girl, and for the first time in my entire dejected life, I felt like I could *be* somebody. Like I could be somebody for *her*. And so, I had to find a way to tell her, to make sure she knew that I was all in, if that was what she wanted. I was prepared to give her everything. All of me. I wasn't sure if this vacation was the right time to give her that type of proclamation—but as soon as we got home, I'd take her out on a real date, and I'd tell her everything in my heart. I'd lay it all out there and pray like hell that she wouldn't run from all my jagged pieces.

When the light of the morning smothered over me from the bedroom window, I got out of bed and quietly made my way to the bathroom to shower and get ready for the day. After dressing comfortably, I headed downstairs to the kitchen and found Nora already there, eating a bowl of berries at the island with Rachel.

Her hair was thrown up like a halo of golden light over her head. She wore a yellow pajama set with little pink hearts that made my chest flip. I watched her as she popped a strawberry in her mouth, the red fruit against her rosy lips driving elicit thoughts through my mind. It was almost unbelievable, to *feel* so damn much from simply looking at her.

When a stair step creaked under my weight, she looked up, and a soft, knowing smile marked her face. "Good morning," she said, her voice warm and soft. There was no trace of anxiety

—nothing hinting at regret over what she shared last night—and my want for her ran right over me again.

"Morning," I said, giving Rachel a small nod as well.

Rachel looked between Nora and I and smiled. "Nora was just telling me about her new tattoo—that you took her to your shop to get it?"

I grinned, the memory of that day flaring. "Yeah"—my gaze moved to Nora—"she was great. Took it like a real champ."

Nora's eyes were stuck on mine for a moment, before she looked down at her breakfast. Rachel continued, "I've always wanted one, but I don't think I could handle it. My pain tolerance is like, zero."

"It's not so bad," Nora said, looking back up at me, her brown eyes shining brightly. "You could handle it."

"Good morning!" Amelia sang from the top of the stairs. Logan stood close behind her, wearing bright blue pajama pants. "Is anyone else up, yet?"

I descended the rest of the stairs and planted myself next to Nora, reaching into her bowl for a blackberry and tossing it into my mouth. She smirked as she watched me chew it.

Rachel shook her head. "No, Adam is still sleeping and I haven't seen Eric or Mackenzie yet."

Amelia pulled a stool out from under the island and sat down. "Okay, good—I want to run through the plans for the day before they come down. We have more games planned, but they're a little more traditional bachelor/bachelorette-type games."

"Ohhhhh do we have penis straws?" Rachel's excitement was bursting out of her. I looked at Logan and raised my eyebrows.

"Are you kidding me? We most *definitely* have penis straws," Amelia assured her.

Logan looked back at me and sheepishly knocked his shoulders up in a shrug.

If the guys at the shop knew just how whipped Logan was for his girl, they'd have his ass on a damn platter. But it was obvious how much he loved her . . . and I was beginning to understand the hold of something like that.

I grinned, trying like hell to hold in my laughter. He narrowed his eyes at me.

THE DAY KEPT everyone busy as Amelia worked hard to celebrate her friends' love story. There were, in fact, a plethora of penis straws in everybody's faces. Even though Nora and I didn't find ourselves alone together once, she kept herself close to me. And it was . . . *nice* . . . to orbit around each other with a vision of what the future could possibly hold for us, without spending so much effort trying to shove it all down.

Nothing felt forced, which was something I was used to feeling in my past relationships. Women always wanted so much more than I was able to give, and it wasn't that I was against monogamy or vulnerability or commitment—I'd just never understood *how* to give more. But now I could see the markings beginning to define themselves. It helped to be surrounded by so many great examples of what real love looked like, because I wasn't sure that I'd ever actually seen it before this group of friends.

That evening, we all sat around the large dining room table to eat a brisket that Logan had been slow-cooking all day. We'd be heading out early in the morning to Wyoming where the wedding would be held tomorrow evening—but that didn't stop the drinks from flowing. Luckily, those magic brownies made no further appearances.

After we'd all eaten, Amelia stood up from her seat and tapped the side of her wineglass with a butter knife, causing all conversations around the table to stop. I felt Nora's arm brush against mine as she turned in her seat to face her, effectively raising the hair on my skin.

Amelia's eyes landed on Mackenzie. "I just wanted to take a moment while we're still here—while it's still just us—to say how proud I am of you, Mackenzie." Mackenzie brought a hand to her own chest, caught off guard by the impromptu speech. "I will never forget a conversation we had during a sleepover at your house in high school, when I asked you how you knew that Eric was worth the trouble." Eric chuckled, shaking his head in jest. "Even all those years ago, I could see the shift. I could see the change in you, and it was because you found him.

"We were so young, and I had no idea how you could have possibly known a thing about true love. But despite the inexperience, I could feel how real it was between you both. You were like magnets, fastening yourselves to each other with no regard for caution. And I'm so thankful I was there to witness it all, because you both taught *me* a lot about love.

"You taught me that when you really love someone, you want to make the world a different place for them—not to sweep over or distract from the ugly side of things, but to make room for it, to ease some of the burden by carrying it together."

Amelia looked to Logan now, her eyes shining with emotion. "You taught me that love is resilient, and that it gives *meaning* to the ugly side, turning it into something beautiful. That you can have the power can change each other's whole world.

"That's what love is, I think. The expanse of one heart, to make room for two. You both gave the rest of us such a great example of what that looks like, and I'm really, really thankful for that.

"So, I know we'll get to the big, celebratory speeches during the wedding, but this one is just to say thank you for leading us. For going first. We all love you so much, and we can't wait to see you conquer the world together." She raised her wineglass and reached to the center of the table, meeting everyone else's drinks. "Cheers to real love!"

Mackenzie took a sip of her champagne and then swiped a finger under her eye. "Dammit, Millie. Give a girl a warning."

Rachel beamed. "Yeah, Millie's out for the heartstrings, tonight!"

"Chordae tendineae," Adam corrected.

Rachel's eyes snapped to him, confusion on her face. "What?"

"It's the scientific term for heartstrings," he replied, matter-of-factly.

Rachel rolled her eyes while Logan snorted. "Dude."

Adam deadpanned. "What?"

Logan stared back at him. "You're killing a good moment with your nerdiness."

"More like neediness," Amelia countered, and Rachel burst out in a giggle.

Adam rolled his eyes and took a drink of his whiskey.

I felt Nora glance at me briefly before looking back toward

the rest of the group, and I couldn't help myself as I reached under the table to wrap a hand around her leg. To anchor myself to her. And I felt her go still at my touch. She smiled into her wineglass before she reached down and placed her hand on top of mine.

And I'd never felt more filled with pride.

Chapter Twenty-Eight

NORA

THE DAY OF MACKENZIE'S WEDDING WAS FLAT-OUT from the moment we got to Eric's family property. The bridal party had been given access to a large wing of rooms as the property was being set up for both the ceremony and reception. Mackenzie, Amelia, Rachel, and I—along with Eric's sister, Melissa, and Mackenzie's mother—had all been set up in various stations around the room for hair, makeup, and manicure services that were provided by the glam consultants Mackenzie had hired.

Two bottles of champagne sat in an ice bucket on a table in the center of the room upon our arrival, and they were both empty within an hour. The third bottle—brought in by an event staffer after Mackenzie asked her mother to hunt one down—lasted a bit longer. We knew it would be in bad taste to get the bride drunk before the wedding even started. Though, as I looked at myself in the full-length mirror, eyes sweeping along the shimmering, gold-beaded dress that hugged my body like a warm embrace, I could feel the edges of my own vision beginning to blur.

"Hey, Mack." I turned to look at Mackenzie, watching as the hair stylist coated her beautiful arrangement of curls in hair spray.

Mackenzie's eyes bounced to mine through the mirror in front of her. "Hey, Nora." She giggled, even more of an indication that the third bottle was probably overdoing it.

"I'm going to sneak out and get some water bottles for everyone. I'll be right back."

She nodded. "*Great* idea. Thank you."

As I left the room and made my way down the hallway, I could hear the murmurs of conversation from the front of the big house. We were half an hour out from when the ceremony was due to begin, so guests were starting to arrive at the grounds. I paused mid-step, looking down at my dress. What were the rules about a bridesmaid being seen before a ceremony? I didn't think it was as big of a deal as the bride being seen. I decided to seek forgiveness later if this was a mistake—we had a bridal suite full of women who needed serious hydration.

I rounded the corner into the lobby and found it almost full of people. My eyes quickly scanned the room, wondering if Andre was here already. Sure enough, it was easy to spot him standing near the open bar at the edge of the lobby, a full head taller than everyone else in the space. Goose bumps scattered over me and I began to move in his direction.

As I got closer to him, I noticed he was making polite conversation with a petite redheaded woman whose bright blue eyes were obviously enjoying the dark and handsome man in front of her. I watched as a flirtatious laugh spilled out of her perfectly painted red lips, her hand reaching up to touch his arm. Andre gave her a small—albeit, stiff—smile before his eyes moved up and, seemingly on instinct alone, found mine.

He went completely still as he looked me up and down, taking in the dress that hugged my curves in a way that I knew flattered me. A true smile pulled his lips up, and I watched as he excused himself from his conversation with the woman without even taking his eyes off me. My gaze was stuck on his as he closed the distance between us, looking incredible in an all-black suit. I had no idea where he'd picked up something so sharp, so clearly tailored.

It felt as if the whole world slowed down, like he was moving toward me in slow motion. There was only me, standing in front of him in my golden dress, feeling more alive and vulnerable than I ever had in my entire life. And him, the column of his throat working as he swallowed, his fingers flexing at his side, as if in restraint from reaching.

"She was pretty," I threw out breezily as he approached, giving him a wry grin.

He tilted his head as his gray eyes pierced mine. "I didn't notice," he said. And then I watched those broodingly sexy eyes make a second sweep down my body. "You look incredible, Nora."

I felt the rush of blood to my cheeks. "You look amazing too. Nice suit."

"Thank you." His throat bobbed, and my eyes caught on the skull in the center of his neck, peeking out from the top of his onyx dress shirt, hawk wings spreading wide on either side to reach behind his ears. The juxtaposition of such a stunning, clean-cut suit against his tattooed skin riled something deep in my bones.

"Sorry that you're here alone right now . . . I actually don't even think I'm supposed to be out here yet, but I need to grab the girls some water and I saw you over here. I couldn't resist saying hi." His wide smile curled even higher.

We'd gotten to Wyoming this morning, and almost as soon as the car was parked out front, the women and men of our group split up. Andre wasn't a groomsman, but he'd been pulled into the groom's suites by the rest of the men, just as Rachel had been pulled in with us despite her not being a bridesmaid.

I'd been missing him all day.

He must have decided to come out here and mingle, probably an attempt to give Eric and the groomsmen some space, to politely recuse himself from their hospitality. "You don't have to worry about me out here, *mariposa*. Go do your thing, and I'll see you after the ceremony."

"Okay." I nodded, smiling. "Yeah, that sounds great." It was refreshing not to feel the pressure of any sort of expectation. That I didn't need to mold myself around my date—even if I *wanted* to. "Thank you. I'll find you after."

"Already looking forward to it, pretty girl." His eyes twinkled as he threw me a wicked grin. "Now go on. Go be there for your friend."

Pretty girl. It was what he'd called me that first night at Jackson's. I accidentally stumbled backward as I moved to walk away from him . . . I couldn't quite turn myself around, couldn't quite unlock my gaze from his. I felt a breathless chuckle float out of me, aware that I was making his effect on me really damn obvious.

I finally pulled myself together and forced my gaze in the

other direction, forced my feet to take the necessary steps toward the kitchen.

After grabbing a handful of water bottles from the catering company, I returned to the suite and found Amelia making final adjustments to Mackenzie's veil. Mackenzie's mom, Ruth, was helping her slip into her heels, and Melissa was taking pictures on her phone of her soon-to-be sister-in-law. Rachel had tucked herself into a chair in the corner, snapping pictures of the whole scene on her own phone.

Mackenzie looked absolutely stunning—the most beautiful bride I'd ever seen.

Amelia's eyes turned to me as I entered. "Oh good, you're back . . . the photographer wants to get some more pictures of us now that we all look like bangin' movie stars."

I set the bottles down in the ice bucket that no longer held champagne. "Sounds great."

THE CEREMONY WAS ABSOLUTELY BEAUTIFUL. It took place outside, in the large and luscious backyard. Tears spilled out of Eric's eyes the second he saw his bride for the first time, walking down the aisle to the moment that would cement their relationship together forever. The sight of his raw emotion made my chest squeeze. It made me realize that, had I said yes to Parker's proposal, I had serious doubts he would have ever looked at me like that.

I'd been escorted down the aisle by Eric's youngest brother, who was still in high school and a full twelve inches shorter than me—but it did nothing to dampen my mood. The love and magic in the air was palpable, like I could wave out a hand and feel it slipping through my fingers. After the ceremony was over, the bridal party was whisked away for pictures while other guests made their way to refresh their drinks and find their name cards in the sea of white tables on the other side of the property. I caught Andre's eyes in the crowd for the briefest of moments before we were shuttled away, throwing him a quick, apologetic look.

Near a colorful garden in the front of the house, it felt like hundreds of pictures were taken of the bridal party, and I was growing impatient with each click of the camera. The need to be back with Andre was unyielding—it was all I could focus on as I smiled until my cheeks felt like they might fall right off of my face.

Eventually, the photographer announced that we'd gotten all the poses and pairings that Mackenzie and Eric had outlined for her, so we were released to join everyone else out back. *Finally*, I could find that handsome date of mine and spend the rest of the evening next to him. We'd hadn't had any alone time together since telling him I wanted him two nights ago, and now I was aching to have him all to myself, to see what my admission might mean for us.

As I walked back through the house and toward the backyard, I began scanning the tables through the windows for Andre. Amelia came up beside me, the sleeve of her dress brushing along my arm. "Looking for our table?"

"Are we sitting together?"

"Duh." She rolled her eyes with a smile, pulling her arm through mine as she led me out to a table near the stage. It was right next to the sweetheart table where Mackenzie and Eric would eat together. The photographer had released the groomsmen first, so Logan and Adam were already seated at the table. Logan stood as we approached to pull Amelia's chair out for her. But my eyes moved to Andre, who'd been seated next to Logan, and I watched as he, too, rose to greet us.

All of the men looked utterly dashing tonight, but while the groomsmen had worn a traditional, crisp white shirt, Andre's black shirt gave him a certain edge of danger that had my blood thrumming. In the light of the setting sun, the sight of those dark tattoos made my final steps toward him a bit . . . unsteady.

Adam and Rachel were seated on the other side of the chair that Amelia was now taking, and I was thrilled to see Gwen seated at the table as well. Mackenzie and I had met Gwen in college—she was a TA in a handful of our classes. She was two or three years older and had mentored us through a few of our courses, though things had quickly turned into an easy friend-ship. As anxious as I was to get to Andre, I took a moment to give her a warm hug and introduce myself to her date, Sean.

When I finally made it to where Andre stood, he grinned down at me, his gray eyes looking more silver against his dark clothing. "There she is," he murmured.

I swallowed. "Thanks for waiting for me." I sat down in the chair he held out for me. "Are you enjoying yourself?"

He nodded, scooting me forward into the table. "Yeah, yeah of course. Thank you."

Amelia's voice flitted from next to Logan. "What have Nora and I missed?"

We soon learned that we hadn't missed much. Adam was thrilled there was an open bar and Gwen and Sean had been catching up with the rest of the table. As the conversation rolled on, we were served an incredible meal of orange-soy glazed scallops, roasted chicken with rice and fresh apricot, and a deliciously creamy vegetable risotto.

As the best man and maid of honor, Eric's oldest brother and Amelia, respectively, took turns giving speeches that left the whole reception in tears, and Mackenzie and Eric shared a gorgeous first dance together to "Beyond" by Leon Bridges. The live band on stage packed a punch in the energy department, and it wasn't long before everyone at the table got up to join the happy couple on the dance floor.

Andre and I hung back while I enjoyed a second helping of the risotto. I hadn't eaten all day, and the food was incredible. Andre didn't seem to mind, sitting beside me patiently while I scarfed it down. But as soon as I was done and had pushed my plate out in front of me, he leaned in to speak over the music.

"Are we going to sit at this table all night, Nora, or are we going to bust some moves out there?"

His question caught me off guard. "You want to dance?" For some reason, I'd figured that he wouldn't be up for it.

The small lines around his eyes crinkled as a wide grin spread across his face. "Are you kidding me? With you looking as good as you do—I would be a fool not to show you off to all these people." He leaned even closer and lowered his voice. "I have *the* sexiest date in the entire damn wedding."

I felt a flush crawl up my neck as I stared back at him. Andre had a way of flirting that could be so honest—so *bold*—that the confidence wrapped around it all was almost blinding. He chuckled at my lack of response, then scooted his chair back and stood up. He took a single step toward me so that his legs brushed against mine, the fabric of his pants lightly grazing the beads of my dress, and looked down at me with an easy smile.

"Nora," he said, his voice like velvet, "would you please make me the luckiest man here tonight?" He held his hand out between us. "Come on, dance with me."

The flush in my neck spread up to my cheeks as I placed my hand into his. He kept hold of my hand the entire way to the dance floor, his warm fingers curling around mine with gentle pressure. My eyes locked on where our hands were joined between us—mine, small and slender inside of his, large and tattooed. The sight of it snapped something that had been pulled taut, loosening the desire that was coiling within my belly.

We stepped onto the wooden dance floor and Andre turned to face me, pulling me in close. I took a deep breath to steady myself through the rush of our proximity, but in the process, I inhaled his scent of clean soap and spice and almost stumbled.

The band's music had slowed, morphing into a sweet melody, and Andre didn't hesitate for a moment as he led us into a comfortable rhythm. I pulled my hand from his to wrap both arms around his neck and heard the hum of his approval rumble between us.

"You know," I said, looking up at him, "you can't be the luckiest man here tonight."

His eyes narrowed. "Oh? Why's that?"

My shoulders lifted in an easy shrug. "It's a wedding. And you're not the groom."

The corner of his mouth twitched. "I said what I said, Nora. And I meant it." He spun me in a graceful turn. Where had he learned to dance like this? "I really do love this dress," he murmured as he brought me in close again, his breath dancing across my neck. I felt the weight of his gaze as he looked down at the shimmering material, skimming my waist with the tips of his fingers.

His touch ignited a frenzy inside of my heart. I wanted to match his honesty with my own—and what better time than now? "When I put it on this morning," I whispered a bit breathlessly, "I found myself hoping . . ." I closed my eyes, trying to concentrate on my words as his fingers painted goose bumps along my arm. My tongue felt foreign in my mouth.

"Hm? What did you hope for, Nora?" His voice was gravely and full of sin. The rough sound of it, the warmth of his body so close to mine, that intoxicating smell of his . . . I wanted to sink my teeth into him.

I opened my eyes and looked up at the dark fan of his long lashes as he continued to gaze down at my dress. He was *everywhere*—I could feel him all over me, enveloping me. "I was hoping you would be the one to take it off," I finally said.

His hand stilled as his gaze jumped up to mine. His eyes flashed before they darkened, flicking down to my lips. "*Nora.*" I felt the palm of his hand press firmly against my waist. "Don't tease me with something like that."

My eyes caught on his mouth as his tongue swiped along his bottom lip. *God* I wanted to kiss that lip. "I'm not teasing."

His eyes danced as his gaze locked in on mine. I watched his throat work beneath the collar of his shirt, and felt the overwhelming urge to loosen his tie. To expose more of his neck. His voice brought my focus back to his mouth. "Do you remember what you asked me that night at Jackson's?"

Of *course* I remembered—I remembered how embarrassed I was the next day for trying to get him to go into the bathroom with me. Heat rose to my cheeks again at the memory. "Yes."

He reached his hand to tilt my chin up, and my eyes found

his. They were dark and stormy, smoky with heat. "Ask me again." I stopped breathing. Anticipation clawed at my belly as my blood sizzled throughout every shaky limb. His eyes blazed as they commanded me. When I said nothing, he spoke again. "Don't play with me, *mariposa*. Ask me again." His tone was firmer. His voice, rougher.

I swallowed. "Do you . . ." I started to ask, feeling the grip on my chin tighten as his eyes watched my mouth say the words. "Do you want to meet me in the bathroom?"

The finger he had on my chin moved to press on my bottom lip, and a small gasp escaped from me. "Good girl," he whispered in my ear, then planted a featherlight kiss to my temple. He sounded pleased, and the effect of his praise sent a burning jolt of electricity straight to my core. The hand he had on my waist was warm as his thumb stroked twice along the small of my back. "There's a bathroom down the first hallway to the right. Meet me there in five minutes."

He stared at me for another long, heavy moment before he smirked and pulled away. I watched him walk toward the doors that led inside the house, looking comfortable and at ease with his hands in his pockets. And I felt like I was on *fire*.

Chapter Twenty-Nine

NORA

OH MY *GOD*.

Mackenzie and Eric's friends and family whirled around me in a joyous haze before I realized that I needed to get off the dance floor. I forced my body to move, finding myself back at our table where Adam and Rachel were both sitting. There was a sheen of sweat along Adam's forehead and Rachel was fanning her flushed face with the name card that had been used to designate her seat. Adam's eyes lifted up to me as I approached, and he shook his head. "Rachel and I needed a drink break from dancing." His tone was so serious and matter-of-fact that it almost made me laugh.

"I think I need a drink break, myself," I muttered instead as I picked up my wineglass and took a long sip. My mind was spinning like a top on a freshly waxed floor. Andre was literally waiting for me inside of the bathroom to . . . *do things* with me in the middle of this wedding, and I was a bumbling mix of so-turned-on and so-damn-nervous that I almost couldn't see straight.

"Where's Andre?" Adam asked, looking behind me, as if he could somehow read my mind.

"Hm?" I said, tripping right over the question.

Adam grinned. "Did you hide Andre somewhere?"

My eyes widened. "No!" I almost shouted. Adam's face notably transitioned to surprise, and I quickly added, "He just went to use the bathroom."

"Ah." Adam nodded, eyes slightly narrowed. "I see."

"I'll be right back," I said rather abruptly, placing the now-empty wineglass down on the table. I looked over to Rachel, finding her totally unfazed by this conversation as she continued to fan herself. *Good.* My eyes flicked once more to Adam's mildly confused expression before I turned on my heel and bounded away.

Smooth, Nora.

Thankfully, I made it inside without running into anyone else. I shot a look behind me to see if anyone was watching, and then darted down the darkened hallway to the right. Most of the doors were cracked open, but the one at the very end was shut tight. It must have been the bathroom where Andre was waiting.

I pushed open the door to find a *very* clean and elegant bathroom, though it wasn't particularly spacious. A deep sink plunged in the middle of a long marble counter, and a shelving unit hung from the opposite wall. Andre's form was leaning against that counter, his shoulder brushing up against a wall that rose three-quarters of the way to the ceiling, hiding a toilet on the other side. His hands were still tucked in his pockets, his stance casual and unassuming. His eyes were his only tell, the only indication of the wickedness he had planned.

I felt the weight of his smoldering gaze while I shut the door softly behind me, and then my eyes locked with his as I turned the deadbolt. The clicking of the lock as it slid into place was the only sound between us, even the thumping music from the reception out back was only a mere echo. I leaned against the door, mesmerized by the beautiful man in front of me. A predator, hungry for his prey.

There was something about the way Andre snapped into burning focus when he was aroused that sent me reeling. As my friend, he pushed me to be selfish, to do things that made *me* happy, reinforcing new habits of standing up for what I wanted in life. But in these heated, stolen moments, he had this delicious ability to both exert control and dominance while still giving me what he knew would make me happy.

Somewhere along the way, he'd learned enough about me to know what I wanted, to know how my body ticked. He *knew* me, and it was thrilling. Because as I looked up at him now, his eyes black with desire as they bore into my own, I trusted whatever he had planned.

He pulled one hand out of its pocket and moved to unbutton his suit jacket as he pushed off and took steady steps toward me. I momentarily lost the ability to breathe, like there wasn't enough air in the room for the both of us. His tattooed fingers easily unfastened the button, and my eyes caught on the letters inked on each finger, the word *LOVE* staring back at me.

Indeed.

After what felt like an eternity, he made it to where I stood at the door, our bodies almost flush. He didn't say a word as he lifted that same hand to my face, grazing the pads of his fingers along my jaw. A soft touch with a rough edge.

If it wasn't for his breathing, he would have appeared calm. Completely in control. As if something like this was routine for him, a typical Saturday night, picking up girls from bars and clubs all over the city. But his chest rose and fell at a pace that almost matched mine, and I knew for certain he was affected by this just as much as I was.

The fingers that traced my jaw moved down to my throat. I felt his warm hand slide down my skin, and it was possessive, the way his hand covered my entire neck.

He leaned his face in to press a soft kiss to my forehead, and it sent a shiver right through me. Anticipation hung heavy around us, and Andre used it to his advantage. Already, he was making me absolutely ache for him.

"Nora," he murmured as his lips moved to brush lightly along my neck, his other hand grazing the outside of my thigh. I realized, somewhat distantly, that he was inching the material of my dress up.

"Hm?" I couldn't focus on anything except his hands—now both of them—trailing up my legs, lifting my dress higher and higher as his eyes burned into mine.

"Can you be a good girl and stay quiet?" His voice was so low that the vibrations from his words reached a place deep inside of me, a place where I was desperate for him. I could feel the tension snapping between us, but his control was sure and steady. He was sin and lust and wild cries, and with just a few light touches, I was already on the verge of imploding.

"Yes," I whispered.

A dark chuckle rumbled from his chest. "Are you sure?"

I felt a chill on my leg, and my mind was torn away from

the hazy pull of his voice as I realized he'd lifted the material of my dress all the way up to my thighs. I looked down to see that he was fisting the fabric as his other hand traveled along the skin of my bare legs.

I couldn't help but shudder as his hand rose higher on the inside of my thigh. He hadn't even so much as kissed me yet and I was already melting into the floor before him. "Yes," I whispered again, more urgently this time. "Please."

His eyes snapped to mine at that word, and I watched as they went completely black.

Before I knew it, his free arm snaked around my waist to turn us both around so I was now facing away from the mirror behind the sink, and he crowded me until the backs of my thighs hit the counter. He lifted me to sit on the counter, and his hands began a feverish exploration of my legs. My dress was hiked so far up around my waist that my entire bottom half was exposed.

His eyes blazed as he watched me intake a sharp breath, and I realized how much I loved this version of him, this man who took control. Who liked to hear me beg. This Andre was different from the kind and gentle friend I'd grown so close to these last few weeks. *This* man was wound tight, and his precision and restraint—his desire to dominate—was unbelievably erotic.

When his fingers skimmed high enough to reach the fabric of my underwear, I couldn't help but gasp again, throwing my head back against the mirror behind me. His eyes were on my face, enjoying the reactions he was luring out of me. "You like that, *mariposa*? You like when I touch you"—his hand cupped possessively between my legs—"here?"

I moaned, and he leaned in to cover the sound with his

mouth. The kiss was feral, his tongue darting against mine as his fingers stroked between my legs over the material of my underwear. The ache was so intense I almost couldn't bear it. I wrapped my arms around his neck to hold on to him, to pull him in closer, and I felt him smile against my mouth.

"Andre," I whispered against his lips.

"I'm right here, baby," he rumbled as he kissed my jaw.

"This . . . makes me happy."

He stood tall between my legs as his hand continued to stroke me. His mouth consumed mine with an urgency that had me reeling, his tongue sweeping along my bottom lip, tasting me. When he pulled away, his beautiful, silver eyes bore into mine. "This makes me really happy too, Nora." I smiled before his mouth was on mine once more, his fingers moving my underwear to the side and stroking me again along my bare skin. He hissed. "I can feel how much you want this, pretty girl." And then, without warning, he plunged two fingers in deep.

I wanted to cry out, but Andre anticipated my reaction and covered my mouth again with his, smothering any sounds from me as his fingers moved in and out with such delicious force that I saw stars.

Chapter Thirty

ANDRE

I was an uncaged animal, brutally desperate to bring out more of Nora's gasps, more of her moans. We'd been playing this cat and mouse game for the last few days, making daring moves in moments where we knew we couldn't yet see them through—but her words on the dance floor, the *clear* indication that she wanted this tonight, that she'd visualized me taking off this very dress—it was my complete undoing.

The sounds that came out of her were breathtaking. Almost as breathtaking as the pink on her cheeks as she looked down to watch my fingers disappear inside her body. She was radiant. A fucking goddess. I wanted to immortalize the sight of her like this, how chaotically beautiful and vulnerable she was. I wanted to brand her into my soul.

The strain in my pants was almost unbearable. Her effect on me was brand-new. No other woman had ever made me feel like this. Not a single one.

She let out another muffled moan as her head fell backward

against the mirror. Her eyes closed as she sucked in a breath, and I could tell she was close to coming unraveled. "Good girl," I murmured softly as I leaned in to kiss her neck. "Come for me, Nora." My voice was thick as my mouth traveled along the column of her throat . . . I was so turned on by her. Too turned on by her.

She opened her brown eyes and locked them on mine as her breathing became erratic. Then she clutched the back of my neck with both hands and rocked her gorgeous hips back and forth along my fingers. The cuff of my suit jacket was drenched from her arousal, and the sight of it drove me fucking wild.

I leaned my body into hers, wanting to be as close to her as possible when she came undone. "That's it, baby," I whispered against her mouth, tasting the air she breathed. I flicked out my tongue and drove it into her mouth, swiping it up and catching it on her teeth, on her swollen top lip.

And then I felt her entire body tense as she began pulsing around the fingers I had inside her, and it was so maddeningly perfect I wanted to fall to my knees in thanks for being the lucky bastard who got to be here with her like this. To do this with her.

I kissed her deeply to stifle her cries and immediately promised myself that the next time we did this, her cries could go unchecked—a song for the stars. For my heart. "Oh my god," she said against my cheek, her chest heaving. "Andre . . ."

I nuzzled my face into her neck, savoring the sweet smell of her, the sound of my name on her lips. The feel of this, having her so close to me. My eyes swept over her—flushed cheeks, swollen lips, strands of hair loose and in her face. *My god*. She was an angel. Sent just for me.

I wanted to press my body to hers and become one, to yield myself to her so completely that I'd never have another single thought without her in it.

After another drawn-out moment of rapid breaths and soothing touches and resisting anything more, I slowly pulled my fingers out of her as I pressed a delicate kiss to the soft spot below her ear. She closed her eyes as I straightened and took a step back, like she felt the loss of our physical connection as much as I did. But that loss of her in my hands was made up by the sight of her, raw and fucked and vulnerable on that counter, completely open to me. It took everything I had to pry my eyes away.

I turned on the sink's faucet and washed my hands—giving her a moment to collect herself. The rustling of fabric filled the room as she stood and let her dress slink back down, pulling herself back together.

Using two sheets of paper towel from the dispenser, I dried my hands and glimpsed at her reflection in the mirror. She was rosy-cheeked and smiling, and I almost crumbled from the squeeze in my chest. Her hair wasn't quite as neatly bound as it had been when she walked in here, and there was no denying the flush that covered her face and chest, but none of it mattered—she was the most beautiful thing I had ever seen.

I couldn't resist putting my hands back on her, winding my fingers back through the beads at her hips. "You look so fucking pretty when you come," I murmured, leaning in for a brisk kiss before pulling myself back.

"I've never felt anything like that in my entire life," she whispered. Her hands ran down the front of my shirt. "I'm not done with you yet."

I chuckled, clasping her hands and holding them at my

chest. "Oh, if you think this is all I have planned, you're mistaken. If I remember correctly"—I plucked at the strap of her dress that rested on her shoulder—"you mentioned something about wanting me to take this off you tonight."

She nodded eagerly, those brown eyes shimmering. "Yes, please."

Hearing Nora say "please" drove me crazy. I wanted to give her anything she might ever ask for. I *would*—I'd find a way, no matter what.

"We should probably head back out there before anyone realizes we're gone," I said, stepping toward the bathroom door and pulling her along with me, keeping a hold of her hand in mine. "But I promise this isn't over, *mariposa*. Not even close."

Nora squeezed my hand as we slipped through the door and walked back through the house together.

IT HAD BEEN ALMOST an hour since I made Nora come in the bathroom, and I hadn't been able to stop looking at her. My god, the way she looked . . . She was perfection in that sparkling dress, and if she gave me the opportunity tonight, I might just say way too much about the way she blurred the sight of anything or anyone else. She was radiant, a bright white angel somehow walking this earth—and I knew I was so damn lucky to just be near her.

I watched as she smiled with Mackenzie, clutching her friend's hands in her own. Looking at her physically hurt my chest. She was ruining me . . . killing me with tiny cuts every time she smiled, with every laugh that burst from her lips. Her touch sank straight into my bloodstream so that all I ever did was burn for more of her.

I was falling hard, the impact reverberating through my entire body, and it scared the shit out of me. Times like these made me wish Gabriel were still here so I could ask him what the fuck to do. I wasn't any good at this shit—I don't know how to lay it all down for a girl, to tell her she was everything I could ever hope for while still being the confident, stable man that she deserved.

As I sat at our table—content in her periphery—I looked down at my hands, and in an odd twist of fate, found the answers written right there on my damn fingers. *LOVE* and *FEAR*.

I almost laughed.

Maybe Gabriel had already given me the answers, and I simply hadn't realized. Long ago, when we were still just kids, Gabriel had been chasing a girl in the neighborhood for months. She was headstrong and practically forbidden—her older brother was a shot caller for the local street gang, and anyone who laid a hand on her was damn near flirting with death. But Gabriel swore he loved her, that he'd marry her someday.

Once, after I'd caught her sneaking out of our basement in the middle of the night, I'd asked him how he could be so brave. Her family was dangerous—what could be worth the risk of it all? And I'd never forget the way he shrugged before he put an arm around me and whispered the words into my ear.

"Love, mijo.*"*

He sat me down and told me that love was the greatest

currency in life, that it conquered all. It was a force bigger than money, bigger than clout. And then he said something that stuck with me enough to get these words tattooed on my fingers:

"Love doesn't exist without fear, mijo. It's like a trade, an exchange to the universe that must be given for a gift so good. When you love something, you fear losing it. If there's no fear, it's not real love. So before you go telling anyone that you love them, you make sure it's real. That you can't stand the thought of losing them. That to lose them would be like a bullet to your heart."

Love didn't exist without fear. That was true for Gabriel, and it was true here, now, with Nora. To love is a risk. It was a painful, maddening risk. It meant giving Nora the power to break me. But I knew, even as the thought crossed my mind, that whether I wanted to give her the power to break me or not —it was already done.

I looked at her again, watched as her face broke out into a laugh at something Amelia said. And if I'd thought she was beautiful before, this . . . this was my heart growing painfully inside of my chest, struggling against the strain of so much goddamn *love.*

Soon, it was time for Eric and Mackenzie's recessional, and all their wedding guests formed a long tunnel from the reception to the back entrance of the house. They'd be staying here tonight—most of the family from both sides would be staying on property for the night while the rest of us were shuttled to a nearby hotel.

Nora stood across from me, sparks dancing all around her from the sparkler in her hand, like a beacon for my heart. And while everyone around us waved their sparklers in the air and cheered for the couple who would be spending the rest of their lives together, our eyes stayed locked on each other the whole time.

An hour later, the sprinter van that Eric had arranged for us pulled up to the western-style lodge that we'd be staying in tonight, and we all piled out with our bags. Logan and I had already run our cars over here earlier this morning so that we'd be all set for the long drive home tomorrow.

Adam bent down to nestle his face in the crook of Rachel's shoulders in the lobby while we waited for Logan and Amelia to check us all in. "Baby, I'm so tired."

Rachel reached up to pat him on the head. "You danced *so* hard tonight."

Nora stood less than a foot away from me, and though we weren't touching, there was a rippling undercurrent teetering between us.

Amelia walked toward us from the reception desk, a stack of room key holders in her hand. She handed one of them to Rachel. "You guys are on the fifth floor. We are too." And then she turned to Nora and handed her a room key. "It looks like Eric and Mack booked you guys in one room together. I hope that's okay?" Despite the question reflected in her features, I could see the glint in her eye as she waited for Nora to answer. "We could always ask if they have any other rooms available."

Nora glanced at me for a moment before taking the key card. "We'll make it work." I *almost* smirked.

Amelia nodded. "You guys are on the eighth floor. Enjoy the view!"

Logan walked up with his and Amelia's bags slung over his shoulders. "They have a complimentary breakfast that starts at six. We should try to get down here to eat before we hit the road. If we leave early enough, we'll make it home at a decent hour."

I nodded. "I plan on going into the shop tomorrow, once we get back."

Logan grinned. "Yeah, me too."

"All right," Adam groaned from somewhere in Rachel's neck. "I need to get into a bed or I will pass out right here."

Rachel giggled, and we all headed for the elevators. At the fifth floor, the elevator car stopped and everyone said good night, reaffirming plans to be downstairs no later than six thirty tomorrow morning. And then the doors closed, and the elevator started its ascent again, and I just couldn't fucking help myself.

I pushed Nora against the wall, and I kissed her.

Chapter Thirty-One

NORA

Andre tasted like red velvet cake and tequila —sweet and dangerous, like the best kind of vice. It made me dizzy, the way his tongue swept hungrily along my lip, the way his teeth grazed against my skin.

Even more dizzying was the reality that . . . this was it. There was nothing to stop us now, and after weeks of heated glances and shaky hands, of this ferocious build-up, this was the culmination of our desire rising to the surface. It felt like slipping into a strong current and letting the water simply take me. No use fighting something so real and untamed, so magnificently powerful.

His hands slid down my body, cupping my ass and pulling me further into him. As if there was any further for me to go. He drew his mouth away from mine and nipped at my chin, dragging his teeth along my jaw toward my ear, where he whispered, "Tell me to stop right now, if you don't want this." His teeth nipped at my earlobe, and goose bumps scattered down my spine.

"Please," I begged. And his hands tightened on my hips as he thrust himself against me.

The elevator dinged and the doors opened, exposing us to an empty hallway. We hardly even noticed, and eventually the doors shut again. Andre's hands wrapped around my thighs as he lifted me into the air, and I tried to wrap my legs around him but my dress got in the way, and the bags he was holding slumped forward and smacked me in the hip, and I couldn't help the giggle that spilled out of my mouth. He smiled into my neck and I felt it in my soul.

He set me back down, and I slung my arms around his neck, pulling him down, greedy for the pressure of him, needing to feel it everywhere. We were like crazed teenagers seeking and exploring ways to make the other gasp.

Suddenly, Andre reared back and looked at me with a crooked expression on his face, his chest rising and falling against mine. "Is the elevator moving?"

Sure enough, the elevator was dropping, quickly re-approaching the first floor. "Shit," I said back to him, laughing.

We did, eventually, make it to the eighth floor—after riding back up to the third with an older man who gave us both a stern expression as he stepped in from the lobby.

It took us nearly ten minutes to find our room after we got turned around down the wrong hallway, distracted by the incessant need to steal more kisses in the shadows. Once we keyed our way through the right door, we stepped into the dark room and it was like the entire world paused.

Andre dumped our bags on the ground, and we simply

stared at each other. At this point, there was no part of me that was left untouched by him. He'd woven his way into all of my dark corners, seen all of my insecurities and vulnerabilities, and he'd never once allowed me to be embarrassed or ashamed of them. He'd made me feel *seen* in a way that I'd never been before, making all of this feel . . . inevitable. Like he was the other side of the same coin, my perfectly designed counterpart.

He made me want to be brave. He made me want to be as fearless as he was.

"Keep your hands at your sides," I said softly. His eyes flared at the command, his mouth rising mere millimeters. I stepped forward. Teasing. Aching.

Needing.

I reached a hand up to pull his tie loose, dragging it side to side until enough of the black, silky material had moved through the knot that I could pull the whole thing over his head. And then I unbuttoned his collar, the skull with roses for eyes looking at me from his throat, and moved all the way down until his shirt was wide open, untucking the bottom from the waist of his pants. Beneath his dress shirt was a black undershirt, and I swiftly removed both, exposing all of the lines and whorls of his tattoos.

I let my eyes fall to his hips, and then to the buckle of his belt. The proof of his arousal was right there, obvious even in the dark, and I could feel my blood begin to pound through me at the sight. My hands moved to unbuckle his belt, and then to unfasten the button of his pants so that they fell into a heap around his ankles and on top of the dress shoes he still had on.

He was wearing black briefs—everything he wore tonight, it seemed, was black. I traced my finger along the skin of his abdomen, feeling him pull in a sharp breath. But he didn't say a word, and he didn't move his hands. He was going to let me do this, let me feel and explore him on *my* terms.

"My, my," I whispered, my voice shaking. "I've thought about this so much. It's already even better than I imagined." He smirked in response, but there was nothing cocky in his expression. His eyes were full of wonder and longing as he watched me pull his briefs down to join his pants around his ankles.

My eyes widened at the sight of him. At the sharp, hard angles of his lust. It was obvious that he wanted this . . . badly. His need was undeniable.

I looked him right in the eyes as I gathered up the skirt of my dress and sank to my knees, the rough fabric of the hotel room carpet cutting into my skin. But the discomfort was nothing compared to my delight at his expression. Keeping my eyes on his, I pressed a kiss against his warm skin.

"Careful, *mariposa*," he grunted out, his eyes falling closed for three heartbeats before they opened again, "it's not going to take much for me to fall apart."

Exhilaration prickled at my senses. His hands were clenched into fists, and I loved seeing that crumbling restraint. It felt . . . dangerous. I knew that at any moment, I might push him over the edge.

I teased him with my tongue, swirling it around him in lazy circles before. When I met his eyes, I found him looking at me like I was . . . his. And then I plunged him all the way into my mouth.

The groan that exploded out of him was feral, rumbling through his chest like a tremor, and his hands were suddenly no longer at his sides. I felt his fingers fist a section of my hair as he thrusted himself further into my throat, and my own plea-sure sang in response.

It wasn't my first time doing something like this, but I'd never enjoyed it until now. This wasn't just some physical act; it was seeing how far I could bend Andre until he snapped. It was an intoxicating game of push and pull that made me feel both vulnerable and powerful.

I swirled my tongue around him again while he was still deep in my mouth, teasing against his senses. His eyes looked down at me like I was a revelation, those stormy gray hues nearly black with lust. I felt him thrust again, seeking a further, deeper place to bury himself inside of me, and I moaned in response.

"Fuck, baby. *Fuck*," he said, as he pulled himself out of my mouth. "I'm going to come so quick like that, and I'm not ready yet." He made quick work of taking off his shoes, kicking out of the pants and briefs that still lay around his ankles, before bending down and scooping me up into his arms.

His mouth found mine with renewed urgency as he moved me toward the bed, setting me down on my feet right at the edge of it. His arm felt around me in search of the clasp on my dress, and he zipped it down to where it stopped at the base of my spine.

He stepped backward, eyeing the dress's strap over my left shoulder before he hooked a finger underneath and helped it down. When he did the same to the right strap, the top of the dress fell, pooling around my waist. Beneath, I wore a lacy nude bra, and Andre's eyes fixated on it.

I watched the column of his throat work before he stepped forward and knelt in front of me. His hands came to either side of my waist, gently tugging the material down, exposing the hemline of my matching panties. He pressed a soft trail of kisses down my stomach, and the featherlight feel of his mouth on my skin was almost too much.

The material finally slid over and beneath the curve of my ass, and his fingertips followed it down along the backs of my legs. I couldn't help the gasp that knocked out of me.

He chuckled darkly. "Do you like seeing me kneel before you, *mariposa*?" All I could do was moan in response. But it didn't matter, because he answered himself a moment later, his eyes hazy as they focused between my legs. He swiftly pulled the fabric to the side and pressed his warm tongue flat against me.

"You sure taste like you like it." He hummed appreciatively before he licked me again, right over the bundle of nerves that had me falling backward onto the bed.

He chuckled again, the vibration of it dancing up my spine as he continued to undress me from where he kneeled. His fingers unfastened the delicate straps around my ankles, and he pressed a kiss into the arch of each foot as my heels jostled to the floor. As the dress came the rest of the way off, he gingerly turned to place it on the chair behind him.

Rising to his full height, I nearly lost the ability to breathe as I took in the sight of him wearing nothing but those tattoos and his desire. He was a fucking masterpiece. And I needed him, needed him bad. "Andre," I whispered.

"Hm?" His eyes raked over my body, taking his time as he appreciated the sight in front of him. "What do you need? Tell me." His voice had an edge, like he was barely controlling himself. Like he might just lose it at any second.

"You," I breathed.

He moved to kneel onto the bed, nudging my legs open

with his knees. I felt his fingertips on my legs as they moved higher and higher and . . . *oh*, my eyes shuttered closed at the feel of those fingers reaching my panty line. My core was still on fire from his tongue. I needed *more*.

I lifted my hips, seeking and reaching for more of him, and he used the opportunity to slide my underwear off me. The bed shifted as he bent, caging me on either side with his hands, as his length nudged against that place between my legs. I gasped, and his mouth was on mine as he plunged his tongue down.

As he kissed me fervently, he reached a hand beneath me to unclasp the strapless bra I was still wearing. His mouth moved to my chin, to my throat, and down to the center of my chest before he lifted himself to look at my breasts. His eyes jumped back and forth as he audibly swallowed. "You're so beautiful, Nora," he said before he teased a nipple with his tongue. "The most beautiful thing I've ever seen. So perfect. So *mine*."

I watched as he readjusted, falling to his knees on the floor next to the bed. His hands wrapped around my legs as he pulled me toward him, sliding me down the mattress until my hips were right on the edge. And then his mouth was back on me, seeking and exploring and driving into me as I fell apart, piece by burning piece. When he swiped a finger against that bundle of nerves, I cried out, wrapping my legs around his head and tugging him in, closer.

Just as he edged me to the brink of utter oblivion, he stopped, turning to reach for his wallet in the pocket of his discarded pants. And I knew it was intentional. For as much as we were both falling apart, he was still exercising control where he could. Winding me up. Making me crazy for more of him.

He pulled out a foil square, swiftly ripping it open with his teeth and gliding the condom down the length of him. And then he stepped back in between my legs, lining himself up so he was right *there*, and bent down to kiss me again.

I could taste myself on his lips, taste my arousal on his tongue. "Are you sure?" he asked, as if there existed a single thing I could have possibly wanted more.

I want you, I want you, I want you, my body sang as it curled around his. "I want you, Andre," I said into his mouth, sharing his breath as I spoke the words that broke him.

In one swift movement, he pushed into me, the pressure of it almost more than I could take. He hissed against my shoulder before he stood up, wrapping his hands around my waist, and began the most delicious assault as he drove into me over and over and over again.

Immediately, I was close—so close. The tension that had been building since we left that bathroom together, the anticipation for another release, was catapulting me higher and higher into the sky. This was devastatingly new, this complete yielding of my body and mind and soul to another.

Andre's thrusts quickened as he increased his pace toward the pursuit of the ecstasy we both knew was so . . . fucking . . . close. "*Andre,*" I gasped.

Abruptly, he paused—his chest heaving, brow slicked with sweat as he pierced a hungry look into my eyes. Again, pausing right on the cusp of oblivion. Right as we were about to tip over. Dark and feral, I watched his eyes snap down to my mouth. "Say it again," he murmured, "when you come for me." He brushed a thumb across my bottom lip and smiled before he wound his hand beneath my back and flipped me over.

He lifted my hips up into the air, quickly slipping back into me from behind. And this was . . . better. Deeper. "Oh god."

His hands roamed all over the front of my body, over my breasts, greedily grabbing and pinching and touching me like I'd never been touched before. One hand reached to where we were joined, and I felt his fingers circle me as his other hand snaked up to my neck, clutching my entire throat in his palm.

It was only moments before I lost myself. He brought me right to the brink of my own existence and as I screamed his name, I felt him fall apart too. And I could feel the change, the rearranging of the very pieces of our souls that danced around us, shifting and coming back together anew.

I knew I would never be the same.

"I love you," I whispered into the curve of his arms. It had lived in my throat for long enough. I felt his muscles tense. His nose grazed along my neck as he pressed a soft kiss against my shoulder. "I love you, Andre."

I turned to look at him over my shoulder, finding his eyes closed and his face twisted into disbelief. Astonishment. Like he couldn't believe I might actually be his for the taking. This went far beyond any of our games, far beyond our blatant lust and desire. And I decided, right then, that I'd make sure he always knew just how special and perfect he was. That he was made for me.

There was a shimmer in those gray eyes that felt like home as he pressed his cheek against mine from where he stood behind me, still inside of me, breathing me in. Collecting himself. "I love you so much, Nora," he said, his voice raw. "I'm yours. I'm all yours."

I smiled, wrapping my arms around his neck above me, pressing a kiss underneath his chin. Holding him and his vulnerability tight. "I'm yours, too."

Chapter Thirty-Two

ANDRE

It felt like we'd only been asleep for twenty minutes when my alarm sounded from the nightstand. I grunted, forcing myself awake, irritable and frustrated that I would have to move to turn the blaring thing off. Nora was curled in my arms—her warm breath curling and winding around my chest as she slept—and the last thing I wanted to do was disturb her. I had to, though. It was already six in the morning, which meant we had thirty minutes before the others would expect us downstairs.

Reluctantly, I grabbed the phone on the nightstand behind me, ending the incessant wailing with a quick swipe. Nora stirred against me, her chin tipping toward her chest as she nuzzled into the crook of my arm. The arm I couldn't even feel, numb from the weight of her. But I didn't care.

With my free hand, I combed my fingers through her hair and watched her beautiful face as she slowly woke. She let out a sigh of pure contentment that filled my chest with pride.

"Too early," she whispered, her eyes still closed.

"I know." I traced my fingers down her nose.

"Don't wanna move."

"I know." I brushed my fingers across her lips.

"Stay here forever?"

I smiled. "Does that make you happy?"

She opened her eyes, and I was immediately lost in them. "Yes."

I leaned in to take her mouth in mine, the need for her coming over me like the crest of a wave. After a few moments of lazy kissing, she pulled herself on top of me, straddling my hips and breathing more love and light into me than I knew what to do with. My hands traced a path around her body, gliding up her spine, down her arms, diving to her hips and thighs.

She broke the kiss and looked at me, still dazed with sleep and want and the long night we'd shared. Her eyes heated as she put her mouth on my chest again, teasing and licking and moving down to where I was already aching for her again, taking me into her mouth as she had last night. I groaned, the feel of her unlike anything else.

It wasn't long before my climax barreled into her with such a force of unyielding ecstasy that I swore the damn earth shook. I could feel her swallowing around me as I came hard and fast, spilling into her throat. The constriction of her mouth as she continued to move—I was going to fucking die from the sensation, from the pleasure of it.

I couldn't even muster the wherewithal to push myself up onto my elbows to get a better look at her. Couldn't raise my body up off this bed to climb over hers and wrap myself around her the way I desperately wanted to. The high was all-consuming, and my limbs were now useless. Spent.

Forcing my head up, I watched as her mouth slowly took me in once, twice more—her pressure softening until her tongue and lips were light against me. And then she pulled her mouth away, looked right into my eyes, and licked her lips.

Licked her fucking lips.

Her eyes sparkled in triumph and it nearly killed me again.

"Holy fuck" was all I could say.

She smiled.

I lay there breathless, trying to piece my mind back together. To remember what the fuck my name was, because all I could think of was hers.

"Nora," I mumbled, closing my eyes.

"Yes, Andre?" Her voice was like starlight.

"I love you."

She giggled. I felt the shifting of the mattress, the pressure of her body bending around my side. "I'm not sure I'll ever get used to that."

"What?" I asked, turning to look at her.

"You. Loving me for me," she said, pressing into my chin with her index finger, "wanting nothing else."

I curled an arm around her and kissed her forehead. How the hell could I ever want anything else? She was everything.

"We have ten minutes to get downstairs," she mused, playfully.

I nodded. "We still have a good five, maybe seven to rest. Stay here. We'll make it."

"I should shower," she noted. "I probably smell like sex."

The thought drove me wild, the animal in me roaring at the idea that I'd marked her in such a way. But she was right, I wanted that for myself. I didn't want Logan or Adam anywhere near her when she smelled like that.

Though my body was still shaky and weak, I forced myself to rise, to scoop her into my arms and carry her into the small bathroom. "Let's get you clean then, *mariposa*."

Today had been a long day, and I was beyond exhausted. Between the lack of sleep last night, the drive home this morning, and the last six hours of work at the shop, I was both wired with delirious energy and on the verge of passing out at any moment.

I needed to burn off some steam, to settle my body down from the buzz that had flowed through me all day, and though I'd dropped her off at her apartment only hours ago, I wanted to see Nora. She was working at the bar tonight—her first real shift as a bartender. Mara had called her this morning during our drive home and asked her if she was ready because another girl called out and it would be a busy night with some event that was going on.

Nora was ecstatic, her face full of joy at the prospect of earning a bartending shift on her own. She'd been training with Mara for weeks, working hard to learn the ins and outs of the popular downtown club, and she was finally vindicated in all that effort. The pride in her smile was evident as she told Mara she'd be there, and when she hung up the phone, she'd turned and squealed in delight.

I couldn't wait to see that joy and confidence tonight. And

then after her shift, maybe we could get naked together—that sounded really fucking good.

I found Manny in the third bay, shoulder-deep in the body of an old, classic roadster. "Manny," I called out over the loud hum of the air compressor that Cameron was using in the next bay over.

Manny pulled his head out from behind the engine, throwing me a goofy-ass smile. "What's good, boss?"

I crossed my arms over my chest, grinning down at him. "I wanted to thank you, for keeping the shop together while Logan and I were out. Logan's name is on the building, and quite frankly he can come and go as he pleases. But I left you without much warning, and I'm really damn proud of how you handled yourself. Whether you realize it or not—you're a natural leader, and these guys look up to you."

His eyes softened as he dipped his head. "Thanks, boss. You know I couldn't have gotten here without you. It's your leadership that drives this place."

The comment hit me right in the chest. Because he was right, and it felt good to hear it. I loved this shop. If Logan hadn't already built it from the ground up, I'd be itching to create an environment just like this. I felt the familiar pang in my gut, the bittersweet knowing that eventually I'd have to say goodbye to this place and help Marisela build her kingdom. "Thanks, Manny. Good work. And again—thank you."

He grinned as he mumbled, bashfully, "Anytime, boss." And then he side-eyed me. "Logan said you both went to a wedding. Hopefully you got some good action? Lord knows your ass needed it—no offense." He winked. "Nothing like a good wedding to get the ladies crawling."

My face twisted. "Manny," I grumbled, "shut the fuck up and get back to work."

Manny laughed. "There he is. I was worried you'd have a permanent smile on your face." Shaking his head, he bent back down into the car.

On my way home, I made a quick stop to see Myrna at the tattoo shop. There was something I needed to do, something to cement this moment in time. No matter how any of it played out in the end, this was a feeling worth remembering later. Plus . . . I had a feeling things would play out the way I wanted them to.

Luckily Myrna wasn't busy, and I was in and out within thirty minutes. At home, I showered off the grease and smell of gasoline before slipping into a black T-shirt and shorts. I gave Marisela a quick kiss on the cheek, and then headed back out.

I had a lady to see.

Larkspur was crawling with activity, a line at the door winding itself all the way around the corner of the block. A banner that hung above the front entrance advertised a foam party for ladies' night—the thought instantly driving tension in my jaw. The last thing I wanted was Nora being oogled at during some out-of-control foam party. But I forced the ire down—she was looking forward to tonight, and I wasn't about to ruin it for her.

Still, I'd happily go toe-to-toe with any of these pretty boy motherfuckers if one of them so much as looked at Nora wrong.

Despite the long line, the bouncer was familiar enough with me that he let me pass right through. I shook his hand in thanks, and turned my attention to the bar in the back of the busy club. My eyes instantly landed on a gorgeous blonde behind the bar who moved with ease, serving drinks to the patrons who crowded around it. She'd kept her hair down, like a blonde waterfall down her back. Her black tank top was tight across her body, and though I couldn't see her legs from here, I imagined they looked incredible. They always made me a little weak.

I couldn't help leaning against the wall and watching her from a distance. She was busy, a little flustered, but radiant all the same. Her joy was unmistakable. Mara was behind the bar with her, moving around like a warrior on a mission, her expression a little harder, a little more no-nonsense as she asked a group of college-aged guys for their order.

Mara was much smaller than Nora, but she packed a fucking punch. I'd seen her handle rowdy customers like they were nothing, and it made me happy to know that Nora had her, that Nora could even learn from her. She'd taken enough shit from people in her life, and I didn't want her to have to do it anymore. Though maybe that was why she liked working here. To practice that effort.

When I couldn't take another moment without those beautiful brown eyes on mine, I pushed off the wall and moved toward the bar. I knew I'd have to wait for an open stool, but I didn't mind. I'd wait forever to see this girl.

Chapter Thirty-Three

NORA

I watched as Andre's long form sat in a stool at the end of the bar, his eyes brightening when they found mine. Larkspur was busier than I'd ever seen it before—Mara had been advertising a ladies' night foam party all over social media and it felt like all her one hundred thousand followers had shown up.

It was a huge success for the bar. Ladies got in for free, and men had to pay a twenty-dollar cover charge at the door. It seemed like an obscene amount to ask of our mostly college-aged crowd, but the swarm of women in here must have been enough of an incentive, because boy did they pay.

I was thrilled with the turnout—I'd easily be bringing home a few hundred dollars in tips tonight. And even though I was running around like a chicken with its head cut off, I was having an absolute blast in the rush of it all.

I set three shots of tequila down in front of a group of young women before I turned to face the dark and dangerous man who now sat and watched me from the other end of the bar. Sauntering toward him—giving my best *confident bartender* impression—I smiled at him as I approached. "Hey, stranger," I greeted, as if I hadn't seen him butt naked this morning. God, I would never get over how incredible he looked under all those clothes.

His eyes wandered all over me, and I clocked when he noticed the tiny shorts I was wearing that didn't quite cover my ass. They were a risk, but they made me feel ballsy—and I wanted to feel ballsy tonight. The column of his throat worked as he swallowed, and he did his best to shake the heat that flared on his face—but I still saw the embers of it.

My own white-hot awareness caused a fierce pounding in my chest, but I worked to shove it all down. Now was most certainly *not* the time.

"Hey, Nora. You look . . . great." He swallowed again, cheeks flushed. "How's the night going?"

I smiled, enjoying that I'd made him a little flustered. "Really good. Busy as hell but I'm having fun. Can I get you a beer? Tequila?"

He flashed a smile. "Beer, please."

I knew what that smile felt like against my navel, knew what it tasted like. And now I was greedy for more.

Turning away from him, I bent down to grab a bottle of beer from the fridge, soaking in the cold brush of air on my face and chest. I pulled a bottle opener from my back pocket and popped the top off before setting it down in front of Andre. His fingers briefly brushed against mine as he picked it up, and it sent a shiver through me.

"Nora?" I heard a male's voice from down the bar, a voice that prickled at my senses, and turned toward the sound. My eyes scanned the faces of the many patrons who waited to be served a drink until they landed on one that was familiar—one that didn't belong here. His blue eyes looked surprised, as if *I* was the one who shouldn't be here, in a downtown bar in Denver.

Parker.

For a long moment, I simply stared at him, my mind trying to piece together how the hell this segment of my past was now standing right in the middle of my present. I hadn't seen his face in weeks, not since I'd watched that horrible interview where he'd called me a self-interested gold digger. The thought drove a rush of frustration right through me.

I looked back at Andre, finding him eyeing Parker with curiosity and the slightest edge of violence. As if he'd sensed the shift in me, the adrenaline running through my limbs. "It's Parker," I said, and his eyes snapped to mine. They roamed my face, looking for any cue to handle the situation his way, which likely included fists and broken bones. "Stay here, okay?" I worked to keep my voice light, my eyes reassuring. He gave me a small nod.

Turning back toward Parker, to where he stood in the middle of the bar's crowd, I walked until I stood right in front of him. "Parker?"

"Nora." He swallowed. "I was really hoping I'd find you here." His eyes swept me up and down as he took in every detail.

"How?" I asked.

"I searched your name online, and found this event." He looked around the club, at the moving lights and DJ booth and hazy smoke that filled the air.

He must have found Mara's posts. She'd asked to take a

picture of me, for "promo" she'd said, but I hadn't realized it would be tied to this. Not that it mattered; I was happy to give her what she needed. "Why?"

Parker ignored my question. "You look . . . incredible, Nora. Different, somehow."

I nodded. "Thank you. I'm happy."

My response landed how I'd wanted it to, and his face fell, his brows dipping in confusion.

I stole a quick glance back at Andre, who was watching our interaction intently, before I looked back at Parker, twisting my expression into a glare. A distant part of my mind recognized that people around us had begun to whisper his name, recognizing him as *the* Parker Hart. "Why are you here, Parker? Are you looking for me to dig up some more of your gold? Chase some more of your clout?"

His eyes flicked to Andre behind me, and I watched as he nervously swallowed. "Nora, I didn't mean for any of it to come out like that. I was hurt, and—"

"*You* were hurt?!" I scoffed. "I gave you *everything*. I gave you entirely too much, if we're being honest. And it still wasn't enough." I stared directly into his blue eyes, the honest confidence that poured out almost knocking me over. "You never respected me for who I was, and you certainly never respected any boundaries I had."

He shook his head, and I noticed that lights had begun to shine in his face, lights that were brighter than the club's lighting. People were using their phones to record us. "That's not true, Nora. I always respected you . . . I wanted to give you everything—"

"You knew how little interest I had in being in front of cameras, and not only did you blatantly disregard my discomfort with them during your *proposal* to me, but then you turned around and used 'clout' and 'fame' as weapons against me after I left. How is that respecting me? You lied to the media to protect yourself. You've never done anything that didn't serve you first, and I finally realized that's all I ever was to you. A way to serve your image."

"Tell him, girl!" someone shouted from behind him.

"Nora, please. Please just come home and we can make this right."

"No," I said firmly. "I'm exactly where I want to be, Parker. I'm building a life on my terms, one that has nothing to do with money or press or pretentious fucking actors. I'm happy here." I looked back at Andre again, and smiled.

His face relaxed just enough for me to see the slightest curl of his mouth.

"*Him*?" Parker spat. The venom in his voice had my head whipping back around. He was looking back and forth between us with disgust in his eyes. "You're with him?"

Ice slid down my spine. "Yeah," I responded, my chest swelling with pride despite the anger roaring in my blood. "I'm with him. And he loves me for *exactly* who I am." Parker stared at me, his eyes shooting daggers. "Go back home, Parker. Or don't, I don't care. But you need to get the fuck out of this club."

The crowd around us whooped and cheered as two bouncers appeared on either side of Parker, pulling him back and away from the bar. He snapped his arms out of their hold. "Get the hell off of me, do you have any idea who I am?"

Frank, the main bouncer and head of security, supplied him with a bored expression. "Nope."

I felt a small, warm hand touch my elbow, and I turned to find Mara's vicious smile next to me. "You okay, Nora?"

I took in a deep breath, feeling my own face morph into a smile. "Yeah. Yeah, I really am."

"Good." She winked. She turned to face the crowd, raising her voice above all the excited energy. "All right, everyone, show's over! Turn those fucking flashlights off your phones and get back to enjoying your night." She tossed me another smile before she began taking orders again.

The bar was even more packed with patrons now, and I knew I needed to help Mara handle it. But I had to check in with Andre first—I had to make sure he was okay.

When I turned, I was surprised to find that the smile on his face was the biggest I'd seen yet. The sight of it stole the breath right out of my lungs. "Hey," I said as I approached. "I'm so sorry about that."

Andre shook his head. "No, Nora. You have nothing to be sorry for. That was . . . that was incredible." The pride that radiated from him was palpable, and it sank into my skin like a tender warmth.

In Los Angeles, I'd let a lot of important pieces of myself fall away to make room for what I thought would be good for me. Sacrifice, they say, can make the ending of a story worth it —you can't have pleasure without pain and all that.

Now I knew sacrifice could be a dangerous sport. It wasn't an investment into the bank of happily ever afters, and I understood now that there could never have been a happy ending with Parker if I couldn't reach it with all of the honest parts of myself still intact.

Hindsight felt like an out-of-body experience, giving me the ability to look through the lens at past-Nora and think,

What the fuck are you doing? This isn't us! This isn't you! Stand your ground and fight *for what you need!* I allowed the wrong partner to let me feel good for my sacrifices, to hold my hand as I crumbled while he soared.

But Andre—Andre helped me realize my worth. He taught me that happiness was self-governed, that no one else could give it to me—it wasn't a gift to be rewarded, not a currency to be traded. It was a spark that lived in the deepest trenches of my heart, its only true kindling the confidence in my choices as I worked to create a life for *myself.*

I didn't bear the burden of needing to make Andre happy, just like it wasn't his responsibility to make me happy. I made myself happy by choosing to be with someone like him—and there was a *huge* fucking difference.

He helped remind me what joy really looked like, what it *felt* like, even in the midst of challenges and pain. He showed me that coming undone inside of the wild currents of love didn't happen so that we lost anything in the process. We came undone so that we could be forged anew with everything we gained. And through *this* love, with him, I knew it to be true.

Love was power, and I was stronger today with Andre standing next to me, knowing that I could hold his hand and still soar at the same time. So much about the joy of loving him was learning who I could be inside of it.

As I stared at him now—at the silver gleaming in his eyes, the mouth that made me lose my ability to breathe—I knew. *This* was my happily ever after.

I would follow him back to the beginning, just to relive the start. I never saw him coming, never expected to stumble into his orbit, right into that smile that made me forget what it was to *not* be myself. And I would never be the same—he was a permanent, golden tattoo on my heart.

He reached out a hand, and I placed mine inside of it. Then he rotated our wrists so that his hand was on top of mine—and I saw it.

My butterfly tattoo. On his hand.

"Andre," I gasped as I lightly swiped my thumb over it. I knew for a fact he didn't have it this morning—he'd gotten it done today.

"A reminder, *mariposa*, of the one I love. Forever."

Epilogue

NORA, THREE MONTHS LATER

I ONLY HAD A FEW MINUTES UNTIL THE END OF MY shift, but Larkspur was busy—busier than normal for a Thursday night. After dropping two pint glasses in front of a couple of out-of-towners, I snuck into the walk-in cooler behind the bar where all the kegs were kept so that I could send Andre a quick text.

> Going to be a little late for dinner. It's crazy here, but I won't be too long. Don't wait for me to eat!

It was less than a minute before he responded.

ANDRE

> Okay, mariposa. But so you know—Gloria just turned the blender on.

I giggled as I tucked my phone into the back pocket of my

denim shorts. Everyone knew how much I loved Gloria's margaritas.

Pushing back through the large metal door and into the roar of the loud music from the DJ booth, I found Mara pulling out a container of prepped limes from the bar fridge to replenish what was already out. She turned back to face me. "You okay?" she yelled over the noise.

I nodded. "Yeah, I'm going to hang for a little longer and help you with this rush."

"You don't have to do that," she called back, but I knew the relief that'd be flooding through her at the prospect; I'd felt it myself countless times.

I smiled. "It's no problem." Mara returned a quick grin, then took off to the other side of the bar, lime wedges in hand, as I locked eyes with a group of women who were clearly celebrating a bachelorette party.

Even in the few months that I'd worked here, it was obvious how much busier the club had gotten—each new week brought in a whole new swarm of first-time customers who'd heard about Larkspur through the word-of-mouth that was winding its way through every crevice of the city. Murmurs that not only was this a great place for fun, but it was also *safe*. Mara made sure that every single woman who walked through those front doors was as safe as possible from any unwanted advances.

We had an entire security team keeping a close eye on everyone who stepped into the club. There were also numerous signs in the women's restrooms advertising a secret menu of "drinks" that were really various signals of distress to the staff. Common ones included a "purple cowboy," which prompted the bartender on duty to call you a cab so that you could quietly slip out and safely bail on a bad date; a "red voodoo" let the staff know that someone wasn't taking the hint to leave you alone, signaling staff to get the security team's eyes on you right away and step in if and when needed; and a "black panther," which was a downright cry for help when something was really wrong. That one got our security team on you within seconds, ready to assess and eliminate the threat to your safety.

The safety aspect made women feel good about being here, and where women congregated—men followed. That, and Mara's social media was fun and flirty and drove a lot of traffic on its own accord. She was single-handedly pouring her own blood, sweat, and tears into marketing this place, as if her life depended on it. And maybe it did—she just so happened to share with me, after we'd each downed two consecutive shots while we were closing down one night, that she had plans to buy the bar from its current owner.

I was learning so much from Mara—not just in regards to bartending, but in managing the bar, her marketing techniques, the way she developed new events to promote. I'd started to pay attention to her influence on every aspect of the business side of things, drawn to the science of what made it so successful.

I couldn't pinpoint, exactly, whether the idea came to me all at once or if it started manifesting over time as I watched Mara drive more bodies into Larkspur than the building could even manage. But nevertheless, once the idea sprouted, I couldn't stop it from rooting deeper and deeper into my psyche.

Especially as I watched Andre silently war with the fact that his sister was just about ready to take the plunge into her own venture in business ownership, which meant he'd have to give up Logan's shop—the place he loved working at so much.

I'd thought everything through to the best of my ability. I'd come up with rough plans about how to make it all work both financially and operationally. Now, I simply had to convince Andre and Marisela to change that finish line they'd been working toward their entire adult lives.

No pressure.

IT WAS after eight by the time I finally pulled my Subaru up to Andre's house. As soon as I got out of the car, I could hear music playing from the backyard and the soft murmuring of happy conversation—Chino and his family were still here, then.

I used the spare key that Andre had given me to unlock the front door and found Chino's kids watching a movie in the living room. The youngest, Rio, looked up at me from where he lay tucked into a dinosaur blanket on the couch. "Hi, Nora!" he said, sweetly.

"Hi," I whispered. It looked like his sister, Jenny, had fallen asleep. "Whatcha watching?"

"*Toy Story*."

"Ohhhh." I nodded. "Good one."

He smiled before fixing his eyes back on the screen.

I set my stuff down on the kitchen table, and then joined the adults hanging out in the backyard. Andre was the first to spot me, and I watched as he unfolded himself from his camping chair and quickly closed the distance between us. "Hey, pretty girl," he murmured as he engulfed me in his arms.

He smelled like the shop and spice and . . . home. "Hi," I replied as my heart beat out of my chest at his closeness.

"How was work?" he asked, running his fingers through my hair.

"So busy," I whined, my eyes fluttering closed from the feel of his hands on me. "But so good. I made literal bank."

I heard the soft rumble of a chuckle in his chest. "Sounds like you can retire me any day then," he teased.

My eyes opened to find his. "Actually," I whispered, keeping my voice low so that only he could hear me, "there's something I want to talk to you and Marisela about—after everyone else leaves."

Andre's brows came together and he opened his mouth, ready to drag more out of me.

"Are you going to hog Nora, or can the rest of us say hello?" Chino came up from behind Andre, peeking at me from over his shoulder. I giggled as Andre rolled his eyes, reluctantly letting me out of his hold.

"Hi, Chino." I greeted him with a hug before giving one to Frances and Mary and Gloria as well.

Gloria slipped a margarita in my hand mid-embrace. "I've been waiting for you, *mija*." She winked.

I laughed. "I've been looking forward to this all night. Trust me," I said, taking a sip.

Tequila burned down the walls of my throat. It was *strong*.

Despite my protests, Marisela went inside to fix me a plate of leftovers; she'd made carne asada tortas and was excited for me to try one. Her delight in cooking and sharing food only strengthened my determination in what I was about to present to her and Andre.

As she set the plate down in front of where I now sat at the patio table, my mouth immediately watered. It smelled like heaven. I picked the sandwich up, some of the meat falling onto the plate from the other end, and took a big bite out of it.

"Mmmm," I groaned. It was freaking delicious.

"Yeah?" Sela asked, her eyes bright.

"Seriously, so good," I confirmed.

She smiled, looking at Andre with such obvious pride it made my chest tight. Andre was right—Marisela *did* deserve for all her dreams to come true. I just didn't want them to be at the expense of Andre's.

"All right, *'mano*." Chino clapped Andre on the shoulder. "I'm going to take the family home, it's getting late."

"Thanks for coming."

"Thanks for having us." Chino moved to give Marisela a hug. "And thanks for feeding us, Sela."

She laughed. "Always a pleasure, Chino."

Andre walked Chino and his family back through the house, and Marisela took a seat across from me at the table. She and I had been spending more and more time together over the last few months, and I considered her a good friend. I felt her watching me as I took another bite, and I looked up to find her brows pinched together. "You look like you have something you want to say," she observed.

"Damn, you're good." I looked at her and clicked my tongue. "Andre's always saying you have a sixth sense."

She shrugged. "It's a gift."

Andre reappeared at the back door, throwing me another

curious look as he walked toward the table. I sighed. *Now or never.*

"Okay, listen," I said, pulling out the chair next to me and indicating for Andre to sit down. "First, let me just start by saying that I hope I'm not overstepping. And if I am, you both have free rein to shoot me down. But . . ." I looked back and forth between Marisela and Andre, suddenly feeling nervous.

"What, Nora?" Andre asked, softly.

"Um. My mom left me some money," I blurted. "And I've been waiting for something to spend it on . . . something that feels right. And I would really like to invest in the restaurant with Marisela."

Andre's gaze flashed to his sister before landing back at me. "Wow, Nora—I . . . we . . . thank you," he said, reaching his hand out to cover mine on the table. "That's really kind of you, but—"

"Before you say no," I interrupted, "hear me out?" Andre paused, leaned back in his chair, and nodded. "Look, Andre, I know how much you love the shop. And I know how much you love the team you work with. You feel strong there, you're happy." His lips pressed together, and I knew it was because the sacrifice was worth it to him, that Marisela's dream mattered more. But even still, he didn't like to think about the things he would be walking away from. So I pressed on. "I have over a hundred thousand dollars."

"Holy shit," Marisela whispered from across the table.

I nodded. "Yeah, it's more than enough to start with. And we can be strategic about the business plan. We can make sure we bring in as much revenue as we can at the beginning. We can plan a soft opening, keep menu options limited at first . . . I have a ton of ideas."

"But, Nora . . ." Andre started.

"Andre, I know you've been saving for this. But I think . . ." I took a deep breath. "I think you should offer your money to Logan, instead."

His eyes narrowed. "What?" He looked . . . frustrated. Confused.

I continued. "Buy into the shop. Ask for him to make you part-owner. You *love* it there, Andre. And you deserve to have your dreams too. You don't have to give any of it up. Let me help."

The look he gave me was so intense, I had to rip my eyes away. I looked at Marisela, and found her face twisted in . . . relief. *Relief.* Like she knew what this was doing to her brother, and she was relieved for him to have a way out. He would have never backed out otherwise—I just had to convince him.

My eyes landed on those silver storms again. "I'd love the opportunity to do this, Andre. Or I never would have brought it up. I need something like this to sink my teeth into, and I *know* Marisela and I can do this. You don't have to give up your own dreams. You don't have to give up the shop. Just say yes. Ask yourself if it makes you happy, and say yes."

I watched as his head tilted to the side, eyes never wavering. And I braced myself for the impact of his denial, his refusal. I knew how important it was for him to take care of his sister—I just . . . I wanted him to be as happy as he was helping me to be.

I swiped my hands across the tops of my jeans, my palms clammy despite the cool autumn air. This quiet anticipation was making me . . . hot. And not in the way being in front of Andre usually made me.

But then I saw the corners of his mouth rise, his eyes

swirling with raw emotion. Before I knew it, he'd jumped out of his chair and wrapped his arms around my waist, burying his face in my lap, his nose grazing along the top of my hands. "Are you sure, *mariposa*? Are you really fucking sure?"

I gently tugged my hands from beneath him, scraped my nails over his short hair. "Yes, I'm really, really fucking sure."

He lifted his head and his eyes found mine, and I saw our entire future in that look. I saw the infinite measures of love and happiness that bloomed so perfectly between our hearts. And I felt more confident than ever about the trajectory of my life.

Except Andre's acceptance wasn't the only one I needed. I turned to face Marisela, and found her eyes filled with tears. I smiled. "Aw, Sela. I hope those are happy tears and you're not, like, bawling about going into business with me?"

She laughed. It was loud and full of hope. And as she stood, as she rounded the table and threw her arms around me, curling over her brother who was still on his knees and wrapped around my waist, she said through her tears, "Fuck the patriarchy. This is women shit."

And I beamed.

Acknowledgments

THIS LOVE story is sweet and sticky with vulnerability, and I couldn't be prouder of how Nora and Andre crack themselves wide open in their pursuit of happiness. Their journey wouldn't have been possible without people in my own life who constantly encourage me to chase my dreams, and I'm beyond grateful to be so lucky.

xo, Michaela

END GAME

A Sneak Peek

"Uh . . . hello? Ma'am? Can I get some help over here?"

Blowing out a breath, I ignored the man standing on the other side of the bar—standing, might I add, shoulder-to-shoulder with dozens of other patrons who'd been waiting patiently for a drink *much* longer than him. He'd sidled up to the wooden countertop only minutes ago, and if he thought he was going to get my attention that quickly, he was sorely mistaken.

Focusing on the task at hand, I added Crown Royal, apple schnapps, and cranberry juice to my ice-filled stainless steel mixer before capping the top and shaking the contents around. The cold mixer dripped with condensation from the ice, and I had to wipe my hand against my thigh before I could pop the cap back off. The sticky-sweet smell of the apple schnapps wafted through my nose, and I wondered if my own sticky-sweet treat would be stopping by tonight. I hadn't seen Charlea in almost a week, hadn't felt her soft curves beneath my hands in too many nights—and after another busy shift like this one, I needed to blow off some steam.

Now that I thought about it, I hadn't heard from Charlea at all since the last time I saw her. Which was . . . five days ago? And even though I'd told her—repeatedly—that my interest in her was of a strictly non-exclusive nature, I'd gotten used to her texts every day. She'd become a real friend. Just . . . with some sexy benefits.

Shit. I hoped she was okay. Making a mental note to text her when things slowed down, I poured the Washington Apple shots into three glasses and pushed them in front of a birthday girl and her two friends.

"Ohmigod!" Birthday Girl squealed as she tucked her shot close to her chest. "I love theeeese." Her lime green birthday sash was backward and falling off her shoulder, reflecting offensively under the neon pink lights that swirled around the bar in time with the dizzying beat of the music.

I frowned, looking at the friend closest to her with narrowed eyes. "How drunk is she?" I asked, giving her a look that said *Don't bullshit me.*

The friend shrugged. "Drunk enough that this should be her last one?" she answered sheepishly.

I nodded, pushing down the irritability that flared in my chest. This was a bar, after all. People came here to drink. That was good, right? More money in my pocket, that's for sure. "Yeah, I'd say so. I'll bring you ladies your tab. You have a ride home?"

The other friend chimed in. "Yep! I just texted Rosie's brother," she nodded toward Birthday Girl. "He's on his way."

I nodded again, and that should have been the end of it. I

didn't know these girls, and I wasn't responsible for them. I should be able to trust that they were capable of getting themselves home. But still, I couldn't resist the next question from spilling out of my mouth. "This brother of hers . . . he's sober tonight? You guys will be safe?"

Both of Rosie's friends nodded vigorously from where they stood on either side of her. "Oh yeah," the first one said, "he's been waiting at home for our call to pick us up. We're solid."

All three of them stared at me as I mulled over their response. And I realized they hadn't taken their shots yet, that I was inadvertently interrupting their fun with my . . . "mothering," as Frank called it. "Let me grab your tab," I repeated as I turned around to face the small computer behind me.

I navigated through the touch-screen system to find and print their tab, and heard Man Child's voice again from just down the bar. "Yo! Could you please slide that fine ass down this way when you're done? Jesus . . . I don't want to keep begging for a fucking drink." This time I let my eyes snap to him, taking in the rogue blonde curl falling into blue eyes surrounded by thick, long lashes.

He was . . . pretty. But I knew those good looks were trouble. He probably lived a charmed life with easy access to most of the things he wanted—typical, really, for a lot of the guys who came in here, used to being fed by a silver spoon. They expected instant gratification after throwing out a *Please* and a sultry wink. But at my bar, that kind of shit didn't fly.

Larkspur was a busy downtown nightclub that hosted hundreds of people on any given night, and tonight was our monthly ladies' night event that only made things crazier. The club was swarming with women who got to enjoy free cover at the door and discounted drinks. And where there were women,

men would come—they never seemed to mind having to pay to get in. Even with three bartenders behind the bar, we were more than outnumbered.

"I see you," I called back to him with a firm tone. "I'll get there when I can."

His eyes narrowed as he scoffed. "What the hell does a guy have to do to get a beer in this place?"

Rolling my eyes, I ignored his childlike display of impatience and turned back to Rosie and her friends, sliding their tab toward them. Rosie looked up at me—well, her gaze made it up to my chin—and said, "Thank you for making this the best birthday *ever*."

I smiled. "I literally didn't do anything. But thanks?"

Each of her friends slipped a credit card into the book and pushed it back to me. "Can you split it down the middle?"

I nodded. "Sure thing." Turning back to the computer, I nearly ran into my newest bartender. "Shit, sorry!"

Nora looked at me over her shoulder, grinning from ear to ear. "It's so fucking busy tonight, Mar."

She was a special kind of freak who thrived on being in the weeds. It was one of the reasons she'd quickly soared right up my list of favorites—especially considering that, until she started working here, she'd never bartended a night in her life. "You doing okay?" I asked.

"Hell yes!" she yelled before booking it back to her end of the bar.

I laughed at her bizarre excitement, closed out the tab for the birthday girl and her friends, then brought their receipts back to them. Just as I turned to greet a smiling couple and ask them for their order, the gremlin shouted out again. "For fuck's sake, woman, I have money I'm trying to spend!"

The man and woman standing in front of me frowned at the attention-seeking display of testosterone leaning on the bar ten feet away. I looked back at the couple and whispered an apology, putting a finger up to indicate I'd be right back.

I turned to my right and made eye contact with Frank, our head of security. We had guys stationed all over the club, but Frank always took the position at the end of the bar, keeping watch over all transactions. I gave a little head-jerk to the side, toward my current bane of existence—a sign he knew well. He nodded, pushing off the wall to head this way.

Frank was our head of security for a reason. He may have a handsome, boy-next-door face, but he also had a body like a linebacker and a mean streak when it counted. I watched as his eyes scanned the rowdy patrons, readying himself for anything.

Knowing he'd be here within seconds, I turned and walked toward Blondie, smiling at him as brightly as I could. "I'm so sorry, sir. Please forgive my *blatant* disregard for your needs."

He tilted his head and peered down at me, that blonde curl bouncing against his forehead. A crooked grin tugged at his mouth as his eyes raked over my body. "That's more like it, sweetness. I was hoping you'd bring me a beer—I'm getting thirsty over here."

"Thirsty?" I smiled wider, winking. "Thirsty for a good time, I hope?"

His eyes flicked to my chest, to the skin exposed from my low-cut Larkspur shirt, before he raised his chin. "What do you know about a good time?"

Fluttering my eyelashes, I looked to where my hands rested on the bar, feigning bashfulness. "Well, I know that for you," I teased, looking back up at him, "it's not here."

His grin faltered, and his eyes dulled in confusion. "What?" he asked.

My own expression shifted to a glare. "You don't disrespect me, you don't disrespect my staff, and you certainly don't disrespect our other customers with your entitlement issues. Whatever you're looking for, *sweetness*, it's not here." I pointed to the door on the other side of the building. "Get the fuck out."

Just as his face twisted in anger, Frank grabbed hold of his shoulders from behind. "All right, pretty boy, let's go."

"What the fuck?" Blondie spat out.

"Bye bye!" I waved as he disappeared into the crowd behind him, Frank keeping a firm grip on his shoulders. The people who'd been standing close enough to hear his tantrum clapped. While I had everyone's attention, I took the opportunity to shout out a friendly little public service announcement. "Listen up, folks! We're so happy to have you here at Larkspur, but make no mistake, if you treat this bar, my staff, or each other with disrespect, you can join Goldilocks out through that front door. We clear?" Cheers erupted again, this time from even more patrons who'd leaned in to hear what was going on.

Content with my point being made, I headed back to the couple I'd left hanging, finding them smiling again. "I'm so sorry about that. What can I get for ya?"

Things didn't slow down until well after one o'clock, and even then, "slowed down" was a stretch. Still, Nora and Sam had practically kicked me out from behind the bar, assuring me that they had things under control for the rest of the night.

I usually liked staying until closing time, but I'd closed the last eleven nights in a row, and I would be lying if I said I wasn't exhausted. I hadn't actually taken a day off in more than three weeks—but Larkspur was my life. Since starting here two years ago, on the heels of the most terrible season of my entire existence, I'd thrown my heart and mind into the nightclub and welcomed the distraction with open arms.

After closing myself out for the night, I stuffed my stack of cash tips—over three hundred dollars' worth—deep into my belt bag and pulled out my phone. I typed out a quick text to Charlea to ask her what she was doing, even though I knew it was late and that she was probably already sleeping. Even still, I wanted to check in and show some effort from my side of our little arrangement, even if neither of us owed the other anything like that.

She was a kindhearted girl, and she deserved to be thought of.

I returned my phone to my purse before slinging the strap over my shoulder and making my way to the back of the building where a small locker room existed, a reminder of the old community center that used to exist in this space. There was a single-stall shower inside, and while I normally didn't bother with it before heading home each night, tonight's shift had been crazy enough to have more than one drink spilled on me.

Making quick work of showering and throwing on some extra work clothes from my locker, I headed toward the front of the club to leave. I said a quick goodbye to Ethan and Mikey, the bouncers who worked the door, on my way out. There were only a handful of people waiting in line to get in, and I smiled at them all as I walked past.

"Oh shit, look, it's Mara!" I heard someone call out. I was

used to being recognized here—I'd built a pretty large social media presence advertising Larkspur on my personal accounts, promoting the events that we hosted alongside candid shots of me working behind the bar. My social media accounts had become one of the driving forces behind the growing popularity of Larkspur as I carved out a digital presence that otherwise wouldn't have existed.

The current owner, an older, long-time investor named Robert, was much more old-school in his business approach. He preferred traditional marketing strategies, like buying advertising space in our local newspapers or paying for billboard spots throughout the city. When I started working here, I'd asked him if I could take the dive into online spaces, and though he didn't think it would amount to much, he let me have at it. Luckily for both of us, it worked.

Robert promoted me to bar manager and marketing director a year ago, and though I was still a core bartender at the club, I'd also worked to develop a huge digital presence that made both of us a lot of money—his in the form of an overall increase in revenue, and mine in bonuses and tips like I'd ever seen before.

It was October in Denver, which meant temperatures were beginning to drop considerably during the late-night hours. A chilly breeze swept around me, goosebumps spreading across my arms and neck, so I pulled my favorite black hoodie over my work shirt and yanked the drawstring tight around my face. My bare legs still shivered thanks to the spandex booty shorts I was wearing, but I did my best to ignore the bite.

My apartment was only a twelve-minute trek through the downtown city streets—a path that I could walk in my sleep at this point. Unhooking my pepper spray cartridge from my bag,

I tucked it into the front pocket of my sweater. Though I took this walk home every night—usually later than this—I was still aware of the risks a big city posed. I promised myself long ago that I would never let anyone make me feel unsafe in my own skin again.

Five minutes into my walk, my favorite late-night convenience store came into view. Rudy's Market was open around the clock, offering scattered grocery options, over-the-counter medications, and fresh sandwiches and pastries from a small deli in the back. Rudy himself worked the night shift, while his younger brothers covered the early morning and afternoon shifts.

I started stopping in to get a post-shift sandwich years ago. My routine was getting it to-go, then stuffing it down at home before crashing until the next afternoon. At some point, though, I'd begun eating my sandwiches in the shop while visiting with Rudy. He was twenty years my senior and loved to reminisce about his teenage years spent in Cuba—all of which were hilarious if not borderline unbelievable.

While it was admittedly a bit unconventional, I considered Rudy to be a friend. I didn't have many of those these days, and he was kind and considerate enough to make me feel comfortable anytime I was in the store. It certainly helped that, while it wasn't technically on his menu, he had a habit of making me strawberry milkshakes.

I decided to stop in and say hello . . . I *was* off early tonight after all. Plus, I hadn't eaten anything since I garbled up some leftover boneless wings on my way out the door earlier this afternoon. Taking a second to look both ways, I crossed the street and bee-lined it for the front entrance.

The soft chiming of a bell sounded as soon as I opened the

door, and Rudy's voice came from somewhere in the back. "Oh, what luck for me—is that Mara, I see?"

I smiled. "Hey, Rudy!" Rounding a display of greeting cards, my eyes landed on where he stood behind the deli counter. He was wearing a navy polo and jeans, his chocolate-brown hair combed over to the side and his smile bright against his russet skin. "How's it going over here tonight?"

Rudy shrugged. "Not too bad, I've had a few customers every hour. Most of them to buy beer."

I smiled wider. "Well, it's a good thing you and I both profit nicely from people who like beer, isn't it?"

"You more so than me, I'm sure." He chuckled and then nodded toward the fridge behind him. "You hungry?"

Nodding eagerly, I rushed out a "Yes, I am," just as my stomach rumbled. "Can I have a turkey and provolone please?"

Rudy chuckled. "Coming right up, *chiquita*."

There were three tables set in front of the deli counter, each with two chairs. It was cramped—there wasn't enough room in here to provide any more seating than this—but I wiggled myself between two of the tables and squeezed into one of the tiny metal chairs. I watched as Rudy pulled out meat, cheese, and veggies from the industrial-sized stainless steel walk-in. "Do you ever get scared of getting trapped in there?" I asked the question before I could think better of it.

Rudy quirked a brow. "No...?"

"Oh, so you're normal then?" I laughed. "Sometimes when I have to change a keg at the bar, I get worried that someone will accidentally lock me in and I'll freeze to death."

His dark brown eyes swam in amusement. "I highly doubt

you guys keep your walk-in cold enough to freeze, or you'd be pouring beer slushies from the tap."

Hm. *Not a bad idea.* I was just about to tell him as much when the bell chimed again.

Rudy lifted his head. "Hello, welcome!" he called out.

I couldn't see the front door from where I sat, but I heard the low, baritone voice that responded. "Good evening, sir." It cut through the air like butter—smooth and rich as it drifted along my senses, sensual and teasing like a long overdue vice. "I was curious if you sell champagne?"

Rudy's brows pulled ever-so-slightly, but he quickly wiped the confusion away with a smile. "Uh, yes sir—one second and I'll show you our options." He rubbed his palms against the apron he wore around his waist and moved toward the front door.

I ducked my head to catch a glimpse of the new arrival through the chip shelves on my right, but only managed to catch a fleeting glimpse of a light gray business suit and large olive hands before they disappeared down another aisle.

"We unfortunately don't have many to choose from," said Rudy, his voice traveling from the other side of the store, "but what we do have is right here."

"Which one is your most expensive?" the man asked. I almost snorted.

"Uh, that would be this one, sir. It's seventeen dollars."

"Mhm." That voice rumbled out a low, pleased hum. I felt the sound somewhere in my limbs, like a spark igniting. "It's perfect, I'll take it."

Sounds of feet shuffling moved back this way before Rudy came into view, carefully holding a bottle of champagne in both of his hands. He made his way behind the register and scanned the barcode.

The man trailed behind, pausing on this side of the counter. He was wearing a three-piece suit, the light gray material looking almost silver under the fluorescent lights. The white collar of a dress shirt peeked from the back of his neck, and soft chestnut waves cascaded around his head, just long enough for the ends to drape over that collar.

From the back, he looked . . . promising. His stature alone called for attention, and I realized he certainly had mine. Which was odd, considering I hadn't felt genuine attraction for a man in a very long time.

How long has it been? I wondered. *Two years?* Maybe longer. Not since Logan . . . but I didn't even really count him. He'd been a soft landing after the worst days—or more accurately, *months*—of my life. Plus, he was technically an ex-boyfriend, the guy I lost my virginity to when we were both sixteen, so our reconnection had been more like the comfort of muscle memory than a new, whirlwind attraction.

"Do you need anything else, sir?" Rudy asked, bringing me back to the too-bright shop.

The man reached into his suit jacket and propped a leather wallet on the counter. "No, thanks. This'll do just fine."

Rudy nodded. "Your total is eighteen dollars and thirty-six cents."

I heard the swipe of a card followed by the *ting* of the register slamming shut. "Thank you so much for coming in, sir." Rudy smiled brightly. "We hope to see you again soon."

The man nodded, his waves rustling with the movement. "Yes, of course. Thank you for all your help." He turned around clutching the bag, but his eyes snagged on where I was sitting in the cold metal chair and as soon as they landed on me, his feet stopped moving.

Want to keep reading Leo and Mara's story? Read the next book in the Love In The Rockies series: End Game!

Read for FREE in Kindle Unlimited!

Books by Michaela Jean Taylor

Love In The Rockies

Only You

This Love

End Game

Saddlebrook Falls

Sunshine

Peaches

Sugar

About the Author

Michaela is a hopeless romantic from the western desert who writes grippingly tender romance novels featuring diverse characters and messy, beautifully relatable storylines.

Stay tuned for exciting announcements at
michaelajeantaylor.com

www.ingramcontent.com/pod-product-compliance
Lightning Source LLC
Chambersburg PA
CBHW030108310726
48970CB00004B/1200